"Whatever threat is jeopardizing the peace of this town and the law, you can be sure I'll be out there fighting it." **Bree pressed her full lips together.**

Jamie wondered what she'd do if he tried to kiss her. His pulse quickened. As unpredictable and unreasonable as she was, she might just shoot him.

Not that kissing those lips wouldn't be worth the risk. Not that he was going to do it. He was in town on serious business. And women were no longer part of his life, anyway. He had too much baggage, too many nightmares. He had no right to bring that into a relationship and mess up somebody else's life along with his.

He was a trained killing machine. That was about it. He planned on living the rest of his life using what skills he had in the service of his country. He stood. "Forget about me and my team."

Although, he was pretty sure he wasn't going to be able to forget about her.

ABOUT THE AUTHOR

Dana Marton is the author of more than a dozen fast-paced, action-adventure, romance-suspense novels and a winner of a Daphne du Maurier Award of Excellence. She loves writing books of international intrigue, filled with dangerous plots that try her tough-as-nails heroes and the special women they fall in love with. Her books have been published in seven languages in eleven countries around the world. When not writing or reading, she loves to browse antiques shops and enjoys working in her sizable flower garden, where she searches for "bad" bugs with the skills of a superspy and vanquishes them with the agility of a commando soldier. Every day in her garden is a thriller. To find more information on her books, please visit www.danamarton.com. She loves to hear from her readers and can be reached via email at danamarton@danamarton.com.

Books by Dana Marton

*Mission: Redemption
**Defending the Crown
***HQ: Texas

MY SPY
&
LAST SPY STANDING

—

DANA MARTON

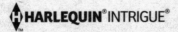

ISBN-13: 978-0-373-69720-5

MY SPY
Copyright © 2013 by Harlequin Books S.A.

The publisher acknowledges the copyright holder of the individual works as follows:

MY SPY
Copyright © 2013 by Dana Marton

LAST SPY STANDING
Copyright © 2012 by Dana Marton

Recycling programs for this product may not exist in your area.

Printed in U.S.A.

HARLEQUIN®
www.Harlequin.com

CONTENTS

CAST OF CHARACTERS

Bree Tridle—When a stalker returns from her past, deputy sheriff Bree Tridle's life is in danger. Dare she accept help from a handsome stranger who has the singular ability to get on her last nerve?

Jamie Cassidy—An undercover operative with a dark past, Jamie is watching the border to catch some terrorists. Seeing Bree in danger doesn't sit well with him, especially since he suspects there might be some serious bad guys after her.

The Coyote—A mysterious and powerful crime lord on the south side of the border. His true identity is unknown.

Katie Tridle—Bree's sister. Since Katie lives with autism, Bree is extra protective of her. No way is she going to let her stalker put Katie in danger.

SDDU—Special Designation Defense Unit. A top-secret commando team established to fight terrorism and other international crime that affects the U.S. The group's existence is known only by a select few. Members are recruited from the best of the best. Jamie Cassidy is part of a six-man team from the SDDU who are stationed on the Texas–Mexican border.

With many thanks to my wonderful editor, Allison Lyons.

This book is dedicated to my readers who are my
support, my inspiration, my true friends, online and off.
Your kindness means more to me than words can say.

Chapter One

He had two weeks to gain the information he needed to stop terrorists with weapons of mass destruction from entering the country. But everything his six-man team had done so far had been a bust.

Undercover operative Jamie Cassidy sat with his back to the wall in the far corner at the Yellow Armadillo, a seedy, small-town bar on the backstreets of Pebble Creek, Texas. Country music streamed from overhead speakers; the place was dark and dingy, the food was fried within an inch of its life. But the beer was cold, the only nice thing that could be said about the joint.

"So you have no idea who the new boss is?" he asked the scrawny farmhand across the table.

Billy Brunswik fingered the rim of the tattered Stetson on his lap, his eyes on his empty glass. A cowboy tan left the top of his forehead white, the rest of his face several shades darker. His checkered blue shirt was wrinkled and smudged with dirt, as if he'd been wearing it for more than a day or two. He silently shook his head.

Jamie had his own cowboy hat and jeans and shirt to fit in, a far cry from his usual commando gear. In a place like this—a known hangout for smugglers—being spotted as a government man could quickly earn you a bullet in the back.

He waved the perky blonde waitress over for another round for Billy but didn't return her flirty smile. His attention was on the man across the table. "It's tough. Believe me, I know." He waited until the waitress left. "In this economy, and they cut off work. Hell, what are you supposed to do? Who do you go to now?"

"Nobody knows nuthin'." Billy set his empty glass down and wiped his upper lip with the back of his calloused hand, then pulled out a tin of chewing tobacco and tucked a pinch between gum and cheek. "I can barely buy groceries for the girlfriend and me, I'll tell you that."

Jamie watched him for a few seconds, then slid three twenties across the table. "I know how it is."

Billy was on the cash like a duck on a june bug, the bills disappearing in a flat second. He looked around nervously, licking his crooked yellow front teeth. "I ain't no snitch."

Jamie gave a sympathetic nod. "A man has to live. And I ain't asking for nothing that would get you in trouble. Just need enough to show the boss I've been working." He shrugged, playing the halfhearted customs agent role.

Billy hung his head. "I do work a little," he admitted. "When nobody's lookin'. Just some weed."

"Who do you kick up to?"

"Ain't nobody there since Kenny."

And no matter how hard Jamie pushed the down-on-his-luck farmhand after that, Billy didn't give up anything. Although he did promise to get in touch if things changed.

Developing an asset was a slow and careful business.

Jamie left the man and strode across the bar, looking for familiar faces as he passed the rows of tables. The two border towns his team watched, Hullett and Pebble Creek, had their share of smugglers, most of them lying low these days. He didn't recognize anyone here today.

He paid the waitress at the bar, stepped outside into the scorching heat then shoved his hat on his head and rubbed his eyes. He'd spent the night on border patrol, then most of the morning running down leads. His legs hurt. The doc at Walter Reed called it phantom-limb pain.

He resisted the urge to reach down and rub his prosthetic limbs. It did nothing for the pain, and he hated the feel of the cold steel where his legs should have been.

He strode up to Main Street, came out by the bank and drew a hundred out of the ATM while he was here, since Billy had cleaned him out. Then his gaze caught on the bookstore across the street. Maybe a good read would help him fall asleep. When on duty, his mind focused on work. But when he rested, memories of his dark past pushed their way back into his head. Sleep had a way of eluding him.

He cut across traffic and pushed inside the small indie bookstore, into the welcoming cool of air-conditioning, and strode straight to the mystery section. He picked out a hard-boiled detective story, then turned on his heels and came face-to-face with the woman of his dreams.

Okay, the woman of every red-blooded man's dreams.

She was tall and curvy, with long blond hair swinging in a ponytail, startling blue eyes that held laughter and a mouth to kill or die for, depending on what
she wished.

His mind went completely blank for a second, while
his body sat up and took serious notice.

When his dreams weren't filled with blood and torture and killing, they were filled with sex. He could
still do the act—one thing his injury hadn't taken away
from him. But he didn't allow himself. He didn't want
pity. Foreplay shouldn't start with him taking off his
prosthetics—the ultimate mood killer. And he definitely
didn't want the questions.

Hell, even he hated touching the damn things. Who
wouldn't? He wasn't going to put himself through that
humiliation. Wasn't going to put a woman in a position
where she'd have to start pretending.

But he dreamed, and his imagination made it good.
The woman of his dreams was always the same, an
amalgamation of pinup girls that had been burned into
his brain during his adolescent years from various mag-
azines he and his brothers had snuck into the house.

And now she was standing in front of him.

The pure, molten-lava lust that shot through his gut
nearly knocked him off his feet. And aggravated the hell
out of him. He'd spent considerable time suppressing his
physical needs so they wouldn't blindside him like this.

"Howdy," she said with a happy, peppy grin that
smoothed out the little crease in her full bottom lip.
She had a great mouth, crease or no crease. Made a man
think about his lips on hers and going lower.

He narrowed his eyes. Then he pushed by her with

a dark look, keeping his face and body language discouraging. Who the hell was she to upset his hard-achieved balance?

He strode up to the counter and paid with cash because he didn't want to waste time punching buttons on the card reader. He didn't want to spend another second in a place where he could be ambushed like this. The awareness of her back somewhere among the rows of books still tingled all across his skin.

"I'm sorry." The elderly man behind the counter handed back the twenty-dollar bill. "I can't take this." He flashed an apologetic smile as he pushed up his horn-rimmed glasses, then tugged down his denim shirt in a nervous gesture. "The scanner kicked it back."

"I just got it from the bank across the street," Jamie argued, not in the mood for delay.

"I'm sorry, sir."

"Everything okay, Fred?" The woman he'd tried to pretend didn't exist came up behind Jamie.

Her voice was as smooth as the kind of top-shelf whiskey the Yellow Armadillo couldn't afford to carry. Its sexy timbre tickled something behind his breastbone. He kept his back to her, against enormous temptation to turn, hoping she'd get the hint to mind her own business.

Then he had to turn, anyway, because next thing he knew she was talking to him.

"I'd be happy to help. How about we go next door and I'll help you figure this out?"

The police station stood next door. All he wanted was to go home and see if he could catch a few winks before his next shift. "I don't think so." He peeled off another twenty, which went through the scanner without trouble. Next thing he knew, Fred was handing back his change.

"I really think we should," the woman insisted.

Apparently, she had trouble with the concept of minding her own business. He shot her a look of disapproval, hoping she'd take the hint.

He tried to look at nothing but her eyes, but all that sparkling blue was doing things to him. Hell, another minute, and if she asked him to eat the damned twenty, he would have probably done it. He caught that thought, pushed back hard.

"Who the hell are you?" He kept his tone at a level of surly that had taken years to perfect.

The cheerleader smile never even wavered as she pulled her badge from her pocket and flashed it at him. "Brianna Tridle. Deputy sheriff."

Oh, hell.

He looked her over more thoroughly: the sexy snakeskin boots, the hip-hugging jeans, the checkered shirt open at the neck, giving a hint of the top curve of her breasts. His palms itched for a feel. If there was such a thing as physical perfection, she was it.

Any guy who had two brain cells to rub together would have gone absolutely anywhere with her.

Except Jamie Cassidy.

"I'm in a hurry."

"Won't take but a minute." She tilted her head, exposing the creamy skin of her neck just enough to bamboozle him. "I've been having a hard time with counterfeit bills turning up in town lately. I'd really appreciate the help. I'll keep it as quick as possible, I promise." The smile widened enough to reveal some pearly white teeth.

Teeth a man wouldn't have minded running his tongue along before kissing her silly.

Another man.

Certainly not Jamie.

Okay, so she was the deputy sheriff. The sheriff, Kenny Davis, had been killed recently. He'd been part of the smuggling operation Jamie's team was investigating. A major player, actually.

After that, Ryder McKay, Jamie's team leader, had looked pretty closely at the Pebble Creek police department. The rest of them came up squeaky clean. A shame, really. Jamie definitely felt like his world would be safer with Brianna Tridle locked away somewhere far from him.

She was too chirpy by half.

He didn't like chirpy.

But if she wasn't a suspect, she could be an ally—if he played his cards right. Although poker wasn't the first thing to spring to mind when he thought about playing with her. He could no longer feel the air-conditioning. In fact, it seemed the AC might have broken since he'd come in. The place felt warm suddenly. Hot, even.

He loosened the neck of his shirt. "Fine. Five minutes."

He held the door for her, regretting it as she flashed another gut punch of a smile. She better not read anything into that basic courtesy. He'd been raised right, that was all. He couldn't help it. He wasn't falling for her charms, no way, he thought as she walked in front of him, hips swinging.

The gentle sway held him mesmerized for a minute. Then he blinked hard as he finally focused on one specific spot. Was that a small firearm tucked under her waistband, covered by her shirt? Hard to tell with his eyes trying to slide lower.

He looked more carefully. Damn if the slight bulge wasn't a weapon. She'd been armed the entire time and he'd never noticed. He was seriously losing it.

He drew in a slow breath as they walked into the station. On second thought, forget developing her as an asset. Working with her would probably be more trouble than it was worth.

He was going to tell Brianna Tridle where, when and exactly how he'd come into possession of the stupid twenty-dollar bill in question. Then he was walking out and not looking back. If he had even a smidgen of luck coming to him, he'd never see her again.

"I REALLY APPRECIATE this." Bree measured up the cowboy with the bad attitude.

Not a real Texas cowboy, actually. He was missing the Texas twang, his general accent making it difficult to pin down from where he hailed. And he wore combat boots with his jeans. It threw off his cowboy swagger. He had shadows all around him, his aura a mixture of dangerous and sexy. He was hot enough to give women heart palpitations on his worst day.

Not that that sort of thing affected her. She was a seasoned law enforcement officer. "And your name is?"

"Jamie Cassidy." He didn't offer his hand, or even a hint of a smile as he scanned the station.

She'd bet good money he didn't miss many details.

Fine. She was proud of the place, clean and organized. The dozen people working there were the finest in South Texas. She would trust each and every one of them to have her back.

While he examined her station, she examined him.

He stood tall, well built, his dirty-blond hair slightly mussed as he took his hat off. When he ran his fingers through it in an impatient gesture, Bree's own fingertips tingled.

He had the face of a tortured angel, all angles and masculine beauty. His chocolate-brown eyes seemed permanently narrowed and displeased. Especially as he took in the metal detectors she'd had installed just last week.

Lena, the rookie officer manning the scanner, held out a gray plastic tray for him.

Bree offered a smile. "We just upped our security. If you could hand over anything metal in your pockets and walk through, I'd appreciate it."

She was in charge of the station until the new sheriff was elected. They'd had an incident recently with a drunk housewife who'd come in to file a complaint against her husband, then ended up shooting a full clip into the ceiling to make sure they believed her when she said she *would* shoot the bastard if he came into her new double-wide one more time with muddy boots.

She'd been a bundle of booze and wild emotions— the very opposite of Jamie Cassidy, who seemed the epitome of cold and measured.

He scowled as he dropped his cell phone, handful of change and car keys into the small plastic tray. "I'm going to set the alarm off." He tapped his leg. "Prosthesis."

That was it, then, Bree thought as she watched him. The reason why his walk had been off a smidgen. "Not a problem, Lena," she told the rookie, who was staring at him with dreamy eyes. "I'll pat him down."

"No." His face darkened as his gaze cut to hers.

They did a long moment of the staring-each-other-down thing. Then his lips narrowed as he fished around in his shirt pocket and pulled out a CBP badge.

Customs and Border Protection. *And the plot thickens.* She tilted her head as she considered him. Why not show the badge sooner?

Maybe it was a fake. She'd worked pretty closely with CBP for the past couple of years. She'd never seen him before. If she had, she would have definitely remembered him.

She widened her smile. Defusing tension in a bad situation always worked better than escalating it. "I need to check you just the same. New procedure. Sorry."

For a second he looked like he might refuse and simply walk away from her. She kept her hand near her firearm at her back, ready to stop him. She preferred to do things the easy way, but she could do it the hard way if needed. Up to him.

But then he seemed to change his mind and held out his arms to the side. She wondered if he knew that his smoldering look of resentment only made him look sexier.

"It'll only take a second." She ran her fingers along his arms first, lightly. Plenty of muscle. If he did change his mind and began causing trouble, she would definitely need her service weapon.

She moved her hands to his torso and found more impressive muscles there. She could feel the heat of his body through his shirt and went faster when her fingertips began to tingle again, a first for her during pat down. What on earth was wrong with her today? She tried to focus on what she was doing. Okay, no shoulder holster, no sidearm here.

"Almost done." She squatted as she moved down his legs, pausing at the sharp transition where the living flesh gave way to rigid metal. *Both* of his legs were missing. Her gaze flew up to his.

He looked back down at her with something close to hate—a proud man who didn't like his weaknesses seen.

"Enough." He stepped back.

But she stepped after him. "One more second."

Awareness tingled down her spine as she pulled up and reached around his waist, almost as if she were hugging him. And there, tucked behind his belt, she found a small, concealed weapon.

She removed the firearm carefully, pointing it down, making sure her fingers didn't come near the trigger. "When were you going to tell me about this?" She checked the safety. *On.* Okay.

"I'm so used to carrying, I forgot," he lied to her face.

Which ticked her off a little.

She dropped the weapon into the gray plastic tray Lena was holding. "You can claim these on your way out." If she let him leave. "This way."

They went through the detector, which did go off, as he'd promised. Curiosity, wariness and even some unwanted attraction warred inside her as she led him into interview room A at the end of the hallway. He was not your average Joe. This man had a story. She wanted to know what it was.

"How about I get us something cold to drink?"

He didn't look impressed with her hospitality as he scanned the small white room. "I'm in a hurry."

She left him anyway, and swung by Lena on her way to the vending machine. "Let me see that." She took his weapon, grabbed two sodas then stopped by her office and ran the gun.

Unregistered firearm. On a hunch, she called her friend Gina at the local CBP office. "Hey, you got someone over there by the name of Jamie Cassidy?"

"Not that I know off the top of my head. Why? Anything to do with the counterfeiting thing you're working?"

"Don't know yet. Might be nothing. I'll talk to you later." She hung up and walked by Lena again, looking at Jamie Cassidy's car keys in the plastic tray.

"You'll need a warrant to look in his car," Lena remarked, now sitting by her computer, answering citizen queries.

"Or his permission. Least I can do is try," Bree said as she walked away.

Mike was coming from the evidence room. "What you up to?"

"Picked up someone with a fake twenty."

"Need help?" He was a few weeks from retirement, but not the type to sit back and count off the days. He was always first to offer help and never said a word if he had to work late.

"Thanks. But I think I can handle him." She hoped. She was ready to roll up the counterfeiting thing.

She was sick of the recent crime wave in her town lately: a rash of burglaries, several acts of unusual vandalism and sabotage, arson even, and then the counterfeit bills showing up suddenly. Whatever she had to do, she was going to put an end to it.

She grabbed her shoulder holster from the back of her chair, shrugged into the leather harness and stuck her weapon into the holster to keep it within easier reach. Time to figure out who Jamie Cassidy was and if he'd come to town to cause trouble.

She had a sudden premonition that prying that out of him wasn't going to be easy. She'd been a cop long enough to know when somebody was lying, and the man waiting for her in interview room A definitely had his share of secrets.

HE WAS SITTING in an interrogation room, fully aroused. That was a first, Jamie thought wryly. Because, of course, she'd *had* to put her hands on him. At least she hadn't noticed his condition; she'd been too focused on his weapon.

He leaned back in the uncomfortable metal chair. The place was small, the cement brick walls freshly painted white, the old tile floor scuffed.

The metal door stood open, but the station was full of uniforms. He wouldn't get far if he tried to walk out, not without violence, and he wanted to avoid that if possible. He watched as the deputy sheriff reappeared at the end of the hallway, her gaze immediately seeking out his.

And there it came again, that punch of heat in the gut.

"Stupid," he said under his breath, to snap himself out of it.

He'd never been like this. Back when he'd been whole, he'd enjoyed the fairer sex as much as the next guy. Since he'd been crippled, he kept to himself. He was half machine, half human. Who the hell would want to touch that?

Yet she'd touched him and hadn't flinched away. She'd felt his prosthetics and her face had registered surprise, but not pity. He pushed that thought aside. What would Miss Perfection know about physical deformity?

He watched as a uniformed cop, dragging a loud-mouthed drunk, headed her off halfway down the hall.

"No needles," the drunk protested, then swore a blue streak, struggling against the man who held him, trying for a good swing, the movement nearly knocking him off his unsteady feet.

Brianna Tridle smiled sweetly.

Yeah, that was going to work. The man needed someone to put the fear of God into him. Jamie could have gotten the job done in three seconds flat. Possibly two. He relaxed and got ready to enjoy watching the deputy sheriff fail.

"Come on now, Pete." She kept up the all-is-well-with-the-world, we're-all-friends routine. "Big, tough guy like you. Remember when you had that wire snap at work and cut your leg open? You didn't make a sound all the way to the hospital when I took you in. Pretty impressive."

The drunk pulled himself together a little and gave her a sheepish look. "It's just the needles. You know I can't stand them, darlin'."

"Tell you what. You do the blood test, I'll drive you home. You won't have to wait here until Linda gets off shift."

"Can't give no blood." He shook his head stubbornly. "I'm dizzy. Haven't even eaten all day."

"I bet Officer Roberts hasn't had lunch yet, either. How about you swing by the drive-through and grab a couple of hamburgers? On me."

The drunk went all googly-eyed. "You'll always be a queen to me, darlin'," he promised, and this time followed Officer Roberts obediently as he was led away.

Jamie stared. *Enforcing the law with sweet talk.*

What kind of monkey-circus police station was this? And then he stilled as he realized he was even now sitting in an interrogation room, where he'd had no intention of being. Hell, the woman had done it to him!

He glared at her with all the resentment he felt as she came in with a couple of drinks. He was out of here.

"Got the money out of the ATM at the bank across the street five minutes ago. You can check their security video." He rose. "That's all I know."

She put a can of soda in front of him with that smile that seemed to have the ability to addle everyone's brain around her. She sat, folding her long legs under her seat. "Just a few minutes. Please?" she asked very nicely. "As a favor from one law enforcement drone to another."

Establishing common ground in thirty seconds flat. Nice work, he had to admit. He sat, but only because he was beginning to be intrigued.

"What do you do, exactly, at CBP?" She fitted her supremely kissable lips to the can as she drank, keeping an eye on him.

"I'm on a special team," he said, more than a little distracted.

"Dealing with?"

"Special stuff."

She laughed, the sound rippling right through him. He resented that thoroughly.

"Why do you carry an unregistered firearm instead of your service weapon?" she asked as pleasantly as if she was inquiring about his health.

She got that already, did she? A part of him was impressed, a little. Maybe she wasn't just surface beauty.

"Took it off someone this morning. Haven't had a chance yet to turn it in," he lied through his teeth. He was in town as part of an undercover commando team. What they did and how they did it was none of her business.

She smiled as if she believed his every word. "All right, that's it, then," she said brightly. "I better clear you out of here so you can get back to work. I know you guys are busy beyond belief."

She stood, taking her drink with her. "Just to make sure I have all my *T*s crossed and *I*s dotted, would you mind if I took a quick glance at your car?" she added, as if it was an afterthought. "With all this counterfeit stuff I'm struggling with…" She gave a little shrug that another man would have found endearing. "It's really helpful to be able to cross people completely off the list."

"Go ahead," he said, regretting it the next second. But part of him wanted to test her. No way in hell she was going to find the secret compartment that he himself built. "It's a black SUV in front of the bank." He gave her his plate number. "You already have the keys."

She walked out, ensuring him of her gratitude and sincere appreciation. And this time, she closed the door behind her. Which locked automatically.

And just like that, he was in custody.

His mouth nearly gaped at her effortless efficiency.

He had to admit, if he was normal, if he was the type who believed in love, she would be the exact woman he might be tempted to fall in love with.

Of course, with everything she had going for her, chances were she was already married. No wedding ring—he couldn't believe he'd looked—but people in law enforcement often skipped that. No reason to advertise to the bad guys that you had a weakness, a point where you could be hurt.

Married. *There.* He found the thought comforting. He liked the idea of her completely out of his reach. Otherwise, the thought of her would drive him crazy during those long nights when he couldn't sleep.

He waited.

Looked around the small room.

Looked at the locked door.

It'd been a while since he'd been locked up and tortured, but the more he sat in the interrogation room, the more uneasy he felt. *It's not like that.* He swallowed back the memories. Rubbed his knees.

But a cold darkness seemed to fill the room around him little by little, pushing him to his feet. *Think about something else. Think about work.*

Plenty there to figure out. His six-man team was putting the brakes on a serious smuggling operation that planned on bringing terrorists, along with their weapons of mass destruction, into the country, information that had been gained on an unrelated South American op.

To stop the terrorists, his team had to work their way up the chain of command in a multinational criminal organization. They'd gotten the three low-level bosses who ran the smugglers on the United States side of the border. What they needed now was the identity of the Coyote, the big boss who ran things on the other side.

He paced the room, forcing himself to focus on what they knew so far. But too soon his thoughts returned to Brianna Tridle. He moved to the door to look out the small window through the wire-reinforced glass. What he saw didn't make him happy.

She was coming back in with a uniformed cop, carrying his arsenal, down to his night-vision goggles that had been hidden in a separate secret compartment from the rest. She called out to the handful of people in the office as she deposited the weaponry on a desk.

He couldn't hear her, but he could read her sexy lips. He was pretty sure she'd just said *terror suspect*.

Oh, hell. That definitely didn't bode well for him.

Chapter Two

"Officer Delancy here is going to take your finger-prints," Bree informed Jamie Cassidy, if that was his real name, once she was back in the interview room with him, feeling a lot more cautious suddenly than the first time around.

"I noticed earlier that you had a wallet in your pocket. I'd appreciate it if you handed that over, please." She kept as pleasant an expression on her face as possible, even if she felt far from smiling.

The kind of weapons he had in his SUV were definitely not standard government issue that CBP would use. And they were far too heavy duty for the kind of criminals she usually saw around these parts. He didn't just have weapons—he had an arsenal with him. For what purpose?

"I need to make a phone call," he demanded, instead of complying.

"Maybe later." If he *was* a domestic terrorist, he could set off a bomb with a phone call. She wasn't going to take chances until she knew more about him. "Let's do those prints first and have a little talk. Then we'll see about the phone."

He scowled at her, looking unhappier by the second. An accomplishment, since he'd been in a pretty sour mood even when she'd first laid eyes on him.

"How about we talk about your weapons first?"

He held her gaze. "How did you find them?"

He clearly hadn't thought she would. At the beginning of her career, it had annoyed her that men tended to underestimate her. Then she'd realized that it was an advantage.

"Just came back from special training with the CBP. They spent three entire days on tips and tricks for spotting secret compartments. Same training you received, I assume? Since you claim you work for them?"

Smuggling had been getting out of hand in the area until a sudden recent drop she didn't think would last. And now with the counterfeit money nonsense… She needed skills that would help her put an end to that. As she watched him, she wondered if he was a CBP agent gone bad. It happened.

"You're making a mistake here."

"Oh, Lord," she said easily. "I make at least ten a day, for sure." She smiled. "Why are you in Pebble Creek, Jamie?"

"I told you. I consult for CBP," he said morosely, but sat back down and let Delancy take his fingerprints.

Consulting now, was it? His story was subtly changing. There was more here, something he wasn't telling her.

"And you needed those guns for…"

"I spend a lot of time on the border."

"Doing what?"

"Monitoring smuggling."

Or helping it along, most likely.

Sheriff Davis was dead, the new sheriff elections mere weeks away. She'd been away for training and out of the loop, way too much dropping on her lap the day she'd come back. Like counterfeit twenties showing up.

She'd notified the CIA as soon as she'd caught the first. They were sending an agent before the end of the week to investigate. Acid bubbled in her stomach every time she thought of that. She wasn't a big fan of outsiders messing around in her town.

And if that wasn't enough, now she had Jamie Cassidy to deal with. She was starting to feel the beginnings of a headache.

He was watching her, his eyes hard, his face closed, his masculine mouth pressed into a line—not exactly a picture of cooperation. If this went the way she thought it would, she'd be here all day and then some. Which meant she'd have to call her sister and let her know she'd be late. Not a good thing with Katie being so bad with even the slightest change in her routine.

"How long have you been in town?" she asked as Delancy left with the fingerprint kit, closing the door behind her.

"A couple of weeks."

Which coincided with the counterfeit money showing up.

He rubbed the heels of his hands over his knees, drawing her attention there. How much did she know about what was really under his jeans, anyway? She'd felt metal. But was all of that his prosthetics?

She stood to walk around the desk. "Would you mind rolling up your pants?" she asked in her friendliest tone.

"In light of the weapons we found in your car, I'd feel more comfortable if I made a full search. Just to set my mind at ease."

If he'd been cold before, he went subzero now, his gaze turning to black ice. Every muscle in his body tensed. She'd definitely hit a nerve.

Would he hit back? She was ready to defend herself, not that she was looking forward to tackling him. He looked strong, quick and capable.

She should have asked Delancy to stay as backup, she thought too late. Jamie was already on his feet.

ANGER AND HUMILIATION washed over Jamie as he stood. He'd played along long enough. He didn't have time for this. "You need to let me make that call."

The next thing he knew, he was shoved face-first into the wall, his right hand twisted up behind his back, his cheek rubbing into the brick. Air whooshed out of his lungs, more from surprise than anything else.

Her transformation from sweet to tough cop was pretty spectacular and stunned him more than a little. For a second her body pressed against his full-length from the back, her soft breasts flattened against his ribs. Another place, another time… Heat and awareness shot through him, pure lust drowning out the aggravation that she would try to manhandle him.

He could have put her down. He could have put her down hard.

But she was an officer of the law, and they were on the same side. And frankly, he was beginning to respect her skills.

"Take it easy," he said. "I'm cooperating."

He let her pull down his other hand and put plastic restraints on him, even if the thought of being tied up made him uneasy. Any undercover commando who couldn't get out of plastic restraints in under a minute needed to quit. He said nothing when she edged his boots apart with her foot.

Then she bent and grabbed on to the hem of his jeans, and that set his teeth on edge. "That's not necessary. I'm not the enemy."

She rolled the denim up briskly. "Just a quick check. Then you give me that number you want to call and I'll call for you. How about that?"

Over his dead body. She called Ryder and Jamie would never live it down that he'd gotten nabbed and interrogated by Deputy Sheriff Hot Chick.

He held still as she moved his pant leg up. He knew what she would see: cold steel alloy, nothing human, a well-engineered machine. He'd received his prosthetics as a major favor from a friend of the colonel his team reported to. It was the best technology Olympic athletes used, taken up another notch. A prototype, the first and only set to receive the designation combat ready.

"Fancy hardware," she commented as she covered up his left leg and moved on to the right. "How did this happen?"

None of her business. "Car accident." He said the first thing that came to mind.

"I would have thought war injury." She finished and straightened, expertly sliding her hand into his pocket and retrieving his wallet. "You move like a soldier."

And suddenly he had enough of her prying into his business. He twisted his wrist to expose the link on his metal watchband that he kept sharp. Another twist, applying pressure to the right places, and he was free.

He reached for her as he turned, caught her by surprise and had her trapped against the wall in a split second, holding her hands at either side of her head, preventing her from going for her weapon.

Their faces were inches from each other, their bodies nearly touching. She stared at him with wide-eyed surprise that quickly turned to anger, then back to calm strength again, the transition fascinating to observe.

God, she was even more beautiful up close—those sparkling blue eyes and all that flawless skin.

"Not a smart move," she said calmly, the words drawing his gaze to the crease in her bottom lip that begged to be kissed. "I call out and there'll be half a dozen officers in here in a second."

"Why don't you?" He knew the answer, the exact same reason why he hadn't given her the number to call Ryder at the office. She didn't want to embarrass herself.

Her cell phone rang in her pocket.

He thought about kissing her, which was really stupid. He held her for another long second before he stepped back and let her go as a gesture of good faith, but took his wallet back.

She pulled her phone out with one hand, her gun with the other, pointing it at the middle of his chest.

She glared at him as she took the call. "Yes. Yes, sir," she said, the look on her face stunned at first, then quickly turning speculative. She lowered her gun. Her sparkling blue eyes narrowed when the call ended, and she turned her full attention back to him.

She stepped around to put the desk between them once again. "Want to guess who that was?"

He raised an eyebrow.

"Homeland Security. I've been ordered to release you immediately, without any further questions. Want to tell me what that's about?"

He winced. He would rather have that nobody know about his brief time in Brianna Tridle's custody, but, hell, he'd take whatever break he could get at this stage.

He sauntered by her on his way to the door. "Looks like you won't get to keep me. Life is full of disappointments, Deputy Sheriff."

HE ALMOST DIDN'T even mind having to see her again, Jamie thought as he ran a quick background search on her once he was back at his office that night, after having caught a brief nap at his apartment.

She hadn't returned his weapons, probably just to spite him. The orders on the phone had been only about releasing him, she'd said. He could claim his property after a twenty-four-hour waiting period, some rule she'd made up on the fly, he was sure.

"So she hauled you in?" Shep, one of his teammates, was asking with a little too much glee.

They worked out of a bulletproof office trailer in the middle of nowhere, close enough to the border to be able to reach it within minutes, far enough from prying eyes in town.

They had a pretty simple setup: one office for Ryder McKay, the team leader, an interrogation room, a bathroom and a small break room in the back, the rest of the space taken up by desks for the six-man team.

Ryder was locked up in his office, on the phone. The rest of the team was out.

Jamie shrugged as he scrolled down the screen.

"She questioned you?"

"Interrogation room." He spit out the two words as if they were broken glass in his mouth. He read the search results on his screen, scanning the scores of photos of her. *Miss Brianna Tridle accepts her crown.* She'd been Miss Texas. No joke.

She'd been younger—different hair, more makeup, but the smile was the same. He felt a tug in places that hadn't tugged in a long time, just looking at her on the screen.

"Handcuffs?" Shep asked.

He refused to answer, opening the next document that detailed everything from her family circumstances to her education. She was single, the sole guardian of one Katie Tridle, twenty-three years old.

Sister?

There was something there, he thought. Normally a person didn't need a guardian at twenty-three.

"Seriously, she had you in handcuffs?" Shep gave a belly laugh. "Oh, man, I would have given money to see that. Why didn't you just call in?"

Because she wouldn't let me, was the answer, words he wasn't about to say. He shut down his computer instead and pushed to his feet. "Patrol time, funny boy. Move it."

Shep picked up his handgun and shoved it into his holster, grinning all the way. It burned Jamie's temper that he had to get his backup weapon out of his drawer because most of his stuff was in the deputy sheriff's custody.

"Good thing she ran your prints and the flags went off in the system." Shep was having way too much fun with the incident to let it go, giving another gloating smirk as he got into his own SUV while Jamie hopped into his.

Yeah, flags had gone off. Homeland Security had called. They'd called both Brianna Tridle and Ryder at the office, unfortunately.

Jamie turned on radio contact as they pulled out of the parking lot. "How are you doing following up on the Kenny Davis angle?" he asked, ready to change the topic of conversation.

"Running into a lot of dead ends."

The Pebble Creek sheriff had been killed in a confrontation with Mo, another teammate, when the sheriff had gotten involved in the smuggling and kidnapped a little boy to use as leverage to regain a drug shipment he'd lost.

Mo did gain some clues out of his investigation: a code name, Coyote, the head of the smuggling operations on the other side of the border, and a date, October 13.

Something, but not enough. They needed to unravel the Coyote's identity and take him into custody, and they needed to figure out what the date meant.

"You think October 13 is the transfer?" He asked the same question they'd asked each other a dozen times since Mo had come up with the date.

"What else?"

"Why would the sheriff reveal it?"

"A sudden pang of patriotism? He knew at the end that he was dying. Money had been his main motivator for going bad. At that last moment, he knew money was no longer any good to him. He did this one thing to appease his conscience."

That made sense. But October 13 was only three weeks away. They had credible intelligence that several terrorists, along with some weapons of mass destruction, were going to cross this section of the border, the few hundred miles they were patrolling and investigating.

Now they had the date. Hopefully.

They needed an exact location.

To get that, they needed to find the Coyote.

"We'll catch as many smugglers as we can. One of them will lead us to the boss on the other side. He'll have the details of the transfer. Once we have him, I'm not worried. We'll get what we need out of him." Shep was more optimistic than Jamie.

"The smugglers we catch are small potatoes. None of them had a straight line to the Coyote so far."

"Patience is the name of the game."

Not one of his strengths, Jamie silently admitted.

They could have called in the National Guard and closed down the border in this area. But the bad guys would see that and simply bring over the terrorists and their weapons someplace else.

Which was why Jamie's six-man team was handling things quietly. According to their cover, they were here to observe illegal border activity and make budget recommendations to policy makers, while closely working with the CBP. In reality, they were a small, fast-hitting unit of a larger undercover commando team that protected national security all over the globe.

They wanted the terrorists to have no idea that they were expected. They wanted the bastards to come as planned so they could be apprehended and neutralized, taken out of the action for good—the only real solution.

Jamie and Shep talked about that and strategy as they reached the border, then radioed Keith and Mo to return to the office. The night shift was in place.

The full moon had come up, illuminating the landscape: some limited grazing land with large patches of arid ground thrown in that grew nothing but prickly pear and mesquite.

The Rio Grande flowed to the south of them, its dark waters glinting in the moonlight. Cicadas sang in the bushes. Up way ahead, deer were coming in to drink, but hearing the two cars, they darted away.

The place could look so peaceful and serene, belying how much trouble this little strip of land was causing on a regular basis lately.

Jamie pulled into a mesquite grove to observe for a while. Shep drove ahead and disappeared from sight after a few minutes. They were at one of the known crossing spots where the river was wide and the water low, the crossing relatively easy.

He got out his binoculars and used those for the first scan, then switched to his old, cracked night-vision goggles he'd grabbed from the office. He was mostly panning the river's southern bank, so he almost missed the three men who stole forward from the bushes on his other side, carrying oversize backpacks and an inflatable raft.

"Got three here," he said into the radio to warn Shep. "Be right back."

Jamie didn't wait for him. He started his car and gunned the engine, caught the trio halfway between the bushes and the water, squealed to a stop then jumped out, aiming his weapon as he rushed forward while they scattered.

"Guns on the ground! Hands in the air! Now!"

But the idiots seemed to find courage in the fact that they outnumbered him three to one. The nearest one took a shot at him.

Jamie ducked, ran forward and fired back, aiming for the extremities. They needed information, which dead men couldn't give.

He hit the guy in the leg and the smuggler went down, then Jamie was on top of him, maybe a little rougher than he had to be. His already damaged night-vision goggles broke and fell into the dirt.

Disarming the idiot took a minute, cuffing him another as the man struggled pretty hard while swearing and complaining about his injury.

"I'll feel sorry for you later." Jamie finished securing him. "Now shut up."

By the time he was done, the one who had the raft was at the edge of the water, the other one running in the opposite direction, back into the bushes where they probably had a vehicle hidden.

"Halt!" he called after him, not that the guy obeyed.

Jamie swore as he pushed to his feet. He'd already taken one down. He could have waited for Shep to go after the others together. But he wasn't in the habit of holding anything back.

He took after the guy who was going for the getaway car. With his prosthetics, he was no good in water, a weakness he hated.

He caught sight of Shep's car flying back, kicking up dust, just as the man he was chasing turned for a second and squeezed off another shot at Jamie.

He slowed, steadied his arm and shot back, aiming at the guy's gun and hitting it, a miracle considering the distance and lack of light. Then he darted forward once again, after the man who had already disappeared in the bushes.

The brush he entered was as tall as he was in places so he slowed, watching for movement up ahead. Nothing. The moon sliding behind a stray cloud didn't help. He had his high-powered flashlight clipped to his belt. Too bad turning that on would just make him a target.

Waiting for Shep and hunting as a team would have been smarter, but once again something—a need to prove himself, pride—pushed him forward.

He moved slowly, step by step, careful not to trip.

Somewhere behind him, Shep beeped his horn to let him know he got his man. That blare turned out to be Jamie's undoing.

He didn't hear the smuggler jump out of the bushes on his right, so he caught the collapsible paddle full in the face.

Pain shot up his nose and into his brain. He sprinted after the bastard anyway, shaking his head to clear it. The uneven ground tried to trip him; he focused on his balance, on closing the distance.

The man dropped his backpack and picked up speed.

Jamie didn't slow to see what he'd been carrying. That could wait.

Dark shadows surrounded them; there was no other sound but their boots slapping on the ground and their harsh breathing. Thorny bushes tore at him, ripping flesh and fabric. He paid no mind to anything but the man in front of him.

When he came close enough, he dove forward. They went down hard onto gravelly ground, rolled. Jamie was stronger, but the guy could maneuver his legs easier. A few minutes passed before he could subdue the smuggler.

"What's your name?" He flipped the guy onto his stomach and yanked the plastic cuff around his wrists. "What are you doing here? Who do you work for?"

But the man didn't respond, just snarled with impotent fury.

Jamie pushed himself up with his hands, then stood, the movement ungainly. Walking and running were his strengths; other things still didn't go as smoothly as he would have liked. He pulled the guy to standing and drew his gun at last to speed things up. "Talk and walk."

The guy did neither, so Jamie shoved him forward.

He picked up the backpack on their way back to the SUV. Judging from the metallic clanking, it held weapons, probably a few dozen small handguns.

Drugs and illegal immigrants were smuggled north; guns and money were smuggled south, in ever increasing quantities, fueling massive empires of crime on both sides and causing untold human misery.

The three they'd caught tonight were a drop in the bucket.

"Got him. Coming out." He called a warning before stepping out of the cover of the bushes.

Shep had been waiting. He lowered his weapon. Looked like he'd already stashed the other two guys in the back of his SUV. He holstered his gun as Jamie came closer.

"You okay? Your nose doesn't look too good."

"Feels like it's been driven into my brain." It really did. He was seeing a couple of extra stars than what were in the sky tonight.

"Broken?"

"Nah." But his cheekbone might have gotten cracked. He flexed his jaw. His face burned like hell.

"Could have waited for me."

Yeah, they were a team. *Whatever.* Just because he was no longer whole didn't mean he couldn't handle a chase by himself. Although that probably wasn't what Shep had meant.

He drew a deep breath. After his injury, he'd spent some time in the darkest pit of depression. Then he'd gotten his new legs and…fine, he'd been overcompensating. "We got them. That's what counts, right?"

Shep was panning the brush with his spotlight. "Did you find their car?"

"Didn't get that far. Has to be back there somewhere. I don't think they walked far." The man he'd chased down had had plenty of energy left in him for a good sprint.

"I'll go and take a look." Shep took off running, keeping both his flashlight and his weapon out.

Jamie shoved the smuggler he'd caught up against his SUV, searched the man's pockets for ID but found nothing but a small bag of weed. He locked the guy in the back of the car then went through the backpack and came up with three dozen brand-new small arms: Ruger .380, the perfect size to be carried concealed.

A small-time operation, but something. These three had to have a link on the other side. And that link would have an uplink. Follow the trail, and it might lead to the elusive Coyote.

He stayed on patrol while Shep ran the smugglers in, bringing Mo back with him so Mo could take the smugglers' car for a thorough search and fingerprinting. They would follow even the smallest lead. The stakes were too high. There were no unimportant details.

They kept an eye out for others. Sometimes smugglers worked in separate teams. They figured if one team got caught, the others would slip through while the border patrol was busy with the unlucky ones.

But the rest of the night went pretty quietly, the borderlands deserted. When Keith and Ray came to take over at dawn, Jamie drove back to his apartment to catch some sleep. His ringing phone woke him around midmorning.

"A friend of yours stopped by to see me earlier," Ryder, the team leader, said on the other end, sounding less than happy.

Jamie tried to unscramble his brain as he sat up and reached for his prosthetics. "Who?"

"Brianna Tridle."

An image of her long legs and full lips slammed into his mind. Okay, now he was wide awake.

"She kept calling up the chain at CBP until they gave her our contact number. Tracked us down from there.

She's demanding to be involved in our investigation. If her town and her people are part of whatever our mission is here, as she put it, she wants in."

"How did she take being disappointed?" With her looks, she probably didn't often experience a man saying no to her. Jamie almost wished he could have been there to see when Ryder had done it.

But Ryder said, "Actually, I agreed."

"Say that again?" His hand halted over the straps.

"She grew up around here, knows everyone. People respect her. Record clean as a whistle. We're pressed for time. She could be an asset."

"More like a pain in the asset."

"Possibly. She's pretty protective of her town. In any case, I don't plan on that being my problem," he added cheerfully.

A dark premonition settled over Jamie, immediately justified as Ryder said, "Since you're the one who got her all riled up, you'll be her liaison on the team."

"I don't think it's a good idea to involve her."

"You have my permission to try to talk her out of it. Tomorrow. Right now I need you to drive up to San Antonio. I got a new name from one of the men you and Shep caught last night on the border. Rico Marquez. He's a known gangbanger."

Which translated to: be ready for anything.

He was just as likely to come back with Rico as he was with a bullet in his back.

"Want someone to go with you? I could pull Keith from border detail," Ryder offered. "This is a pretty promising lead."

Chapter Three

Jamie tracked Rico to an abandoned warehouse where the man was apparently hiding out at the moment due to the fact that a rival gang member was hunting him. Information unwittingly supplied by his mother, who'd thought Jamie had come to help her son.

Jamie picked the lock on the rusted emergency door on the side of the building and eased inside little by little, as silently as he could manage. The temperature had to be close to a hundred; there was definitely no air-conditioning here. The cavernous place smelled like dust and machine grease.

The carcass of a giant and complicated-looking piece of machinery took up most of the floor; the ceiling was thirty feet high, at least. A metal walkway ringed the building high up on the wall, and some sort of an office was tucked under the corrugated metal roof in the back.

Jamie caught sight of a faint, flickering light up there—a TV?—so he moved that way. Where the hell were the stairs?

He walked forward slowly, carefully, listening for any noise that might warn him that he wasn't alone down here. Nothing.

Once he was closer to the back wall, he could hear the muted sounds of the TV upstairs. Good. Maybe they wouldn't hear him coming.

Now all he needed was to find a way up. He wished he had more light down at ground level, but all the windows were up high, just under the roof, and all were covered with enough grime to let through precious little light.

There were a million hiding places for someone to wait to ambush him. Then again, he'd also have plenty of cover if it came to a close-quarters shootout in here.

He scanned all the dark corners and found the stairs at last, hiding behind a bundle of foot-wide pipes that ran up along the wall. He approached it with as much care as possible.

The corner was a perfect place to ambush someone if anyone was down here, watching him. But he reached the bottom of the stairs without trouble.

Next came the tricky part—he had to go up the stairs. No more cover. He'd be in plain sight the whole time. The metal steps would rattle, drawing attention to him. He could be picked off with a single shot.

He took his gun out and moved up facing the main floor, ready to fire back if anyone took aim at him. Maybe he could keep them pinned down until he reached the top. But he made it all the way, walking backward, without anyone taking a shot at him.

Okay. That had to mean there were no lookouts on the lower level. If there were, they wouldn't have let him get this far, not when taking him out would have been a piece of cake.

So far, so good. But the next step was even more

difficult—sneaking by a wall of office windows that stretched from floor to ceiling and left no place to hide as he made his way to the door.

Anybody in the office would see him as soon as they looked this way.

He stole toward the windows and stopped as soon as he reached glass. He poked his head out a little to see what waited for him inside the room.

Overturned office furniture and stacked-up file cabinets cut the office space in two. He could see behind them through the gaps, could see part of a television set in the far corner, a mattress on the floor and naked bodies entwined in the act of lovemaking.

He blinked. Okay, that was unexpected. *Awkward.*

But also lucky.

He could make it across the walkway, passing in front of all those windows, without being seen. Nobody was paying the slightest attention to him.

He twisted the doorknob. Locked, which he'd kind of expected. But it was a simple office door lock and he had it picked in a flat minute.

Heck, a secretary with a hairpin could have done it.

He moved inside silently and kept down as he inched forward, using file cabinet for cover. Any noise his boots made was covered by some moaning and a lot of heavy breathing, not to mention the TV running a Mexican soap opera and a fan that was going somewhere behind the pile of furniture.

The scent of sex hung in the air, which made him think of Deputy Sheriff Bree Tridle, for some reason.

He pushed her out of his mind as he pulled his

backup weapon and stepped forward with a gun in each hand. "Freeze!"

The woman screamed and scampered off her man in a panicked rush, nearly kicking him in the head as she grabbed for the sheet to cover herself.

Jamie's eyes were on the guy. "Freeze! Hands in the air!"

Rico was in his early twenties, covered in gang tattoos, his gaze rapidly clearing as he grabbed for the handgun next to the mattress. He wasn't concerned with modesty.

Jamie shot at the gun and the force of the bullet kicked the weapon out of reach. Rico went for a switchblade that had been hidden under his pillow, apparently. He was nothing if not prepared.

He lunged toward Jamie.

"No! *Mi amor?*" the woman screamed, scampering farther away from them, looking shocked and horrified at the scene unfolding in front of her.

Jamie deflected the knife and knocked Rico back. "I don't want to have to shoot you, dammit!"

That slowed the guy down a little. "You no come to kill us?" He held the blade in front of him, ready for another go.

Jamie kept his gaze above neck level. "Customs and Border Protection. I'm here to talk about the smuggling your gang is involved in. You look like a nice couple. Nobody has to die today."

Wow, he was getting downright soft here. He sounded almost as optimistic as the deputy sheriff.

Rico didn't look convinced. "Her brother didn't send you?"

Jamie stashed his backup gun into the front of his waistband, then reached for his CBP badge and held it up. "I'm only here for information, man."

Rico raised his knife and his chin, sneering with contempt. "I don't talk to pigs."

"That's generally a good policy. Snitches don't live long in this business." Jamie glanced for a split second at the young woman who was white with fear, pulling her clothes on with jerky movements, and he did some quick thinking. "But it looks to me like you have something to live for. What if you two could get away both from your gang and your father?"

"Mi amor?" The woman's gaze flew to Rico, hope mixing with alarm in her voice.

"Can't be done." Rico reached for his jeans, didn't bother with underwear. He was tough enough to rough it, seemed to be the message.

Since he wasn't sneering anymore, Jamie took that as a good sign. "A chance at true love, the two of you together. What's that worth?"

Rico considered him through narrowed eyes. "You let Maria go. Right now."

"Okay," Jamie agreed, as a gesture of good faith. Maria probably had zero useful information for him, anyway. He looked at the woman. "Go."

She cast a questioning glance at Rico, who repeated the order in Spanish and explained that he would find her later, but she stubbornly shook her head.

A rapid argument followed before she finally ran for the door. They could hear her footsteps on the metal walkway, then down the stairs.

"I could kill you now," Rico said, still holding the

knife, a nasty-looking piece that had probably seen plenty of business on San Antonio's backstreets.

"You could try," Jamie answered calmly, feet apart, stance ready. He actually preferred Maria out of the way. No sense of her getting in the middle of this and maybe being killed.

Rico measured him up again. Swore in Spanish. "What the hell do you want from me?" he asked at last.

"I'm looking for a man called Coyote."

"Don't know him." But the corner of his left eye jumped.

"Any information would help. All I need is a link I could follow to him."

"And if I give you this, me and Maria go to witness protection?"

He nodded.

"Where?"

"Someplace where nobody can find you. You can get rid of the tattoos. They'll hook you up with a job and a place to live. You can get married."

Rico still hesitated.

"Ask yourself this," Jamie gestured at the ratty, messed-up room with his free hand. "Is this the life you want for your children? Or do you want something better? Doesn't she deserve more than this?"

God help him, he was appealing to true love. Something he wasn't even sure he believed in. But maybe Rico did, and that would be enough to settle matters here.

The man lowered his knife and filled his lungs, his ink-covered shoulders dropping as he exhaled. He looked pretty damn young with all the bluster gone out of him. He barely looked twenty. "There's no way out for guys like me."

"There is now. This must be your lucky day."

Tension-filled silence stretched between them.

"Okay," Rico said. "Let me think. I might be able to get something for you. If you can keep us safe. Maria the most."

An opening. "I'll talk to my people. But I need a solid lead."

More silence, then, "How do I find you?"

Jamie reached into his back pocket, pulled out a business card with his number on it and tossed it on the mattress between them.

Rico didn't move to pick it up. He'd do that when he was alone.

"Don't wait too long to call," Jamie warned. "I found you once, I will find you again. If I have to track you down, I'll be coming to bring you in." Then he backed away, gun still in hand.

He didn't relax until he was down the stairs and out of the building.

Damn, he hoped this would get them results. Because otherwise he would have to explain to Ryder why he wasn't taking Rico back to the interrogation room with him.

He'd just taken a hell of a gamble.

BREE WAS HEADING back to her office with her first cup of coffee of the morning, thinking about the talk she was giving at the middle school later about crime prevention, when Jamie Cassidy strolled into the Pebble Creek police station.

"I'm armed and I'm not handing my weapon over," he advised Lena by the metal detector, looking as surly and aggravated and sexy as ever. He took off his cowboy hat and ran his fingers through his hair to straighten it.

"Let him through," Bree called out before Lena could tackle him.

Or something. The officer had that dreamy-eyed look again that said she wouldn't mind seeing Jamie Cassidy on his back. There were probably a million women out there who shared the sentiment, although today he looked somewhat worse for wear.

Bruises and cuts marred the right side of his face— looked like he'd taken a beating since Bree had last seen him. Given his attitude and general disposition, she could see how a person would be tempted.

She flashed him her "this is my station and I'm the boss here" look, but when she spoke, she kept things cordial. "Mr. Cassidy. Nice to see you again. Why don't we talk in my office?"

"Jamie." He strode in past her, his mouth set in a line that was suspiciously close to a snarl.

A part of her that was apparently easily distracted wondered what it would take to make him happy. Not that she was volunteering for the job. Not even if those sharp eyes and those sculpted lips of his could have tempted a saint.

She closed the door behind them. "Please, take a seat. How can I help you today?"

He lowered his impressive frame into the nearest chair as he gave a soft growl of warning that he probably meant to sound threatening.

She found it kind of sexy, heaven help her. "Are you all right? What happened to your face?"

"Somebody whacked me."

"While the rest of us can only dream," she said sweetly. "Life is nothing but unfair." She set her mug down. "Came to share information?"

"Came for my equipment."

"Heavy-duty stuff." She didn't want him to leave until she got at least *something* out of him, so she grabbed the first-aid kit from the bookshelf on the back wall and went to stand in front of him, half sitting on her desk. "Let me see this. Look up, please."

He did, but only to send her a death glare. "I'm fine."

"Of course you are, mucho macho and all that. Which is how I know you won't be scared of a little sting."

He'd cleaned and disinfected his injuries from the looks of it; the smaller scrapes were already scabbed over, but she didn't like the larger gash over his cheekbone where his skin had split.

"I assume you didn't go get stiches because you don't have the time, not because you're scared of the needle?"

He shot her a dark look. He did that so well. Must have been part of his training.

"Why don't I slap on some butterfly bandages, as long as we're both here. Then you won't have to go see a doc. You'll save a ton of time that you can use to glare at people. I'd hate to see you slip off schedule."

His eyes remained stoic, but the corner of his sculpted mouth twitched. "Make it quick."

"How about you tell me who you guys are for real? Who do you really work for?"

"That's on a need-to-know basis."

"You're in my town, on my turf. I need to know."

"I don't think you have the right clearance, Deputy Sheriff."

He said *deputy sheriff* as a slur, as if he was calling her *babe* or maybe some other word that started with a *b*.

She focused on the disinfecting and the butterfly bandages to keep herself from engaging in contact unbecoming a police officer. When he was good to go, she closed her kit and walked back behind her desk.

"How about you tell me the basics," she suggested. "Something to get started with."

"I'm here for my equipment," he repeated.

Okay, then. He wasn't going to be an easy nut to crack.

She shoved aside a manila envelope somebody had left on her desk and folded her hands in front of her. "Just so we're clear on this one thing, this is my town. You make trouble here and I'll know why."

Being a Southern belle and a lady came naturally to her. She'd been raised on the beauty-queen circuit, but some days she did have her lapses. Looked like it was going to be one of those days.

His eyebrow slid higher. "Do I look like trouble?"

"Double serving. With whipped cream and cherry on top."

A bark of laughter escaped him, softening his face, and she caught a glimpse of what he might have been at one time, without all the darkness he was now carrying. It took her breath away.

Phew, all righty, then. She shook her head to clear the image.

So unfair that she would find him attractive. He was in her town doing secret things. He was about as pleasant as a wild boar with a toothache. He was high-handed. She didn't want to like him, not even a little.

"What's your team really doing on the border?" she asked again, and waited.

And waited.

"Ryder McKay said that you'll be my liaison. Liaise." She raised her eyebrows into her best schoolmarm look.

He still waited another couple of stubborn seconds before he finally said, "We're here about the smuggling."

"But not to make policy recommendations," she guessed.

He shook his head, watched her, measured her up again. "We're here to intercept a special transfer."

"And you work for Homeland Security?"

He just stared at her.

So, okay, she could pretty much guess the rest. Whatever his team had come for probably had something to do with terrorism. "Is my town safe?"

"Yes."

"And you know this how?"

"We have *some* information. You're not a target."

Made *some* sense. Terrorists would be going for one of the major cities.

Anger coursed through her. She was a patriot and a Texan, sick of people who tried to mess with her country. "Is there anything I can help with?"

He hesitated for a moment. "Maybe. I'll let you know if we come across something where we could use your assistance."

"And you'll let me know of any developments?"

He hesitated longer this time, but said, "Yes."

"Thank you." She pulled out the bottom drawer that was about filled to the rim with his weaponry and one by one set them on the desk between them, grabbing an old canvas bag from under the desk and dropping it on top. "I'd appreciate it if you carried that loot out of here concealed."

He gave a brief nod and stepped forward to pack up his things. The string on his night-vision goggles caught on her manila envelope. They reached for it at the same time, their fingers touching.

She barely had time to register the zing as she jerked back, the contents of the envelope spilling all over her desk.

She stared at the photos for a disjointed moment as her brain registered the images: snapshots of her in her kitchen, taken from outside her house. She grabbed for them, but not fast enough.

He snatched up the last one and took a good look at it before holding it up for her. "What the hell is this?"

The photo showed her standing in her bedroom next to the bed, changing, wearing nothing but a skimpy bra and blue jeans, holding her favorite checkered shirt.

She grabbed the picture from him as her heart sped suddenly. *Oh, God. Not again.* She so didn't have time for her past to rise up to claim her. "That's on a need-to-know basis."

HE DIDN'T LIKE the way she suddenly paled, or the idea that she had a stalker.

"When do you think these were taken?" Jamie asked.

She didn't think about it long. "Last night. That's the shirt I was wearing yesterday."

"And you went to see Ryder McKay earlier in the day?" He gave her a pointed look.

"The two have nothing to do with each other."

The hell they didn't. "Smuggling is a multibillion-dollar business. It's a dangerous business."

"Really? I must have been sitting behind my desk, filing my nails, and I missed that briefing," she said with that overly sweet smile he'd come to learn meant she was mocking him.

He shot her a look that told her he wasn't amused. "Look, people around here know we're investigating smuggling. Someone saw you visiting the office. They didn't like it. You need to stay out of what we're doing."

"I'll take the risk."

"I'm not asking. I'm telling you. Don't involve yourself. Forget everything we've talked about earlier."

"Or what?" A laugh escaped her and trilled along his nerve endings. "You'll spank me? For heaven's sake. I'm an officer of the law. I'm trained to handle myself."

The visual of the spanking bit left him both speechless and breathless for a second.

"I'm a big girl, Jamie." She switched to dead serious and ticked off in a split second, which did nothing to lessen the wave of lust that threatened to drown him. "Whatever threat is jeopardizing the peace of this town and the law, you can be sure I'll be out there fighting it." She pressed her full lips together.

He wondered what she'd do if he tried to kiss her. Throw him against the wall again? His pulse quickened.

On the other hand, as unpredictable and unreasonable as she was, she might just shoot him.

Not that kissing those lips wouldn't be worth the risk, he decided. Not that he was going to do it. No way. He was in town on serious business. And women were no longer part of his life, anyway. He had too much baggage, too many nightmares. He had no right to bring that into a relationship and mess up somebody else's life along with his.

He didn't have much left. He was a trained killing machine, that was about it. He planned on living the rest of his life using what skills he had in the service of his country.

"Stick to speeding tickets," he said as he stood. "Forget about me and my team." Although he was pretty sure he wasn't going to be able to forget about her. He was going to try, anyway, he promised himself as he walked away from her.

His shift was starting in half an hour.

He walked out of the station to his SUV parked up front. At least he'd gotten a possible lead in San Antonio.

He would have to figure out the witness-protection thing with the U.S. Marshals Service. And Rico had to think about what he had and come up with enough that would buy him two witness-protection tickets.

Jamie needed to talk to Ryder about that. And forget about Bree. He would. After he made sure she was safe.

Chapter Four

Stick to speeding tickets, Jamie Cassidy had said. He had a singular ability to get under her skin, Bree thought as she went about her business.

She didn't have to worry about speeding tickets, as it turned out. Just as she finished her crime-prevention presentation at the middle school, the town's streetlight system went down, snarling traffic, cars barely inching along. She spent most of the rest of her shift cleaning up the mess.

A dozen fender benders got tempers flaring; a couple of arguments ended in fistfights before it was all over. Bree didn't have too much time to think about Jamie Cassidy, and thank God for that, because the man was enough to raise any sane woman's blood pressure.

She was exhausted by the time she made it back to the station, and then a whole other hour went to waste with writing up reports. She'd just finished when Hank, the contractor whose company managed the town's traffic-control system, walked into her office.

"Hey, Bree." He was short and round, the mocha-skinned version of Danny DeVito, a family guy who was always hustling, always working on something, if not for his kids and small company then for the town. He was a tireless volunteer.

"Everything up and running?"

"Almost. I wanted to talk to you about something." He stopped in front of her desk. "Looks like several of our control boxes were shorted out on purpose."

She stilled. "Are you sure?" Why on earth would somebody want to do that? "Can you give me the locations?"

He rattled off the crossroads and she wrote them down. "I'll look into it. Thanks for letting me know. Can I get you a coffee from the break room?" The least she could do. She appreciated the work Hank did and the fact that he took the time to come in to talk to her.

"Lena already fixed me up with coffee and a Danish." He patted his round belly with a quick grin. "I better get going. I still have a couple of things to fix."

She gave him a parting wave. "Thanks. I really appreciate it. Give me a call if you run into any trouble."

"Will do. Say hi to Katie for me," he said as he left her to her work.

She shrugged into her harness and slipped her weapon into her holster as she stood and scanned the major intersections on her list. Several stores in those spots would have external security cameras. She needed to check the footage.

Most of the officers were out on calls and the station was close to deserted.

"I'm off to look into the traffic-light business," she called to Lena on her way out. "Back in an hour, I hope. Want anything?"

"A hot guy with an oil claim on his ranch?"

"If I see one, I'll send him your way."

The traffic was clearing up at last so she didn't have any trouble reaching the first address, just three blocks from the station. The owner of the small pawnshop handed over his security video without insisting on a warrant. Bree had cut him a break a month or so ago when he'd taken in stolen merchandise without knowing.

She moved on to the next address, a place that sold used video games and gaming equipment, and got the recording there, too. She'd been buying Katie games there for years. She knew her community and was nice to people. And they were nice to her when she needed something.

The next place after that was a specialty shop, selling high-end, artisan cowboy boots, run by one of her old schoolmates.

Rounding up the half-dozen recordings took a little over an hour, including taking some time to talk with people. She liked knowing what was going on in her town.

Then it was back to the office to view the footage. Another half an hour passed before she had her men, two twenty-somethings from Hullett—Jeremy and Josh Harding, brothers. She knew them from a round-up brawl that had sent six men to the E.R. last year.

She headed out to Hullett to pick up the boys. She let them sweat it out in the back of her police cruiser— didn't start questioning them until they were in the interview room.

They both wore scuffed boots and jeans and identical ragged T-shirts, no brand, cheapest stuff money could buy. They looked down on their luck. If they were going to commit a crime, why not one that would benefit them financially? Try as she might, she couldn't figure out the traffic-light angle.

"Little old for pranks, aren't you?"

Jeremy shot a meaningful look at his younger brother before looking back at her. "Dunno what you talkin' about."

"What do you Hullett boys have against Pebble Creek these days?" They had an arson investigation going, the fire started by someone just like these two, last week. Then there were the half-dozen cases of random vandalism she couldn't tie to anyone. Investigations that kept her busy, like she needed extra work with smuggling and the counterfeit money coming in.

"You're messing up my crime-rate statistics," she told them, putting away her softer side. "I don't like it."

The younger one, Josh, brightened. "We are?" He sounded a little too eager. Even pleased.

She looked from him to Jeremy. "Okay. What's going on here?"

"We have an alibi. We were at a friend's house, hangin' out and shootin' beer cans," the older brother said, smug as anything.

"Is that so?" she asked calmly. "Because I have half a dozen security tape recordings showing you two messing with the traffic-light control boxes."

The younger brother paled. "I can't go to no jail. Jenny's gonna have a kid. Ma's gonna skin me alive if I get into trouble again. She said it."

"Shut up, idiot," Jeremy barked at him.

Bree raised a placating hand. "How about we start

with cooperation, then discuss restitution? Things don't have to come to jail."

"Sounds good, ma'am," Josh hurried to say, all manners, suddenly.

His older brother whacked him on the shoulder. "You don't even know what it means."

"Can't be worse than jail."

Bree shook her head. "It means you two have to pay back the repair costs, and then never cause trouble in my town again." She thought that was a fair deal, but Josh's shoulders sagged.

"We ain't got no money. That's why we did it in the first place," he whined, earning another smack from Jeremy.

They were only about ten years younger than she was, but she felt like she should ground them or something. "No more hitting." She held up a warning finger. "Now, explain to me how you make money from stopping traffic?"

They looked down. Looked at each other.

She pulled out her cell phone. "How about I just call your mother?"

"The mill," Josh blurted out, then slumped as Jeremy shot him a dark look that said, "I'll make you regret this later."

"The wire mill?" Hullett had a wire mill. She failed to understand what Pebble Creek traffic had to do with it.

"It's going under," Josh explained.

Not a surprise. The owner was in prison for human trafficking. A shame for the workers and their families. The Hullett wire mill was the town's largest employer.

"You two work there?"

Jeremy pressed his lips together and sulked, but Josh responded. "We already got our pink slips."

Bad timing with the baby coming, she thought. "I'm still waiting on how this connects to traffic."

"Word is, there's gonna be a paper mill comin' in. Choice is between Hullett and Pebble Creek."

She knew about that. Some rich Chinese guy, Yo Tee, who owned a big paper mill on the other side of the border, was thinking about building a smaller one over here. Probably to get a tax break or whatever. He had some team that was scouting for a location. She'd run into them the week before when an overeager citizen spotted them at an abandoned factory and reported it as a possible burglary.

"We want the paper jobs in Hullett," Josh told her. "They could put new machines into the wire mill and keep the workers on. We could do trainin'. We ain't stupid."

Clearly. She narrowed her eyes at him. "So you're making a mess of my town to make Hullett look better. Is that it?"

He looked down at his hands sheepishly. "We need the work."

They went about it in a completely wrong and idiotic way, but she could certainly understand their motivation. "What else?"

Josh looked up, confusion on his face.

"What else have you done?" she clarified.

"The lights were it. I swear."

He looked earnest enough that she believed him. But she would bet good money that Pebble Creek's recent troubles with vandalism had been caused by some of his buddies—bunch of geniuses.

She told them she'd take them to holding, one at a time, while she figured something out. She took Jeremy first, then Josh. With Josh, she swung by the break room on their way to holding.

He walked with his head hanging. "Just don't call my ma, all right? She can't pay no bail."

"Want some coffee?"

He looked up with surprise. He'd probably expected chastisement. "Thank you, ma'am. I would."

"How about something to go with it?" She gestured toward the box of doughnuts on the counter.

"For real?"

"I'm not here to abuse people whose biggest crime is wanting to work."

Relief filled his face as he cautiously reached into the white paper box for an apple fritter.

She drew a slow breath. "But you and your brother did go about it the wrong way. Replacing those fuse boxes will cost a mint."

Josh looked like the first bite got stuck in his throat. "I told you, we ain't got no money."

"And the baby's coming," she said with sympathy. "I'll talk to the judge. You could be booked and released today, no bail. I could put in a strong recommendation for community service only. You and your brother could work off the damage." She paused. "Thing is, if I'm that nice, I need to know everything you know."

But instead of giving her information on other recent vandalism in Pebble Creek like she'd expected, he said,

"I know about the bad money they were talkin' about on TV." He looked around nervously.

Pay dirt.

She hurried to the door and closed it, all ears. "Sit." She put the whole doughnut box in front of him.

But he looked really scared now, just holding on to his fritter. "If anyone finds out…"

"Not from me. I promise."

He swallowed hard and looked to the door as if to make sure nobody was coming in. "I was at Ronny's house last week for some grillin' and beer." He paused.

"Ronny who?"

"Brown. Down by the reservoir."

She knew Ronald Brown. They were old friends. She'd arrested him on drug distribution last year. He'd gotten off on a technicality. "How is he linked to the fake money?"

"I don't know. I swear." Josh put his free hand to his chest. "I went into the house to take a leak. He was in the kitchen with this other dude. The other guy was givin' him a roll of twenties and tellin' him they needed to be spent slowly and carefully."

"That's it?"

He nodded. "I didn't think nothin' of it until they said about bad money on the news."

"What did the other man look like?"

"Mexican. Short and scruffy. He had some tattoos. Ain't never seen him around before."

"How about you look at some pictures for me?"

She led him back to her office then had him look through the mug shots on her computer.

Scrolling through the pictures, and doing a lot of

handholding so Josh wouldn't renege on his promise to help, took some time. By the time they ran out of mug shots to look at and she'd processed then released the brothers, her shift was over. Too late to go and see Ronny Brown. She put away her files. Tomorrow was another day. Right now, she had to go pick up Katie.

The drive over took less than ten minutes.

"Did you have a good day?" Bree asked when they were in the car, heading home.

Katie worked at a facility that employed handicapped people. They shipped small machine parts all over the country and were responsible for wrapping and packaging. The people running the place were fantastic with the employees. Katie loved going to work since all her friends were there. They had fun together.

"Mrs. Mimms said I did good work," Katie said. "I think she was happy. She made the happy face."

They'd been working on emotions with cue cards and internet pictures in the evenings. Katie was high functioning, but she did have autism. She had trouble with emotions, both displaying them appropriately and telling the mood of others.

"I'm sure she was very happy. Did you have a good lunch?"

Food was a touchy subject. Katie only liked a handful of things, and she wouldn't eat at all if the food on her plate was touching.

"Chicken fingers. Good."

Bree relaxed a little. It worried her when Katie skipped meals. She was such a skinny little thing already.

"We got someone new," her sister informed her.

"He's just like me. Except he doesn't talk to anyone. His name is Scott."

"Do you like him?"

"He's quiet."

Which meant she liked him. She gave a full report on the way home, then went through her coming-home routine, putting her things away, washing her hands, setting the table, while Bree made some hamburgers for dinner.

"Can we do a puzzle later?"

"Sure." Bree pulled the French fries from the oven— baked to save some calories—and thought how much she liked their evenings together. Katie was sweet and gentle, and part of her life irrevocably.

She didn't care if the few boyfriends she'd had over the years couldn't deal with that. They'd wanted her, but they hadn't wanted her "baggage," as the last one had put it. Thing was, she would rather have her sister than a jerk in her life, anyway. She *had* said that. With a Southern-belle smile on her face.

Still, the good things in her life far outweighed the bad.

She thought of the pictures in the manila envelope, the first time she'd allowed herself to think of them since she'd gotten them away from Jamie Cassidy.

Trouble was coming again.

Just thinking about that made her tired.

Why now?

She would end it for good this time, she promised herself. She wasn't going to let this touch Katie, put her in danger.

As she turned to put the food on the table, movement outside caught her eye.

Did someone just step behind her garage?

She set the fries on the table. "I'm going to put the garbage out, then we can eat."

"Okay," Katie called back, cheerful and oblivious to danger, which was the way Bree meant to keep things.

She bagged up the garbage. Then she slipped her service revolver into her waistband before she walked outside through the back to confront her past that was rising up once again to claim her.

Chapter Five

Her mother's oversize garden sculptures populated the backyard, same as the front, their shapes too familiar to look eerie, even in the twilight. Bree opened the door without a sound and ducked to the right, into the warm evening air and the cover of the bushes. And then recognized the man standing by the shed—Jamie Cassidy.

You have got to be kidding me. She ground her teeth together.

She nearly sprung up to yell at him. But maybe teaching him a lesson would be a more productive way to prevent him from spying on her again. So she kept down, skulked around the rock garden and snuck up behind him, using the statues as cover.

She didn't have much in the backyard as far as tall plants went, just a few butterfly bushes, with more color added by generous clumps of black-eyed Susans and asters that were putting on quite a show of yellow and purple this fall.

She moved as silently as a copperhead, raising her gun when she was but a step behind him, anticipating the jolt he'd give when she pressed the cold metal against the back of his skull. That ought to take the cocky bastard down a peg.

Except when she was an inch away, he said, "Hey, Deputy," and reached back at the same time, clamped his fingers over her wrist and shoved her against the side of the shed, holding her hand above her head, their faces inches from each other.

His cheekbone had turned purple since she'd last seen him. He still wore her butterfly bandages. And he still looked too handsome by half. *Deal with it.* She normally wasn't a shallow person.

"What are you doing at my house?" She shoved against him with her free hand but he wouldn't budge. "I could have shot you."

"I didn't think you were the type to shoot a fellow law enforcement drone."

"How did you know I recognized you?"

"You never took the safety off your weapon."

Dismay and aggravation tightened her jaw. He'd probably seen her and tracked her movements from the moment she'd come outside.

She didn't often get caught off guard. That Jamie Cassidy had had her back against the wall twice now in the space of a week aggravated the living daylights out of her. "What are you doing here?" She repeated the question he still hadn't answered.

"Trying to catch whoever took those pictures. I think this might be connected to your visit to Ryder. Someone doesn't want you to share your local expertise with my team. Whoever is trying to mess with you might be just the guy we're looking for."

"You're just trying to scare me off so I don't stick my nose into your team's business."

"One can dream," he said lightly.

"Maybe *you* sent the pictures to intimidate me," she said, although she knew that wasn't the case.

He leaned another inch closer. His sharp gaze raked her face. "When I want to scare someone, I'm a lot more direct about it. I don't leave them guessing."

His powerful body completely blocked any escape, his fingers holding her right hand above her head as effectively as handcuffs. He wasn't trying to look threatening, she didn't think. The words had been said straight-faced, yet alarm tingled down her spine nonetheless.

Okay, and a little bit of lust, too. She didn't think he was going to harm her. He could have done so already, countless times if that was his intention. The twinge of attraction she felt was a pure evolutionary response of a female to a display of power from the alpha male.

So unfair.

She tried to resist the magnetic field that drew her to him.

The faint scent of his soap tickled her nose, mixed with some barely there, understated aftershave. She could almost swear she could smell the testosterone coming off him, he was so ridiculously male.

He had a warrior's body, a warrior's stance, a warrior's eyes. And definitely a warrior's strength. She tried to pull away and failed once again.

"You're trespassing," she pointed out, a little testiness mixing with the twinges of lust she didn't appreciate.

He opened his mouth to respond, but Katie appearing at the back door stopped him short. He let Bree's hand go immediately and she moved out of the shadows while he disappeared into them. She appreciated that tremendously. She didn't want him upsetting Katie.

"We're having dinner," Katie said. "It's dinnertime."

"Yes, it is, sweetie. I'm coming." She hurried toward her sister. Having her schedule interrupted could send Katie off-kilter for the rest of the evening. Better to keep everything running smoothly.

She glanced back from the doorway one last time, but Jamie Cassidy had disappeared completely.

She wasn't enough of an optimist to think permanently.

JAMIE WENT AROUND the back of Bree Tridle's modest two-story home. He'd gone off and grabbed something to eat, then came back. This time her upstairs lights were all out; there was just one light on downstairs, in her kitchen. He knocked quietly on the back door before trying the doorknob. Unlocked.

"Bree?" He didn't want to get shot.

"In here."

He moved down the dark hallway and came out into the kitchen, bathed in light. The space was plain and spotless, Mexican tile floor, simple pine cabinets. A handful of small, crystal unicorns hung in the window.

She sat at the kitchen table, a bottle of beer and a bottle of strawberry wine cooler in front of her. Looked like she'd been expecting him.

"How did you know I'd come back?" he asked as he sat, taking the beer.

"You don't look like the type who walks away without getting what he came for."

He leaned back in his chair. "I like smart women. I'm glad we understand each other."

"Let's not get carried away." She drank straight from the bottle.

Good. He didn't have the patience for prissy women. She was trying his patience in so many ways already, the last thing he needed was for her to start putting on airs.

"So why are you here, exactly?" she asked.

"I need that envelope." He should have taken it when he'd been in her office. He'd been distracted. By her. That wasn't going to happen again. He was here on a mission.

"Why would you think I brought it home? Things like that are entered into evidence."

He watched her for a long second. "You strike me as the kind of woman who would handle her personal business herself."

"I'm glad you understand that it *is* personal. I'll take care of it."

She said that with a little too much confidence. He watched her for a moment. "So you know who your stalker is?"

She shifted in her seat, reaching for her bottle again, saying nothing.

Okay, she did know. "Has this happened before?"

She gave a reluctant nod. "Back when I was competing."

Beauty pageants, she meant. She looked different now from the super made-up, big-hair pictures he'd found on the internet. She was still beautiful without a doubt, but in a hometown-girl kind of way.

She wore her hair in a simple ponytail, the blond her natural color, he was pretty sure, little makeup, dressed plain and comfortable. The kind of woman who could dazzle the hell out of a guy yet somehow make him comfortable when sitting with her. And could probably beat the stuffing out of him if he got fresh with her.

"Want to tell me about it?" he asked.

"If it gets you out of my hair."

He promised nothing. Not about keeping out of her hair, or her pants, for that matter. There was a part of him, getting louder and louder, that wanted to keep his options open.

"When I was doing the pageants," she said after a minute, her expression turning sober, "I had a young fan, Lilly Tanner, who wanted to be just like me. She wrote me several times, and I wrote back. We even met. Her room was apparently covered with my posters. She wore T-shirts with my picture on them."

She paused to draw a slow breath. "She was bullied in school and ridiculed. They called her ugly, and worse. A lot worse. Just really mean and nasty stuff." She folded her hands on her lap. "She ended up committing suicide."

"And one of her friends blamed you for it."

"Her twin brother, Jason. He's not—" she paused "—he doesn't always understand what he's doing. He was born with some mental disability and the added depression pushed him off balance after Lilly's death."

Not a comforting thought. "You need to make him stop before this escalates."

"I know." She took a drink. "I called his parents while I was waiting for you to show. They don't know where he is. He moved away from home six months ago and only keeps in touch sporadically. I'll find him."

She didn't seem scared or upset as much as sad.

"You feel some responsibility for the sister," he guessed. "The parents lost their daughter and you don't want to be the one to put their son in prison."

"Maybe." She glanced toward the stairs. "I met him before. He wasn't some evil kid. He just didn't know how to relate to the world around him."

"I don't think you're taking this seriously enough."

"We'll just have to agree to disagree."

That little crease in her bottom lip kept drawing his gaze. He looked up into her eyes. "I don't do that when I'm right."

She raised an eyebrow. "Are you ever wrong?"

"Not that I can remember."

He got the quick laugh from her that he'd been aiming for. He hadn't liked the darkness on her face, the idea that she would carry the guilt over the girl's death. She had nothing to do with that. Her happy, peppy personality might have annoyed him before, but it looked good on her. She needed to go back to that.

If anyone had a past to feel guilty about, it was him. An entire family had been killed because of him: husband, wife, four kids. He pushed away the memories, rubbed the ache in his knees, even if there was nothing there but metal.

"I like modesty in a man," she observed, irony in her tone.

He almost asked what else she liked in a man, but

decided he'd better not. He needed to focus on the business at hand. "I'm going to need that envelope."

Her forehead pulled into an annoyed frown. "I know who sent it. I said I'll take care of it."

"I still need our lab to confirm whether any prints on the envelope really belong to your old stalker. Once I know this has nothing to do with my job, I'll cross it off my to-do list and you can handle it any way you want to."

"I don't need your permission to do that." But she got up and walked to the kitchen counter and pulled out an evidence bag with the manila envelope inside it. She grabbed a plastic bag from the counter, carefully transferred the photos into that and kept them. She gave him the envelope only.

He didn't feel like arguing with her for the rest. He took the bag and walked to the door. "I'll be in touch."

"Phone is good," she said.

He lifted an eyebrow as he looked back at her. "Why, it's almost as if you didn't like me, Deputy Sheriff," he said as he left her standing in her kitchen.

He walked across her small front yard, where she had almost as many garden statues as she did in the back, mostly unicorns and angels. He wondered what the story behind those was, but he couldn't wonder for long. His phone interrupted.

Rico Marquez.

"Made up your mind?" Jamie asked as he got into his car.

"Yeah, man. I got something."

"I'm on my way. Same place as before?"

"At the chop shop across the road. Come in through the back."

He hung up, then sent a text to Ryder to let him know where he'd gone. At this time of the evening there wouldn't be much traffic on the roads, but it'd still be well past midnight before he made it to San Antonio and back.

He had plenty of time to think on his way into the city. Mostly he thought about whether the meeting was a trap. But no matter which way he turned it in his head, he didn't see what reason Rico would have for taking him out. Unless his whole plea was bogus and he wanted a high-score kill to get a promotion within his gang. A possibility.

Yet the chance that he did have something on the Coyote and he was willing to share it was worth the risk. So Jamie made sure his weapons were checked and ready and that he was wearing his bulletproof vest before he pulled into the dark alley behind the chop shop and got out, sending his exact location to his team first, as insurance.

He got out of the car slowly. When he didn't immediately get hit from one of the windows, he counted that as a good sign.

The rusty steel door opened before he could knock, and Rico gestured for him to hurry inside. The lights were off in the main bay, and the smell of motor oil hung in the air. Rico led him to the office in the back but only turned on the small desk lamp there. It barely illuminated the room. The cavernous shop stretched in darkness on the other side of the glass partition.

Rico scratched his tattoo-covered neck. Pretty much

every part of him that was visible was inked, including the backs of his hands. "Anyone follow you here?"

Jamie shook his head.

"You wired?"

Jamie pulled up his shirt.

Rico's glance caught on the gun first, tucked into the waistband, before he raised his gaze to scan the rest. That they would both be armed had been understood from the beginning.

Jamie dropped his clothes back into place. "What do you have?"

Rico rubbed his fingers over his mouth. "If this checks out, I get protection? For both of us? "

"That's the deal."

The man shifted from one foot to the other. "You said you're looking for the Coyote. What for? He's bad news, man."

"Let that be my problem."

Rico measured him up. A couple of seconds passed in silence.

"Last year I was in the can," he said at last, then drew a long breath. "Enrique led the gang then. He wanted to move some of our guys down south, take over. Wanted to control both sides. He wanted to be king."

"So?" Gangs looking to expand weren't exactly big news. "Where does the Coyote come in?"

"In prison, the man in the cell next to me worked for the Coyote."

Jamie leaned forward and listened.

"He wanted revenge. The Coyote killed his brother. He said he'd pass information to Enrique, help Enrique take territory from the Coyote."

"Did he?"

"He got stabbed the next day." He banged his fist against his chest several times to demonstrate. "The guards never figured out who stabbed him, but I know. A guy called Jimenez. On the Coyote's orders."

"Where is Jimenez now?"

"Nobody knows. He went underground when he got out. Might be he was killed."

Another dead end. But there was something else here. Orders got delivered through visitors. All he had to do to find the Coyote's messenger was search the visitor records at the prison, see who'd come to visit Jimenez just before the murder. Then the messenger could lead him to the Coyote himself.

"So when do we get out?" Rico asked. "I don't want to wait. Maria's ready. Tonight?"

"Give me a couple of days to finalize everything. I'll call you to let you know how and when to come in."

The thought that they would soon have a direct link to the Coyote was enough to keep Jamie awake on the drive home, no coffee needed. Even if they couldn't dig up enough evidence to charge the man with smuggling, they would have murder one if they could prove that the Coyote had ordered the execution of that man in prison. It didn't much matter under what charge the bastard was put away, as long as he was taken out of circulation.

And, most important, once they had him, they would do whatever it took to get enough information out of him to catch the terrorists they were hunting.

He thought about that, and about Bree's stalker. He didn't like the idea of Bree in danger. She was way too nice. If some bad guy came into her house she'd be more likely to offer him coffee than shoot him between the eyes.

Yet if anyone could talk her way out of a situation with smiles and politeness, it was her. He didn't fully understand how she did what she did, but he had to admit it worked.

That was a whole different approach from how he operated. He'd been trained to identify the enemy, aim, shoot and kill. She needed someone like that to back her up, just in case.

Not that he was volunteering.

He just wanted to make sure her stalker wasn't connected to her recent cooperation agreement with his team. He hoped she was right. He hoped it was something else, a misguided regular Joe, like she'd said, and not some professional criminal sent to harass her.

He had work to do and she was a distraction. He wanted to figure out what was going on so he could close the door on the whole business and walk away from her. As soon as possible.

Chapter Six

She'd planned on going out and finding Ronny Brown to ask him about the suspicious roll of twenties Josh had seen him receiving, but by the time Bree dropped off Katie at work and got to the office the morning after Jamie's surprise visit to her house, she had a visitor waiting. The CIA had sent an agent in response to her call about the fake twenties.

He was a full head taller than she, clean shaven, blond hair cropped, black suit crisp. He carried a black leather briefcase and wore the exact kind of CIA sunglasses actors wore on TV. He had a strong jaw, straight nose, good build.

Hot, Lena mouthed from behind him, grinning. Looked like she wouldn't have been against a full-body search if the opportunity presented itself. Not that she was a lecher or anything, or someone who flitted from guy to guy. She just had a cheerful personality and a zest for life, and she noticed and appreciated pretty things and hot guys and whatever else made life good to live. She fostered rescue puppies and went skydiving on the weekends. Working with her was fun, because she was fun, and because she was also an extremely competent officer.

Sexy, she mouthed next with a wink.

Not as sexy as Jamie Cassidy, Bree thought. Not that she was here to check out men. Or that she was interested in either of them. But she wasn't blind. Especially to Jamie, whose dark gaze had managed to haunt her dreams all night, damn him.

The visitor nodded at her. "Deputy Sheriff."

"You must be Agent Herrera." She shoved Jamie out of her mind and returned the agent's smile as she showed him into her office. Since he was already holding a disposable cup he'd probably picked up at a drive-through, she didn't offer him coffee. "Why don't you take a seat?"

She turned on her computer, then unlocked her top drawer and extracted the three evidence bags that held the three twenty-dollar bills she'd seized so far. "I have time and date, and the circumstances of how and where the bills were obtained, including names and contact information."

"I appreciate it. It's always good to work with competent people." The agent held one of the bags up to the light and examined the banknote.

"Can you tell anything just by looking at it?"

"Just that it's pretty good quality. We'll have to run some tests. Could be leftover from an old batch we've already seized."

She thought about Ronny Brown, the clue Josh had given her. What had Josh seen in that kitchen? Somebody handing over a roll of bills. Ronny hadn't been caught with any fake money, and most vendors in town were checking. She'd put the word out right after the first case.

More likely than not, the money Ronny had received had to do with drugs. That was his usual speed. She would check him out before she said anything to Agent Herrera and look like a small-town rookie, too eager to jump the gun. The agent wouldn't appreciate having his time wasted.

And she didn't need to look like a fool just before sheriff elections. Not that she was running. Being sheriff took more time than she could give. First and foremost, she wanted to be there for Katie. But the new sheriff would be her boss, and she didn't want his first impression to be that she was an imbecile.

"You find a lot of counterfeit money?" she asked the man.

"Not that much. But when we do, we take it seriously. Out of every ten thousand dollars in circulation, about three are fake."

He glanced through the window of her office at Lena, who caught the look and smiled at him. The agent's gaze lingered.

Well, what do you know? "Will you be staying?"

"For the rest of the week." He laid his briefcase on his knees, opened it then carefully placed the three evidence bags on top of some papers before looking across the desk. "If I need a place to interview people?"

"Feel free to use our facilities." Lena could show him around.

"Thank you, Deputy." He stood. "I'll be in touch." He pulled a card from his suit pocket and set it on her desk.

"If you come across any information that might be relevant to this case, I'd appreciate it if you'd let me know."

"Of course."

He left with a parting nod.

Okay, definitely handsome, if a little dry for her taste. But Lena was a big girl and had the right to pick her own poison, Bree thought with a smile as she stood to go for coffee.

The corner of a manila envelope in her in-box caught her gaze.

Her stomach clenched.

So stupid. Now she was going to be scared of envelopes? It could be anything.

But she used her shirtsleeve to carefully tug the envelope from the pile. Unmarked, it was the same size and color as the one the photos had come in. Lumpy. *Not pictures this time.*

She stepped over to close her door, then pulled two rubber gloves from the box in her drawer and put them on before she opened the clasp.

Visual first. She peered inside and could see some kind of fabric. Dark. She carefully tilted the envelope, holding it by the corners until the contents dropped onto her desk.

Black lace panties, she registered a split second before recognizing them as hers.

Jason had been in her house. Anger and concern pulsed through her in alternating bursts, her teeth clenching.

He was getting braver. Of course, he was nine years older now—no longer the adolescent kid she remembered, but a man.

When her phone rang, she picked it up without looking at the display, her attention still on the slip of black cloth in front of her. She eased it back into the envelope in case someone came in, while balancing the phone between her shoulder and ear. "Bree."

"Just wanted to make sure you got to work fine and everything's okay," Jamie said on the other end.

Because an arrogant outsider keeping tabs on her was what she really needed. He was on some superteam. If he thought just because she was a small-town deputy and a woman she was clueless, he had another think coming. She didn't need his "protection."

"Thanks for the concern, Mr. Cassidy." She exaggerated her Texas drawl. "I might have strained my pinky, holding it out while I was sipping tea. Also, my corset pinches a little, but other than that I'm okay."

A moment of heavy silence passed. "Don't mock me." Then another pause. "And don't talk to me about corsets."

The deep timbre of his voice as he said that sent a not-altogether-unpleasant tingle down her spine. She was as bad as Lena out there with Agent Hottie. Uh-uh, not going to happen. She didn't even like Jamie Cassidy. And she had way too much going on to get tangled with a man right now.

She filled her lungs. "Is there a particular reason you're wasting my time this morning? Did your team find anything you'd like to share with me?"

"Any new contact from the stalker?"

She shoved the envelope into her top drawer. "No." She didn't want or need Jamie Cassidy's help. He was too much of a distraction.

"You hesitated."

She rolled her eyes, even though she knew he couldn't see it. "My stalker is my problem."

"Not until I'm sure he's not coming after you because you got involved with my team."

He was like a dog with a bone. She closed her eyes for a second. "He's not. I told you."

"We'll see when the envelope comes back from the lab. I'm on border patrol today. I'll stop by tonight to talk about whatever happened since I last saw you."

"Nothing happened."

"Put another beer in the fridge for me," he said before he hung up on her.

She was an upbeat person normally. She really was. But Jamie Cassidy was getting on her last nerve. If he showed up at her house tonight, they were going to have to have a serious talk about boundaries.

She was *not* going to let him keep on distracting her. She drew a deep breath and refocused on her work, then walked out of her office to check with Lena about a bail-bond issue they hadn't yet resolved from the previous week. Then she would track down Ronny Brown.

Lena was just hanging up the phone when Bree exited her office. "Discharge of a firearm at the Yellow Armadillo," she said in a "what else is new" tone.

"Bail-bond agent come in yet?"

"All taken care of."

"I'll see about the Armadillo." And off Bree went, without her morning coffee.

Traffic was light, the sky a clear blue, yet tension stiffened her shoulders. Jason was going to be trouble. And Jamie Cassidy… Not thinking of him on her drive over to the bar was more difficult than she'd anticipated. Those eyes and that fallen-angel face...

She was normally pretty good at self-control. The fact that he was rapidly getting under her skin aggravated her more than a little. She put all that away when she reached the Yellow Armadillo.

She found about two dozen guys wasting away their lives inside the dingy space when she walked in with her weapon drawn. She focused on Ronny Brown, who was standing in a group of three people in front of the bar. Okay, so maybe her day was turning for the better. Except for the small problem that two of the men had their guns drawn.

"Just the guy I want to see," she told Ronny in her calmest tone. He was the only one in the group who was unarmed, and he looked less than happy about that, his gaze darting around as he tried to find a way out of his predicament.

She flashed them all her best smile. "Gentlemen, what seems to be the problem here?"

A young Mexican guy with gang tattoos she hadn't seen before was pointing his gun at Ronny. Both their lips were bleeding. Shorty, the bartender, a grizzly ex-oil-rig worker who stood over six feet tall, was holding the mother of all rifles on them, keeping them in check.

"How about we all put our weapons down? Just as a matter of common courtesy." She was trying to set a good example by lowering her own.

Tattooed Guy swore and swung his gun to point at her then squeezed off a shot. As she ducked, not shooting back since there were people all over the bar, the bartender squeezed the trigger on his rifle. The boom made glasses rattle all over the tables and her ears ring.

But instead of hitting Tattooed Guy, Shorty somehow ended up shooting Ronny, who must have gotten in the way. Ronny went down screaming. A light hit in the leg, nonfatal, Bree registered, yelling, "Somebody call 911!" as Tattooed Guy ran for the back door.

"Keep Ronny here." She threw the words at the apologetic-looking bartender, as she took off after the gangbanger. "And, for heaven's sake, nobody shoot anyone else," she called back as she ran. "I mean it!"

She burst through the back door into a narrow alley between rows of buildings, into a wall of heat and the stench of garbage. The place hadn't grown any more pleasant since the last time she'd made a bust back here.

Tattooed Guy was dashing forward a hundred yards ahead of her, somewhat encumbered by pants that had been below his waist earlier but now were slipping lower. Not the first time she was grateful for the stupid pants-on-the-ground fashion. It was definitely a boon for law enforcement.

"Stop! Police! Drop your weapon!"

Instead, he shot back over his shoulder.

The bullet slammed into the wall next to Bree, sending wood slivers spraying. She felt a sharp sting at her neck but didn't bother to check. Injuries would have to wait until later.

Feet set apart, she braced both hands on her weapon. *Aim. Shoot. Bang.*

She took the shot without emotion, the only way to do it—no aggravation now, no anger, nothing but the job. The man sprawled onto the gravel face-first, sliding another foot or two, carried by his momentum. He was going to leave some skin behind, she thought as she ran forward.

She'd hit him on the back of his right arm. Blood leaked from the sleeve of his T-shirt. But he pushed himself up, ready to run again.

Too late. She was on top of him by then.

"You have the right to remain silent," she started, and kept on going with his rights as she tied his hands behind his back, ignoring his moaning and complaining, yanking him up just as he progressed to threats.

Fortunately for him, she was a good enough shot to have caused only a light injury. Unfortunately for her, that meant he was well enough to dish out a heap of verbal abuse.

"Hey! Is that any way to talk to a lady? You kiss your mother with that mouth?" She had a badge and she had a gun. She didn't need to take sass from anybody.

She got him back to the bar but pretty much had to shove him the whole way. The bartender still had Ronny at gunpoint. Ronny sat on the floor, pale and looking as if he was in shock, holding his bloody thigh with both hands.

She looked around at the patrons, most of whom had gone back to drinking and talking, although they were keeping an eye on her and the proceedings. "Anybody else hurt?" she called out.

"Nah."

"No, ma'am."

The replies were all negative.

She shoved Tattooed Guy onto a chair and made sure he wasn't bleeding heavily enough to bleed out before the ambulance got there. Then she hauled Ronny up and cuffed him before letting him drop back down to the floor.

She glanced over her shoulder. "Dammit, Shorty, put that rifle away. I got this. They're not going to cause any more trouble." She searched the men's pockets and dropped the contents into separate evidence bags: money, bullets, cigarettes. The stranger was Angel Rivera, according to his driver's license.

She turned back to the rest of the patrons when she was done. "All right, cowboys, start lining up for your witness statements."

She called Lena, then took statements painstakingly, had each person sign theirs, not that she got much out of them. Ronny and Angel had apparently been sharing a drink in one of the more secluded booths when they'd started arguing. Then Angel had fired a shot at Ronny before Shorty took matters into his own hands and restored the peace.

Lena arrived at about the same time as the ambulance. Bree let her take over Shorty and the witnesses while she went to the hospital with the two men.

She started grilling them while waiting for the E.R. doc. No sense in wasting time. There'd be a dozen new things waiting for her when she got back to the office. Crime didn't take a break just because she got busy.

She started with Ronny. "Want to tell me what that was about?"

The man shrugged.

"The Angel guy looks like bad news to me. He disliked you enough to take a shot at you. And that was before. Now he's going to the can for it. How much you think he's going to like you when he comes out?"

Ronny stayed silent.

"Looks like a gangbanger to me. You know his type. They come with a lot of close friends, and revenge is their middle name."

Ronny was beginning to look nervous, squirming on the bed—a good start. A little more motivation and he would probably break.

"I don't like outsiders coming into my town, causing trouble," she said, hinting that she was willing to take Ronny's side on this.

That seemed to help.

"He says I owe him money," Ronny said at last, then swore colorfully and at length. "Lyin' bastard. I ain't owe him nuthin'."

"Where is he from? I haven't seen him around here. His tattoos don't look familiar." She knew most of the gang tattoos for the groups that were active in her county.

"San Antonio."

"I don't like it," she said, half to herself, half to the man. San Antonio gangs moving down this way was the kind of trouble she didn't need. "Are you getting into something over your head, Ronny?"

His shoulders sagged, his expression turning miserable. "My leg hurts."

"I know. They'll look at you in a minute." She patted his arm. "Look, I got enough problems already. CIA's here, pain in the neck. They're investigating all that counterfeit money business. I got my hands full.

How about we clear this up right fast and we all go our own way?"

His gaze cut to hers, panic crossing his face. "CIA's investigatin' here? In Pebble Creek, you mean?"

"Yeah." She shrugged. "They take counterfeiting seriously. Thing is, you've kind of been implicated. I've been looking for you, actually."

He cast a desperate glance around, opened his mouth, closed it, opened it again. "I have nothin' to do with it, I swear."

She nodded. "Then none of the bills I took off you will have any trouble going through the scanner? You know I'm going to have to check them."

He froze, panic written all over him. Then Angel cleared his throat on the other side of the green divider and Ronny caught himself, sat up a little straighter in the propped-up bed. "I don't know anything about that."

"I have an eyewitness."

He closed his eyes and grimaced, then, after a moment of hesitation, lifted his hands, palms out. "It was all Angel, I swear," he said, obviously having come to a decision. He was more scared of the CIA than his gangbanger associates, apparently.

Something rustled on the other side of the green divider hanging from the ceiling. "Shut up," Angel called over, his tone plenty threatening.

"I'll get to you, Mr. Rivera. You just hang in there," she told the man and made sure she didn't turn her back to him.

He could try to grab her—even with one hand cuffed to the bed—if he was stupid enough to go for it.

She made sure she was ready for anything as she

tried a few more tricks with Ronny, but he really did seem to be clueless. He got the bills from Rivera, and that was all the information he had.

When she was done with him, Bree pulled the divider open and stepped over to the other bed. "How about you continue the story? Ronny got the money from you. How did you come by it? You just took a shot at me. That's assaulting a police officer. You want to be very helpful now." She waited.

"No hablo inglés."

"Yo hablo español. See? It's your lucky day." She flashed him her nicest smile, even though she didn't feel like it.

But Angel just stared daggers at her and wouldn't answer any questions no matter what language she asked them in or what she promised or threatened. If looks could kill, she would have been lying at the foot of the bed in a sticky, red puddle.

She kept on until the doctor finally showed up to check on the men. While he did that, she stepped outside and called the CIA agent to fill him in. Now that Ronny had confirmed a connection to the fake money, she had something solid to pass on to the agent.

She might not have gotten a ton of information, but they were one step closer to the source of the bad money. Progress.

Agent Herrera could come and see if he might get further with the two dimwits if he felt like it. She also called Delancy to stay with Rivera until the man could be taken into custody. She needed to get back to the office and take care of other business.

BORDER PATROL WAS a bust: no movement all day. Jamie used some of the time to call the lab to check on Bree's envelope. Several times. They had a partial print, too smudged to be of much use, but they were trying to digitally enhance it before running it through all the databases again.

At least he made some progress with setting up witness protection for Rico Marquez and his girlfriend, calling around to make sure all the pieces were in place for a problem-free extraction.

He could have left it to the U.S. Marshals Service; they ran the program just fine. But he'd given Rico a promise, so he made sure he kept an eye on the process and was part of the decisions. He sure hoped Rico would have something usable for him in exchange.

When his shift was over, Jamie swung by his apartment—a utilitarian, sparsely furnished space he basically only used for sleeping—took a shower and changed before heading over to Bree's place. He checked the perimeter first. She kept her property tidy, as did the rest of her neighbors. Seemed like a nice, family kind of neighborhood. She should have been safe enough here.

When he was sure all was clear and nobody suspicious was hanging around, he walked up to the front door and knocked.

"I should have locked you up for that fake twenty and all those weapons," she said as the door opened. "Just to keep you out of my hair."

She wore a pink T-shirt with jean shorts, her long shapely legs making his mouth go dry as they caught his attention, his brain barely registering the words she was saying. Then he blinked and caught up.

"You think of me and you think of handcuffs?" He wanted to see her off balance for once. "A man could take that as encouragement."

But she just burst out laughing.

She was way too cheerful by half. Thing was, he kind of liked it. He'd lived in darkness for so long, she felt like sunshine on his face.

As she lifted her chin, he caught sight of a bandage on her neck and his whole body went still, his protective instincts plowing forth like a steam engine. "Are you hurt?"

She raised a perfect eyebrow. "Chill. Just a scrape. The bullet didn't even hit me."

He didn't like the thought of a bullet anywhere near her. He wanted to ask how it'd happened, but he was interrupted.

"Who is that?" came a call from somewhere in the house.

He had thought they would be alone, that her sister would be asleep by now.

"That's Katie, my sister. She stays up late to watch her favorite shows on Fridays." Bree eyed him with hesitation.

He had no doubt she wanted to kick him out. But she was too much of a lady to do it—the beauty of Southern hospitality.

"It's been a long day." He piled it on. "Hot out there on that border. I sure could use a cold drink."

Her sister stepped into the foyer and stopped, her eyes fixed on Jamie. She looked a lot like Bree in her coloring but shorter and slighter. She wore jeans and a T-shirt with a pink unicorn in the middle.

"Katie, this is Jamie, a friend from work," Bree said.

"Are you a police officer?" She watched him without blinking, as if she had X-ray vision.

"Kind of," Jamie answered. "How are you, Katie? Nice to meet you."

"I'm watching my show," she said after some time, then padded away, barefooted on the Mexican terracotta tile.

"She likes you," Bree said, a frown smoothing out on her forehead. "If she didn't trust you, she would have stood there until you left to make sure you were out of our space."

He followed her into the kitchen, spacing out a time or two when his gaze slipped below her waist. Those shorts should be illegal. Then again, she was wearing them in the privacy of her home. He was the idiot for coming here and asking for trouble.

Katie paid little attention to them, sprawled on the rug on the living room floor in front of the TV, watching some crime show as intently as if she was memorizing every word.

Bree brought him a cold beer, along with a glass of orange juice for herself as they sat down, the same as before.

She caught his gaze on Katie. "Autism. She's very high functioning. She really doesn't need a lot of help," she said with a proud, loving glance toward her sister, not as someone who was bitter or embarrassed. "She's as good as you and I in a lot of things, and in some things she's better."

He wouldn't doubt it. "You're lucky to have each other."

She tilted her head, her shoulders relaxing. "Most people say she's lucky to have me." She watched him for a second or two. "They don't know anything."

"I have seven brothers and a sister."

She muttered something that sounded like, "God help the women of the world," under her breath.

He added a silent amen. His brothers were… His gaze slipped to her legs. With a view like that, who could think about his brothers?

"Seven brothers and a sister," she repeated, sounding more awed than snarky this time around. "That must be great."

It was, even if he'd spent the past couple of years pushing his family away. He'd been in a dark mood after he'd come back from Afghanistan without his legs.

"We have our moments."

He didn't ask if she was from a big family. He'd read her file. She only had Katie. Her parents had both passed away a decade ago in a house fire. He glanced at Katie, who was watching her show, completely mesmerized. "You're close."

Part of him envied that connection. He'd had that before. And he couldn't blame anyone for losing it. He'd been the one to push his family away.

"That's the best part of having a sister." She was smiling, but a shadow crossed her eyes.

"And you would want to keep her safe." He came around to the purpose of his visit. "So if there was anything strange going on, you'd tell me."

She straightened in her chair. "I don't need your protection. Seriously, Jamie, you're handsome and all, have that whole warrior thing going, but we have to stop meeting like this."

She thought he was handsome? That tangled up his thought process for a few seconds. "Where would you like to meet?" A certain part of him was voting for her bedroom.

"On the phone when you call to update me on what your team is doing in my town," she said deadpan.

She was a tough nut to crack. Good thing he didn't mind a challenge. "How about your case? Any progress with the counterfeit money?"

"The CIA is here." She gave a small shrug. "I caught two guys today who are connected. One doesn't know anything, the other one isn't talking."

His gaze slipped to her neck again, the muscles in his face tightening as he reached out and touched the edge of the bandage for a second before drawing back. "You had a tough day. Might as well tell me about it. Chances are, if I get what I came for, I'll leave faster. I want to know about what's going on with your stalker."

She rolled her eyes at him. But then her face grew somber as she thought a little before saying, "I got another envelope today."

His body tensed as he watched her closely. "More pictures?"

She shook her head. "Something more personal. He took something from the house this time."

His fingers tightened on the cold bottle. "He's escalating. He came in. He's getting closer."

"I don't think he'll make contact. He didn't before."

Which meant absolutely nothing. "What did he take?"

"None of your business."

He had to ask. "Anything that could be considered sexual?"

She nodded with reluctance.

Anger cut through him. "You know what that usually means in cases like this. He wants you and he hates you at the same time. It's not a good combination."

"I know. I thought about that. He was an adolescent boy the first time he became obsessed with me. Now he's all grown-up."

He turned that over in his head a couple of times, considering the implications. "Why come back now, after all these years?"

"He's been living with his parents until recently. He took off without notice. I'm guessing he stopped taking his meds."

More bad news. "What if he pushes even closer?"

"I'm a trained officer of the law. I'm always armed. Katie is never home alone. If I have to go back to the office for something, Eleanor, our neighbor, comes over. And Jason is not after Katie, anyway. He's after me. He just wants to scare me and have a good laugh about it. He gets off on showing how clever he is."

"You're sure it's Jason Tanner?"

"Pretty sure."

He hoped so. A messed-up average Joe would be easier to handle than if the smugglers, ruthless killers, were coming after her.

"You got the envelope for me?"

She got up and brought it to him with a resigned shake of her head.

"Whatever he took is still inside?"

"Not a chance, buster."

Of course, the more secretive she was, the more his imagination tortured him. He watched her from across the table, held her gaze. There were enough sparks between them to set her kitchen on fire.

He wasn't sure what to do with all that heat. He'd never wanted anyone with this intensity before. He would have liked to think he had enough self-control to not cross certain lines, but the hell of it was, he wasn't sure.

"I'm not relationship material," he said, just so they understood each other. If anything were to happen, he wanted her to be forewarned.

She flashed him an amused look. "Good thing I'm not looking for a boyfriend. I'm not looking for a man at all, in fact." She tilted her head. "Your being here is more like harassment than a date. We're clear on that, right?"

"I don't want you to be upset."

"Because you don't want to be my boyfriend? I think I'll live."

"I meant if we end up sleeping together."

She was just taking a sip of her juice, which she coughed up, some of it through her nose. She grabbed for a napkin and dabbed her face, then wiped the droplets of juice off the table. "You think we're going to sleep together?" She looked at him, bewildered.

She'd never looked sexier.

"I'm pretty sure," he said miserably, with all the resentment he felt. She was the one who'd barged into his life at that bookstore. He hadn't asked for any of this.

"No."

"Okay." He nodded. "That's good." He didn't need that kind of grief.

BRIANNA TRIDLE, THE most beautiful woman in the world, had a guy in her house.

The man watching her from the outside didn't like that. His hands tightened on his camera as he observed through the kitchen window, hidden in the darkness. Clouds covered the moon, and he'd picked a good spot, wedged between two tall bushes. He was good at hiding. He was good at a lot of things. He didn't care if people called him stupid.

Brianna was inside in the light. She was pretty. He wanted more pictures of her. He liked looking at her. He always had. But he didn't want pictures of her with the other man.

She belonged to him. She was supposed to be waiting for him. He'd come back to forgive her. But she was betraying him.

Rage washed over him so hard it had him grinding his teeth.

The doctor said he had to control his rage. The doctor said a lot of things. He didn't like the doctor. He wanted to do what he wanted to do, and not what other people told him.

Chapter Seven

Tracking down Jimenez—Jamie's one lead to the Coyote—proved to be a difficult task. He'd been released from prison two months before, unfortunately, current location unknown. Jamie was running down leads all day, calling Jimenez's family and dropping in on his known associates, trying to get a bead on him.

Nobody knew where he was or, if they did, they weren't telling. He drove back to the office in a bad mood, which didn't improve when the first thing he heard was, "Why the long face? Deputy Hot Chick slapped the cuffs on you again?"

Shep grinned at him from behind his computer. "She can do a full-body search on me anytime she wants," he finished.

"Beauty Queen Babe?" Keith joined in, coming from the back with his coffee. "Oh, man. She's a walking fantasy.

"Watch it before you get lovebug fever," Shep shot at Keith. "It's going around in the office."

He wasn't lying. Ryder and Mo, two guys as tough as they came, had recently been bitten.

"You look at a woman too long, next thing you know

you're shopping for a ring," Shep warned Keith, the youngest man on the team.

"Not me, old man," Keith vowed as he plopped into his chair. "Spending your life with one person is like… medieval. Who does that anymore?"

Keith had a playboy side. He was young and full of energy, and had the looks to pull it off. Jamie had seen women walk up to him and hand over their phone numbers on more than one occasion when they'd been in town together, running down leads.

Not that Jamie'd had any trouble in that department, either, before. He'd meant to get married. Coming from a big Irish family, marriage and kids had always been the assumption, the expectation, even. He'd been in love, or he'd thought he'd been. He'd been on the verge of getting engaged.

Then he'd come home without his legs and given Lauren her freedom back. She hadn't protested. And her leaving hadn't destroyed him.

He hadn't been seriously interested in anyone else until now. Good thing he and Bree had been able to clear the air between them. There was some attraction, fine, but neither of them wanted to see where it might lead.

They both had other things to do. They were both content with the way things were. Big relief.

He booted up his laptop and let Shep and Keith argue over the merits of serial dating. He tuned them out when he saw that he'd been emailed the prison visitors' log for the day he'd requested. Since he couldn't find Jimenez, he had to figure out who carried the hit order to him from the Coyote.

But as he opened and scrolled through the file,

he soon realized that the logs weren't overly helpful. Jimenez had had two visitors on the morning of the day when he'd killed the inmate who'd been about to betray the Coyote.

Neither of the visitors were fellow gang members, but a priest with a prison reach-out program, and Jimenez's girlfriend, Suzanna Sanchez. Jamie checked the address given in the log—San Antonio—looked up the phone number online and made the call.

"I'd like to talk to Suzanna," he said when the line was picked up on the other end.

"Wrong number." The male voice sounded elderly.

He confirmed the address and was assured he'd gotten that right. And after a few moments of conversation, it became apparent that he was calling an apartment building where tenants rotated in and out on a regular basis.

He thanked the man and hung up, entered Suzanna's full name and last known address as well as approximate age into the most comprehensive law enforcement database he had access to. He had a new address and new phone number within seconds. As luck would have it, she was living farther south now, less than twenty miles from Pebble Creek.

This time he hit the jackpot.

"I need to talk to you about your boyfriend, Jimenez, ma'am."

"You found the bastard, ay? You gonna make him pay child support now?" She misunderstood him.

He didn't correct her assumption. "Could I stop by so we could talk in person?"

"*Sí*. I'm at home. Where else would I be? He left me

with three *niños*. I can't afford no daycare to go work
no more." She went on cursing Jimenez both in English and Spanish.

Keith was still trying to convince Shep of the beauty
of open relationships. Jamie tracked down information
about Jimenez's other visitor, the priest, via the internet,
grabbed his address, too, then took off to see Suzanna.

She lived in an immigrant neighborhood where people ran into their houses when they saw Jamie's truck
roll down the street. They were afraid of immigration.
He slapped his fake CBP badge on. Better if they think
he was here checking on her immigration status than if
they thought she was snitching on her old boyfriend to
law enforcement. Jimenez was a hard-core gang member. His buddies wouldn't take well to traitors.

He checked his gun before he got out, then walked
to the patched-up trailer that looked like it was on its
last legs; the roof was repaired with corrugated steel,
the siding was missing in patches. One good storm and
the thing would collapse. He didn't like the idea of little
kids living in a place like that.

When he knocked, a young woman in her early
twenties came to the door with a baby on her hip and
two toddlers clinging to her legs. She wore thrift-store
clothes, nothing but suspicion on her face.

Her gaze slid to his badge.

"I'm green-card citizen," she said. "My children all
born here."

"May I come in, ma'am?"

She stepped aside to let him in and closed the door
behind them. She didn't ask him to sit. "You said you
wanted to talk about loco bastard Jimenez."

"When was the last time you saw him?"

"In the spring. I went to visit him in prison. Told him I needed money for the *niños*."

"Was that all you discussed?"

"He said he give me money when he free. But he never came here when he got out, not even a once." Frustration tightened her voice, tears flooding her eyes. "He's no good *hombre*. You see him, you tell him I want to put knife in his heart."

The anger seemed sincere. "Did anyone ask you to take him a message?"

"No, *nada*. He no family here. His mother lives in Mexico. His brothers all shot dead." She crossed herself.

"How about his friends?"

She rolled her eyes. "He no let me meet no friends. He's jealous man. He hit me if mailman brings package to door. He wants me to him only. Much love before." She shook her head. "Now he want me no more."

He stayed for another twenty minutes, asking what she knew about Jimenez's job, his friends, the people the man hung out with. He asked about messages in prison again, but she knew nothing and he believed her. She didn't seem like a seasoned criminal, just a woman on the edge after making too many bad choices.

Jamie ran the information he had so far through his head as he walked to his car. Jimenez executed one of the Coyote's men in prison, one who'd been on the brink of betraying the Coyote. Jimenez was one of the Coyote's men, but couldn't be found. If Jamie caught the messenger who took him the hit order, that guy could lead him to the Coyote instead.

Jimenez's girlfriend didn't pan out. Jamie drove up

to see the priest at the mission next, which was nothing but an abandoned pizza store in a strip mall.

The front windows were busted, possibly shot out, now patched up with cardboard. Father Gonzales, an older man sitting inside, sported a blue sling, but his face immediately stretched into a smile as Jamie walked in.

Jamie introduced himself then gestured at the windows with his head. "Rough neighborhood?"

"We do gang rescue," the sixty-something priest said. "The gangs don't like it. The Lord's work is not always all puppies and rainbows, I'm afraid."

The priest seemed to have a good sense of humor about it, even if sitting in a storefront unarmed while ticking off some of the most ruthless criminals in the state didn't seem like a smart plan to Jamie. He kept his opinion to himself. He asked about Jimenez instead.

The priest remembered him. "A troubled young man. Yet so much to live for. All things can be forgiven."

"Did you try to convince him to leave his gang? Is that what you were talking about when you went to visit him in prison?"

"That and Jesus. You'd be surprised how many of these young men wear the cross. I try to convince them to live by its principles. We talked about that and his children's future."

"Do you keep in touch? Have you talked to him since his release?"

"No." He sounded genuinely saddened. "I'm afraid I wasn't good enough. We might have lost him. But the Lord doesn't give up on anyone. And neither will I."

"You might be fighting a losing battle, padre."

But the old man smiled with full conviction. "That

cannot be. It's too important a battle to lose. There are thirty thousand gangs in this country, did you know that? Eight hundred thousand gang members. Do you know what the life expectancy is for these young men?" He paused for a second before he went on. "Twenty years. Just enough to leave some orphans behind."

The sad truth. "Jimenez has three small kids."

The priest shook his head. "I lost contact with the mother. I would have liked to help her. She moved at one point. I think paying the rent is difficult for her."

Jamie considered him. He seemed like a good guy. "I can give you their new address. They looked like they could use a little help."

He talked to the priest some more to get a better feeling for him. He definitely seemed to be the genuine article, believing in what he was doing, even willing to give up his life for the men he was trying to save. Jamie couldn't see him passing a kill order.

But then, who?

Could be the order hadn't gone straight to Jimenez. It could have gone to one of his buddies inside, then passed on to him. Who did Jimenez hang with in prison?

Rico Marquez might have the answer. And he wanted that new chance through witness protection enough to cooperate.

Jamie called him on the drive back to Pebble Creek but Rico didn't pick up his phone. He'd have to try again later.

He returned to the office just in time to go out on patrol with Shep.

"I'll meet you by the river," he told his teammate

as they got into their cars. "I need to check on something first."

He wanted to drive by Bree's place to make sure everything was okay there. He tried to make a habit of doing a drive-by check every time he was passing within a few miles of her house.

Not because he liked her. She was annoyingly cheerful. She fought crime by being nice. What was that? Utter nonsense. She was a disaster waiting to happen. That was the only reason he was checking on her. *Not* because he cared or had more than a passing interest in her.

Yet his blood ran cold as he turned the corner and saw the police cruisers lining her street.

Her front yard was destroyed. Tire marks crisscrossed her rock garden, her collection of garden statues scattered around in pieces. Violence and destruction hung in the air.

He noted her car in the driveway as he came to a screeching halt and jumped out, Officer Delancy running to block his path. He was about to shove the woman out of the way when Bree appeared in the doorway.

She had a tight look on her face, her beautiful smile missing. "It's okay. You can let him pass."

He hurried to her, assessing the damage, trying to figure out what he'd missed. "What the hell happened here? Why didn't you call me?"

"Just got home. I have to get back inside. Katie is upset." She turned back in.

When he followed her, she didn't protest.

"We need to talk." They needed to have a serious discussion. Her stalker was progressing from bad to worse pretty fast. He'd gone from watcher to invader to violent attacker in the space of a few days.

Whether she wanted to admit it or not, she was in serious trouble.

BREE WATCHED AS Katie rocked herself in the living room, tears rolling down her sweet face.

"The unicorns are broken," she repeated.

The mess outside was a major disruption in her life, and she didn't deal well with disruption.

Bree wanted to give her a hug, and she could have used a hug herself, but Katie didn't like when people touched her in general, and she didn't allow anyone to touch her at all when she was upset like this.

"What can I do to help?" Jamie asked quietly behind her.

"She's—" Bree folded her arms around herself, her throat burning. "Those statues are pretty much the only thing we have left of Mom. She made her own molds. It was her hobby. She made all those unicorns because they're Katie's favorite."

She drew a slow breath and let her arms down. She needed to be strong and to take charge. They couldn't get stuck in this terrible moment. They had to keep moving forward, get past it.

"How about we get ready for dinner?" she called to Katie, trying to sound as cheerful as she possibly could. "Let's start cooking." They needed to get back to their regular schedule. The familiar chores would offer comfort.

"You need to go someplace safe," Jamie said in a low voice that only she would hear.

She'd thought about that already. "I don't know if Katie could handle that right now. She's not good with change under the best of circumstances. I asked for police protection. We should be okay here as long as we have that."

"You need something 24/7."

She shook her head. "That might be overkill, I think. Jason has done what he set out to do—he scared us. I really don't think he'll come back."

He frowned at that assessment. "And if he does?"

"I can handle things when I'm home. If I have to go in and leave Katie with Eleanor, there'll be a cruiser sitting by the curb with an officer." Bree had responsibilities at the station. Her job didn't always conform to a nine-to-five schedule.

Jamie was watching her with worry in his eyes. "What can I do?"

She searched his face. He seemed to genuinely care. She didn't want to be touched by that, but she was, anyway. "I don't know."

"But you'll let me know?"

Why? They weren't friends. They were nothing to each other. And yet, she nodded.

"I have to go on patrol."

"Go. There's nothing you can do here right now. It's all over." She hoped.

He didn't look convinced. He left her with a dark look on his face. Through the window, she could see him check over her yard and talk to Delancy before he got into his car and drove away.

"Everything's okay," she told Katie. "We'll fix this. We always fix everything, right? We're the superteam."

They'd gotten through worse, like their parents' deaths in the fire.

Yet whatever they'd faced in the past, they'd never been in physical danger.

She went to the kitchen and started preparing dinner. Regaining normalcy was the key. "How about you set the table?" she asked Katie again. They needed to get back to the mundane. She needed to settle Katie down before she could start thinking about how to solve their problems.

She wanted to be out there, securing the crime scene, taking tire casts, looking for prints and clues. But her sister would always come first.

She could hear her front door open. Probably Delancy. She called out, "Back in the kitchen."

"Just me." Her neighbor, Eleanor, shuffled into view, wearing one of those ankle-length flowery dresses she preferred. She was in her sixties, kind faced with pixie-cut hair and lots of artsy jewelry.

She always cheered Katie up, as she did now. Katie stopped rocking as soon as she saw her.

"How are you, Katie, sweetie?" Eleanor asked her.

"Somebody killed my unicorns."

"Oh, I don't think so, honey. Unicorns are magic. I bet they're just sleeping."

The distress on Katie's face didn't ease. "Magic doesn't work. It's a trick."

"Sweet mackerels, did you hear that nonsense on TV? You just wait. Unicorn magic is special." She winked, pulling a bag from behind her back. "Guess what I brought you?"

"Chocolate-covered pretzels!" Katie sounded excited at last. Then turned to Bree. "I can't eat dessert before dinner."

"That's right." Not that she wouldn't have let Katie eat absolutely anything to cheer her up, but rules were an important thing for them, something that provided Katie with stability in a world she didn't always understand.

"Here." Eleanor gave Katie the bag. "You keep this safe until after dinner. You're in charge. Somebody has to be the boss, right?"

Katie looked pleased about that.

Eleanor walked out into the kitchen. "How can I help?" she asked Bree.

"I think we're good. She's calming down. But I'm not looking forward to her going outside tomorrow morning and seeing the destruction again. She's going to Sharon's house to hang out." Sharon was Katie's oldest friend. They'd grown up together, and now they worked together.

She looked from Katie back to Eleanor. "Thank you for calling the station."

Eleanor reached a hand to her chest. "He was crazy. Shook me up." She shook her head. "Plowed right through the lawn with his big pickup. And then back and forth, back and forth. Sweet mackerels." She sank into a chair as if just thinking about it drained the strength from her. "Had to be drunk as a warthog."

"Did you see his face?"

"Young guy. I already told Officer Delancy. Honestly, I was too far away to get a good look at him. And he was turning back and forth, backing over things. Was he on drugs, do you think?"

"I don't know. But we'll definitely find him." Bree pulled a pizza from the freezer and popped it in the oven. "Why don't you stick around for a slice?"

"Don't want to be in the way." But she looked pleased as peaches at the invitation.

She lived alone, not that she was lonely. She had a flock of girlfriends and they were always off to some garage sale here or a flea market there. They had big dreams of finding something rare and making a big splash on *Antiques Roadshow*. Half of them were in love with the furniture-expert twins.

"You know we love you. And we love your company," Bree told her.

So she made the pizza, tossed a salad to go with it and they all ate together, and shared the chocolate-covered pretzels before Eleanor went home. She liked to turn in early.

Bree watched Katie's favorite prime-time crime shows with her and opened a new puzzle to keep them busy during commercial breaks. When Katie remembered the statues and got upset again, Bree gently guided her back to the picture they were putting together piece by little piece, a modern-art painting titled *Sisters*.

Not until Katie was asleep did Bree go out to Delancy. The others were gone by then, Delancy taking night shift for the protection detail. She didn't have much information, just that the forensic teams had done a good job and they should have something by the next day.

So Bree went back inside. She wanted to stay close

to Katie. Sometimes, when she went to bed upset, Katie had nightmares.

Bree thought about the attack, about how serious the danger was that they were in, about what she could do if things escalated further. While she'd been telling the truth when she'd told Jamie she didn't expect this to get any worse, she was smart enough to know that it paid to have a plan B, just in case.

If they needed to go somewhere for a while… She needed to make plans ahead of time, start talking to Katie about it now, prepare her that they might be leaving. Jamie would approve. He seemed to have been genuinely worried about them.

He seemed to always be here, whether she wanted him to or not. Not that long ago, she'd found that aggravating. But today, his checking up on her had felt nice, actually.

And then, since she'd thought about him just before bed, of course, she dreamed about him. In her dream, she definitely wanted him. She wasn't even surprised that he was the first person she saw in the morning when she looked out her window as she brushed her teeth.

Chapter Eight

It looked as if he'd come here straight from his shift on the border. He'd definitely been there for a while, because half the statues had been repaired and were back in one piece. The front yard no longer looked as if someone had swung a wrecking ball around. Huge, huge improvement compared to the night before. Bree couldn't believe her eyes.

She ran a brush through her hair, then checked in on Katie, who was still fast asleep. They didn't have to get up early on Saturdays since neither of them worked. She threw on a pair of jeans and her favorite red tank top, jumped into flip-flops and hurried outside.

Boy, it was getting hot already. But with Jamie there, she didn't spend much time thinking about the weather. He had a way of commanding a person's full attention.

"Thank you," she said as she reached him. He didn't have any new bruises, didn't look like he'd been in any fights last night with smugglers.

"You're messing up your lines," he said as he straightened, his clothes covered in dust. "Usually you ask me what the hell I'm doing here."

She made a face. "It's so unmanly to cling to the past like that."

And he almost smiled, which was big progress for Jamie Cassidy. He wasn't exactly the type one would expect to break out in a song and dance. Although if he did, she'd definitely watch.

"Thank you," she said again as she examined his handiwork. She could barely see the cracks. He'd fitted everything back together nearly seamlessly. There was something sexy about a man who knew how to do stuff. As far as she was concerned, competence had always been an aphrodisiac. "How do you know how to do this?"

"My grandfather was a mason, came over here from Ireland. I helped him build all kinds of things when I was a kid. He used to hire me in the summers. We worked on a couple of old churches together." He brushed a mortar-looking plop of white off his knee. Not that it made a difference. He was pretty much covered in grime.

She was a Texas country gal. Dirt never bothered her.

He wore dusty blue jeans and a black T-shirt with a sweat stain on his chest. Who knew sweat could be so sexy? Her gaze caught on his bulging biceps as he lifted a chunk of unicorn back onto its pedestal.

A decade ago, the kitchen fire that had killed her parents had taken the house. A tragic, freak accident. Katie had been on her first sleepover at Sharon's place. Bree had been away at college.

The fire marshal had said afterward that it looked like their mother had been overcome by smoke at the top of the stairs. And their father wouldn't leave the house without her. He was found with his arms around her, protecting her to the end.

The house had been the least the Tridle sisters had lost that day.

Everything had to be rebuilt, an exact same replica of the old house for Katie's sake. Bree had even replaced the furniture with similar pieces. She'd done a fair job, but it was only the statues that were part of the original property. Katie treasured them. They provided good memories and continuity.

Bree watched Jamie as he worked without pause, his focus on the job. "This will make Katie happier than I can tell you."

"It's good to be moving a little after sitting in the car all night on patrol. I don't have to be at the office until noon. I should be able to finish here."

She was pretty sure between night patrol on the border and office duty he was supposed to squeeze some sleep in there somewhere. Yet she didn't have it in her to send him away. Having the statues fixed would mean the world to Katie.

"I'm making breakfast," she told him. "Why don't you come inside in a little while and have something with us?"

He watched her for a second. "Will Katie be okay with that?"

She smiled. "She will when she sees this."

And then she walked back toward the house, her heart a little lighter. She walked by Delancy's cruiser and thanked the bleary-eyed officer for her help, then sent her home to rest.

"Are you sure?"

"Jamie will be here for a while."

Delancy shot her a curious look.

"It's not like that," she said.

"Sure it isn't. He's obviously just a concerned by-stander," Delancy said with a suddenly saucy grin, then drove away with a wave.

Bree went inside and cooked breakfast: scrambled eggs with salsa mixed in, home-style bacon and skillet cakes. She put on some coffee, too. Lord knew she needed some, and she had a feeling Jamie probably did, too.

Katie came downstairs just as Jamie was entering the house.

"You're Bree's friend," she said thoughtfully. "Your name is Jamie Cassidy."

"Yes it is. Is it okay if I visit?"

"Jamie is fixing Mom's statues," Bree told her sister, and watched as Katie ran to the window, her eyes going wide. She clapped her hands at the sight that greeted her.

Bree could barely talk her into coming to the table to have some pancakes. "Come on now, or they'll get cold and you don't like that."

That did the trick. Katie ran to the table and plopped onto her chair. "Unicorns sneeze Skittles," she said, her gaze snapping back to the window every five seconds.

"Mom used to say," Bree explained. Katie had loved unicorns for as long as she could remember. Because unicorns were different, but great. Just like Katie. Not worse than other people at all, just different and special. Her mother used to say that to her when she'd been younger and asked why some kids at school made fun of her.

There wasn't much bullying. For one, Katie's teachers simply didn't stand for it. And also because they'd had a neighbor kid at the time who was in the same grade and always stood up for her. Bree had been too many years ahead of Katie to be of much help. They had never been in the same school building together.

"Skittles come from unicorns? That's awesome." Jamie was playing along.

"Only not these ones," Katie explained with all seriousness. "Because they're made of stone. And also because unicorns are imaginary. They sneeze Skittles in our imagination. Having imagination is a good thing. And Skittles are real."

"Well, thank God for that," Jamie countered, not a trace of his dark looks and surliness in evidence.

Katie nodded as she ate. During breakfast her gaze kept straying back outside, then returning to Jamie again. They stuck to small talk, mostly Katie asking questions. She was good with questions. She wanted to know everything.

She would have made a good detective. Maybe that was why she liked crime shows. She followed a different one every night, had a TV schedule she stuck to religiously. She could usually guess the killer halfway through the story.

"What kind of car do you have?" she drilled Jamie.

He told her. "It's the blue one, out by the curb." He nodded toward the window.

Katie looked, nodded, then turned back to him. "Where do you live?"

"Are you married?"

"Do you have kids?"

"Do you have a sister?"

The questions kept coming. She was impressed with the seven-brothers-and-a-sister thing.

Then it was time for Bree to take her to Sharon's house, just a few blocks away.

Jamie was still working in her yard when she came home. He was pretty close to finishing. The improvement he'd made was amazing. With some minor cleanup on her part, the front yard would be back to normal in no time.

"I'm so grateful that you're doing this," she told him. "Katie is very impressed with you, by the way. She couldn't stop talking about you to Sharon."

He shot her a questioning look.

"Sharon is a friend from work. They hang out Saturday mornings together. We don't have a big family. I want her to have friends." Especially since she worked for the police. She wanted Katie to have a support system if anything happened to her.

He put the last chunk of concrete in place and smoothed down whatever white cement mixture he was using to glue the pieces together. The unicorn looked fully recovered. Even jaunty. Her mother would approve, she thought out of the blue, and the thought made her smile.

"Why don't you come inside to clean up?" she offered.

He looked down on his clothes. "Okay. That might be good. Thanks. I'll just go out back and clean off these tools with the garden hose first."

She went with him, helped then they walked inside together. She led him to the sink in the laundry room and brought him a towel. "Anything interesting happen out on the border? I see nobody whacked you," she teased. "Must have been a slow night."

"It was pretty quiet," he said as he cleaned himself up, taking the jab in stride. "Every night is not a full-blown monkey circus, thank God."

She had stepped to the window when she'd shown him in, which she now regretted. The space was too small for the two of them and he blocked her way out as he peeled off his T-shirt, washed it under the water then hung it on a peg while he cleaned off his amazing upper body.

Oh, wow. He was incredibly built. And scarred. She tried not to stare, but was pretty much failing miserably. Water droplets gathered on his dark eyelashes, making them look even darker.

When he was done, he shrugged into the wet T-shirt.

"I could toss that into the dryer for you," she offered, finding her voice.

"In this heat, it'll dry as soon as I go back outside. Actually, a little cold feels nice. I don't mind. It's been a hot morning."

It was still pretty hot, as far as she was concerned.

He finger combed his wet hair back into place. "How is the counterfeit investigation going?"

"The CIA agent is doing his stuff. How about your op?" She was so proud of herself for still being able to think. She definitely deserved a pat on the back for that one.

"More dead ends than you can shake a stick at. I got a lead, kind of." He shrugged, the movement of his muscles accentuated by the wet T-shirt. "It's a long shot, but it's better than nothing."

Quit staring. Say something intelligent. Semi-intelligent. Okay, anything that doesn't have to do with rippling muscles.

"Did I see your car up by the mission yesterday? I was up there at the tackle shop to pick out a pole for one of the officers who's retiring. Mike. We're doing a group gift. He likes fishing," she added inanely.

He watched her for a moment as he hung up the towel to dry.

Oh, right. "You probably can't say what you were doing up there."

But he came to some sort of decision, and said, "I was running down a lead on a prison hit. Someone from the outside brought the hit order during a visit. I need to find out who. Father Gonzales was on the visitor log so I checked him out. Do you know him?"

The thought of Father Gonzales being involved in any kind of criminal activity made her laugh out loud and distracted her from his body, at last. Okay, partially distracted.

"He's as antiviolence as they get. He would give his life for you, but participate in murder?" She shook her head. "No way. I've known him all my life. I'd stake my career on it that he didn't have anything to do with an ordered hit."

"Pretty much the impression I got." He nodded, frowning. "Except, here's the thing—there were only two visitors, the priest and the girlfriend. Every instinct I have says she's clean, too. So where does that leave me?"

"The message could have been transmitted through a third party. It might have gone to another inmate first, then he passed it on to the actual hit man."

"That's what I've been thinking. I need to follow up on that today. Man, that's gonna be a time killer. It's a big prison with a ton of inmates." He didn't look happy. "We don't have extra time on this."

"What does your ordered hit have to do with the border?"

"Nothing you need to worry about."

She stepped forward, her dander rising. "I thought we've been over that. Everything that happens in my county I worry about. Does this have to do with smuggling? I could help you with that. I have a pretty good grip on the usual suspects. I know the players. Look, I've been doing this for a long time before you got here."

His gaze dipped to her lips, and she realized she might be standing too close, but she didn't want to step back and have him interpret the move as her backing down.

"It's smuggling related," he said after a moment, with a good dose of reluctance.

Oh, she thought as she recalled his team's purpose here. She narrowed her eyes. "Does this have anything to do with terrorists?"

And then he kissed her.

For a brief second, she wanted to shove him away and demand answers. And then suddenly she didn't have it in her to pull away. A small part of her knew he was probably kissing her only to distract her, but most of her didn't care.

It was sooo good. *Oh, sweet heaven.*

His lips were firm and warm on hers. She hadn't been kissed in a long time, and it'd been even longer since she'd been kissed by a guy who could make her skin tingle just by being in the same room with her.

One second it was just kind of a brushing of lips, then his mouth slanted over hers and he went for it.

Sweet mackerels, as Eleanor would say.

The heat was crazy sizzling. She wouldn't have been surprised if her hair started smoking.

Why now? Why him? He was anything but uncomplicated.

She wasn't the instant-attraction type. She didn't fall for every handsome face. She was friendly when it came to…friendship. But when things went past that… It took her forever to warm up to a guy that way.

All the instant heat now caught her by surprise.

He tasted her lips, slowly, carefully, doing a thorough job of it. By the time his tongue slipped in to dance with hers, her nipples were tingling. She was helpless to do anything but open up for him. He sank into her with a soft growl that was out-of-this-world sexy.

As he tasted her fully, all her blood gathered at the V of her thighs. And he hadn't even put his hands on her yet. She was in so much trouble here.

Her head swam. Ridiculous. Deputy sheriffs didn't swoon. It had to be against regulation. Maybe the eggs she'd made for breakfast were bad. She'd rather consider food poisoning than admit that Jamie Cassidy could undo her like this.

Desire washed over her, again and again, in ever-strengthening waves. He made her want things that…

Her brain stopped. Her body took over.

Wow, okay, she missed being with a man.

HE WAS SO turned on he couldn't see straight. Lust took over his body. Testosterone flooded his brain. What few brain cells were still working were overtaken by confusion. And surprise that he could still respond to a woman like this.

He wasn't sure if he felt hopeful or resentful about his body's overwhelming response to her.

Plain and simple, she knocked him on his ass.

He wanted her now, here, hard and fast. He couldn't see beyond that.

He eyed the washer hopefully. He could lift her on top of that, wrap her endless legs around his waist. His body hardened for her. "I want you," he said in a rusty whisper as he pulled his head back a little.

"Yeah, I think I got that," she responded in a weak tone.

Her beautiful eyes were hazy with passion, turning him on even more.

He swallowed a groan. "I don't want to want you." He didn't want the complications that would come with it. He kissed her again, anyway.

It felt a lot like falling. He didn't like falling. He'd spent months falling all over his face in physical therapy after he'd gotten his new legs. Thinking of that made him think of what would come next, in a normal encounter between a man and a woman who wanted each other.

Taking off their clothes somewhere upstairs.

She melted against him. Some feeling that was a lot

softer and lighter than he was used to lately pulled him forward. He pulled back. She made him want things he didn't want to need.

SHE WAS BREATHING hard and hoping he wouldn't notice. *He didn't want to want her.* Well, other than the part of him that obviously did. Was it pitiful that she desperately wanted him, aching with need between her legs?

She was so damn stupid. She'd tried this before. It never worked. And it was her fault. She would always put Katie first and whatever guy was in her life would want to come first. Completely reasonable.

The kiss had been great, but she couldn't, shouldn't, go too far down this road with Jamie. The longer she let this go on, the more hurt she'd be at the end. One guy she'd fancied herself in love with had asked her to put Katie into a home so he could move in and they would have some privacy.

That had caught her off guard, broke her heart, made her feel stupid that she'd thought he was different than the others. And here she was, thinking the same again, about Jamie.

"I'm sorry. I shouldn't have done that." She shouldn't have kissed him back. "This is not going to work between us. It's not working for me."

He stared at her. Shook his head. "I apologize if I read you wrong."

He hadn't. He'd read everything right, had done everything right. She'd wanted him, wanted him still, even right now, wanted nothing more than to go back into his arms and be kissed silly all over again.

She was tempted beyond words to throw all caution

to the wind and just do that, let the chips fall where they may. Except she'd done that before, and the chips always fell on heartache. She was an intelligent woman. She wasn't going to make the same mistake over and over again when it came to men.

He didn't need to know that her knees were still weak from his kiss.

Quick. Say something unaffected and clever.

Not a damn thing came to mind.

Then she blurted, "Did you check both lists?"

He blinked, looking at her as if she was from another planet. "What both lists?"

"The prison keeps two separate visitors' logs. One for general visitors, the other for the attorneys and whatever. That's maintained separately. And they won't show what attorney visited what prisoner."

The heat in his eyes simmered down little by little. "That sounds stupid."

"It's to maintain attorney-client privilege," she told him, proud of herself for sounding like a professional instead of a moonstruck teenager, even if on the inside she felt more like one than she cared to admit. "Could be Jimenez's lawyer was the one who took him the hit order."

Chapter Nine

On his way home, Jamie called into the office and asked Ryder to put in a request for the new set of visitors' logs. There also had to be court records that would show who had defended Jimenez during his incarceration. They would have to jump through a couple of hoops and wait for warrants, but they could definitely get the information. *Progress in the case.*

Which was a good thing, especially since his liaison with the deputy sheriff was getting worse and worse. He was definitely going in the wrong direction with Bree. She was completely right. He'd been way off base, way out of line.

He wasn't looking for a relationship. There was absolutely no reason to stir things up with her. Good thing she had a sober head on her shoulders and saw their mistake for what it was.

He'd gotten carried away with her. It wouldn't happen again.

The kiss… He drew in a slow breath then released it as he pulled into the parking spot in front of his apartment. It wasn't going to happen again. Definitely.

Maybe she'd forget.

Maybe she barely noticed, he tried to tell himself as he drummed up the stairs. Then he swore at his own stupidity. While the kiss had been completely unprofessional, it was also utterly unforgettable.

He'd been a hairsbreadth from pushing further. Common sense, mission objective and regulation be damned, he'd wanted her, then and there, all the way. Which meant one thing: time to take a giant step back from Bree Tridle.

He showered using a plastic chair since he couldn't stand under the water, drew the blinds, went to bed. He refused to think about her or how she'd felt in his arms, but then, of course, he dreamed about her. In his dream, their interlude didn't stop with kissing. He woke a little while later in a haze of heat and lust, pulled the pillow over his face and forced himself back to sleep.

This time, his dreams turned darker. He was in the torture chamber in the hills of Afghanistan, in the cave that had been converted into a prison just for him. Outside the iron bars, enemy fighters held the family who had sheltered him after his chopper had gone down. He was the sole survivor of his team. With two broken legs.

The first week, they tortured him to gain intelligence. He resisted. The second week, they tortured the family: husband, wife and children. He almost talked then. The third week, when the family had been reduced to bloody corpses, his tormentors had turned their attention back to Jamie once again.

They moved from hooking him up to batteries to chopping off body parts. They'd leave his tongue for last, so he could tell them what they wanted to know, they'd said. Everything else was fair game. They'd started from the bottom up.

By the time he was rescued, he was mad with pain and more than half-dead from blood loss. And a different man from the one who'd taken that chopper in.

Ex-beauty queen Brianna Tridle needed a man like him about as much as she needed a shot in the head, Jamie thought as he woke, then dressed grimly and got ready to go into the office, then out on patrol again.

He needed to pull back from Bree and keep his distance.

BREE HAD JUST gotten home with Katie when she got called into work.

"Jesse called in from the liquor store. He caught a fella with a fake bill. He's holding him at gunpoint. I can handle it if you want," Lena offered.

Bree always had the weekends off so she could be with Katie. She drew a deep breath as she thought for a second, then came to a decision. "I better go. I'm supposed to liaise with Agent Herrera on the counterfeiting." She watched Katie go into the kitchen for a snack. "I'll call Eleanor over to stay with Katie. I need someone to watch the house."

"I'm on my way."

"Thanks. I appreciate it." She hung up and called Eleanor. "Any chance you could come over for an hour or so? I have to go out on a call."

"Anytime, hon," her neighbor said on the other end. "You know how much I love that sweet girl. Spending time with her is a pleasure. I'd just be sitting home all lonesome, anyway."

"You're going to run into a good man one of these days."

"I'd take the one you had out in your front yard yesterday." She chuckled. "If you tire of him, you just send him my way."

"He's not my boyfriend or anything," she started to say, but Eleanor was already ringing the doorbell. "Okay, I'm out here."

Bree opened the door and they put away their cell phones simultaneously.

"Thank you. I really appreciate this."

"Just as long as you have cookies in the cupboard." Eleanor's sweet tooth was as bad as Katie's.

"Always."

"Hi, Katie, sweetie." The older woman walked in. "I was a little lonely tonight. Mind if I come over? I like your TV better, anyway. It's bigger."

That's how they played it lately, since Katie, twenty-three now, had been asking why she still needed a baby-sitter. Bree wouldn't have hurt her feelings for the world, but she wouldn't compromise her safety, either.

"I'm going to run out for a minute. You two have fun," she told her sister. "Leave me some cookies."

Eleanor walked her to the door to lock it behind her.

"Lena will be by in a few minutes," Bree said. "I just… With the vandalism thing…"

"We'll be fine," Eleanor said. "Don't you worry about us, hon." Then she added, "So about your young man?" And watched Bree speculatively.

"It's not like that. He's just a friend."

"Honey, a man puts in that kind of labor on your

front yard and he doesn't send you a bill in the mail, it's more than friendship."

"It's not the right time for me for anything more."

"You can't still be thinking that. It doesn't have to be either Katie or a man, Bree. You're so reasonable and flexible about everything else. You know what a guy like this is called?"

"Jamie?"

Eleanor gave a quick laugh. "A keeper. Think about it."

She promised nothing, but walked to her car and got in. She glanced back at the house as she waited for Lena.

She wasn't terribly worried about safety. Jason wanted *her*. If he ever escalated to the personal-attack stage, he'd be coming after her, and she could handle him.

She waited a few more minutes. Called Lena.

"I'm five minutes away."

"All right. I'm going to get going here. I don't like the idea of Jesse holding anyone at gunpoint."

He was an ornery old geezer who'd had a father and grandfather in the bootlegging business. Jesse had cleaned up his act and took his status as the first up-standing citizen in his family seriously. He was way past retirement age. He claimed he'd owned his small store since before the flood. He protected his turf. He'd been known to put the fear of God into any kid who showed up for liquor with a fake ID.

She called Agent Herrera on her way over. "Got a new counterfeit bill. I'm on my way to pick it up and take a statement from the person who tried to use it."

"I'll drive over."

She gave him the address, then turned down Houston Ave.

A small crowd had gathered in front of the liquor store by the time she pulled up front, gawkers watching through the glass as Jesse kept a young, gangly guy pinned in place by the checkout counter.

"Deputy Sheriff." She flashed her badge, although most of the people there knew her. "Nothing to see here. Please, disperse." She got out of the car and strode straight to the door.

She wasn't scared. It was South Texas. Most everyone out in the country had a gun or two. Most knew how to use it. Jesse was cantankerous, but he wasn't a hothead.

"It's Bree. I'm coming in, Jesse."

She put her hand on the door handle, pushed it in an inch, then said again, "Jesse? It's Bree. I'm coming in."

"Come on in, darlin'. I got you one here."

"I appreciate it. How about you put the gun down?"

Jesse lowered his rifle. "You takin' him in?"

"You bet." To get the man away from Jesse, mostly. She turned to the younger guy. This one she didn't know. "I'm Bree Tridle, deputy sheriff. How about we go down to the station and talk about that twenty?"

"Yes, ma'am." The kid seemed mighty motivated, looking between the door and her.

"Do you have ID?"

The kid dug into his pocket and handed over his driver's license. Garret Jones, age twenty-two, lived a few towns over.

"All right, Garret, I'm going to take you in for a short

interview." She looked at Jesse behind the counter and gestured toward the twenty in front of him. "Is that it?"

Jesse nodded. "Yep."

She pulled a rubber glove from her back pocket, an evidence bag from the right and bagged the money. "I appreciate the call. Go easy with the gun next time. Just a call would be fine," she added, just as Agent Herrera walked in.

He looked Garret over.

"You want him?" she offered.

"You take him in," he said. "I'll ask a few questions here, then I'll be coming in, too."

"See you later, then."

"Thank you, Deputy."

She got the kid in the back of her cruiser without trouble. He didn't say a word all the way to the station. She didn't push him, either. Agent Herrera would be questioning him, although she would ask to sit in on it. Whether counterfeiting fell under the CIA's jurisdiction or not, whatever happened in her town was her business.

Another hour, she figured. Then she'd be heading back home to Eleanor and Katie. Maybe she would take them to the mall for window shopping. They were all in need of a break.

JAMIE DROVE DOWN the deserted dirt road along the border. Everything was quiet. He'd been watching the flat expanse of arid land, keeping an eye out for the slightest movement as he talked to Shep over the radio.

"Ever been in love?" The words popped out of his mouth without warning, surprising even himself.

"Repeat that?"

"You ever been in love?"

A stretch of silence followed. "I had girlfriends."

"I mean real love."

"Hell, no. Who needs that aggravation?"

Exactly. "Come close?"

Another stretch of silence. "Kind of liked someone. Didn't work out. Bad deal all around."

"How bad?"

"She cost me my job, stole my car and set my house on fire. That's all I'm going to say about that," he added gruffly. "And I'm going to have to kill you if you ever repeat it."

"Understood," Jamie said with full sympathy, sobered more than a little. This was exactly the kind of confirmation he needed. Walking away from Bree was the right thing to do. He'd known that all along. And now Shep agreed.

His phone was buzzing. He glanced at the display. "Gotta go."

The labs at Homeland Security worked around the clock, and he'd marked his evidence "contact with results immediately." They were calling back.

"All right, give me the good news," he said.

"Both envelopes were sent by the same person. Jason Tanner."

Bree's old stalker. She was right. Better this Jason guy than the alternative. At least the mess at her house wasn't connected to the smugglers.

"Thanks." He hung up, a little relieved. Her stalker had nothing to do with the smuggling. He was free to walk away.

Except, no way was he going to be able to do that,

not after kissing her, not after meeting Katie, not after seeing the destruction in her front yard.

Despite his best intentions, he'd somehow gotten tangled.

Oddly, the thought of that didn't bother him nearly as much as he'd thought it would. Bree was one of a kind. She was… All right, so he had a soft spot for her. There, he'd admitted it. Didn't mean he had to act on it. Ever again.

While that thought felt very self-righteous, it also felt incredibly depressing.

He was about to call her to let her know about the fingerprints when his police scanner came on. He caught the code first.

Fatal shooting.

Then came the address in a staticky voice, and his blood turned cold. He whipped the car around and shot down the road like a rocket, calling Shep.

"There was a shooting at Bree's place."

"Go. I can call Mo to cover for you."

"Thanks."

His car couldn't move fast enough as he flew over the uneven road, his heart thundering in his chest.

When he hit the actual paved roads and had to worry about other cars, he kept hitting the horn in warning, flying around them, putting every bit of his training to use. Then he reached her street and saw the police cars in her driveway for the second time in two days.

Caring about someone was a heart attack and a half, he decided.

He squealed to a halt and jumped out, his blood running cold as he registered the shattered living room window. He pushed his way inside, but an officer stepped in his path.

Then Officer Delancy, coming in behind him, spoke up for him. "He's with Bree."

"Where is she? Is she hurt?"

Delancy shook her head.

He could breathe again. "Katie?"

"It's the neighbor woman."

He hurried down the hallway and into the living room. An old woman lay on the floor, her chest bloodied, cops securing the crime scene.

He went in as large a circle around them as he could, ran up the stairs. "Bree?"

"In here." The words came from the back.

He caught sight of a neat master bedroom and sparkling-clean bathroom as he made his way to her, to Katie's room where Bree was sitting next to her sister on a pretty pink bed.

Katie was rocking, wide-eyed, talking too loudly. "Eleanor. Eleanor. She. She. She…"

"Shh. I know. It's okay."

Katie's gaze flew to Jamie, and the look in her pretty dark eyes broke his heart. "Eleanor is not sleeping."

"No."

"You can fix her. With unicorn magic."

"I can't, Katie. I'm sorry."

She rocked harder and moaned, ground her teeth.

He flashed a helpless look to Bree. "What happened? What can I do to help?"

She had shiny tracks on her face. She shook her head as she stood.

He walked over to her, then stopped short. He'd almost pulled her into his arms. But she didn't want that. She'd been pretty clear about it. He shoved his hands into his pockets instead. That bullet had been meant for her, he knew without a doubt, and the thought about killed him.

"I have to stay with her," she said in a low tone. "Could you go downstairs and check out what's going on? There's an address book in the top drawer of the TV stand. Could you bring that up? I want to be the one to call Eleanor's brother."

He nodded. "We're going to talk about this. It's gone too far. I'm going to upgrade your security." She might not want his kisses, but she would have his protection. He had a team. They each could spare a few hours here and there. Starting with him.

She didn't protest. A good thing, because no way was she going to talk him out of this.

"DOES IT HURT?" Katie asked.

Bree knew what she meant. "She's not hurting. It's not like when you cut your finger. There's no pain at all in death."

"She has blood. When I cut my finger, it bleeds and it hurts."

"Only when you're still alive."

"She's dead."

"Yes, she is, honey."

"Why?"

The question was killing her. *Jason Tanner.* It had to be him. And if he'd been the one to shoot that gun, then she'd been the target. She'd underestimated him, underestimated the danger he posed. But she wouldn't do that again. She was going to bring the little bastard in.

Sitting inside while other officers processed the destruction outside her house had been difficult the other day. Sitting up here while they processed the crime scene downstairs was nearly impossible. She was a cop, had been a cop for a long time. Everything she was pushed her to go, to hunt, to bring in the man who'd done this.

"Where did Eleanor go?" Katie asked. "The window broke and then she fell down. And then she wasn't there."

No, not in the lifeless body, Bree thought. Katie had always been very perceptive about things like that. Looked like the shooter had pulled up to the front and shot Eleanor from his car. An easy distance, and she'd been standing in a lit room.

"She went someplace else," she told her sister.

"I don't want her to go someplace else."

"Me, neither," she said and blinked back tears. "Do you want to turn on the TV?" She wanted to give her sister something else to think about. Katie wasn't good with emotions. Grief was hard for her to grapple with. It would take a long time and a lot of talking, a lot of getting used to.

"We don't watch TV now."

No. Their favorite shows weren't on until later. "Maybe we'll catch a rerun. Something good."

"Okay."

She turned on the TV and found a repeat episode of *Bones*. Katie liked that. Bree wanted to hug her sister, wanted to be hugged in return. She'd almost run into

Jamie's arms earlier, would have done it, but he'd held himself so obviously aloof.

She'd been the one to push him away.

And yet, the fact that he didn't pull her into his arms still hurt. The exact kind of unreasonable female logic she always hated. She wasn't a drama queen. She was a deputy sheriff. She was strong and capable. Because she'd always had to be strong and capable for her sister.

But just now, some emotional support would have been great.

A small part of her honestly regretted pushing Jamie away.

Maybe Eleanor had been right and she saw things too much in black-and-white, at least when it came to her private life. Just because her life wasn't optimal for a long-term relationship, maybe it didn't mean that she couldn't have anything.

Except it did. Because she wasn't the one-night-stand type. When she fell for someone, she fell completely, which always ended up in heartbreak.

She'd accepted that. Accepted that she would give relationships up.

But it hadn't hurt so much until today.

Jamie popped his head in, address book in hand. He handed it over. "Why don't you go take care of what you need to. I'm beat. I wouldn't mind sitting for a sec." He glanced at the TV. "Hey, that's my favorite show," he told Katie. "Mind if I watch?"

Katie shook her head seriously, and Jamie dropped to the floor in the middle of the room. He was alpha male, a warrior, a doer, the kind of man who would always be first in the line of fire and liked it that way. Yet he understood what she needed, that she needed to be there to handle this. And he pulled back so she could have it.

She moved toward the door. "Thanks." And then she left, secure in the knowledge that whatever she found downstairs, whatever else happened, nothing would get through Jamie to get to her sister.

Chapter Ten

Agent Herrera was waiting in her office when Bree walked in on Monday after she'd dropped Katie off at work.

"Heard you had trouble at home. Let me know if there's anything I can do to help," the agent said.

"I appreciate it. Get anything out of Garret about the fake twenty?"

He shrugged. "He got the money at a gas station. It checks out." He scratched his jaw. "But Angel Rivera will be a decent lead, it looks like. He's actually involved, as opposed to coming into connection with the bills unwittingly."

"Did the hospital release him yet?"

"He'll be released in an hour or so. I'm taking him into custody and back to Washington."

"Hope he'll be more forthcoming with you than he was with me."

"He'll talk. If nothing else than for a deal. We got enough on him to put him away for a while. Found a couple of dozen counterfeit bills at his place this morning. Search warrant came through, finally."

"So are the bills from an old print run, just turning up now?"

He shook his head. "New. High-tech paper and ink. We'll definitely be tracking that. I expect we'll find a serious operation."

"Any clues so far? Are bills showing up anyplace else?" She really didn't want any of this connected to her town. The last thing she needed was the CIA descending in large numbers.

"I just got a call about similar bills showing up in Arizona and New York. That's why I'm heading back to the main office. I'll be putting together a task force and widening the investigation."

"Did you find out how Angel Rivera is connected?"

"Not yet. But Rivera works in transportation. He drives a truck for a produce distributor that brings up truckloads of fruit from Mexico. His routes are all over the South and up the Eastern seaboard."

"So the origin of the money could be south of the border?" Honestly, as long as it wasn't her county, she'd be happy.

But the agent shook his head. "Could be, but unlikely. The technology on these notes is pretty amazing. It's not some handmade printing machine some Mexican farmer threw together from spare parts in his shed."

"There's a paper mill south of the border, not far from here," she told him.

"We'll investigate that to be on the safe side, but this looks like something we usually see from even farther south."

"You mean South America?"

He gave a brief nod. "I'm looking into that. I'll be in

touch. I just wanted to come in to thank you for your help. And ask for one more favor."

She waited.

"Angel Rivera has a brother in prison down here. He went in just a few weeks ago on drug charges. He used to work for the same shipping company. Any chance you could look in on him? See if you can push him into admitting to being involved? He's locked up. He'll be more motivated to talk. Maybe in exchange for a reduced sentence. Let me know if you get anything from him."

He shoved his hands into his pockets in a frustrated gesture. "I don't want to wait around, setting up an appointment with the prison when his lawyers can be present and all that. I want to get moving with this. Putting together a task force will take time and paperwork, approvals. I need to be back at the office and set up a serious op. We need to find the source of the money and stop it."

She could certainly understand that. "No problem."

"Even if the younger Rivera doesn't talk, we might be able to use him to soften Angel up a little. Maybe the older brother will give us something in exchange for a promise to make his little brother's life behind bars easier. Prison is a risky place for gangbangers. Not all who go in come out."

She nodded, thinking of the prison hit Jamie was investigating.

"I appreciate the help. We'll keep in touch." Agent Herrera walked to the door of her office, but then turned back before opening it. He watched her for a second before he said, "The other day, I was leaving here when a man was coming in. Is it possible he was Jamie Cassidy?"

Okay, she hadn't expected that question. "You know Jamie?"

"What's he doing here?"

"Consulting for CBP. How do you know him?"

"I was involved in one of his other consulting gigs," he said after a couple of thoughtful seconds.

She had a fair idea what that might have been. "At a time you can't specify, at an undisclosed location, on a mission of indeterminate nature?"

A smile hovered over the agent's lips. "Something like that."

"Was that where he lost his legs?"

The agent shook his head. "He had them there, and put them to good use. It's good to see him back in action. He was the hero of the day."

"Hero, how?"

"I'm sorry. That's confidential information."

"In generalities? I'm assisting his team with something. He's my liaison. I'd like to know what kind of man he is."

He still hesitated for a long second. "Without any specifics… There were bad guys and they land mined a whole village. Jamie's team moved in, at night…." He shook his head. "He was the rear guard. When his teammates were blown up, he rushed in, under heavy gunfire, and dragged them out one by one. He kept going back and getting hit. He didn't stop until he bled out to the point of falling unconscious in the middle of the village. But he got everyone out who could be saved."

She wondered who had saved him. Maybe reinforcements came. She wanted to ask more, but the agent lifted his hand to cut her off.

"This stays between the two of us."

And Bree nodded. "So you don't know how he lost his legs?"

"Not a clue," the agent said. "But I wouldn't be surprised if he threw himself on a grenade." And then he left to go about his business.

She sat behind her desk, thinking for a while about Jamie, about the kind of work he did. Then she set that aside and made a note to figure out what prison the younger Rivera was vacationing at presently. She was going to call his lawyer and see about an appointment to visit later. But first she needed to find Jason Tanner.

Eleanor was dead. Jason couldn't be allowed to hurt anyone else ever again.

She hadn't taken him as seriously as she should have. Her mistake. But she wasn't going to make another with the man. She was going to use every tool at her disposal, call in every favor, track every lead until she found him and put him away.

JAMIE LOOKED THROUGH the database of images he'd been granted temporary access to that morning. Bree had an APB out on Jason Tanner and his red pickup truck, but Jamie had something better: access to military satellites.

No way in hell was he going to let the bastard get within striking distance of Bree again. Jamie needed to track him to his lair.

Jason would be staying somewhere close enough to swing by to see Bree, but not in town where Bree could run into him. Jamie made the whole south part of the county his target. The satellite identified ninety-six images of pickups the color, make and model Tanner was driving, information Eleanor had given the police after the vandalism on the front lawn.

Jason would be holed up in a motel, most likely, so Jamie went after those. He identified seven matching vehicles in motel parking lots and printed the list of addresses.

"I'm off to check on something," he called out to the office in general as he stood from his desk.

Keith and Mo were on office duty, the rest of the team out on the border or following leads.

Mo looked up. "For the deputy?"

Jamie nodded.

"Let us know if we can help," Keith put in, no teasing this time.

They'd all sworn to protect and serve, and the hit on defenseless women didn't sit well with them.

"I appreciate it." He walked out and made his way to his car. He had hours before he had to go back on duty again. Plenty of time to check the addresses on his list.

He first went to the nearest motel he had marked, drove around it, found a red pickup like the one he wanted in the back, but it wasn't Tanner's. This one didn't have a scratch on it.

He was looking for one that had a smashed-in front grill, at least. Those unicorn statues had to have left their mark.

The next address didn't pan out, either. The next after that didn't have a red pickup. Whoever had it might have moved on already.

Jamie made note of that. He would come back if none of the others panned out. For now, he just wanted to do a quick rundown on his list.

He found what he was looking for at the Singing Sombreros Lodge half an hour later. Grill busted, hood dusty, the pickup was hidden in a narrow place between the lodge's two main buildings, parked with its back to the road so the damage in the front wouldn't be easily seen.

Jamie walked around it, tested the door, found it locked. He looked through the window. Nothing incriminating in sight. He could see nothing on the seats beyond fast-food bags and empty beer cans. He left the pickup and walked into the lobby of the main building, flashed his CBP badge.

"Do you have a Jason Tanner registered?"

The clerk, an older man, bald with a Santa Claus beard, scanned the computer screen. He had an antique banjo hanging on the wall behind him. "I'm sorry. I don't see anyone with that name listed."

"Do you know who has the red pickup?"

He frowned. "Some young guy." He looked at his log. "Wait a minute. John Tansey. Here it is. I keep telling him to park that pickup in the lot where it should go. He doesn't listen."

"Room number?"

"Is he in trouble?"

"Yes, he is."

"The guy's having a bad week, I guess. He hit a deer day before yesterday. Banged that nice truck right up. Didn't even save the deer. He's traveling, I suppose. Still, other people would have been happy to take all that venison off his hands. Don't like no waste." He shook his head mournfully. "Room sixty-eight."

"Appreciate it." Jamie looked down the hallway. "Place is full?" He didn't think so, judging by the handful of cars in the lot, but better to double-check. He didn't want anyone getting hurt. It'd be easier for him if the lodge was mostly deserted.

The old man shook his head. "Rodeo crowd cleared out yesterday."

Jamie thanked him again then walked down the hallway toward room sixty-eight. He checked his weapon before he knocked. No response came, but he did hear movement in there, a chair scraping.

"Open up. Customs and Border Protection."

He heard the window open inside. "Put your hands in the air! I'm coming in." Gun in hand, he kicked the door in and caught a flash of a man's back as he jumped out the window.

Jamie dashed across the room and jumped after him. He landed in some landscaping done with stones and cacti, his prosthetics unable to balance on the uneven ground with gravel rolling under his boots. He went down, but was up the next second.

Still, the time wasted added to Jason's lead. He'd already made his way to his pickup and was behind the wheel and driving away, nearly running over Jamie as he ran in front of the car instead of taking a shot at it. He wanted this done without a fatality if he could help it. He and his team were supposed to keep a low profile.

He dove out of the way, rolled and jumped up and ran for his own car. He'd left it unlocked and the keys in the ignition just in case, which came in handy now. He was behind the wheel and after the man within a minute.

The lodge was on the edge of one of the dozens of small towns north of Hullett, the traffic sparse, a straight country road ahead of them. Tanner would have nowhere to go to get out of sight, nowhere to hide. It didn't stop him from running.

The red pickup sped up, sixty-five, seventy, seventy-five, eighty. Jamie kept pace. They were up to ninety-five in another few minutes, Jason running cars that were in his way off the road.

Okay, he was putting other people's lives at risk now. Jamie pulled out his weapon, but didn't aim it at the back of Jason's head.

Even if he wasn't trying to keep a low profile, he only killed if it was an absolute necessity. Tanner wasn't a trained soldier; he wasn't a terrorist. He was a stalker with a mental disability. Catching him would take more work than simply taking him out, but Jamie wanted to give that a go first.

He waited until they came to a stretch of highway that was for the moment deserted save the two of them, then shot out the pickup's back tire.

The vehicle spun almost immediately, went off the road, swerved all around, kicking up a dust cloud as it ran one wheel up a sizable rock that helped to flip it on its side, the tires still spinning as the pickup stopped at last.

Jamie ran his own SUV off the road and circled back, stopped a hundred feet or so from the wreck and got out, keeping his car between him and Jason until he measured up the situation. Jason had to be considered armed and dangerous.

"Come out with your hands in the air!" he called out.

Nothing happened.

"Customs and Border Protection. Come out with your hands in the air, Jason."

But once again, Jason didn't stir. As the dust settled, Jamie moved forward carefully, keeping his weapon aimed at the pickup, watching the cab and the driver's-side door that now pointed skyward, the only possible exit point.

He went around until he could look in the front window. Jason lay flopped over, blood on his forehead. The smell of gasoline filled the air.

The ignition had to be shut off and fast.

Jamie rushed forward, but climbing up the pickup wasn't easy. A long minute passed before he made it up on top. Then he needed both hands to pull the heavy door open, against gravity, seconds passing by during which the both of them could have been sent sky-high by an explosion.

He reached in and turned off the engine first before grabbing for the man. He got hold of an arm and started hauling him up. This was where legs that felt could have come in handy. Finding leverage was difficult like this, on a surface that was uneven, unstable and slippery.

"Come on. Wake up and push, dammit." He gritted his teeth and pulled as hard as he could.

He'd had to decide at one point, after the depression, after he'd fought his demons, that he wasn't going to let anything stop him, and he wouldn't now. Not even when Jason's shirt ripped and Jamie lost balance and fell back off the pickup, the fall rattling his tall frame and knocking the air right out of him.

He got back up and climbed again, this time making sure he got a better hold on the man. He got Jason out halfway, then all the way, lowered him to the ground, slipped down next to him then dragged him a safe distance from the gasoline fumes. On a hot day like this, the sun alone could be enough to ignite something.

"Hey, wake up." He pulled up the guy's eyelid to check his pupils.

And then the man was coming to at last, moaning as Jamie searched him.

No weapon.

"Where is your gun?"

Another moan came in response. Not altogether helpful.

Jamie swore. They were going to need the murder weapon. He wanted a conviction. He wanted to make sure the guy could never come after Bree again. So he ran back to the pickup, climbed back up again, down into the cab and looked for a gun.

Nothing.

Maybe Jason's weapon was still at the hotel. Maybe in his rush to escape he didn't have time to grab it. Or maybe he'd discarded it after the hit, thinking it'd served its purpose.

Did he even know that he'd hit the wrong woman?

Jamie scampered out of the overturned vehicle and went for Jason, who was sitting now and holding his head, still moaning. "Help."

"Stay down." He called Bree. "I got Tanner." He gave

his location and a brief explanation. Then he called 911 and asked for paramedics.

GRIEF AND ANGER swirled inside Bree as she watched from behind the two-way mirror as Delancy and another officer questioned Jason Tanner. He'd changed since she'd last seen him. He'd grown taller and filled out, and a five-o'clock shadow covered his face. He fidgeted on his chair, his eyes darting around the room. He was definitely off his meds. When he was taking them, he had an eerie sort of vacant look.

Since she was personally involved in the case, she couldn't go in there. Conflict of interest. At least they had him. And she had Jamie Cassidy to thank for that. She could have kissed him when she'd caught up with him by the side of the road.

The paramedics had already been checking Jason out when she'd arrived. He was scraped up and shaken but hadn't sustained any serious injuries. They'd pronounced him well enough to be taken in.

And now here they all were. Delancy didn't pull her punches as she questioned him.

"I had nothing to do with that," he whined. "My head's hurting."

Jason had admitted to the stalking and photos, even to the vandalism, within minutes. But he denied the shooting. Of course he would. He might have had some mental issues, but he wasn't stupid. He wasn't going to admit to murder.

Bree itched to march in there and confront him. Eleanor was gone, dammit. For what? A decade-old obsession? If she was the crying type, she would have cried over the unfairness of it.

She pushed to her feet and might have barged in on the interrogation if Lena hadn't opened the door and whispered, "We've got a problem."

Bree hurried out to the hallway. "What is it?"

"Bank alarm just went off. Got a cell-phone call, too. There's someone at the new bank with explosives."

Explosives. Bree stared at her. *Seriously? Now?* "A bank robbery?" She wanted to stay and watch the interrogation unfold.

"Don't know. Sounds like it."

Mercury must have been in retrograde. She glanced around the office, trying to pick who to take with her. There was nobody around. Brian and Delancy were with Jason. The others were out on calls. She couldn't take Lena. Somebody had to stay and man the station.

The insanity never stopped. Welcome to a cop's life. Well, she couldn't complain. She was the one who'd chosen it. And she did love it. On most days.

Chapter Eleven

Her gaze landed on Jamie, who was coming out of the break room with a cup of steaming coffee, watching her.

He'd come in with Jason Tanner. She didn't think he would have waited, but he had, apparently. And he'd heard everything Lena had said. He was walking straight toward them.

"Who's your bomb expert?" he wanted to know.

"Pebble Creek is too small to have its own SWAT team or bomb squad. We call in the pros." Bree nodded to Lena to do just that, then took off running for her car.

If she had to go alone, she had to go alone. Crime didn't stop just because they were at full capacity.

But Jamie was running behind her. "Hang on, I'm coming."

"Not your jurisdiction." She should have stopped him, but she didn't want to spend time arguing. She jumped into her car and took off for the bank, leaving him to do what he wished.

A cruiser was already waiting in front of the bank by the time she reached the building. Mike Mulligan's. Then she saw him, a thirty-year veteran of the force, pushing bystanders back and making sure everyone was safe. Bree parked her own cruiser strategically, so the two would begin forming a barricade to take cover behind.

Jamie, pulling in behind her, did the same. He jumped out and ran toward her. "I can help if you need someone. I know something about explosives."

Of course he did.

"Start evacuating the adjoining buildings," she told Mike, then turned to Jamie. "All right. Fine. Stay back here. I might have to call for you." Then she rushed forward in a low crouch toward the bank's entrance.

She ducked down outside the front door, opened it a crack, held her badge up so whoever was inside could see.

"I'm Bree Tridle, deputy sheriff. I'm here to give you whatever it is you need."

"Too late," came the response from inside—an older male, judging by the tone. He sounded raspy, maybe a smoker.

She didn't recognize the voice, and couldn't see inside very well through the UV-protection film that covered the glass. All she could make out were shapes.

"How about I come in so we can talk about this?"

"No."

"I can help."

"Can you help me get justice?"

Oh, damn. One of those. Why couldn't it have been over something easy, like money? Justice was a very subjective thing.

"Is killing innocent people justice? Women and children in there?" She could make out two smaller shapes, she thought. Might be kids clinging to their mother.

A moment of silence passed. "Why should I care about them? Nobody cares about me."

"I do. I wouldn't be here if I didn't. Let them go. We'll trade. Me and whatever I can do to help, for them. I'm a cop. I signed up for this. Those people in there didn't. One injustice won't erase another." Whatever it was he thought had been done to him.

More silence stretched between them.

"Those people can't do anything. They can't order anyone to do anything. They have no contacts. No power. I do. I'm the deputy sheriff."

"No trade." His voice shook a little this time. He was getting frustrated.

Okay, no time to waste.

"Then just let me come in. You'll have one more hostage."

And, after an interminable moment, the man said, "Fine." He cleared his throat. "You come in, hands in the air. Leave your gun outside. I see a weapon and we all go to Jesus today."

"Forget her," Jamie called out a foot behind her, scaring the living daylights out of her. How on earth had he snuck up on her? "You don't want a woman in there who'll faint in panic at the first thing that goes wrong. I'm coming in to help. Unarmed."

She shot him a death glare and whispered, "Go away." She could have killed him. They were in the middle of a hostage situation. This was no time for meddling.

"Who the hell are you?" the man inside wanted to know.

"Jamie Cassidy. I work for the United States Government. I can get you things you'll never get from a small-town deputy."

Oh, no, he didn't. Did he just disparage both her sex and her position within the space of a minute? She sent him a Texas death glare.

"Both of you, inside!" the man ordered. "Hands high above your heads."

She turned back to the bank, pulled her weapon from the holster and dropped it on the ground, pushed the door open wide enough to step inside and tried to kick Jamie backward but missed. "We're so going to talk about this," she said under her breath, in a hiss.

He pushed in after her anyway.

In the middle of the main area of the bank, in front of the teller booths, an old man sat in a wheelchair, holding a panicked woman in her twenties in front of him, a handgun pointed at her.

Her eyes wide, her face pale, she looked to Jamie instead of Bree. "Help me!" Her high-pitched voice echoed under the extrahigh, ornately decorated ceiling.

The old man shook her to quiet her. "Untuck your shirts, pull them up and turn around in a slow circle," he ordered in his raspy voice.

Behind him, about a dozen civilians lay face down on the pink marble floor, hands over their heads. Bree sincerely hoped none of them carried concealed weapons and had a mind to start trouble. An amateur shootout was the last thing she needed.

Then again, if someone did have a weapon, they would have probably done something by now.

"Everything is going to be okay," she said to the man

with the gun, as much to as the hostages, as she reached for the hem of her shirt.

Jamie did the same, showing off the fact that he'd come in unarmed.

"You should let these people go," Bree said as she tugged her shirt back down. "Whatever complaint you have, I'm sure it has nothing to do with anybody here."

The man watched her for a long moment, exhaustion and desperation in his eyes. He might have thought about what he was going to do here today, but reality was always different. She hoped he was beginning to see at last that this wasn't his best idea.

"Listen. Why don't we just end this now, peacefully, before anybody makes any mistakes? Everybody's scared and tense. But honestly, nobody's hurt." She flashed an encouraging smile. "This is a damn good place to quit."

"You go over there." The man gestured toward the corner with his head, appearing not the least touched by her plea and sound reasoning.

She did as she was asked, and so did Jamie. They slid to the floor next to each other, kept their backs to the wall. The old man in the middle swung the gun to point it at Bree, but he still hung on to the young woman with his other hand, ignoring her whimpering.

Bree stayed as relaxed as she could under the circumstances and prayed that Jamie would put aside his macho commando instincts for a minute, stay still and not do anything stupid.

Don't escalate. She glanced at him, trying to send him the telepathic message, hoping he got something from the look in her eyes before she turned back to the man in the wheelchair.

"I'm Bree Tridle, as I said, and this is Jamie Cassidy," she added, very nicely. "Would you mind if I asked your name?"

"Antonio Rivera."

She drew a slow breath. Like Angel Rivera? What were the chances it was a coincidence? Very slim.

"You took my son away from me," he yelled at her weakly. "You shot him."

Connection confirmed. Now what? How could she use this to her advantage?

"Only just barely," she said. "Flesh wound. And he shot at me first. He'll be fine." She widened her smile and did her level best to look positive.

"He'll be in jail. His brother is already in jail. What do I have left?"

She had no idea. No wife, she guessed, and scrambled to come up with something.

"Bank's taking the house," the man went on, his face darkening. He adjusted his grip on the gun.

"I'm sorry. Maybe I can work something out with the manager. Do you know Cindy Myers? She sure has a lot of pull at this place. She's very nice, actually. She has two boys, too. Younger than yours. We went to high school together. She'll help you if she can. She's very good that way."

The old man spat on the polished marble floor. "You're just saying that so I let everyone go. I ain't stupid."

"You're holding an entire bank hostage. I know you

can figure things out," she said to placate him, while she tried to see what kind of bomb he had.

She spied half a dozen sticks of dynamite. They weren't difficult to come by, unfortunately. Ranchers used them for all kinds of things, including clearing large boulders from their fields.

However, she couldn't see what kind of setup he had under the duct tape that ran around his chest, holding everything in place. She had no idea what he was using for the trigger mechanism, and no idea what to do even if she could spot it, honestly.

She glanced at Jamie, hoping he was catching more than she was, maybe even working on a plan. They sure could have used one of those. She had no idea whether the SWAT team had arrived yet or when they were coming.

The young woman Antonio held was trembling.

"And what's your name?" Bree asked. Making Antonio realize that she was a real person with a name, somebody's daughter, might help somewhat.

"Melanie."

"Do you have anybody from your family here?" Bree pushed further.

Melanie shook her head and began to cry.

"Shut up," Antonio barked at them.

She couldn't do that, Bree thought, so she took a gamble. "What happened to your legs?"

He might get mad, or he might start talking. Either way, it would gain her time until reinforcements got there.

"What's it to you?" He glared at her, but then he said, "Wire mill."

"I'm sorry. That must have been difficult." She acknowledged him and his troubles. "But you came through it. You'll come through this. Your sons will get out of prison. I'll help you find housing if we can't talk sense into the bank. There's always help available."

"I don't want help," he said darkly. "I just want this to be over with."

The way he said that, the tone of his voice, the bleak look in his eyes, troubled her. Because she knew he meant it. His coming here had never been about getting the bank to change their minds. This was suicide, pure and simple. He just didn't want to go alone.

She drew a slow breath, trying desperately to think of a way out of this, something, anything she could say or do so the standoff didn't end with a bunch of mangled bodies.

"Do you want to speak to Angel? I could probably get him on the phone." She had Agent Herrera's number. "You tell him to cooperate. I'll do anything I can so that he gets a fair deal. Maybe even a reduced sentence."

"Too late." His voice was cold with determination, as bleak as his face.

Melanie sobbed out loud. Some of the hostages squeezed their eyes shut; others stared wide-eyed. A middle-age man was hyperventilating. There was a new kind of tension in the air and they all knew it.

At least there weren't any kids in the bank. She'd been mistaken about that, thank heavens.

But they were out of time.

Jamie shifted next to her.

No, no, no. Her gaze went to him.

He probably had a hidden backup weapon somewhere on him. He would go for it, then Antonio would set off the bomb, for sure, and they would all die.

EVERYTHING HE WAS pushed him to attack. He'd been trained to charge forward and take down the enemy. He was a warrior. He'd been trained to fight with guns and explosives. His brain and body were weapons.

Jamie shifted again, looking for an angle, a split-second opportunity.

But if he tackled Antonio, the man would set off the bomb. Bree and Jamie were sitting the closest. They'd be toast, for sure. He wasn't as worried about himself, especially if he thought a move like that might save the hostages, but he wasn't willing to risk harm coming to Bree.

"Let me tell you something," he began, and couldn't believe he was talking. It didn't feel even half-right. He was a soldier. He'd been rough and tough pretty much from the beginning and, all right, fine, he might even have been overcompensating a little since he'd been cleared for active duty again.

He didn't have a softer side. For him, to show softness meant to show weakness, which was the dead-last thing he wanted to show, wanted to be.

And yet when Bree's life was at stake...

His usual M.O. of pushing harder wasn't going to work here.

"None of us are here because we want to be," he said. "I'm guessing you'd be doing something a little more fun if you had other choices."

The man glared at him.

Not exactly progress but, hey, they were still alive.

"Between the three of us, we should be able to figure a way out of this," he said, even as part of him was still looking for the man's weak spot, a way to rush him.

SHE SAW HOW he was looking at Antonio Rivera. Bree was pretty sure Jamie would attack, and soon. She wanted to warn him not to, but he wouldn't look at her, and she couldn't say anything out loud for fear of setting off Antonio.

But instead of making his move, Jamie kept talking, his voice low and calm. "I know what you mean. I've been where you are now. Hell of a place."

Other than his words, there was dead silence in the bank, the hostages pretty much knowing this was a Hail Mary effort.

Antonio shot him an angry look. "You haven't. So shut up."

"All right. I'll shut up." He raised his hands into the air, then pushed to his feet slowly. "But let me show you something."

She held her breath, along with the rest of the hostages.

Antonio moved his gun to point at Jamie's chest.

Slowly, carefully, Jamie reached to his belt, unbuckled it, then unbuttoned and unzipped his pants and let them drop to his ankles.

Antonio stared, along with pretty much everybody.

Jamie's shirt came down to the edge of his boxer shorts, but left the end of his stumps in open view, the skin puckered, white and red scars crisscrossing his skin. For the first time, she got a good look at the straps that held his prosthetics in place.

A couple of women gasped.

She very nearly did, too. Seeing both the living parts and the metal somehow made the sight starker than when she'd rolled up his pant legs before and had seen only the prosthetics. Those were somehow sterile, removed, cold metal. But his scars, the terrible destruction of his living flesh… She swallowed the lump in her throat.

"I didn't want to live," Jamie said in a low voice. "At the field hospital, I begged them to let me die. When they didn't, I promised myself I'd take care of it as soon as I recovered enough and had the strength."

Antonio listened.

"You get to this dark place," Jamie went on. "And it's bad. When you're there, it doesn't seem possible that things will ever get better again. It's like the life outside, the things other people do and see, that's not real. You almost don't even see it."

The hostages watched him silently, barely daring even to breathe.

"Like when you're over there, in the mountains for years on end, people shooting at you, you killing, blood every day. Every day one of your buddies gets blown to pieces. And it seems like that's the only world. Like back here, this was just a dream, the houses and the family and the rain, the banks and the malls and teenagers who go shopping. It's a dream or a fantasy. It doesn't exist. Not to you."

Antonio still pointed the gun at him, but his arm sagged a little.

"Thing is—" Jamie bent slowly and pulled his pants

up, buckled his belt "—the other world…it's there. It's real. And the people in it hurt when you leave them."

"Ain't nobody will hurt for me," Antonio said, but his voice wasn't as hard as before.

"Your sons will," Bree put in, talking around the lump in her throat, thinking about Jamie's seven brothers and the sister he would have left behind if he'd been a weaker man and taken the easy way out. "They cared enough about you to take care of you. They'll hurt."

She drew a slow breath. "And all the families of all the people in here. They are going to hurt and they are going to grieve. People in here have fathers and mothers and kids. They didn't get to say goodbye. Don't make them go through this."

Then everything happened at the same time. Antonio shoved the young woman away from him so he had use of both hands.

Jamie dove for him, but he was too late.

Chapter Twelve

The man blew his own head off a split second before Jamie reached him. As the hostages screamed, all he could do was secure the bomb.

He ignored the blood and gore and the crying and focused on the mechanism. No timer. He looked over the manual control with a flip switch—clearly a home-made job, but with enough of a punch to take out most of the building.

Thing was, as primitively as it was put together, he couldn't guarantee that it wouldn't go off if someone tried to move Antonio. Or if the man's lifeless body slid out of the wheelchair. So he kept working on it as a SWAT team rushed in and spread through the bank, a dozen men dressed in black, holding assault rifles, shouting.

"Everybody down! Everybody down!"

Some of the hostages had leaped to their feet when Antonio had discharged his gun but now flattened themselves to the marble floor once again.

Bree stayed where she was, her hands in the air. "It's okay. Everything's under control. I'm the deputy sher-iff. My badge is in my left back pocket."

One of the men checked it for her. "She's okay."

She lowered her hands. "This is Jamie Cassidy. CBP consultant, explosives specialist. He came in with me."

"Status?" the team leader asked.

"One perpetrator. Antonio Rivera. Self-terminated."

"The bomb is still active," Jamie put in as one of the SWAT members rushed over to him, probably their bomb expert. "Simple trigger mechanism. It's a pretty shoddy job. You need to get these people out of here."

The guy checked out the sticks of dynamite and twisted jumble of wires as the rest of his team jumped into action, helping the hostages up and rushing them toward the exit.

"Want to take over?" Jamie offered.

The guy shook his head. "You've got your hand on the wire. Go ahead."

That was pretty much standard operating procedure. The chances of success went up exponentially if the man who started a disarming op was the one who finished it. It wasn't something easily handed over midrace.

He focused on the wires, tracing each to their connections, careful not to set off the trigger. The SWAT guy held Antonio in place, making sure the body wouldn't flop.

"All right. Okay. Almost there."

Then, finally, the last wire was detached.

By that time, there were only three people inside: Bree, Jamie and the man helping him. The SWAT team had cleared the building.

"Well done," the bomb expert said, putting the explosives into the safe box someone had dropped off at some point. "I'll take it from here." He walked away with his precarious charge in his arms.

For the moment, until someone came for the body, Jamie and Bree were alone. They walked away from Antonio, but didn't step outside. Press waited out there, cameras flashing, the news team recording everything. The last thing he needed was his picture on TV. He was an undercover operative.

Bree's eyes were haunted, her face grim as she glanced back at the prone body. "He didn't have to die."

Dead bodies didn't bother Jamie. He was used to the carnage of battle. But for her... Two violent deaths in the space of days were probably way more than the small town of Pebble Creek was used to seeing. She'd had a pretty tough week.

While he was comfortable with death, he wasn't comfortable in the role of comforter. Yet something inside him pushed him to be just that, for Bree. He filled his lungs and waded into unfamiliar territory.

"We did what we could. It could have been worse. The bomb didn't go off. You kept him distracted for a good long time," he said. He really was impressed with her. "What you did gave the SWAT team a chance to get here."

Her head dipped in a tentative nod. "I thought for sure you were going to rush him, right at the beginning. I thought for sure we'd be toast if you did."

"I thought about it. Then I thought maybe I should try your technique of sweet-talking him. You must be rubbing off on me. I hope there's a cure for that," he teased, hoping it would lift her spirits a little.

"Wouldn't exactly call what you did sweet talk," she said, but gave a tremulous smile.

He reached for her, gratified when she went willingly into his arms. He brushed his lips over hers, relieved beyond words that they were both alive. He had no idea how Mitch Mendoza, his brother-in-law, handled going on joint missions with Megan before she'd taken some time off for the baby. Seeing Bree in danger had been nearly more than Jamie could handle. He would definitely not want to be in a situation like this ever again.

Her fresh, subtle scent, soap mixed with a light perfume, was in his nose, her curves pressed against the hard planes of his body. She was one of those good things he'd given up on at one point in his life. It seemed surreal that here he was, with the woman of his dreams in his arms.

But she was real in every way. And for now, she was with him, lifting her face to his. So he kissed her lightly. Because he really needed to feel her warmth and life and the reality of her being.

Antonio Rivera hadn't been able to let go.

Jamie rested his forehead against hers. He had let go of some things, but not everything, he thought. What if he could let it all go: the past, the pain, the idea that he was a fighting machine and only that?

She made him want to reexamine his assumptions and the way he lived these days. He didn't know if he could, if he should. But he wanted to, for the first time ever.

He dipped back for another taste of her lips.

She tasted so sweet, so right. She was infuriating. He'd nearly had a heart attack when she'd run up to the bank's door to offer herself in exchange for the hostages. Yet, in hindsight, he should have seen it coming. She was no coward. She did whatever she thought had to be done.

She took care of her town; she took care of her sister. He admired her, he realized.

The kiss deepened, yet it still wasn't nearly enough. What would be enough? Would anything ever be enough where Bree was concerned?

He had no idea, he admitted to himself as he pulled away. He had so much darkness around him. In some ways, his past still bound him. She was all light and smiles. He was a surly bastard. He didn't want his darkness to touch her. Temporary slip of willpower or not, he simply wasn't the right guy for her.

He would have told her that, but people were filing in through the door. Some of the SWAT team were coming back to finish their business.

A BOMB IN a bank, with a fatality added, required enough paperwork to make her head spin. She would have more follow-up work the next day, but she had to set that aside and go get Katie, so Bree powered off her computer and locked up her office.

Jason Tanner was in holding, his parents notified. They retained a lawyer for him. He'd confessed to the photos and the unicorn massacre, but he would not budge on the shooting. Maybe tomorrow, Bree thought. Tomorrow was another day.

The station was buzzing; some of the bank hostages were still there, giving statements, something Lena and Mike were more than capable of handling.

"Tell Katie I said hi," Lena called over as Bree told them she was leaving for the day.

The events at the bank crowded into her head as she drove, as she went over what she could have done to achieve a better ending to the standoff. She was the one who'd caught Angel Rivera. Angel had made bad choices. So had Antonio, in the end. Could she have done anything differently?

She was deputy sheriff, but she couldn't say she was happy when someone went to jail or died, even if they were criminals. First and foremost, she was a peace officer. She wanted peace for her people. Which was why she made sure crime prevention was a very real program in the county, not just a political hobbyhorse to be dragged out at sheriff elections.

She looked in the mirror to make sure she looked okay before she picked up Katie. She drew a deep breath and forced a smile on her face. *No bringing the job home.* The only fast and hard rule she never broke.

She pulled over in front of the big yellow building where her sister worked, and Katie jumped into the car and started talking about her day immediately. Katie lived in the here and now, always. It was an amazing way to live, one that Bree sometimes envied. No worries, no regrets, no self-blame.

"Mrs. Springer brought cupcakes today," she was saying. "They were chocolate with chocolate frosting. They had chocolate sprinkles."

Bree pulled into traffic. "You can never have too much chocolate."

"That's what she said. Except when you're a dog,

because chocolate kills dogs. Then even a little is too much."

"Very true."

"We don't have a dog."

"No, we don't. We have unicorns."

"Scott said once they had a burglar and their dog chased it away."

Bree glanced at Katie then back at the road. They'd had some scary vandalism, then a fatal shooting at the house within the space of a week. Just because Katie lived in the now didn't mean she didn't have logic. She did, and plenty of it. And maybe logic said that if bad things could happen at their house as they had, they could happen again.

"You know the bad guy we talked about?"

Katie nodded.

"We caught him today. Jamie did, this morning. The bad guy is going to jail. All locked up."

"And can't get out."

"That's right."

"Scott was in a car accident once," Katie said. It was a non sequitur, and they talked about that next.

She saw Jamie's SUV in front of her house as soon as she turned onto her street. He'd gone into work after they parted at the bank. He only had half a shift, as Mo had to do something with his stepson and they'd traded time.

His seat was tilted back, she saw as she came closer. He seemed to be asleep. Good. He deserved some rest.

Katie got out and went straight to the front door with the keys. She loved locking and unlocking things, and any kind of lock mechanism. She could play with a combination lock for hours when she'd been younger.

She had a whole collection she'd accumulated over the years. Some she'd picked up with their mother on garage-sale outings—their standing Saturday morning mother-daughter date that had since been replaced by hanging out with Sharon. Many other locks since, even antique ones, had been given as gifts by friends— several by Eleanor. Katie could remember the combination to every single one of them.

Bree walked over to Jamie's car. He had all the windows rolled down, probably to catch a breeze.

His eyes were open by the time she reached him. "Hey."

Her gaze caught on a bundle of yellow police tape on his backseat. He'd gathered that up from around her property. So Katie wouldn't have to see it and remember.

Her heart turned over in her chest. "Hey."

"Thought I'd stop by to make sure everything was okay."

"Jason's in jail. Thanks to you. I think we're done with trouble for a while. Hopefully."

He nodded, looking tired and rumpled with bristles covering his cheeks; he was so incredibly sexy, he took her breath away.

"What are you going to do about that busted living room window?" he wanted to know. "It doesn't look too safe the way it is."

She glanced at the empty frame. The contractor who worked with the police station, people who cleaned up crime scenes, had taken away the broken glass when they'd come to clean up the blood inside. She'd recommended them to families of victims many times in the past. They did excellent work. But they didn't do repairs.

"I called it in. Should be fixed tomorrow. It's a standard-size window, so at least I didn't have to do special order." That would have taken forever.

"How about I hang out on your couch tonight?"

He was asking and not telling her. Definite progress from Jamie Cassidy.

"It's not exactly a high-crime area. And I'm well-armed. I'm kind of the deputy sheriff."

The corner of his mouth lifted a little. "For my peace of mind, then."

Because he cared?

There went that funny feeling around her heart again.

"You're just here for the triple-winner breakfast," she joked. "Nobody can resist my salsa egg scramble."

His lips tilted into an almost smile. "Maybe." And then he got out, unfolding his long frame, and followed her in.

Katie was already going through her predinner routine.

"Jamie is having dinner with us." Bree took off her gun harness and hung it in its place, out of reach, although she didn't have to worry about Katie. Her sister was excellent with remembering and following rules to a T.

"Hi, Katie."

"Hi, Jamie." She glanced through the hole in the window at her unicorns, and seemed to have no problem with Jamie being there. She skipped to the kitchen cabinet and grabbed another plate.

Bree went upstairs and changed into a pair of jeans and a tank top, then padded back down to start dinner. Fried chicken steak, an old Texas staple, was one of Katie's favorites.

"What can I do to help?"

She stopped for a moment to look at him. "When was the last time you slept?" He worked long hours for his team, then he was helping her in between.

"I'm good."

"I have a well-oiled dinner routine with Katie. How about you lie down on the couch for a minute?"

He raised an eyebrow. "So because I'm a man, you assume I'd be no good in the kitchen and you're telling me to stay out of the way? Very sexist."

"Deal with it." But she was smiling as she shook her head. "You'll get to do manly things later," she said, without really thinking about how that sounded until his face livened up.

"Not what I meant." She tried to backpedal, laughing.

He looked skeptical, one dark eyebrow rising slowly. "What did you mean, exactly?"

"Like chopping wood out back." Or something like that.

He didn't look convinced.

So she turned to the stove while he walked off to take a predinner nap.

She didn't think anyone could sleep through the pots banging and Katie's chatter, but he did. He must have been truly exhausted. But he rolled right to his feet when she finally finished the gravy and called him to dinner.

She could barely concentrate on the food. She was too distracted by the man at her table. He had a presence that filled up her kitchen. But while he filled Bree with awareness that tingled across her skin, Katie was acting as if he was a member of the family and his eating dinner with them happened every day. For some reason, maybe because of the great unicorn rescue, she had accepted him fully and unconditionally.

"Excellent dinner. I appreciate the invitation," he said over his plate. And ate like he meant every word.

He probably didn't get many home-cooked meals, she supposed, liking that he appreciated her cooking.

"He's making the happy face," Katie put in.

"Yes, he is." Bree put a happy face of her own into play.

Her awareness passed after a while, and she began enjoying their dinner together. There was such a warm, homey feeling, such a normalcy to them sharing a meal. Maybe because of his nap, maybe because of the meal, the harsh lines on Jamie's face relaxed for once and stayed that way.

She liked this. She liked it a lot.

Not smart. She sighed. *Heartbreak ahead.* Her head sounded the warning.

Too late. She was enough of a realist to know that there was nothing she could do to stop herself from falling for him.

WHAT THE HELL was he doing here? Jamie thought as he lay on the couch in Bree's living room in the middle of the night, staring at the ceiling.

She didn't need him. She was a good cop. She could

take care of herself. Jason Tanner was in jail. And as she'd said, she lived in a pretty good neighborhood.

He hadn't been lying when he'd asked to stay for his own piece of mind. Bree mattered. And so did Katie. She was a sweet kid. Quick, too. She'd put together a puzzle of Klimt's *The Kiss* before he finished a small corner.

Of course, the painting the puzzle created put kissing into his mind. And Bree. And he hadn't been able to clear those images out of his head since. His emotions and thoughts were in a jumble. He didn't like that. He was used to always having a clear battle plan.

Except, this was no battle.

So why was he fighting his own feelings?

He rolled to his feet. He hadn't taken his prosthetics off. While it was unlikely that anyone would break in, he wanted to be ready if there was trouble.

He walked across the room then stopped, thought some more about what he was doing. He was very likely making a mistake. He walked up the stairs, anyway.

He knocked as quietly as he could, prepared to go back down if there was no answer.

"Come in."

He pushed the door in slowly, not entirely sure he should.

She sat up in bed, the worn police academy T-shirt she wore as a nightgown covering most of her, except for her amazing legs. He could have stood there staring at her forever.

She swung her feet to the ground as if to stand up, but then she didn't.

He moved to her without words and sank to his knees

in front of her, pulled her closer, her legs on either side of him as he rested his forehead against her collarbone.

"I couldn't sleep," he said against her T-shirt, breathing in her soapy scent. He liked the way she smelled, the way she felt, the way she fit against him.

Her head lowered, her lips coming to rest in his hair. "Me, neither."

He looked up into her face, which was illuminated by the moonlight. Time for the naked truth. "I want you."

For a nerve-racking moment, she didn't say anything, but then she smiled.

Oh, man. Maybe it would have been better if she sent him away. "I don't know how it's going to work."

Her smile turned into a wicked grin. "A virgin? Don't worry. I'll be gentle."

And he couldn't help but smile back. She could make him smile like nobody else. It was a miracle. He really had been a grouchy bastard over the past couple of years.

To be honest, he almost did feel like a virgin. She was like no other. He didn't want to mess this up. He didn't want to repulse her.

"Step one would be to lock the door," she advised him.

And he got up to do that. When he came back to her, he sat next to her on the bed.

"Okay, so the first part is called foreplay." She shifted onto his lap. "Tell me if I'm going too fast and you don't understand something. We'll go back and repeat whatever step you're having trouble with."

"You're a good instructor," he said as his arms went around her.

"I train rookies at the station all the time."

He threw her a questioning look.

She smothered a laugh. "Not in this!"

"I hope not," he said with a sudden shot of jealousy, as he pulled her head down to his for a kiss.

She was in his arms, her lips pressed against his, her arms wound around his shoulders. His entire body was alive and hardening with desire within seconds.

He deepened the kiss and took what he needed. She didn't protest. When she dug her fingers into the short hair at his nape, desire rippled down his spine.

He wanted her. She was the only woman he'd wanted in a very long time. This was not something spur of the moment; this was not trivial. The two of them in this room meant something, something he wasn't sure he was ready for.

But he couldn't walk away from her.

He shifted them until they were lying side by side on the bed.

Okay, that was smoother, so far, than he'd expected. He was up on one elbow next to her, their lips still connected. He had a free hand. He was a soldier, trained to take advantage of every tactical advantage.

"I don't know what you're doing. Here with me. You're perfect. I'm…" He was going to say messed up, but she cut him off.

"Stubborn?"

"No way."

"Surly?"

"When warranted."

Then he forgot what they were talking about as he tugged up her T-shirt and put his hand, fingers stretched out, on her flat stomach. Her skin was warm and smooth and begged to be explored. He moved his fingers upward.

She gave a soft groan and lifted her chest.

He wanted to be inside her so badly it hurt.

His hand cupped her breast; there was no bra, just warm skin and a pebbled nipple that he was ready to taste. He pulled up the soft material and lowered his lips to the tight bud.

Her hands kneaded his shoulders, her head tilted back.

"Take it back. I'm not perfect," she said in a whisper.

"What?" His mind was in a haze. He lifted his head.

She shifted to look at him. "I'm not perfect."

"A whole state begs to differ. You were Miss Texas. Don't you miss the beauty-queen days?"

She looked away.

"What is it?"

"My mom wanted that." She turned back to him. "She wanted me to be extraperfect, maybe because Katie wasn't…. I didn't really like the beauty-pageant thing."

He watched her, the emotions crossing her face.

"When my parents died in the fire, I was devastated. Then a few days later, when we were picking through the ashes, I came across some of my pageant wardrobe, all charred. And I thought, with Mom gone, I'd never have to go up on stage again. And I had never before felt such relief in my life." Her voice broke.

He held her closer. "And you felt guilty."

"I wasn't relieved that my mother was dead."

He kissed her. "You were relieved that you didn't

have to live a life you never chose. It's not like you shirk responsibility. You take care of Katie."

"That's different. I want to. I love being with her."

He kissed her again, amazed that she would share this with him, that she trusted him enough to open up. This was about more than sex, a warning voice said in his head. For the both of them.

He ignored the voice. His body wanted what it wanted. He went back to kissing her soft skin.

His mouth made the trip back to hers, lingering on her delicious neck in between, then back down to the other nipple. He wanted to keep kissing her for hours, but the urgency building in his body pushed him to take things to the next level.

He rolled her under him, pulled up her knees, one then the other on either side of him, pressed his hardness against her soft core and groaned with the sharp pleasure of the contact. He rocked into her, kissed her over and over, and that was enough for a few more minutes. Then it wasn't.

He shifted them again and pulled her shirt over her head, while she did the same with his, their arms tangling. She was down to her skimpy underwear, her soft skin glowing in the moonlight, bared for him.

She reached for his belt buckle. Because there was no hesitation in her, he didn't feel any, either. He helped her.

She tugged down his pants. He reached for his prosthetic leg on one side. She watched what he did and helped him on the other side, her fingers frenetic and impatient.

Because she wanted him.

With everything he was and he wasn't.

Then the metal was gone, then her underwear, then his. She whisked out a foil wrapper from her nightstand and helped him with that, too.

He loved the feel of her hands on him.

He moved to cover her amazing body with his. Then his erection was poised at her opening for a second before he sank into her moist, tight heat. His mind exploded first, then his heart.

The distance, the walls he'd built, the darkness he'd carried, they all fell away.

There was only Bree.

Chapter Thirteen

Bree woke alone, and after a second, she could vaguely remember Jamie kissing her goodbye before he went into work at dawn.

Her body felt like…cotton candy—a big fluff of happiness. She couldn't stop grinning. Even the toothpaste ran down her chin while she brushed her teeth.

She dropped Katie off at work, went into the office and did some more paperwork regarding the incident at the bank the day before. She wanted to talk to Jason Tanner, still in lockup, but thought better of it. She didn't want to mess up this case. She didn't want him to get off on a technicality.

He needed to be held responsible for what he'd done, be locked up and get help for his mental problems. As he was now, he was a danger to society.

Instead of going back to his holding cell with her questions, she called around to see when she could go over to the prison to talk to Angel Rivera's younger brother. She wasn't looking forward to having to tell him about his father's death at the bank. Angel would have to be told, too, so she sent off a quick email to Agent Herrera about that.

Since she couldn't talk to the younger Rivera without his lawyer present, she tracked that information down first.

"You gotta be kidding me," she murmured as she took in the screen. Steven Swenson. Or Slimeball Swenson, as he was known in law-enforcement circles.

He had very little regard for the law, and none whatsoever for the police. He'd sued probably every police department in the county at one point or another. Everything the cops did was an "overreach of power" in his book, and he was happy to cause as much trouble as humanly possible.

He was famous for his utter lack of cooperation. She so did not look forward to having to talk to him. She made the call, anyway. When he didn't pick up, she was almost relieved, even if she knew she'd have to try again. She left him a message.

She went through some more paperwork, handled some walk-ins then braced herself and called Swenson again. Still nothing. The guy didn't call her back, either. He wouldn't. The word "helpful" was completely missing from his dictionary.

The next time her phone rang, it was Jamie on the other end.

"Hi. Sorry I left so early."

Her heart leaped at the sound of his voice, images from the night before flashing across her brain. Parts that had no business tingling when she was on duty came awake. "You had work."

"I just don't want you to think I was doing the 'guy runs away in the morning' thing. I wanted to stay."

The quiet admission made her heart swell. "I can't

see you running away from anything. You're not the type."

"Neither are you."

"No," she agreed.

He hesitated for a moment. "So what are we going to do about this?"

"We figure it out as we go," she said tentatively, expecting him to come up with ten reasons why a relationship between them couldn't work. Heck, she could have come up with twenty on her own.

But instead, he said, "Okay." Then he said, "Lunch? I can probably get away for half an hour. I'm on office duty today."

"I'm going to take a working lunch. I need to see a guy's lawyer."

"Have fun."

"Not with this one. It's Slimeball Swenson." She was going to drive by and see if she could catch him in person.

"Hostages are suing already?"

"No. Nothing to do with the bank. It's about the counterfeiting case. I'm tying up a loose end for the CIA agent in charge."

"I'll see you tonight?"

Her heart leaped again. "Like you ever asked permission before for barging into my life without notice?"

He chuckled on the other end.

She'd wondered once what it would take to see him smile. And now that she'd seen him smile… She was rapidly falling for him.

Don't get ahead of yourself. Don't get your heart broken. It was one night. Neither of them wanted anything permanent. They both had their lives set up in a way that worked for them.

"I'll see you tonight, then," he said. "Especially if you have leftover chicken steaks."

And even if it was something temporary, whatever they had between them, she felt a thrill at the prospect of spending another night with him. "You only like me for my cooking."

"I pretty much like everything about you, Bree."

Her heart gave a hard thud. "Now you're just angling for dessert." She made a joke of it, even though she was ridiculously pleased.

After they hung up, she called Swenson again. Maybe he was with a client and that was why he wasn't answering. She left him another message, telling him she was coming over.

But before she could get away, a couple of teenagers were brought in: a drug bust. She handled that; one set of parents was belligerent, blaming everyone but their offspring, the other apologetic.

A full hour passed before she could drive off to see Swenson over in Hullett, her mind wandering to how incredibly good Jamie and she had been together and what she was going to do about that. A complicated question, so she drove the back roads, giving herself a few extra minutes to think.

She was so preoccupied that she was at the reservoir by the time she noticed that a dark van was following her. All the windows were tinted, so she couldn't make out the faces in the front, only two menacing dark shapes.

They were the only two vehicles on the abandoned

road. She sped up. So did the van. It kept gathering speed, closing the distance between them.

"Just wanted to see how you were doing," Jamie told his sister, Megan, over the phone as he sat behind his desk at the office. "How is baby Bella?"

"As grouchy as you are. She's teething." His sister made some nonsensical baby noises on the other end.

You couldn't tell now that she was a tough undercover operative. In fact, she'd met her husband on a South American op where they'd nearly killed each other before they'd fallen in love.

"Oh," she said. "You should see her. You wouldn't believe how fast she's growing. She's a little champion at breastfeeding. Aren't you, my little moochy-woochy?" She cooed.

He winced.

He'd only seen the baby once, in the middle of a screaming fest. He had no idea why people had babies. Forget mortal combat, babies were scarier.

"Are you calling to volunteer to babysit?" his sister wanted to know.

Right. Maybe in an alternate universe. "Sorry, too busy saving civilization as we know it."

"Sure, use that old excuse," Megan said in a droll tone, but then she laughed. "How are you? Is working stateside strange? How are the guys? God, they're hot. Don't tell Mitch I said that. How is the job?"

"Good."

She waited.

"Everything's okay."

"Well, no sense singing a whole ode about it. You

know how I hate when you talk my ear off. Sheesh, what are we, like girlfriends?"

"Very funny."

"I'm known for my sense of humor. And loved for it." She cooed to the baby again before returning to him. "So you're calling to tell me what, exactly?"

"Just to see how you all are doing."

A moment of silence passed. "Is there a woman?"

"What? On earth? Over three billion and counting. Some of them are pretty annoying."

"I know for sure you're not talking about me." She paused for a second. "I think there's a woman. You're softening. Is she the type to babysit?"

Probably. "There's no woman."

"Well, she's obviously good for you," Megan went on, ignoring his declaration. "When do we get to meet her?"

Family. A synonym for people who stick their noses into your business and enjoy it. "Oh, look. I better go. Terrorists are attacking. They're coming out from all over the jungle—"

"Yeah, whatever. You're calling from your office phone. I can see the number on my display and—" The baby cried in the background. "All right. But we'll talk about this mystery woman later. Take care of yourself. We all love you, Jamie."

His throat closed up suddenly. "I love you, sis. Give a kiss to my favorite niece for me."

He hung up and thought about his family, the rest of them. He really should be in touch more often. He thought about the baby. He should send her a gift. He would have to ask Bree what would be appropriate.

She would know. She was good with family. She was good with pretty much everything. He would ask her for some advice tonight.

With that resolution made, he turned back to his computer, to the task he'd interrupted to make the spur-of-the-moment call.

He so wasn't the spur-of-the-moment, check-on-family kind of guy. Maybe Megan was right and he *was* softening. Great. Just what he didn't need.

He looked through the secondary list from the prison where Jimenez had been recently incarcerated, scanned pages the warden's office had emailed him and checked the list of attorneys visiting clients on the day the kill order had been passed to Jimenez. A name jumped out at him: Steven Swenson. Might be Slimeball Swenson, the attorney Bree had just mentioned on the phone.

He tapped his finger on his desk as he stared at the screen, bad premonitions sneaking up on him.

So the same lawyer was representing the guy she was investigating for counterfeit money, and the guy Jamie was investigating for doing a hit for the Coyote. If Slimeball Swenson was the one who'd carried the hit order to Jimenez from the Coyote, then he was one of the Coyote's men, too. From what they knew about him, the Coyote worked with some of the most ruthless killers in the business.

And Bree was on her way to Swenson.

He dialed her number, a thousand fears cutting through him while he waited for her to pick up.

"Jamie!"

The sickening crunch of metal that followed the single word had him on his feet. "Where are you?"

"On the old mining road by the reservoir. There's a van behind me."

"Steven Swenson," he called to Shep as he ran for the door. "Local attorney. Find him. He's the Coyote's man. Send someone to pick him up." Then he was through the door, clutching the cell phone to his ear. "Are you okay?" he asked Bree.

"They're trying to push me into the water. I don't think—"

Another sickening crunch came.

"Bree?" He ran for his car and shot out of the parking lot, heading for her.

She didn't respond. Maybe she'd dropped the phone. She probably needed both hands on the steering wheel.

The way he was driving, so did he, so he switched to Bluetooth and tossed the phone onto the passenger seat. He could hear her yelling on the other end, car tires squealing.

His heart pounded.

"I'm coming," he said, in case she could somehow hear him. "Hang in there. I'm on my way."

Thank God the back roads were clear. He made the half-hour drive in fifteen minutes, the longest fifteen minutes of his life. He got there just in time to see Bree's cruiser tumble into the dark water of the reservoir, pushed by the van behind her.

He rolled down his window and shot at the van with his left hand. He had no hope of hitting anyone, but if he could scare them off, it would be enough.

He kept shooting, emptying his clip, slammed a second one into place and shattered the van's back window at last. He could see two men in the front, hunched over the dashboard to avoid his bullets. One of them shot back, but then they finally decided they wanted to stay alive and the van sped away.

Then he was at the water's edge, jumping from his car, kicking off his pants, taking off the metal that would have dragged him down, and dove in, sinking.

He'd learned how to swim without legs, but not well enough. He'd focused too much on the other aspects of his physical therapy, like regaining his balance on dry land and how to adjust his hand-to-hand combat skills so his moves would still work with the new reality of his body.

Now he wished he'd spent more time in the pool.

He used his arms to maneuver himself forward in the murky water toward the spot where he'd seen Bree's cruiser sink. If all he could do was help her out of her car and somehow push her up, even if he stayed on the bottom, he'd be happy.

BREE FREED HERSELF from the car just to get tangled in a giant ball of wire someone had dumped into the reservoir. Probably illegal dumping from the wire mill. She was so going to issue a ticket for that. If she lived.

She struggled to swim, dragging the heavy ball of metal behind her. She bumped up to the surface for one quick gulp of air before the weight dragged her back down.

She doubled her efforts and made it up to the air again. But with the tangle of metal hanging from her left foot, she couldn't stay afloat. She went back down again.

She could go up a few times, she realized, but when

she got tired, the wire would permanently anchor her to the bottom. She gritted her teeth and went down instead of up this time, trying to untangle herself from her anchor.

The inch-wide wire was slimy with rust and algae. Her fingers kept slipping without being able to find a good grip.

When her lungs began to burn, she abandoned her efforts and swam up for another gulp of air, dragging the weight with her. She could only stay up for seconds before the wire pulled her down again. Her arms and legs were tiring.

How many times could she do this? One more time? Twice? Certainly no more than that.

Desperation squeezed her chest.

The wire cut into her ankle, into her fingers as she tore at it. This time, when she went up for air, she had to struggle harder to make it.

Chances were she was going to die here, she thought on her way down again. There were only two things she regretted. That she would leave Katie alone, and that she hadn't told Jamie Cassidy that she cared about him.

But even as she thought about Jamie, he appeared in the murky water next to her. He scared her half to death for a split second before she recognized him and sharp relief washed through her.

He helped her with the wire, shoved her up even as he sank a little. She got hold of his arm, then kicked away toward the surface.

Then she could breathe again, and he was right there, the two of them dragging, pushing each other toward shore like some weird, desperate tag team. When they finally made it out, they could do little more than lie in the mud on their backs and gasp for air.

"I didn't get them." He coughed up water. "I let them get away."

Her lungs burned. She was ridiculously grateful just to be alive. "I'm so glad you showed up. I was running out of steam fast. You saved my life."

"It's not enough. I want to know who's after you, dammit. I should have caught those men."

She brushed the wet hair out of her face. "Oh, well... As long as you're playing God, maybe you can do something about the drought. I'm sure a lot of Texas farmers would be grateful."

He turned his head from her.

A moment passed before she realized he was looking at his prosthetics, a few hundred feet away. He got up and maneuvered himself that way, supporting his weight on his hands.

Her gaze caught on the way his wet shirt stuck to his back and upper arms, outlining his muscles. Those were the arms that had saved her. He had an incredible body. She didn't think she could ever get tired of looking at him.

He strapped his legs on then pulled up his pants.

"You know, we do have a public-indecency ordinance in place. You seem to have a habit of going pantless in public," she remarked as she stood and squeezed water out of her hair and clothes.

He glanced back as he got to his feet. "You going to arrest me for that?"

She sighed. "I kind of like it. Does that make me shallow?"

Surprise crossed his face, then a half smile formed. "You're not what I expected."

"Is that good or bad?" she asked as she caught up with him.

But instead of answering her question, he said. "Don't drown again. It makes me feel…" He shrugged.

She watched him for the rest, but he didn't finish.

"Were you scared for me? Is this a mucho-macho thing? Not admitting to being scared? For the record, I was terrified."

He reached for her, caught her arm and pulled her close. He dipped his head to hers and brushed his mouth over her lips. "I was scared for you. I don't think I've ever been this scared."

"I'm a tough Texas deputy."

He gave a rare full smile at that. "I know. And the stupid thing is…" He glanced down then back up to hold her gaze. "I feel like I don't want to let you out of my sight. Ever."

Oh. Warmth spread through her chest. It quickly turned to full-on heat when he kissed her.

They were wet and dirty from lying in the mud. There was a van with armed men out there somewhere who wanted her dead. Since she figured the chances of catching up with them at this stage were ridiculously slim, she gave herself over to the kiss.

Live in the moment. She'd learned that from her sister.

And after a few seconds, she could barely remember where they were or how they'd gotten here. The thing about Jamie was he could transport her in an instant to some place where she could barely remember reality.

He was a seriously good kisser. He kissed her as if she was the most important thing in the universe to him, the only thing.

That kind of stuff could go to a woman's head.

They fit together perfectly. They moved in unison, each knowing what the other wanted without a word having to be said. She'd never felt like this with anyone before.

"You're not what I expected, either," she told him when they finally pulled away.

He looked her over. "I'll take you home. You need to change."

"Will I see you tonight?"

He nodded.

"I'll have dinner ready." God, they sounded like an old married couple. It pleased her to no end.

But he didn't show up that evening. He was called in to deal with some smugglers on the border, so she spent the night alone, having to be content with only dreaming about him.

Chapter Fourteen

The following morning, Jamie sat in his SUV outside Steven Swenson's house, Bree next to him. Swenson worked out of his converted garage, which served as his home office. He was a one-man law firm. Maybe nobody wanted to work with him. According to Bree, he was pretty much a jerk.

Jamie's team, as well as Bree's, had searched the house and office the day before, but the man had been gone.

Taped to Jamie's dashboard were printouts of half a dozen versions of what he might look like if he came back wearing a disguise. With a beard, with a bald head and so on. Bree's idea. She had some computer program at the station.

Swenson had small, close eyes, a crooked nose and a cruel mouth topped with a mustache that was yellow from smoking. Tall and skinny with a slightly bent back, he even looked like a weasel.

"He'll be back," she was saying, watching the house. "It doesn't look like he took much. He left in a hurry."

They hadn't found anything incriminating either in the house or in the office. Then again, Swenson had passed the bar exam, presumably, at one point. He was probably smart enough not to keep a log of his illegal business with the Coyote.

Because life was never easy.

"You called to let him know that you were coming over," Jamie said. "He probably thought you were onto some of his dirty dealings. He panicked, ordered a hit then took off until the dust settles."

"I'm betting he's connected to the counterfeit money."

"And to the Coyote, too. Should have figured those two were linked." Why not? The Coyote ran human smuggling, guns and drugs. It made sense that he would have a hand in everything that was illegal and big business. He controlled a large area and a veritable army of criminals.

Not for long; Jamie's team always got their men.

"What if Swenson doesn't come back?" Bree asked.

The bastard had tried to have Bree killed, Jamie thought as he looked at her. He could never look at her without being a little dazzled. "Then I'm going to track him to the ends of the earth."

She shook her head at him. "You know, from anyone else that would sound like fake action-movie dialogue, but when you say it, I know you actually mean it."

He smiled at her. She got him. He liked that. He liked way too many things about her.

"He didn't go south," she said as she glanced at the abandoned house once again. "Border agents are watching for him. I put out an APB yesterday. He could be holed up somewhere else."

"He owns no other properties beyond this place. He

has no siblings. Mother and father dead. Never been married." Jamie had run the guy through the system as soon as he'd gotten back to the office the day before.

"He could be with friends," she said, then thought for a second before continuing. "Who does he trust?"

"A guy like that? Probably nobody. I wouldn't if I was in his place." If he was caught, the law was the least of his problems. He knew very well that the Coyote could reach people in prison, have them killed.

"He's lying low somewhere. We have a state-wide APB out on him and his car. Every cop in Texas is looking for him. I'm betting he knows that."

Jamie drummed his fingers on the steering wheel as he ran a couple of possibilities through his brain. "He represents criminals. Most of them are in prison. Which one of his clients has a place that stands empty?"

He pulled out his phone and called that in, talked to Mo on the other end. Mo and Keith were in the office, with access to information a regular sheriff's office could only dream of.

"I'll run some queries," Mo said. "I'll call you back when I have something."

"Thanks." Jamie put the phone down, trying to think what else they could be doing.

Bree shifted in her seat, turning to him. "When your top-secret mission is done here, will you all be leaving?"

"The office has been made permanent. The border needs to be monitored. CBP is set up for illegal immigration. Terror threats are a whole different level, and the problem is not going to go away in the foreseeable future. It needs different people with different training."

"I'm glad," she said. "That you and your team are

here. I wasn't at the beginning when I first found out about it."

They talked a little more about that, how times were changing. They kept watching the house, seeing no suspicious movement. Half an hour passed before Mo called back.

"I have an address for you. I found a couple of things, but I think our best chance is a remote farmhouse. One of Swenson's clients inherited it from his parents recently. The guy's sitting in federal prison. Swenson is trying to sell the place for him to cover legal expenses for an appeal."

"Thanks. We're heading over. I'll call in to let you know what we find when we get to the place." Jamie punched the address into the GPS and took off.

"You need backup?"

"Let's wait and see if he's even there. And I've got Bree."

"Thanks," she said as he hung up.

"For what?"

"For treating me as an equal partner."

He wasn't sure what to say as he flew down the road, heading for the highway.

"This way." She pointed in a different direction. "I know a dirt-road shortcut."

Which was why he looked at her as a partner. She knew what she was doing. Still, as much as he trusted and admired her skills, he did feel a sense of protectiveness at the thought of her going into danger.

Maybe he should have asked for that backup. "What if he's not alone? What if the men who pushed you off the road are with him?"

"I really hope so," she said as she checked her weapon, flashing the first scary smile he'd seen on her.

In another five minutes he reached the dirt road and turned onto it. His SUV bounced over the gravel. In a little while, they could see the abandoned farmhouse in the distance, surrounded by outbuildings. A red-and-blue For Sale sign greeted them from one of the front windows.

"Swenson's last stand," Bree said.

He scanned the ranch. "No cars."

"He'd be smart enough to pull his car into the barn. He knows we're looking for him. How close do we pull up?"

He could see tire tracks in the gravel driveway in front of them. Somebody had definitely been out this way lately. Of course, it could be anybody, even people who were looking to buy the place.

"We'll pull up all the way. I don't think he'd start shooting right away. He'll hope we think the place is abandoned and drive away. He's a lawyer, not a sharp-shooter. He hires out his dirty business. He'll try to avoid a shootout with law enforcement if he can. He knows the odds are not on his side."

"So what's the plan?"

"We pull up, keeping in the cover of the car as we get out. If there's no attack, we'll walk around the outbuildings first." He slowed the car as they reached the end of the driveway, the gravel crunching under the tires.

"We'll make our way to the shed," she said. "That's closest to the end of the house. He might only have a small bathroom window there, or none. I'll stay somewhere visible from the front windows to distract him. You sneak up to the side."

"Exactly." Man, it was easy to work with her. She had a quick mind.

"How do I know when to come after you?"

You don't. You stay where it's safe, he wanted to tell her, but he knew her well enough to know that she wouldn't accept that. And he did trust her to handle herself.

"If things go well, if he's in there, I'll bring him out through the front door. If things go badly, you'll hear the shots." They were both wearing Kevlar vests.

"All right. Let's get him."

He stopped the car and pulled his weapon out, waited. Nobody shot at them. So far, so good. He opened his door. No movement in the house. He stepped to the ground but stayed behind the open door for a second as he scanned his surroundings. Still nothing. Then he stepped to the side and closed the car door.

He was out in the open.

If Swenson was in there and he was going to do something stupid, this was the time to do it. But nothing happened. Jamie nodded to Bree. She got out on the other side.

They both had their weapons ready as they moved forward, walking a few paces apart, ready to provide cover for each other. But all remained quiet as they passed by the house, checking it from the outside only, from a dozen or so yards away. The curtains didn't move, and there was no sign that anybody was watching them from inside, yet Jamie's instincts prickled.

They walked to the barn. Bree covered for him as he

stepped inside into dusty darkness. They listened. No sound or movement anywhere in the dim interior. They turned on their flashlights to see better and panned the cavernous area in front of them. The stalls stood abandoned, farm tools and moldy hay taking up most of the space.

The old, wooden ladder to the hayloft looked promising, but rickety, to say the least, leaning more than a little. Bree tested it then shimmied up, keeping her gun out. She weighed less than he did. Still, he stood ready to catch her should the ladder break under her.

She disappeared over the edge of the hayloft. The wooden floor creaked under her as she walked around, checking every corner, sending dust sifting down between the cracks of the floorboards.

"Nothing up here," she called down before reappearing at the edge and climbing back down with care.

They left the barn and checked out the rest of the outbuildings. No sign of cars, although the grain silo was definitely big enough to hold a vehicle. Or more than one. It had no windows to look inside, and the door stood padlocked.

They moved on to the shed, according to plan. This they found unlocked. They went inside together.

The light coming through the open door and small window was enough; they didn't need their flashlights here as they looked around. Old, rusty equipment took up most of the space; things were piled randomly and perilously on top of each other. Jamie popped open the small window in the back and climbed through. Bree walked back out to distract whoever was watching them.

Keeping low, Jamie rushed over to the side of the house—no windows on this side, so nobody would see him—then moved around to the back. He stopped under the first window there and inched up. He saw a sparsely furnished bedroom, but there no sign of anybody and nothing was out of place.

Disappointment tightened his jaw. Maybe they were wrong about the old farmhouse. Maybe Swenson had gone someplace else.

He snuck over to the next window—open a crack—and popped up to eye level. This bedroom was just as deserted as the first one, but clothes lay scattered on the bed here.

Bingo.

He wedged his fingers into the opening and pushed the window up inch by slow inch, then climbed inside without making a sound, careful with his boots on the old, hardwood floor. He registered the clothes: faded jeans and a light shirt. Could definitely be Swenson's.

A duffel bag had been half kicked under the bed. He edged it open with his gun carefully and found more clothes, a box of ammo, some pill bottles and a stack of twenties held together by a rubber band, several thousand dollars' worth.

Things were looking pretty good.

He left the bag where he found it and moved to the closed door. Voices filtered in from the other side, at least two men talking.

Okay. They had Swenson, but the man wasn't alone.

Jamie pulled out his cell phone and sent a quick text to Mo, asking for backup. A month ago, he would have gone in, waiting for nobody. But he no longer needed to push the envelope every single time just to prove something to himself.

Now he had Bree, and that changed things, too. And Bree had Katie. So, no, he didn't always have to do everything the hard way. The smart way was better.

He put his phone away and turned the knob silently, hoping to hear what the men were talking about while he waited for reinforcements. Whatever intel he gained would come in handy later, and could be used against the men in interrogation.

"Nobody saw our faces," someone said. "And we had the license plate covered with mud. Ain't nobody gonna recognize us, no way. I'm telling you, man."

There was a long pause, and then a different voice said, "I can't take any chances. I'm sorry."

Then a gunshot, and Jamie had to sprint forward, because he knew the gunshot would bring Bree running.

He burst into the living room to find Steven Swenson holding a gun while a man lay bleeding on the floor, looking pretty much dead.

As Jamie burst in, Swenson swung the gun toward him, his face startled, eyes wide. "Who the hell are you?"

"Put your weapon down! Customs and Border Protection," Jamie ordered.

Swenson's gaze darted back and forth, calculating. "Hey, man. I've been ambushed by a burglar. Clear case of self-defense. I'm an attorney. I'm not illegal."

"Put down your weapon."

Swenson hesitated, swallowing, measuring Jamie up, almost as if he was waiting for something.

What the hell was he waiting for? "Put down your weapon!"

Then the door banged open and another man came through, looking a lot like the one on the ground. They could have been brothers. The newcomer had Bree, one hand around her midsection, another holding a gun to her head.

As he took in the body on the floor, rage contorted his face. He yelled in Spanish, cursing Jamie and all his ancestors, assuming he'd been the one who'd fired the fatal shot.

"Calm down," Swenson advised, probably still thinking he could somehow come out of this clean if he only played his cards right. "Everybody calm down!" But he didn't sound too calm himself.

The guy with Bree didn't seem to be listening. His weapon hand was shaking as he swore at them all in Spanish.

The tension was escalating out of control, seconds from where it would hit conflict point.

And Jamie froze.

The bastard had Bree.

For a second, all he could think of was that family in the Afghan mountains. He couldn't save them. People on his team had called him a hero, but he hadn't been able to do anything heroic back with that family. He'd let them die. His fault.

And he blamed himself even more because nobody else wanted to blame him.

The only thing worse than being called a hero and put on a pedestal was being a failed hero.

And here he was again. The old darkness came back

all at once and hit him hard. The thought of another failure paralyzed him. Bree meant more to him than he'd admitted, even to himself. And she was a split second from a bullet.

She looked at him with nothing but trust in her eyes. And at long last, in her eyes, he found himself. Not the overly tough guy he played to avoid pity, not the scarred mess he hid from others, but something truer and better.

His mind cleared.

"Hey." He lifted his hands into the air, but hung on to his weapon. "Nobody needs to die here."

The man holding Bree kept swearing, crying now, but Swenson looked interested. He shifted his weapon to his buddy. "You let her go."

As soon as Bree was free, he would shoot the guy, Jamie was pretty sure. Then there'd be no one to point a finger at him. Jimenez was gone, either lying low someplace or dead. Swenson would have nobody to testify against him.

"Everybody, put down your weapon," Jamie said in his best field-commander voice. "Let the deputy sheriff go." He shifted so he'd have a better angle on the guy who held Bree. She was not going to get hurt here, dammit.

"I have the right to defend myself in a home invasion," Swenson yelled.

His goon flashed a confused look at him. Swenson tightened his finger on the trigger.

He was going to go for it. And since he wasn't a professional, chances were pretty good he'd hit Bree by accident.

Jamie had to act first.

If he shot Swenson, the other guy would be startled and might pull the trigger on Bree. Which meant Jamie had to take him out now.

Straight in the middle of the forehead was his only option, or he might twitch and squeeze the trigger before he died.

One, two, three. He held his breath, so even that wouldn't interfere with his aim, brought his hand and weapon down and shot at the bastard.

Unfortunately, Bree, having correctly read Swenson's intentions to make a move, did some self-defense maneuver at the same moment. She jerked forward with a sharp cry then dropped herself to the ground, which jostled the man as he grabbed for her, so Jamie's shot went into his shoulder.

The man shot at him as Bree rolled away behind the cover of an ancient recliner, even as Swenson shot at his own guy.

Jamie ducked behind the couch, hitting the lawyer in the arm on his way down. He couldn't go for a kill shot. They needed information from the bastard, dammit. He pulled his backup weapon from his boot and popped up long enough to throw it toward Bree, then flattened to the floor as a hail of bullets came at him.

Bree must have caught the gun because the next thing he heard was her yelling, "Freeze! Pebble Creek P.D. Drop your weapons!"

Jamie came up for another shot at Swenson just as the young gangbanger squeezed a shot off at Bree. Dammit, it was like the O.K. Corral in there. She shot back, springing up, but got hit, the bullet knocking her on her back.

Something snapped inside Jamie.

"Drop your weapons! Drop your weapons!" He rushed forward, yelling at Swenson. He was ready to put a hole in his head if he threatened Bree in any way.

The gangbanger was dead, he registered, lying in blood next to the other one. Bree had gotten him even as he'd gotten her.

Swenson shot at Jamie, missed, and then Jamie was vaulting on top of him, bringing him down, smacking him hard to make him go still.

"Bree?" he called back as he disarmed the man, flipped him, then handcuffed him.

"Bree?" He could turn back at last.

She was still on her back. His heart stopped.

But then she moved and sat up slowly. "That hurts."

And he could breathe again.

She was shaking her head and rubbing her chest through the Kevlar that had protected her.

"Man, I hate this part. It's going to leave a bruise, I know it."

He went over to her and helped her up. "Are you okay?"

"I'm fine. Let's finish this." She strode straight to Swenson.

"You have the right to remain silent." She read him his rights while Jamie went to check on the bodies, checking pulses to make sure the men were as dead as they appeared.

Bree was back in cop mode, calm and matter-of-fact, pulling the lawyer to his feet, efficient as always while Swenson whined about the bullet that had gone through his arm, tossing out words like "police brutality" and "liability" and "legal protection."

She didn't let him rattle her one bit.

Man, she was hot in action.

Jamie wanted her. And it wasn't just the adrenaline rush.

He wanted her forever.

"All right," she said. "Let's take him back to the station."

He straightened. "Sorry. My team will want to talk to him first."

She narrowed her beautiful eyes at him, then relaxed her stance and gave a blinding smile that had his heart beating double. "I'm sure you agree—"

"Don't even try the sweet-talk thing. It's a matter of national security." Four SUVs tore down the driveway as he said that, all belonging to his team. He hoped they impressed his point on her.

"Fine." She didn't look happy, but she handed Swenson over. "I can be reasonable. How about we share him?"

"Make you a deal. You can have him when we're done with him."

She was still smiling at him. "We make a good team."

Yes, they did. They were good together in every way. He needed to think about that instead of running away from it. But not now.

Mo, Ryder, Keith and Shep were jumping out of their cars and came running.

Chapter Fifteen

"I want the Coyote," Jamie told the man in the interrogation room.

The small space was hot, the air-conditioning cutting out from time to time. Swenson was sweating.

He had been protesting up a storm, demanding his rights and barely taking a breath. "I'm injured. I need more first aid than your idiot buddies handed out. This is the United States of America, not a third-world country. Who the hell are you, anyway? I'm going to be suing every single one of you for this unbelievable treatment. Count on it. You're going to answer for this."

He claimed he didn't know the two hit men at the farm. They were intruders, he'd said. He insisted that any shots fired by him had been fired in self-defense. If any bullets had come near Bree or Jamie from his gun, that was by accident. He was scared and he wasn't good with weapons.

"When are you going to let me go?" he demanded.

Jamie shook his head. "This is how it goes. I'm asking the questions here." He said the words slowly so Swenson would understand. "We'll stay right here, in this room, until you give me what I need. It's as simple as that."

"I have rights. I know the law. I want a lawyer." Swenson shot him another outraged look. He had quite a repertoire. He could have made a career on the stage. His acting ability had probably come in handy in the courtroom in the past, but was gaining him nothing here. He stomped his feet as he said, "I have the right to know what I'm being charged with."

Jamie drew his lungs full and let him have it. "Aiding and abetting terrorists."

That shut the idiot up.

He paled a shade. A moment passed before he fully recovered. "You're all crazy. I want my lawyer. I demand legal representation. That is my right as an American citizen."

"You'll find the procedures are different for a terror suspect. What do you know about the Coyote? When was the last time you saw him?"

Swenson shot to his feet. "We live under the rule of law in this country. I have rights." Apparently, he still didn't understand the kind of trouble he was in.

"Too bad you didn't remember those laws when you were breaking them."

"Do you understand who I am? I'm a prominent attorney in this county. I have friends who are judges and politicians."

Jamie stood, too, running out of patience. "Do you understand how little I care? Do you know how many good men I've seen ripped to pieces overseas by our foreign enemies? And then here you are, an American, and you're betraying your country? Want to know how I feel about that?"

He braced his hands on the table and leaned forward, his voice cold as he said, "I'm not a great fan of traitors. So here are your choices. Do you want to leave here alive or in a body bag?"

That got through to the man at last. His shoulders dipped, his words losing that tone of outraged superiority as he dropped back onto his chair. "I have no idea what you're talking about. I don't know anything about terrorists. I swear."

"Yet you work for a man who's setting up an operation to smuggle terrorists into the country. How far are you involved with the Coyote?"

More sweat beaded on Swenson's forehead.

"Look," Jamie told him. "This is about the last chance you have to be smart here. You don't want to further align yourself with him by protecting him."

The man swallowed hard and wiped his forehead with the back of his hand. The indignation on his face was replaced by worry lines and fear.

"All I know about is the counterfeit money. I swear. I didn't have a choice. When someone like that sends you a message that he wants your help, you help," he rushed to say, eager to speak now. "I want a plea bargain. I tell you about the money, you drop any charges that have to do with terrorism. There's no way you're going to pin that on me. No way."

He jumped up, but immediately sat back down again. "I want to cut a deal."

Jamie flashed him a dispassionate look. "I think you're under the mistaken impression that we're negotiating here. I want to know everything you know about the Coyote. Let's start with his real name."

"I don't know. I really don't."

"Where does he live?"

"I don't know."

"Here is a hint. You'll fare a lot better if you prove yourself useful to us. So let's try again. What do you know about the Coyote?"

The man stared at him, his entire body tight with tension, desperation in his eyes. "He tells me what he needs through messengers who come then disappear."

Jamie waited. "Solitary confinement," he said after a minute.

"What?"

"You give me that bastard and I'll arrange that you don't go into the general prison population." Meaning he might have a chance to survive the first week.

Swenson stared at him. Shook his head, but then almost immediately said, "Okay. Solitary confinement." He drew a deep breath. "I know where he'll be Monday morning. He needed to have something done. Medical. I hooked him up with a doctor friend who doesn't always keep patient records."

Somebody who was willing to take bullets out of criminals and gangbangers, most likely. What did the Coyote want with him? With the kind of money he had, he could have afforded the most expensive Swiss clinics. But the *why* wasn't as important as the fact that they finally had a straight link to the bastard.

Two days from now.

With enough information, they could set up an op to

grab him. They would have enough time to make him talk, enough time to set up a trap for those terrorists.

For the first time in a long time, Jamie relaxed a little. The lack of progress over the past couple of weeks had gotten to them all. But now they had some actionable intelligence, finally. "Start talking."

This was it. They'd finally caught a break, and they were ready for it.

BREE LOOKED UP as Jamie walked through the door at dinnertime. He looked about as happy as she'd ever seen him. He wore blue jeans, a black T-shirt and his ever-present combat boots that she'd learned were fitted to his prosthetics to provide him with extra stability. He'd left his cowboy hat in his car. He was carrying a shoebox full of cookies.

"You bake?"

"Very funny. It was a gift."

"From a woman?" She hated the jealousy that bit right into her.

"I sent a young couple into the witness protection program today. She was grateful, that's all."

Just as long as they weren't going to see each other again. She took the box he offered and set it on the counter. They looked great—a bunch of different Mexican fiesta sweets.

"Any progress with Swenson?" she asked. "I want him when you're done with him."

"That won't be for a while yet. He's talking." He watched her for a second as if wanting to say more, but then he didn't.

Fine. She knew what kind of work he did. He'd never

be able to share everything with her. She was okay with that. She understood it.

"We found the van that pushed your car into the reservoir," he said. "DNA evidence will link it to the two goons Swenson had at the farmhouse with him, I'm pretty sure. Ballistics already linked one of their guns to the bullet that killed Eleanor. Jason Tanner wasn't lying about not being the one who shot through your window."

She stared at him, various emotions mixing inside her. Jason's parents were in town and had made an appointment with her for tomorrow. At least she didn't have to tell them that their son was a killer. The family had suffered enough already, so she was happy for that.

Jason needed meds and to be in a facility where his movements were monitored. Mental illness wasn't a crime. He needed the kind of help he wouldn't be able to get in prison.

"So the men who shot Eleanor are dead. How do you feel about that?" Jamie asked, watching her.

"Good." While Jason had her sympathy, those two killers definitely didn't. They'd known what they were doing. They'd gone after her to stop her from investigating the counterfeit money business.

Jamie nodded, then looked around, up the stairs. "Where's Katie?"

"Over at Sharon's house for a sleepover. It's Sharon's birthday. Katie is not big on sleepovers, but she wanted to try. If I get a call in the middle of the night, so be it. I want her to have as many normal experiences as possible."

"She'll do fine. She's a sweet girl," he said. "How was your day?"

"All party and cakes. Mike had his retirement shindig."

"Liked his fishing pole?"

"You bet. I thought he might sneak out of the party to go and try it. It'll keep him out of Bertha's hair." Bertha was nearly as excited about the pole as Mike. She grinned.

Talking to Jamie like this felt nice: sharing their day, just being together without being in mortal danger.

He was standing in front of the living room window, which had finally been fixed, the late-day sunlight outlining his body—tall and wide shouldered. The man was pretty impressive, prosthetics or no prosthetics.

"A hero returning from the day's business." She said out loud the words she was thinking.

But instead of taking the compliment in the spirit in which it was offered, he frowned. "What are you talking about? I'm nobody's hero."

"You're mine. And I'm sure there are plenty of other people who feel the same."

"You don't know anything about my past."

"I know you've seen hard times. I know you risked your life for others."

"People died because of me."

"They shouldn't have plotted to attack our country."

He shook his head, a haunted expression coming over his face. "Innocent people."

"It wasn't your fault." She believed that with everything she was. He was good to the core, and honest and honorable.

"A whole family," he said. And then he told her a story that made her heart bleed and had her blinking back tears.

"The bastards went slow, made them scream. For days. And they would stop, they told me, if I gave them the location of my unit."

"They wouldn't have," she told him.

"I know. They meant to kill them from the beginning, to teach the rest of the village a lesson. And yet, I—"

"You couldn't have done anything to make a difference. If you'd given up information, more people would have died."

He rubbed a thumb over his eyebrow. "Sure, that sounds all reasonable and logical. Except in the middle of the night when I'm startled awake because I'm hearing their screams." He shoved his hands into his pockets. "I never told that to anyone before, not even the shrink at Walter Reed," he finished, and stood aloof, as if not sure how she would react.

She wanted to rush into his arms, but she wasn't sure if he would want it. Last time they talked about things between them, each had been adamant that there could be no relationship, nothing beyond the professional. Yet it was too late. They were friends, at the very least.

And more. If she said she felt nothing beyond friendship, she would be lying. "I wasn't sure you'd come."

He raised an eyebrow.

"Tanner is in jail. You have Swenson. His goons are dead. I no longer need a bodyguard."

"You never really needed one. I know you can handle pretty much everything yourself."

She narrowed her eyes. "Who are you, and what have you done with the real Jamie?"

He smiled. "I kept coming because I like being here with you."

Her heart rate picked up.

He looked at her, turning stone serious in a split second. "Do you want me to leave?"

Her heart sank. "Do you want to leave?" Then she laughed out loud. "I can't believe I just asked that. Could I sound more like a high school girl?"

The smile came back onto his handsome face. "I definitely don't want to leave."

"Good." She drew a deep breath. "Not that I have the faintest idea what we're doing here."

"We're having a relationship."

They were? "I didn't want a relationship."

"Me, neither. But I stand my ground even when I'm scared. Not that I'm scared. I'm just saying, in case you are."

"Really? You're going to play the 'who's chicken' card? Now who sounds like a high school kid? Where's the mucho-macho stuff?"

He came closer, caught her by the waist. He wiggled his eyebrows. "I can show you my manly ways. If you'd like."

"So you want me to ask for it? You think you're so hot you can make me beg? That's what you really want, isn't it?" she teased him, giddy with happiness that he was here and she was in his arms, that they had a whole night in front of them.

His gaze focused on her mouth. "I just want to stop

you talking so I can kiss you," he said as his lips descended on hers.

He kissed so good. So unfair. How was she supposed to think and come back with some snappy response? Her knees were going weak; her brain was getting rapidly scrambled as he tasted the seam of her lips then teased his way inside, claiming her mouth fully.

She melted into his arms. There were times to be tough deputy chick, but this wasn't it. Her entire body tingled. She felt so incredibly good. Giddy, happy. She wanted this. She wanted him. She wanted more with every passing second.

When she was past all reason, he pulled back. Just enough to look into her face. He kept his strong arms around her waist.

His intense gaze held hers. "Why don't you want a relationship?"

"Oh, sure," she said weakly. "Ask questions when I can't think."

"I thought about it on the way over. I don't want this just to be a casual thing."

Nothing about Jamie Cassidy was casual.

"It's that..." she started to say, then stopped to figure out how to word it. "I'm pretty busy with work on the average day. And now we have sheriff's elections. Katie doesn't like change. If I ever got seriously involved with someone, I picture it as someone with a steady schedule and a stable job." She drew a deep breath. "Someone who might take care of Katie if something happens to me in the line of duty."

His arms tightened around her, his voice rough as

Send For
2 FREE BOOKS
Today!

I accept your offer!

Please send me two
free Harlequin Intrigue®
novels and two mystery
gifts (gifts worth about $10).
I understand that these books
are completely free—even
the shipping and handling will
be paid—and I am under no
obligation to purchase anything, ever,
as explained on the back of this card.

❏ I prefer the regular-print edition
182/382 HDL F435

❏ I prefer the larger-print edition
199/399 HDL F435

Please Print

FIRST NAME

LAST NAME

ADDRESS

APT.#   CITY

STATE/PROV.   ZIP/POSTAL CODE

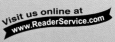
Visit us online at
www.ReaderService.com

NO POSTAGE
NECESSARY
IF MAILED
IN THE
UNITED STATES

BUSINESS REPLY MAIL
FIRST-CLASS MAIL   PERMIT NO. 717   BUFFALO, NY

POSTAGE WILL BE PAID BY ADDRESSEE

HARLEQUIN READER SERVICE

PO BOX 1867

BUFFALO NY 14240-9952

he said, "Nothing's going to happen to you. That's an order. Do you understand?"

"You're not the boss of me."

His eyes narrowed.

She narrowed her own right back. "Your job is more dangerous than mine. As little as I know about it, I figured that much out. So if I can put up worrying about you all day, you can put up with worrying about me."

"Fine," he said, not looking the least bit pleased. "I care for Katie. I don't think she minds me. I would do anything to protect her. You know that."

She supposed she did, but hearing the words still made her feel better. "I've never seen her warm to someone as fast as she warmed to you. She has this sixth sense to know instinctually who's a good person. That's a big point in your favor. Among others."

He brightened at that. "There are others? What are they?"

She tried to pull away. He wouldn't let her.

Oh, for heaven's sake. "You do a fair job at kissing," she admitted reluctantly.

He pulled himself to full height. "Fair?" And then he dipped his head to hers and stole her breath away.

By the time he pulled back again, she would have admitted to being the tooth fairy, let alone that he was a good kisser. She probably looked fairly bamboozled, because he had a pretty proud look on his face.

"You're not bad yourself." He winked at her. "We'll figure the relationship thing out. I would do anything for you and Katie. You know that, right?"

This was the man who'd carried wounded teammates

out of a war zone until he bled out to the point where he could no longer stand. Yeah, she believed him.

"Why?" she asked anyway.

"Because I'm falling for you." He held her gaze. "And I play for keeps. So let that be a warning."

Okay, he'd certainly laid his cards on the table. Warmth spread through her. Her heart seemed to swell in her chest.

"My life is never easy. Katie will always have to come first. I'm all she has. I'm responsible for her. You might not realize what you're taking on."

"I'll be around. I can promise that much. I'm permanently stationed on the border. But life is never a cakewalk. Mine has its own glitches."

Yes, it did. She so didn't care. She wanted him. So she reached up and, bold as you please, pulled his head back down to hers.

This kiss was softer, deeper, even more spine-tingling than the last, a confirmation of what they were feeling for each other.

He picked her up and her legs wrapped around his waist, his hardness pressing into her. He carried her toward the stairs, but she ran her hands up under his shirt as she hung on to him and they didn't make it.

He ended up pressing her against the wall in the hallway.

Heat suffused her as he rocked against her.

"Take off your shirt," he demanded.

She did.

He trailed kisses down her neck, to her collarbone, down into the valley of her breasts.

A moan escaped her throat.

"Yeah," he said, and brought up his hands to push her bra down, holding her against the wall with his pelvis.

Then his lips were on her nipple that was so hard, it ached. For him. And he did this thing with the tip of his tongue, a rapid back and forth movement that took her breath away. That was before he suddenly enveloped the nipple in the wet heat of his mouth and sucked gently. Pleasure exploded through her body.

She hung on to his shoulders for dear life.

Her entire body begged for him. She ground against him and he ground back, the need at her core intensifying to an unbearable level.

"We're not going to make it to the bedroom," he said in an apologetic, raspy whisper as he switched to the other nipple.

By that time, she could barely even remember that the house had another floor.

He teased her and suckled her until she was cross-eyed with need, tearing impatiently at his shirt, then at his belt buckle.

He slid her to the ground, but only until they had both stripped out of their clothing—in frenetic, jerky movements, working zippers with one hand, still reaching to touch each other with the other, their lips barely separating. Sweet mackerels, he was gorgeous.

He produced a small foil wrapper from somewhere and stumbled with it as he opened it without looking.

His body was carved from granite, every muscle perfect, and he had a lot of them. She wanted to touch him and never stop, her hands moving from his chest to his rock-solid abdomen and buttocks.

She couldn't help herself. Fine, she didn't *want* to help herself. She squeezed.

He groaned and lifted her again, up against the wall. She wrapped her legs around his waist, his hardness pushing deep inside her, stretching her, caressing her from the inside, filling her completely.

"Oh, wow," she said, barely able to catch her breath.

"You can say that again."

She simply moaned, because he began to move inside her and she was suddenly beyond speech.

The sex was amazing. He was amazing. Pleasure raked her body. She wanted to touch every inch of his skin and she wanted him to touch hers. She wanted his lips on hers and she wanted to never stop kissing.

Oh.

The man knew how to move.

Wave after wave of pleasure began where they were joined, then rippled through her body. Then the pleasure reached a crest and washed over her completely, her body contracting around him as she called out his name.

He stilled, held her, kissed her, caressed her.

She'd barely come back down to earth when he started up again, a steady rhythm at first, then gathering speed.

She was utterly spent. "Jamie?" She couldn't take more of this.

Or could she?

Okay, she could, she realized as delicious tension coiled inside her all over again.

Then she remembered how long he'd been holding her up like this, how long he'd been supporting her weight. Did that feel uncomfortable for him? Was it hurting him?

"Do you need a—" Her breath caught and she couldn't finish.

But he somehow knew what she'd been about to say. "My legs never get tired," he said, and grinned. Then he pushed deeper into her, sending her body soaring all over again.

Later, when they were spent and both still breathing hard, she slipped her feet to the ground, and they leaned against each other, supporting each other, holding each other up.

"I want to say something."

"Okay." She pulled back so she could look into his eyes.

"You're the light of my life." He gathered her close against him. "I love you, Bree Tridle."

"I love you, too. But don't let it go to your head and get all protective. I'll still be deputy sheriff, even if I'm your girlfriend. So no putting on bossypants."

He laughed out loud before he kissed her. "No, ma'am."

* * * * *

Don't miss the exciting conclusion of HQ: TEXAS,
*by award-winning author Dana Marton,
when SPY IN THE SADDLE
goes on sale next month.
Look for it wherever Harlequin Intrigue books
are sold!*

CAST OF CHARACTERS

Megan Cassidy—She is full of secrets and on a desperate mission in the South American jungle. This is difficult enough without making a formidable enemy in Mitch Mendoza, a no-nonsense undercover operative who awakens impossible needs in her.

Mitch Mendoza—Member of a top-secret military group (SDDU). He is on a rescue op, his only goal being to find his target and take the man home. But everything gets a lot more complicated when a sexy, mysterious woman shows up in the middle of the jungle and stands in his way.

Zak Goodman—The son of the governor of Kansas, Zak chose a different path than his father. When he's involved in a drug deal gone bad, he finds himself the prisoner of a powerful drug lord south of the border.

Juarez—A powerful drug captain, he controls a large chunk of the jungle.

Don Pedro—He's the top boss of the drug business in the region, with several captains reporting to him. They fear and loathe him at the same time. With good reason.

SDDU—Special Designation Defense Unit. A top-secret military team established to fight terrorism and other international crime that affects the U.S. Its existence is known only by a select few. Members are recruited from the best of the best.

Colonel Wilson—Mitch's boss. He's the leader of the SDDU, reporting straight to the Homeland Security secretary.

This book is dedicated to Karen Micek, a wonderful friend.

With many thanks to my editor, Allison Lyons.

Chapter One

The unforgiving South American sun scorched Mitch Mendoza's neck as he watched three men on the hillside below him through a pair of high-powered binoculars.

His current mission had only two rules. Rule number one: don't mess up. Rule number two: if you mess up, don't leave witnesses.

The three men, aka the witnesses he wasn't supposed to leave, moved at a good clip. They were local, used to the jungle terrain and the humidity that made breathing difficult for outsiders who had no business being in these parts. Outsiders like Zak "Kid Kansas" Goodman, who gasped for breath as he tried to keep up with Mitch.

"We can't let them reach the river." Mitch let the binoculars drop against his chest and looked back at the twenty-two-year-old trust-fund jerk whose only ambition seemed to be finding trouble and annoying as many people as possible in the process.

The boy was a long way from his fancy college fraternity—scratched and gaunt, wearing the signs of his recent imprisonment. "They're just a couple of goatherds. Let them be."

Mitch didn't think the kid had developed a conscience—although, that would have been nice. More likely, he was just too lazy to pick up the pace, too soft to put in the effort that would be necessary to catch up.

"I'm hungry. I want a break." He was worse than a three-year-old whining, "Are we there yet?" from the backseat.

"Soon." Mitch moved forward, adjusting his half-empty backpack.

Their food had run out the day before. Neither of them had washed since last Friday. Not that he would have said they were roughing it. They still had a bottle of drinking water between them, and a tent to keep out the poisonous creepy crawlers that liked to pay jungle trekkers nighttime visits.

"Watch your step."

The faster they went, the more careful they had to be. Snakes hid in the undergrowth; stones blocked their steps on the uneven ground. Neither of them could afford a twisted ankle. They needed to catch up with those goatherds. Quickly.

Word that two Americans were trespassing through infamous drug kingpin Juarez's part of the jungle could not reach the nearest village. Or the head of the local *policía*. If the police chief was corrupt, he'd report right back to Juarez. If he was clean, he'd report the info to his superiors. Mitch didn't need complications like that. Enough had gone wrong already.

The trip should have been a simple in-and-out rescue op, except that Zak wasn't the clueless victim his file had indicated. Mitch had found him in a shed on

Juarez property just as the kid had shot the drug lord's second in command. Juarez's brother-in-law, in fact.

That wasn't going to be forgiven.

Juarez was going to move heaven and earth to find the idiot. What had the kid been thinking anyway? He'd shoot his way out of camp and make it out of the jungle? He would have been dead within the hour if Mitch hadn't been watching the camp for days, and if he hadn't been ready to grab the kid and run with him.

He pushed forward and knew without having to turn around that Zak was falling behind. The kid made a lot of noise.

"Keep up and keep quiet." His mission was to get Kid Kansas, aka Kansas governor Conrad Goodman's son, out of the South American jungle in one piece without anyone knowing that he'd been there in the first place.

They didn't exactly have authorization from the local government. Mitch didn't have authorization from his own government, for that matter. Just a request from Colonel Wilson. The governor and the Colonel went way back, to a double tour of duty in 'Nam. They were blood brothers.

That the Colonel trusted Mitch with the mission was an honor. Mitch would have walked through fire for the man.

He looked up at the sun and prayed for a little luck, although he was used to his prayers going unanswered. But maybe this was his lucky day, because suddenly the three men he was following stopped. It looked like they were going to have a bite before crossing the river.

"Let's move." He set the pace even faster.

"I can't."

"Should have stayed home, then."

"It's not my fault I was kidnapped," the kid snapped. He was getting his spirit back and then some.

Right after he'd shot Juarez's brother-in-law, he'd been ready to fall apart, panicking when Mitch had busted into his prison. But in the past two days, once he'd realized his escape had been successful, he'd come to consider himself some sort of an action hero—or, at the very least, Mitch's equal.

"I don't deserve any of this," the boy kept on whining.

"You didn't come to Bogotá for sightseeing."

The governor had bought that line from his spoiled son. Mitch didn't. But Zak's lies were an issue for another day. Right now, he had bigger fish to fry. The men in front of them weren't his only problem. Juarez's soldiers were hunting for Zak, and they couldn't be far behind.

He got the kid down the hill in twenty minutes, stashed him in some nearby bushes then moved toward the men's camp. The goatherds had already lit a fire to warm water for their *yerba maté,* a favorite herbal drink of most South American natives.

They seemed simple men, each traveling with a single bag, wearing worn, mismatched clothes under their equally tattered ponchos. Their only crime had been being at the wrong place at the wrong time. Then again, better men than these had been killed for lesser reasons. And how many truly innocent men hung out in this part of the jungle? Where was their herd, for starters?

What had they been doing that close to Juarez's camp? The day after Mitch had rescued Zak, he'd stashed him out of harm's way and left the idiot for half an hour, so he could double back and see how close their pursuers were getting. Zak's only job had been to sit tight. But when he'd heard people moving through the woods, he'd lost his head and panicked. He'd run, yelling for Mitch in English. The goatherds had seen him.

And for that, they would have to die. Mitch checked his gun with distaste. He didn't condone senseless killing. And he hated having his hand forced by Zak, who should have simply followed him out of the jungle, quietly appreciating the rescue along the way.

He shook all that off and focused on what he was about to do. He would take these men out because he had to. But he wasn't going to shoot them in the back. He took a deep breath and stepped out into the clearing.

The next second, ponchos were shoved aside and the men—definitely not simple goatherds—were aiming AK-47s at him. Mitch's index finger curled around the trigger of his weapon, adrenaline shooting into his bloodstream.

But instead of all hell breaking loose, everything became absurdly surreal as a blonde suburban housewife stepped out of the bushes at the edge of the clearing. She wore khaki capri pants and a matching tank top, blond waves tumbling around her heart-shaped face, translucent amber eyes as wide as they could be. She looked like she'd come straight from a backyard barbecue or a kid's birthday party. The only things missing were the oven mitts.

"Excuse me. I'm sorry. Can you help me?"

Then their moment of grace was over and the "goatherds" opened fire on Mitch. They apparently didn't consider the woman much of a threat. Mitch dove for the bushes to avoid the flying bullets. But one nicked him in the shoulder. He ignored the burn as he shot and rolled, careful to avoid Blondie.

Lucky for her, he was good at what he did. The fight ended in seconds.

She stood in the same spot, her feet frozen to the ground, her entire body trembling. And he noticed now that her clothes were stained in places, her hands dirty.

"Oh," she said, as he came to his feet, blood trickling down his arm. Her full lips trembled faintly. "I think I'm going to be sick."

"Don't move." He patted her down, feeling surprised, and a little guilty, that he enjoyed it. Her eyes went even wider, and her cheeks blushed pink.

When he was done, he slipped the small designer backpack off her shoulders and checked over the contents: a small first-aid kit, bug spray, suntan lotion, extra clothes and a water bottle with a filter that made even mud puddles safe to drink. No weapons.

He gave the bag back. Damned if he knew what to make of her. "Okay. Get sick if you need to."

She ran for the bushes she'd come from, and a second later he could hear her retching.

He turned to the bodies on the sand, then to Zak, who was inching forward from his hiding spot. He looked green around the gills, too. He threw a questioning look toward the bushes, where they could still hear their mysterious guest.

Mitch shrugged and collected the weapons. "Go see what they have in their bags." Food would be welcome.

He looked with regret at the *yerba maté* that had been spilled.

"Hey, check this out!" Zak held up a two-kilo bag of white powder a minute later, grinning from ear to ear.

Mitch leveled his gaze on the idiot. "Rip it open, then dump it into the river."

"What? No way."

Mitch went stock-still. "Dump it into the river or I'll leave you here to rot."

A long minute passed before the kid sprinkled the white powder over the water, his stance belligerent. He took a quick sniff from the back of his hand when he thought Mitch wasn't looking.

The governor of Kansas was a decent man, but too softhearted. He was going to have to learn tough love in a hurry if he wanted to straighten out his son. Mitch didn't envy him.

He collected the AK-47s and tossed them into the river. He had plenty of ammo for his own gun and didn't need the extra weight to carry in this heat. No way he was giving one to the kid.

The bushes rustled as Blondie returned, none too steady on her feet. She kept her distance. She was too pretty to look truly pitiful, but she looked tussled—in a curvaceous, wholesome way. "Are you Americans?"

She wasn't the kind of woman Mitch could relate to. He didn't exactly lead a suburban lifestyle. He fixed Zak with a look to keep him quiet. "Who are you and what are you doing here?"

"Megan Cassidy. From New Jersey. I'm on a South American orchid tour." She swallowed hard. "We were attacked in the jungle."

Here? What was she on, the kamikaze boat run by Stupid Tours? He swatted some bugs away. "How many people?"

"Twenty-two of us tourists…" Her voice faltered. "Plus the two guides."

He felt infinitely tired all of a sudden. He didn't have time to rush into the jungle. He couldn't. It wasn't part of his mission. He asked anyway. "Survivors?"

"Just me." Tears spilled over and ran down her alabaster skin.

He didn't trust tears. He never knew when they were genuine and when they were used to simply manipulate a man. Her crying made him uneasy.

What did people like her think they were doing in the jungle? Hell, she shouldn't have been allowed in the country. Women like her should stick to attending PTA meetings, sipping double lattes while strolling through the mall and playing golf at the country club.

"I need to go home." She swallowed a sob. "Could you help me find the nearest town? I need to get to the police and an airport. Please?"

An unwanted complication at a time when he couldn't afford to be slowed down. "When did all this happen?"

She blinked rapidly. "This morning."

"How far away?"

"I don't know." She sniffed. "I kept running."

He hadn't heard gunshots, but the dense greenery muffled sound—the jungle formed solid walls in places. It all came down to this: he had no way to figure out where exactly the massacre had taken place. And he had no time to look for it.

He finished considering his options and shot Zak a look to remind him to keep quiet. "I'm Mitch and this is Zak here. From Panama. We're hiking buddies. Just got on this trail when these drug runners ambushed us," he lied with practiced ease.

He didn't want to have to kill her and didn't have the heart to leave her, either. But he would, if she became a threat to his mission. "About that attack on your group…"

She folded her arms around her slim midriff, her skin tightening over her cheekbones. "Would you mind if we didn't talk about it? Just right now, I mean?" Her amber eyes begged him. There went those trembling lips again.

The sight of her twisted something in the middle of his chest, an unfamiliar sensation he didn't care for. He supposed his questions could wait. "You can come with us as far as the nearest town."

She looked ready to melt with relief. "Thank you. I won't be any trouble, I swear."

He didn't believe that for a second.

Her shoulders straightened as she visibly pulled herself together. "What can I do to help?"

All right, she got a point for that. He'd yet to hear that question from Zak.

"Take whatever food and water you can find and store it in our backpacks," he told her. He nodded at Zak to help her, then went to see about the bodies.

He searched their clothes, but found little beyond cigarettes. No ID on any of them. The last thing people like this would have wanted, if they were caught, was for the *policia* to be able to identify them.

Ten minutes later, the current carried the bodies of

the three goatherds-slash-drug runners downriver. Another minute and the bags were packed. Mitch's had been hit, his GPS/radio unit among the casualties. It would have been a lot worse if he'd lost that on his way in. But from this point on, the way back out was fairly straightforward.

As he swung his backpack over his shoulder, he caught Megan looking at him.

"Let me see to your wound." She stepped closer, her movements hesitant, but her gaze determined.

His shoulder. Back at home, he would have ignored something this small, but it wouldn't be smart to risk an infection in the jungle.

"All right." But he watched her carefully. She hadn't taken the earlier gunfight well. He didn't want her to faint at the sight of his blood.

She seemed more together now as she peeled back the torn fabric of his shirt, took a good look then went for her first aid kit.

Zak wiggled his eyebrows at Mitch from behind her. He glared back at the kid, who seemed to have little on his brain beyond drugs and women. He looked decidedly less tired than he had before Megan had shown up. His gaze kept returning to her, lingering on her curves.

"Try to focus on something useful," Mitch told him. "It tends to increase the chances of survival in a place like this."

He rolled his eyes, but asked, "Where do we cross?"

"I'll figure that out. Don't you worry."

The woman's glance darted to the river, concern in her eyes, before she returned her attention to the task at hand, her movements quick and efficient. He wouldn't even have felt her light touch as she cleaned and bandaged his wound if he wasn't so damned aware of her. He closed his eyes so at least he wouldn't have to watch those long, slim fingers as they touched his skin.

He stepped back the second she finished. "Thanks."

She couldn't have been much older than the kid was. No more than late twenties. In some ways, he felt ancient compared to the two of them. A couple of years of black-ops duty had a way of aging a person. But not enough, it seemed. He definitely wasn't too old to appreciate the way she moved. He caught himself. He wasn't any better than Kid Idiot, the two of them ogling her as she packed away her emergency kit.

He cleared his throat and glanced up and down the river, evaluating the height of the opposite bank and the speed of the current. "We'll cross right here," he decided after a moment of deliberation.

If the locals had picked this spot, it had to be the easiest crossing in the vicinity. He looked back at the jungle behind them, watching closely for a few seconds. Listening did no good—the noise of the river blocked any distant sounds. He didn't see any flocks of birds suddenly taking flight or movement in the vegetation. That didn't guarantee anything, but he'd learned over the years to trust his instincts. He felt reasonably sure that Juarez's men hadn't caught up with them yet. Crossing the river should be safe, as long as they didn't stay out in the open longer than was absolutely necessary.

"Let's go." He reached for the woman's small hand and nodded for Zak to take the other one. They strode into the water, the three of them forming a human chain.

"If we get separated and washed downriver, turn on

your back and aim your body toward the other shore at an angle. Don't fight the current. Work with it." He had to raise his voice to be heard over the rushing of the river now that they were standing in the shallows.

The water wasn't high, but it moved fast in its narrow bed. Which was better than slow water and the pools it formed. At least here they didn't have to worry about piranhas, poisonous water snakes or alligators. All they had to contend with was the current and any logs that might wash along under the water. Being hit by one of those wouldn't be pleasant. He knew from experience.

Soon they were in up to their knees and Mitch fought to keep his balance. "Remember, if the water breaks you loose, stay on your back."

"Why?" Megan had his hand in a death grip, her delicate fingers folded tightly around his.

"To protect your vital organs. There might be sharp rocks on the river bottom, or logs and other junk being swept along under the surface."

She paled.

"You'll be fine." He tried to find the right words to reassure someone like her but came up empty. He felt like he should carry her out of the jungle without letting any danger touch her. He felt guilty that he couldn't, then angry with himself for feeling guilty. He hadn't asked for any of this.

He couldn't let her mess with his head. He had no time to mollycoddle her. He swore under his breath. She was definitely going to slow them down, despite her promises.

But she did keep up in the water. He didn't have to

drag her or anything. She did slip once, but he was quick to haul her up against him.

Wet top. Award-winning curves. Man, it'd been a long time since…

He made himself look away.

Zak's eyes were seven kinds of shiny and glued to her. Mitch frowned at the kid and kept going, testing the river bottom with his foot at each step before putting his weight on it.

In the end, he was the one who messed up. When she slipped again and this time went under, he was suddenly all thumbs, not wanting to grab anything, um, delicate. A moment of hesitation, but it cost him. As she scrambled to right herself, her frenetically moving legs kicked his legs right out from under him.

Zak pulled her up. Mitch let go of her, not wanting to pull her back down with him. He tried to stand, but finding purchase on the muddy bottom was no easy task. His feet couldn't find purchase on the slippery silt.

The current carried him downriver.

"Get to shore. I'll find you," he shouted back to them, trying not to swallow too much of the frothy water.

Zak looked green with panic. She didn't. Probably because she didn't know enough to realize how much trouble they were in—two complete amateurs in the middle of a raging river.

Chapter Two

An eternity seemed to pass before Mitch crawled up the muddy bank on the other side of the river, exhausted from battling the current. He scanned the hillside behind him.

No sign of Juarez's men. Yet.

He could see Megan helping Zak out of the water a few hundred feet away. She hadn't panicked. In fact, she had enough presence of mind to even help the kid. *Maybe she isn't as helpless as she looks,* he thought as he began marching toward them.

"Better get into the woods and out of this sun." He took charge when he reached them, leading them into the cover of the trees so they wouldn't be seen from the other side. They could use some rest, and this place was as good as any.

On closer inspection, she did look shaken. And more than a little lost. She kept casting worried looks at him. He couldn't blame her. This morning she'd been on a bus tour that she'd thought was safe. She had no way of knowing that the only roads up here were the ones cut into the jungle by loggers who were little more than criminals, clearing the jungle illegally. Traversing those roads without permission from the local crime lord could be deadly. Without protection, the bandits who controlled the area would consider anyone on them free prey.

Whoever had put her tour together was running an irresponsible operation, exploiting tourists who didn't know better. He'd probably figured he could take a few people in and out quickly without being seen. Idiot.

And so were the people who would sign up for a trip like this. You couldn't hire the first local guide that showed up at your hotel. Nor should you get on the first rickety bus that promised a grand adventure. He had half a mind to tell her that, but she looked like she'd already paid plenty for her error in judgment. She'd almost paid with her life. The thought set his teeth on edge.

"What did your husband have to say about you coming all this way for a flower?" he asked once they were settled on a big rock, shaking water out of their boots. He wanted to know what kind of man would let a delicate woman like her come to a dangerous place like this.

"I'm not married." She finger combed her hair, then pulled her clothes away from her skin. She seemed to be trying to air-dry the fabric, but it wasn't going to happen anytime soon considering the humidity level.

He tried not to look much, but it wasn't easy. She had perfect proportions. Everywhere. And a pretty face, with symmetrical features, thick lashes and full lips. She radiated a kind of wholesome innocence he didn't know what to do with.

He took the cheese and chunk of flatbread that they'd taken from the goatherds out of his waterproof backpack, and divided the food between Zak and Megan. "You go ahead. I'm not hungry."

He'd eat grubs if he got desperate. He had a feeling the other two wouldn't.

"You two hike a lot in these parts?" she asked between bites.

"Here and in other places." His missions took him all over the world.

As far as the kid went, this was Zak's first trip to South America. Based on the scant information he'd been given, Mitch knew Zak had graduated from being a pothead to more serious vices and decided that as long as he was using, he might as well get into the business. He'd probably taken one too many college business classes and fancied himself an entrepreneur. And since he'd learned from his father that when you wanted to get something done, you went to the top, he'd bought a ticket to South America.

Big mistake.

"How far is the nearest town?" Megan wiggled her toes in the sunshine. They were tipped with nail polish and looked like candy. Her pants were rolled up to above her knees.

He looked away. Her dainty toes and long legs were none of his business. "We should be there by nightfall."

"Do they have an airport?"

Sure. Right next to the day spa. "We'll be lucky to find a phone and a shack to sleep in. We're in a sparsely populated area. There isn't any industry around here, and little agriculture. The natives farm a little, but mostly they live off the jungle's bounty." He didn't mention the criminal element, didn't want to remind her.

In the morning, he would hook her up with a dependable guide who'd take her to the nearest city. She couldn't come with them any farther. When he contacted the Colonel, they'd get a military transport out of the country, which wasn't something she could be allowed to see.

"But they have shops, right?" She tugged on her top, her eyes filled with embarrassment. "This outfit is completely ruined. Everything else I have is soaking wet from the river, too."

Educating her on the local realities didn't seem worth the energy. She'd be out of his hair tomorrow morning. Simpler for him and safer for her. She was a babe in the woods. Megan Cassidy had no business being someplace like this, around men like him.

THEY REACHED THE TOWN at twilight, walking out of the rain forest tired and dirty.

Mitch wiped the sweat off his forehead as he led his small team toward the largest wooden building he could see. Kids ran around in the dust, chasing dogs and small, black pigs. The hum of generators filled the air, providing the few-dozen houses with electricity. A couple of ancient bicycles leaned against crumbling walls. A beat-up, rusted-out pickup—probably the only car in the village—hid in the shade of a fruit tree.

He scanned the scene before him carefully, but everything seemed as it should be. He couldn't spot anyone paying them undue attention. Juarez's influence may or may not extend as far as this place. But even if Juarez *was* looking this far afield, he'd have people watching for a young man, not two men and a woman. They had that going for them—a definite advantage.

"Hola!" They reached the building, and he slowly pushed the door in.

The local guesthouse had four rooms, the toothless old man who shuffled out from the back explained, but one had burned out and two were permanently occupied, so only one was free. He didn't have a phone, but there was one in the next village, fifty kilometers to the east. Mitch paid in advance, took the key then led the others down the hallway to the room the man indicated.

"This is it." The door stood ajar. He nudged it open with his boot, his hand near his weapon, ready for ambush, ready for anything. Juarez's men could have cut in front of them.

But as he looked around, it didn't seem they did. Nobody waited for them in there save a handful of cockroaches that skittered across the floor. A single bed took up most of the room, covered by a torn blanket that might have had bright-colored stripes at one point in the distant past, but was now beyond faded.

He could hear Megan swallowing behind him.

"Didn't the sign on the front say *LUJO?* Doesn't that mean luxury in Spanish?" Her voice was a touch faint.

He felt sorry for her. She was so far out of her element.... "We have our own bathroom. And you'll be in a nice hotel by tomorrow this time. Hang in there just a little longer."

She nodded bravely.

He walked forward to the open door in the corner and took in the small shower that probably had only cold water. The chipped toilet had no seat. The pipes were rusty, but none of them were leaking. And he didn't have to worry about water quality as long as they had their filter bottles.

Not that Megan appreciated their good fortune— having a roof over their heads and all. Her eyes were unnaturally wide and brimming with something that looked suspiciously close to tears. Even Zak was looking around with a dubious expression on his face.

He couldn't allow them to fall apart now. "Sit."

They both obeyed.

"This is what we're going to do. We'll clean up, then have a decent meal. Then we'll get some rest." He looked at Megan. "You should wait to report the attack until you reach a bigger place. The *policía* in a village like this is probably one man. He won't be able to do much. And he might even be in league with the bandits."

Plus, he didn't want any part of the police report. If they were together when she went to the authorities, the police would also want to talk to him and Zak.

She went a shade paler, probably remembering the attack, but she nodded.

He couldn't let her think too much. "All right. Let's get on with the cleaning up. I don't know about you, but I'm pretty hungry. The sooner we get ourselves in decent enough shape to go out and look for food, the better."

Zak went first. He didn't take long, then settled in front of an ancient radio bolted to the wall, trying to make it work while Megan took her turn. She didn't loiter, either, confirming Mitch's suspicions about the water being unheated. He was about to ask Zak, but then the bathroom door opened and she stood there wrapped in nothing but a worn towel.

His tongue got stuck to the roof of his mouth.

She had legs a mile long. Lean pink thighs. Zak stared at her wide-eyed with a stupid grin on his face. She tugged the towel down in a self-conscious gesture that nearly caused her breasts to spill out on top. She looked desperate and embarrassed, the hottest thing Mitch had seen in years. Or ever.

Stop staring, get moving, he told himself, and after a few seconds he actually did it.

He moved to grab his gun off the dresser, but she moved toward her bag on the bed at the same time, getting between him and his weapon.

In nothing but a towel.

Which would have been just fine—more than fine— if she were a different sort of woman, if they were alone and he wasn't in the middle of a clandestine mission.

He practically ran for the bathroom, needing that cold shower ASAP.

"I'll be out in a minute," he called through the closed door, wiping the sweat from his forehead.

He peeled off his clothes, stepped into the shower and let the cold spray hit his head. Exactly what he needed. He tried not to think of Megan Cassidy in that flimsy towel, those legs or those wet, soft locks framing her delicate face.

Morning couldn't come too quickly. She needed to get far away from places like this and men like him.

He quieted the little voice in his head that said he should put Zak on the military transport then stay behind and personally escort Miss Cassidy back home to make sure nothing bad happened to her.

That voice had nothing to do with her long, lean thighs. Rescue missions just ran deep in his blood. He couldn't help it if his instincts were to rescue her, too.

She was the proverbial damsel in distress, a scared, lost little thing who'd gone through considerable trauma in the past day. She collected orchids in New Jersey. This was probably the first massacre she'd ever seen.

He couldn't relate to a life that sheltered.

He was drying off when he heard a crash come from the bedroom. He didn't stop to dress, just burst through the door without thought, ready for fighting. He swore viciously at the sight that greeted him.

Zak was tied up on the bed, a rag in his mouth keeping him quiet. Megan stood in the middle of the room, dressed in shorts and a black tank top, boots on, hair pulled back into a no-nonsense ponytail, looking like the lead character in a kick-butt video game. A fierce scar ran from her ear to her throat, a pink line her tumbling locks had covered up until now.

All uncertainty was gone from her fiery amber eyes, all paleness gone from her face as she glared at Mitch and pointed his own gun at him. She held a matching weapon in her other hand.

Where did she get that from? "Put them down," he ordered.

Instead, she stepped closer.

"Who are you?"

"Who are *you*?" She turned the question on him. "Definitely not a hiker from Panama." She shoved one weapon into the back of her waistband, pulled a plastic cuff from her back pocket—one she had to have stolen from his backpack—then gestured toward the water pipes in the bathroom behind him.

"No." He measured the distance between them, judging it too great to be covered in a single leap. He was going for it anyway.

Or not.

She squeezed off a shot that passed so close to his ear he could feel the wind of the bullet.

"Hey, all right." He stepped back, knowing no help would be coming. In a place like this, people knew enough to walk away from gunfire, not toward it.

She tossed him the plastic tie. "The pipe."

He took a step back, held his left hand up to the pipe and cuffed himself to it. He swore under his breath, not taking his eyes off her for a second. He'd been had. He couldn't remember the last time that had happened.

What in hell had he been thinking? But, of course, he hadn't been thinking at all. She'd short-circuited his brain the moment she'd stepped into that clearing.

He flashed her his most lethal glare. "The money I have on me ain't worth it, honey. I'm going to track you down. That's a promise."

She gave him a cocky smile, keeping her gaze above his shoulders, then turned away, leaving him handcuffed and naked.

But if he thought this was about cash, he realized his mistake a second later when she untied Zak roughly and yanked him to his feet, not paying any attention to the boy's muffled groaning.

"You let him be," Mitch ordered in a voice that usually brought results.

She didn't even bother with a backward glance as she shoved Zak out the door. The next thing Mitch heard was the door slamming behind them and the key turning.

The sound of a car's motor coming to life reached his ears a minute later, as he desperately searched the bathroom for a tool that could set him free. Under his breath, he cursed Megan Cassidy—if that was her real name—a hundred different ways, each singularly inventive.

Chapter Three

The rumble of the ancient motor drowned out the sounds of the rain forest, but not the strange noises the kid made behind the gag.

"Are you going to keep quiet if I take it off?" Megan glanced over as she drove the geriatric pickup down an uneven dirt road that cut through the jungle.

Zak glared at her and sounded as if he were trying to swear around the cloth.

"Then I'm sorry, but you're going to stay this way." Not that she enjoyed making anyone uncomfortable on purpose.

But he could breathe. She was going to save herself from having to listen to more of the threats and the names he'd called her when she'd tried to take out the gag the first time. She wasn't going to put up with that from some two-bit drug dealer who got on Juarez's bad side.

She didn't know who he was and she didn't care. All she cared about was returning him to the boss and getting that next promotion, the next level of trust that would allow her to accompany Juarez to the meeting at Don Pedro's hidden stronghold next week.

The logging road she was on was about to end, which meant they would have to hoof it thirty miles south to the next passable road she knew, the one she'd left her ATV on before she'd cut through the jungle to cut off the kid at the river. She had figured that would be the way he would go if he knew anything.

Unfortunately, she hadn't found him alone, which had required some quick thinking and cost her a lot of wasted time. Mitch was… Never mind that. She didn't have all the details and she didn't need them, not even if he had the most amazing body she'd ever seen and the most dangerous bedroom eyes she could imagine. Juarez's orders were only for the kid.

She drove to the point where the jungle became impassable, left the pickup and shoved Zak forward on the foot trail ahead. His head was red with fury as he dragged his feet.

She shoved him harder. "I'd prefer if you walked. It's easier than dragging a dead body over terrain like this. Of course, the boss probably wouldn't want the whole body."

She pretended to ponder the point, then put a smile on her face. "As long as I take some vital organ that proves you're dead, it should be enough for him."

The kid's eyes went wide. He picked up the pace.

She undid the snaps at her hips and rolled down her pant legs, transforming her shorts into long cargo pants, the bottom of which she tucked into her boots to keep herself safe from bugs and scratches. Then she pulled a light shirt from her backpack, completing her preparations for the jungle. And she did it all on the go, without missing a step.

She kept an eye on their surroundings as they pushed ahead, looking for anything edible, alert to possible danger. "Watch for snakes on or near the trail. And poison frogs."

Her stomach growled for the meal they'd missed at that guesthouse. The small chunk of bread and goat cheese they'd eaten after crossing the river hadn't been nearly enough. But she didn't have time to leave the trail and forage right now. Night would be falling soon, and before that happened, she had to find a place to camp and make a platform that would keep them off the ground while they slept.

Even a raised bed didn't guarantee that they wouldn't awake with a snake or a tarantula up their pant leg, but at least it would improve the odds in their favor. Regardless of what she'd threatened the kid with, she intended to take him back to Juarez alive and in one piece.

Which meant they were going to sit the night out. Walking through the jungle after dark was suicide. She wasn't foolish enough to attempt that. And they both needed rest, anyway. You got tired, you made mistakes. Then you were no help to anyone.

They walked an hour before she found a good spot, a clearing with bamboo nearby and big-leaf palms that had gathered rainwater she could collect in her safe-filter water bottle. She'd forgotten to fill it at the guesthouse. Okay, not forgotten. But once Mitch had been cuffed to the pipes, it hadn't seemed too smart to go near the sink.

She wasn't going to think of the way she'd left him. Naked.

She'd almost dropped her guns when he'd busted out of that bathroom, all muscles and tanned skin.

"Here." She hung her backpack on a branch and used her short machete to cut enough bamboo for a double bed and enough vines to suspend it. When she was done, she pulled the rag from Zak's mouth.

"Keep quiet," she ordered before she showed him what she wanted him to do. "I'd recommend you do a good job. You don't want to sleep on the ground here, believe me."

She wasn't a great fan of the jungle. The past year hadn't been fun, exactly. But she would have put up with worse to achieve her aim. She scanned the trees and moved toward one that seemed to have potential, all while trying not to think of Mitch—and failing.

"Where are you taking me?" Zak called after her. Dirty and exhausted, he sounded a lot more subdued than when he'd screamed choice obscenities at her earlier.

She ignored that question as she started working on the bay leaf palms locals used for thatching to keep the rain out of their huts. "We need a roof to keep us dry overnight."

"Why does it rain so much here?" he whined, pulling his shirt away from his neck where the wet clothing had rubbed the skin raw.

She had some salve that would work on that.

"Because it's a rain forest." She kept Zak in sight as she worked. When she dragged the palm fronds back, she helped him finish the beds—he hadn't gotten far—then put the roof on, thatching it as best she could. The sky was already darkening by the time she finished. They had only minutes to start a fire.

She grabbed a dry cotton sock from her backpack and used that as kindling, wondering how far Mitch was behind them. Far enough, hopefully. She hadn't seen another vehicle at the village.

Getting a fire going in a place that dripped with moisture was quite the trick, but the burning sock dried the bamboo shavings she piled on, and then that caught fire at last. Just in time. The jungle around them was already black. Because of the tall trees, night here was a sudden thing. You'd better hope you were ready for it.

"Here, put this on your neck." She tossed the small jar of salve to the kid, then tied his left foot to the platform with some vines and one quick hook.

"You can't do that to me!" He yanked his bonds, his face turning red with outrage. "What if some wild animal attacks us? How do I escape?"

She put more wood on the fire then climbed onto her side of the platform, stashing the guns so they were at hand for her but out of reach for the kid. "If any trouble comes our way, I'll take care of it."

He swore viciously, but did it under his breath this time. And he didn't try to attack her, mindful of her weapons. Good. He wasn't an all-around idiot then. He seemed to have the ability to learn.

"Where are you taking me?" he asked again.

"Back to the camp."

"I have money— My father has money—"

She needed sleep. "No." However much drug money the kid and his family had, there weren't enough greenbacks in the world to tempt her. Something a lot more important was at stake.

Zak fell into sullen silence. Bugs began their night serenade. A macaw cried somewhere above them in the canopy.

She closed her eyes, ignoring her growling stomach. In the morning, as soon as there was sufficient light, she would find something to eat.

Her dreams were jumbled, and mostly involved Mitch. In some of the dreams, he was naked in her bed. In others, he was trying to kill her.

She woke in the dead of the night to a noise that didn't fit in with the rest of the sounds of the jungle. Or had she dreamed it? She listened carefully. No. Even the insect chorus was off. Something was disturbing their nightly routine.

Their fire had burned down to embers, providing little visibility. She reached for her weapon as quietly as possible and waited.

SHE WAS AWAKE but she hadn't seen him yet. Mitch crouched in the cover of some bamboo. The smartest thing would be to shoot her right now, but he wanted to know who she was and who she worked for. She intrigued him; he couldn't deny that. It kept her alive. For now.

"Drop both guns to the ground," he told her without showing himself.

After a moment of hesitation, she did, then slipped from her shelter, searching the darkness in the direction of his voice. "How did you find us?"

He'd followed the logging road on the *policía* man's

motorbike, then tracked their trail through the jungle. "I could smell the smoke of your fire from miles away."

"I didn't think you'd be so close behind," she admitted, then pulled a machete from behind her back and came at him.

How in hell did she see him?

The first blow almost took off his nose. He dropped the old pistol he'd bought in the village, knowing he wasn't going to use it, not yet, not until he had some answers. And for that, he needed both hands to restrain her.

He grabbed her wrist and held the machete away from them. She launched herself at him again and they ended up grappling on the ground in short order, which was a really bad idea, considering all the poisonous bugs and snakes. The sooner he got her under control the better.

"Quit it," he snapped at her.

She ignored him.

He kicked the embers as they rolled and the flames livened up, giving them both a little more light. He could see Zak from the corner of his eye, working madly on the restraint on his leg.

"You stay where you are," he growled at the kid. The last thing he needed was for the idiot to pick up one of the discarded guns and shoot him by accident.

That small diversion—his attention on Zak for a split second—was enough for her to make her move. She flawlessly executed a flip he remembered from special-ops training. *Interesting.* And where would she have learned that?

He responded with a move a martial arts fanatic

taught him while he'd spent two years deep undercover in Thailand. That made her eyes go wide and got him control of the machete at last.

He tossed the weapon aside and pinned her to the ground, embarrassed to be breathing so hard. Her firm breasts pressed into his chest. That image of her at the guesthouse wearing nothing but a towel popped into his mind. He batted it away. "Where did you get your training?"

"Where did you get yours?" She strained against him, taxing his focus.

"Who do you work for?" *Don't think lean pink thighs.*

"Same guy everyone works for around here." She grunted with frustration as she tried to heave him off, undaunted by the sixty or so pounds he had on her.

He kept her firmly in place, ignoring the interesting ways her body moved under his. At another time, in another place… *Focus.* "Not me."

"Let me guess, you're Cristobal's."

Cristobal was a rival drug lord who controlled vast territories north of the river. He had the reputation of being a ruthless bastard who didn't hesitate to burn whole villages if someone crossed him.

"Guess again." He transferred both of her wrists to one hand, then reached out with the other and grabbed his gun from the ground, feeling much better with a weapon handy.

She stared at the barrel and turned all soft under him, her large eyes filling with tears. "Juarez is going to kill me if I don't bring the kid back. You don't know my situation. You have to help me. Please."

He went slack like an idiot at the sight of her tears.

She immediately shoved her knee where sharp knees had no business going. Her elbow slammed into his chin, and before he could begin to breathe again, she was out from under him and running into the jungle, taking a split second to sweep down and pick up her own weapon.

What was wrong with him? He was the most cynical man he knew. He could usually smell a trap or a scam from a mile away. But something about her kept sneaking under his defenses.

He rolled to his feet and tore after her, limping, determined not to make the same mistake again. They were both playing with their lives like this, dammit. He couldn't see her in the darkness—the thick canopy above didn't let through much moonlight. He fired a warning shot in the general direction where he could hear her moving.

Then he could no longer hear her. Could he have shot her by accident? So much the better. Except part of him didn't like the idea of Megan Cassidy dead, no matter how much grief she'd caused him. He caught himself. There he went again, thinking stupid thoughts.

He stole forward step by slow step. At last he spotted her figure emerging out of the darkness. She faced him head-on, her legs slightly apart, her gun in both hands, aimed directly at him. A movie-poster combination of dangerous and sexy. She made a fine-looking enemy, he had to give her that.

But he was done letting that affect him. He pointed his own gun right back at her. "Now what?"

"One of us shoots the other and gets what she wants."

Everything about her was cocky, from her stance to her voice.

It turned him on, God help him. But he was a professional. "Juarez will kill Zak if he gets him back," he said, deciding to reason with her instead of using brute force and threats. He could always fall back on those. Maybe he could appeal to her feminine compassion. "He's just a kid."

For a moment she wavered. But only for a moment. "That's between the two of them."

All right, so she wasn't interested in compassion— not that big a surprise. Maybe she was interested in money. "I'll pay you for him."

"I'm not after money," she snapped, as if offended. "Why do you want the two-bit crook? You two business partners? He screwed the big boss over. He's going to do the same with you."

He thought for a long moment, trying to figure her out, then decided to take a calculated gamble. "He's not a two-bit crook, exactly. He's the son of a U.S. governor."

That gave her pause. "Which one?"

He told her, and again she wavered.

"The reward would be substantial," he pushed.

She didn't even bother to acknowledge that. "So you're U.S. law enforcement or something."

He calculated how far they'd come from Zak. Far enough. The kid should be out of hearing distance. "Or something."

For a second she took her eyes off him to scan the black jungle behind him. Her gun never moved, however. "Where is the rest of your team?"

"Where I come from, we don't waste a whole team's time on a quick little job like rescuing a politician's idiot son."

She considered him for a long time. "Are you one of Colonel Wilson's men?"

He went still. Now that was a question he hadn't expected. Who the hell was she? "How do you know Colonel Wilson?"

The Colonel headed the Special Designation Defense Unit, SDDU, a top-secret team of commando soldiers who ran various secret missions around the globe without anyone knowing. So how did she know?

"You're not CIA. The FBI never sends just one man. If you were a mercenary, you wouldn't have helped me. There was no money in it," she added. "So that didn't leave much."

Sound logic. But it didn't explain how she'd come to know about his team. Very few people knew about the SDDU. A handful of top government officials, and the few FBI and CIA agents who'd done joint missions. Had she?

"Who do *you* work for?"

She pressed her generous lips into a tight line as she glared at him without saying anything.

"Have you infiltrated Juarez's band of criminals?" He couldn't help being a little impressed.

"You're ruining an undercover op a full year in the making," she snapped at him. "I need Zak."

He reported to the Colonel, not to anyone else. "You can't have him."

"There'll be a meeting between Juarez and the big boss, Don Pedro, next week. No outsider has ever been to the don's secret stronghold before. We know he deals weapons to terrorists from there. I need to know what kind and how much. I need to uncover his connections. These are weapons that could march straight north, across Mexico and then through the U.S. border."

She was hunting terrorist connections abroad. A CIA spook, then. He should have guessed. She'd ruled out the CIA for him first, because that was her outfit and if he was with them, she would have known it.

He was beginning to understand her better now. She was trusted at Juarez's camp, but not enough for Juarez to include her in his personal retinue. Except if she did something his other men couldn't accomplish, like bringing back the kid who'd killed his brother-in-law...

Her plan wasn't bad. She was working on an important mission. But his orders weren't to accommodate other important missions he came across. He only had one order from the Colonel: bring the governor's son back.

"I'm sorry," he said, and he meant it. "You'll find another way."

But instead of accepting defeat, she shot at his foot, apparently not done with this way yet. A miracle that she hadn't maimed him. He had no choice but to shoot the gun out of her hand. He did just that, then lunged forward, and they went rolling on the ground again.

"This doesn't feel like progress." She had the presence of mind to joke with him, even though her hand must have smarted.

It might not have felt like progress, but it sure felt like one hundred percent pure, curvy female to Mitch. He wouldn't have minded the prolonged body contact so much if the ground wasn't full of danger. He couldn't afford to get injured, and he didn't want her hurt, either.

"Could we have a civilized discussion about this?" he suggested between a flip and a roll.

"Worried that you can't win by sheer force alone?" She grunted and heaved.

"Stop." He pinned her down at last. "You roll into a sharp branch and your mission goes nowhere."

She gave it another try before she stilled. "Fine. A civilized conversation it is. In the morning." She blew out a breath. "So you're an extractor."

"*The* extractor. When someone needs a target removed unseen from an impossible situation, I'm the go-to guy." She might as well know that he wasn't going to give up or give in to her.

"Do you always get them?"

"Always." He didn't compromise.

"It's that important to you. Interesting." She gave him a calculating look. "I'm guessing you lost someone close to you at one point?"

A discussion they weren't going to have. He moved back slowly and let her go, then offered her a hand.

She sprang up on her own and dusted off her clothes. "Just for the record, you called truce first."

She sauntered off toward her makeshift camp without looking back at him. Unfortunately, not enough moonlight filtered through the canopy for him to fully enjoy that tempting image.

"Take a picture. It'll last longer," she called over her shoulder.

She must have attended some CIA training on how to be thoroughly irritating. But if she thought she was going to be the last spy standing here, she was sadly mistaken.

He headed after her, hoping Zak hadn't done anything stupid like untying himself and running off into the jungle. They'd had enough excitement for one night.

As luck would have it, the kid was where they'd left him. Mitch checked his restraints and, despite loud demands, left them in place.

"Up," he ordered next, nudging Megan onto the platform and tying her wrist to the other end the same way she'd tied up Zak. Then he lay between them, snug, his gun resting on his chest, finger on the trigger.

He didn't like the idea of the other two guns, plus the machete, scattered out there, but he'd have to wait for daylight to look for them and secure them.

"You can't be serious about this." Megan snarled the words at him.

He settled into the uncomfortable bed. "Try to get some rest."

"There's not enough room," Zak grumbled. "Untie me now. You can't treat me like this. I'm the victim here."

"I could knock you out, if you prefer," he offered.

"You can't touch me. You're getting paid to save me."

"This is cozy. Think of us as one big happy family," he told the kid.

Megan turned to her side, jabbing him viciously in the side with her elbow in the process, probably not by accident.

He let it go. Couldn't be mad at her when they were pressed against each other full-length. She smelled like the rain forest and the cheap soap they'd all used at the guesthouse. Not a combination that would turn the average man's head, but for some reason it got under his skin.

He shook off the tension that had pushed him forward since she'd left him tied to the sink. Then he grinned into the night as the breeze moved her hair and it tickled his chin. At least, chances were, he was going to have pretty good dreams.

An honest-to-goodness spook, looking like a teenage video gamer's dream come true. Thank God for small favors. When he'd thought she was a lost suburban housewife, he didn't know what to do with her. When he'd thought she was a heartless criminal, one of Juarez's lackeys, he didn't want anything to do with her. But now that it turned out that they were almost on the same side… Their chance encounter suddenly brimmed with possibilities.

For after.

When they were both done with their missions and back in the U.S., he wouldn't mind asking her out for a drink. He was ready to sink deeper into that fantasy when he heard something moving in the jungle, circling their small camp.

Megan heard it, too. She went instantly rigid.

So much for a good night's sleep.

"Give me your gun," she whispered under her breath.

Not going to happen. But he did reach up and untie her wrist. He had firsthand experience with the kind of damage she could inflict, even unarmed. If they were attacked, she would be far from helpless. That was all he could do for her. He didn't trust her enough to arm her, at least not until he knew what kind of danger they faced.

He listened.

Four men. He used military hand signals to pass on the news.

She nodded and pointed west.

He slipped from the makeshift bamboo bed and pulled back into the jungle just as the four shadows snuck into the clearing opposite them. They moved forward, then one of them signaled to the others to stop.

Mitch was ready to open fire at the first sign of aggression. He could take them out in a second.

"Is that you, *chica?* What are you doing here?" the one in the front asked with a voice raspy from too many cigarettes.

"Dammit, Paolo." She swore an impressive blue streak in Spanish. "Ever heard of giving warning? I almost shot you."

Megan jumped off the bed, brazen as anything, pretending to shove her nonexistent gun into the waistband at her back. And as dark as the night was, it seemed she managed to fool the others, because nobody called her on it.

If he weren't careful, he was going to start admiring her or something stupid like that, Mitch thought.

"I'm taking Juarez's young friend back to him," she told the men, tossing wood on the fire, looking around surreptitiously.

Paolo checked out the sleeping platform behind her. "We've been looking for the bastard all day. We made camp east of here a couple of hours ago. Upwind, or we would have smelled your fire. Heard the shots, though.

Figured we better investigate." He knocked Zak to the ground and took his place.

The kid had to stay where he fell, with the ankle restraint still tethering him to the platform. He couldn't do much more than squat and look scared.

Paolo patted the bed next to him and flashed a grin at Megan. "How about you come back to bed?"

Mitch took a silent step forward. He wasn't quite out of cover, but he was close enough to take swift action if needed.

"How about you give up? As I said before, I don't mix business and pleasure."

"Give it a try. I promise you'll like it." Paolo's tone took on a menacing edge. There were four of them and one of her. He probably knew that she, too, would have the odds figured. "Come on."

Mitch stepped into the clearing, not bothering with stealth. He wanted them to see him.

Immediately, four guns pointed at his chest. Four pairs of hard eyes said they wouldn't hesitate to pull the trigger.

"Friends of yours?" he asked Megan as if he'd just gotten back from a bathroom break.

"Who the hell is he?" Paolo came off the bed.

"An old friend." Megan stepped closer to Mitch. "I knew he was in the area so I called him in for help."

"The boss don't like strangers in his business," Paolo warned her, then turned to Mitch. "Who do you work for?"

"Whoever pays best. Right now, I'm protecting a logging operation north of here." All logging in the area was illegal, so that should give him the right credentials. "Gun for hire, soldier of fortune, that kind of thing," he added.

"Which timber boss?" Paolo wanted to know.

Mitch kept his demeanor friendly and his hand close to the weapon tucked into his waistband. "He doesn't like his name passed around."

Tense silence stretched between them.

But when Paolo lowered his gun, so did the others. "Forget logging. You'll come with us. I know a man who pays well and needs some extra muscle."

And just like that, his chances of getting Zak out of the country swiftly and unnoticed dimmed. Sure, he'd taken on four men in a gunfight before. When he'd been on his own. But if all hell broke loose now, in the dark, Zak or Megan could get killed, and he wasn't going to take that chance.

Under the smile on his face, his jaw clenched. Instead of taking Zak to safety, he was going to have to stand by as the men took the kid back to the lion's den.

Megan could have been helpful, but damned if he knew whether he could count on her. She seemed determined to care only about her own mission and nothing else. He had hoped to convince her once morning came, but they weren't likely to get time alone for that now.

And the balance of power had shifted anyway. The men had played right into her hand.

Regardless, he *would* get Zak home. *With or without her,* he thought as he surveyed the drug lord's lackeys for weaknesses. He never left a mission incomplete.

Chapter Four

By the time morning came, Mitch had a plan. He'd thought about it all night long as he'd slept in spurts squatting by the fire. He could take the men out during their long trek. Getting another look at Juarez's compound might have provided new intelligence he could pass on to the Colonel, but Megan had already seen the place and had probably passed on all kinds of intel to the CIA. They could deal with Juarez.

His job was to deal with the kid. Which meant he would have to take out Paolo and the others, then turn around and continue north with Zak. He'd call in for military transport the second he could make connection.

Megan Cassidy was welcome to do whatever she pleased. As long as she didn't stand in his way.

They marched forward silently, in single file. Paolo led the way, with Sanchez, his second in command, behind him. Then came Megan, Zak, Mitch then the other two men.

Mitch reached into the opening of his shirt and plucked a leech from under his collar, slowing his steps as he disposed of the little bloodsucker. He needed to fall to the back of the line. He didn't like anyone with a weapon behind him.

He made a point of scratching a couple of times before stopping altogether and stepping aside. "Damned leeches in my pants."

One of the men laughed at him, another winced with sympathy and the rest didn't bother to respond. Nobody stopped to wait. He messed around with his belt and zipper for a while until they passed him, then he fell in step behind them.

Step one completed.

Yet the setup was far from ideal. Since they were walking single file, he'd have to take out the men in the back first as they blocked sight of the others up front. But if he took out the men in the back, the two in the front would start shooting at him. Which would leave Megan and Zak in the crossfire.

Not that she was a factor. Megan Cassidy was nothing more to him than the possibility of some carnal fun. His unhelpful fascination with her had to stop before it got him in trouble. She could take care of herself. And yet, on some level, he cared. Not because she was another American; God knew he'd been stabbed in the back more than once by his own countrymen. And definitely not because she was CIA. He'd been caught up in their intrigues before. Their wheeling and dealing had once cost the life of a good friend and nearly his, too.

He had allegiance to his country, not to its corrupt systems. He took orders only from the Colonel. He was loyal only to his team. He trusted very few people beyond that circle. Friends outside the job were too much of a risk.

His family thought he was dead. Better that way for everyone. They hadn't gotten along too well when they'd thought he was alive. This way, his work didn't put them in danger, and they didn't get on each other's nerves.

He was too busy to be lonely.

Except, back when he'd thought Megan was a traumatized tourist he was leading out of the jungle, she'd sure made him wish for… He wasn't sure what, but an empty little spot suddenly opened up in his chest.

He looked at her as she marched on resolutely and felt a funny kind of tingle on his skin.

Maybe he was getting jungle fever. That would explain why his thoughts were getting jumbled all of a sudden. He wasn't the type of man who lost his head, and consequently his life, over a pretty woman.

He had a small box of emergency medicine in his backpack, antibiotics and malaria pills among them. He'd take some meds when they next stopped, Mitch decided as he marched forward, watching where he stepped, until sharp cries pulled his attention to the canopy.

Howler monkeys were passing by high above the ground, flashes of gray streaking through the emerald green of the foliage. He watched them for a second before returning his focus to the path in front of him and the four men he had to neutralize before he could complete his mission.

"Are your wrists okay?" Megan was asking Zak up ahead. Paolo had tied the kid's hands thoroughly that morning. She checked his skin and reached into her backpack, pulled out a jar and put some kind of a salve on Zak's wrist.

The kid's response was lost in the noise the monkeys made.

She was a strange one. Taking the kid back to Juarez where he'd be shot, yet worried about the ropes cutting into his wrists. She didn't seem hard-hearted. But definitely focused. She would do whatever it took to achieve her aim.

So would he.

The men looked up at the monkeys. Mitch looked at the men. His best chance would be if one of the two up front stopped for a bathroom break. Both at the same time would be outstanding, but he wouldn't hold his breath for that. He would take whatever opportunity presented itself.

His break came sooner than he'd expected. The howlers were crossing right above them. The man in front of him slowed as a shot went off.

Paolo had decided to go monkey hunting. But he'd only managed to wound the animal, which clung to a branch, emitting a keening sound of pain.

Mitch took aim and ended the animal's suffering. Then their line scattered at last, Paolo going for the monkey, taking charge of it, even though it hadn't been his kill. "Let's eat!" Others moved off into the jungle to gather wood for a fire. Mitch used the distraction to get closer to Megan.

"Are you with me?" He kept his voice below a whisper. He felt better just standing next to her. Didn't understand why. He barely knew her. She'd scammed him.

A lock of hair had escaped her ponytail and curled

against the scar on her neck. His fingers itched to tuck that lock behind her ear. He didn't.

He watched regret come into her eyes as she said, "I can't. Not in this."

So she wouldn't fight to help him. But would she fight against him? Or would she stay out of it all together? He didn't have a chance to ask.

"Hey, gringo," Paolo called him over, working at skinning the monkey. "Look at this. Big sucker, eh?" He puffed his chest out. "What do you think?"

"I think we're about to have some lunch." He faked an enthusiastic grin.

Twenty minutes later, the fire crackled under the roasting meat. When it was done, Paolo divided it and handed out the portions. Mitch ate in silence, filling his stomach for the first time in two days. Now if he could only get some decent sleep. As soon as he and Zak could make their escape and get far enough away from Juarez, they were going to take a serious break.

From the corner of his eye, he caught Megan sneaking off into the woods. Probably for a bathroom break. The men had taken theirs as they'd walked, barely bothering to step off the path before aiming at the nearest tree.

Mitch gobbled up the rest of his portion, noting the position of every man, the whereabouts of every weapon. Now was his chance. He could take them without having to worry about Megan. He reached for his gun, ready to yell at Zak to duck.

If he weren't watching the men so closely, he wouldn't have caught the exchanged look between Paolo and Sanchez. A second later, Paolo melted into the jungle, following the path Megan had disappeared down a minute ago.

"All right." Sanchez stood. "Better get going."

The others washed down their food with some water, then picked up their backpacks and fell in line. One yanked Zak onto his feet. The kid shot a plaintive look at Mitch, but he was more concerned about why Paolo had taken off after Megan.

He made sure he was the last to head out, bringing up the rear. Then he silently fell behind without anyone noticing. They were slowed by the heat and humidity as much as their full bellies. Catching up with them again wouldn't be too difficult. Their job was to bring Zak back to Juarez, so unless the kid did something stupid, he'd be safe for the moment.

In five minutes, Mitch had returned to the remains of their abandoned fire, drops of water sizzling on the coals as rain began to fall. He moved forward in the direction Megan and Paolo had taken.

He was a pretty good tracker, and they hadn't bothered to mask their trail. Another minute or two brought him close enough to hear the two of them, and he soon realized they weren't talking. They were fighting. Mitch rushed forward, finding them rolling in the undergrowth, glaring and swearing at each other. Paolo was doing his best to gain the upper hand while Megan fought like crazy to prevent that from happening. They were a blur of growling faces and entangled limbs.

For a moment he hesitated, unsure if Megan would want him to interfere or if she needed to beat the man herself to maintain her status on the team. He didn't want to mess up her mission if he didn't have to.

But then Paolo grabbed her between the legs and reason flew from Mitch, a swift wave of anger pushing him forward without allowing him time to think. The cold fury that leaped to life inside his belly surprised him. "Get your hands off her."

Paolo glanced back with a dark look on his weather-beaten face. "You wait your turn."

Two more steps forward and Mitch was lifting him off her, tossing him aside with more force than was necessary. He went for his gun at the same time as Paolo. Mitch squeezed the trigger first.

The shot rent the silence and sent birds flying. Monkeys screeched in the distance. Paolo's eyes went wide and stayed that way.

"And now how are we going to explain this?" Megan's cheeks turned pink with outrage. She didn't seem to notice or care about her injuries, but the welts on her neck and forehead pumped a fresh supply of anger through Mitch.

His jaw tightened. "How badly are you hurt?"

She was on her feet already and searching for her gun among the decaying leaves. She found it, stashed it then stamped over to Paolo.

Mitch didn't need to check the body. He always hit what he aimed at. If he meant for a man to be dead, the bastard was dead. End of story.

Paolo no longer held his attention. Megan did.

"Shot through the heart. Great." Annoyance roughened her voice. "You had to do that? Seriously?"

Her clothes were wet and muddy, outlining her tempting figure. She shook some stray leaves from her hair with an impatient flick of her head. "Did I ask for help? I could have handled it."

He hadn't expected gratitude, but he didn't deserve getting chewed out for what he'd done, either. "Forget I came back."

He tried to stare her down, but she stared right back, holding his gaze without flinching. She was fierce and wild, and he had the sudden impulse to stride right up to her, yank her into his arms and kiss her. Anger and frustration morphed into hot lust in the blink of an eye. He wanted to feel those full lips crushed under his, wanted a taste of her.

Whoa. Rein it in. He stood down and shook his hare-brained impulses right out of his head. For one thing, she'd just been attacked. She sure didn't need more of the same from anyone. For another, even if she were willing, even if she were begging for his touch, he needed to stay *far* away from her. He was here on a top-secret mission, not on some singles vacation.

Her chin sunk back down, her shoulders, too, as she calmed herself. "How is your shoulder? I didn't want to ask in front of the others this morning."

She didn't want to alert them to any potential weakness on his part. Smart. Too bad he was beyond appreciating the gesture just now.

"Forget it." Lust and frustration had him on edge. He turned on his heels and marched away.

She caught up quickly. She, too, seemed to be humming with tension. "We'll tell Sanchez that we heard people moving through the woods and Paolo went to investigate, sending us back to let the others know. He'll expect Paolo to catch up eventually. When he doesn't, he'll assume that some wild animal or one of Cristobal's men got him."

He didn't like it that she'd come up with a plan first. Ever since they'd met, she'd always been a step ahead of him. It bothered him more than it should have. Why? He occasionally worked on teams. He wasn't always the best and the quickest. But with her—

Was he trying to impress her? Now that would be stupid.

"How about the gunshot?" he thought suddenly. "They had to have heard that."

"Maybe not. The vegetation is thick enough to swallow the sound. There's a river up ahead. If they were close enough to it when your gun went off, the sounds of the water could have drowned out the shot."

They followed the trail in silence for a while until it stopped on the bank of a river she'd been talking about. For a second he wondered if it was the same one they'd crossed yesterday, winding its way through the jungle. If it was, then they were farther upstream. The riverbed was narrower and shallower than where they'd crossed before. Then he noticed a deep gouge in the sand that showed where a canoe had recently been pulled into the water.

Oh, hell, no.

They could only see a few hundred feet ahead where the river disappeared around a bend. No trace of the men anywhere.

He swore. This couldn't be happening. He slammed his backpack into the mud as steam gathered inside him.

"Juarez has boats and weapons stashed all over the jungle in case of emergency." Megan's voice was filled with a level of frustration that matched his. "I left an ATV twenty miles or so from here. I was hoping Paolo would lead us that way, but of course he had to choose otherwise. Now we have no choice but to follow the river."

He stared at the water, his mood getting darker by the second. The men were gone and they'd taken Zak along with them. He paced the shore, not quite able to believe it. He'd saved Megan, who didn't in the least want to be saved, and in the process he'd lost the kid.

HE LOOKED LIKE he was ready to strangle her. Fine, so she'd stolen Zak from him at that guesthouse. But, hey, nobody had told him to rush to rescue her from Paolo. "You should have stayed with the kid and made them wait."

His lips narrowed further. His nostrils flared. He reminded her of a bull in the arena, pawing the ground. All in all, she preferred this look to the one he'd presented back in the woods.

Back there, he'd looked like the hero out of some big-budget Hollywood action flick as he'd broken through the bushes and challenged Paolo. She wasn't used to rescue. She couldn't say her heart hadn't fluttered just a little. It must have been some basic, primitive female reaction to the macho display of an alpha male. But she didn't appreciate the interference, and she definitely didn't appreciate the flutter. That simply couldn't happen again.

Mitch Mendoza was nothing but a giant monkey wrench in her plans. That he was hot was beside the point. She'd just have to ignore the way her hormones stood up to salute him every time she looked at him.

Because of him, Paolo was dead, and his absence might make Juarez suspicious, regardless of her cover story. And now she wouldn't be the one to bring Zak to the mighty drug lord. Sanchez would get the credit instead.

No way. She *had* to get the brownie points. Juarez had to take her with him to see Don Pedro.

Her mind flipped through all the possibilities until she hit upon an idea that might work. "There are some rapids up ahead. They'll have to take the canoe out of the water and carry it around. It'll make them lose whatever time they gained on the river. If we move fast enough, we can catch up to them."

He rolled his neck and his shoulders and adjusted his backpack. "Let's move out," he called, taking the lead.

Typical man.

When she tried to cut in front of him—hello, she was the one who knew the terrain, she'd traipsed all over this jungle in the past year—he picked up speed to prevent her.

Fine. She fell in line behind him. Carrying that massive ego around was going to get too heavy sooner or later. He followed the river, logically, so he wasn't leading them off course. She could afford to humor him. One of them had to be the mature adult. With eight younger brothers, she was used to the role. She could handle it.

"So out of curiosity," he asked over his shoulder, "you would have let Paolo beat you up or worse to keep your cover?"

"This happens to be an important mission." But that was only part of it. She worked for the CIA, but she had her own reasons for being here. Reasons that would likely end her government career when the truth came out. The home office didn't appreciate operatives with private agendas, regardless of the worthiness of their cause.

"You're tough."

His acknowledgment meant nothing. She squashed the small thrill she got from it. "Don't you forget it."

"Tough for a girl, I mean."

"Well, that just ends all the goodwill we've been building," she deadpanned.

"A sense of humor, too," he mocked her. "So with all that, how come you're not in a safer job in a nicer place?"

"I'm exactly where I want to be."

"All things considered, I'd rather be on my couch with a cold beer, watching a game on the big screen."

She didn't believe him for a second. He had the look of a man who lived for action. He was always on, always ready, mind and body honed in combat. You didn't get this good at something without liking it. "How often does that happen?"

"Once a year if I'm lucky."

She didn't know much about him, only that he was one of Colonel Wilson's men. The colonel was running some commando group that flew so deep under the radar, even Congress didn't know about it. Which was a neat way to avoid congressional oversight, she supposed. They did lone-wolf operations, deep undercover, took care of problems nobody else dared to tackle.

The grand sum of her knowledge about the team didn't amount to much, despite the fact that at one point, she'd tried all her CIA resources to find out more. She'd been stunned at how fast doors had been slammed in her face.

Clearly they were in the black-ops business. She wasn't impressed. The United States had enough law enforcement and military branches already. They didn't need a new batch of yahoos who thought they were above the law and interfered in the legitimate agencies' business. And it was dangerous, too. She thought of Jamie at home, of the way he was now. Sorrow filled her swiftly. She put thoughts of her eldest brother away.

"Why don't you go home?" she suggested to Mitch. "After I'm done with what I've come to accomplish, I'll take Zak back to the U.S. with me."

"You'd leave him behind in the blink of an eye."

She shrugged. "He's grown on me."

He shot back an amused look. "How about me?"

"You leave now, and I'll let you know if I miss you in a couple of weeks."

He snorted. Then he got serious. "Without me, Zak will be dead within ten minutes of reaching that compound."

"I'll keep an eye on him."

"He's not your top priority."

He was right about that. She was here to rescue someone else. So she changed the subject. "How long have you been in the commando business?"

"Too long. How long you've been with the company?"

"Since college."

"Spook University?"

"Yale."

He gave her the once-over. "Come from big money?"

"No money at all and nine kids in the family. Went to school on scholarship."

"You must be the eldest."

"How did you know?"

"Bossy and stubborn."

She looked at the ground for something to throw at his wide back and found nothing but composting leaves. "I grew up with eight younger brothers. They needed positive direction. Anyway, being decisive is a positive trait."

"All the bossiness could be the reason why you don't have a man. Ever thought of that?" He was baiting her on purpose now. He seemed to get some sick satisfaction out of needling her.

"I've got someone back home."

"You haven't been home in over a year," he reminded her.

Not that she needed a reminder. Her relationship with Vincent hadn't been that great to start with. She had no illusions about him waiting for her. Not when she hadn't been able to tell him where she was going or how long she would be staying.

"I'm sure your life is chock-full of women," she shot back.

"You have no idea how grateful some of those damsels in distress I save can be." He smirked. "You realize that since we've met, I've saved you once a day?"

Okay, he'd gone too far with that one. She didn't need saving. Ever. Her self-sufficiency was a matter of pride. He was possibly the most infuriating man she'd ever seen, and she had eight brothers to compare him to, not to mention dozens of colleagues. She did work in a male-dominated field.

"The first time around, you weren't saving me, I was scamming you." She set the record straight. "And if you'd stayed with Zak instead of interfering with Paolo, we wouldn't have lost the kid." She would have been able to fight Paolo off. Probably.

If she hadn't rolled her eyes, she wouldn't have noticed the movement on the branch above Mitch. He didn't. He'd been paying too much attention to annoying her and missed the snake. Just as it dropped out of the tree, she leaped forward and swiped at it with her machete.

He spun, alerted by the noise she made. The snake's body fell around his neck with a small thud, the head landing at his feet. He stood frozen to the spot, wideeyed, color creeping into his stubble-covered cheeks.

"You scared of snakes?" Megan smiled. So he did have a chink in his armor. She softened a little, closing the remaining distance between them with a short step and slipping the still-wriggling body from around his neck to throw it into the underbrush. "No good for eating. This kind has a bitter taste."

His chestnut eyes were way too close.

His gaze fell to her lips.

The jungle heated around them. Breathing seemed extra difficult for a moment.

An electric charge ran through her. She wasn't sure what she should hope for, that he'd kiss her or that he wouldn't.

His tongue darted out and moistened his lower lip. His Adam's apple bobbed up, then back down as he swallowed.

Then he stepped away.

SHE HAD NO IDEA how hot she was. How was that possible? She just about short-circuited his brain every time he looked at her. Seeing her in action… She had to be getting male attention 24/7 at Juarez's camp. Of course, it was probably unwanted attention, more worrisome than self-esteem boosting. Or downright dangerous, like Paolo had been.

"Thank you," he told her as he moved forward. "That's what you do when someone saves your life, by the way. Acknowledge it instead of denying it."

"If you ever save my life, I'll be sure to express my gratitude," she said in snarky tone behind him.

He allowed himself a small grin. He didn't normally work with a partner. She was annoying at times, definitely tested his patience on occasion, but she was also entertaining. And hot. Something about her made hormones flood his brain. *Great.* He was in the middle of a mission. He'd lost his charge. And now his thoughts made him feel like a teenager.

He'd better fix that, and quickly, before he kissed her or did something equally stupid. The snake hadn't bothered him, but when she'd stepped that close—to be that near to those lips…

They marched on in silence for a while, pushing as hard as they could. He walked in front. Walking behind her would have provided too much distraction. He needed to keep his mind clear and keep up the pace.

Catching up with the men before they reached the compound was crucial.

They didn't even stop when they came upon a mango tree. They filled their pockets as they walked. Their forced march expended a lot of energy. Replacing that was vital to remain in top fighting shape. They ate as they hiked, but also saved some for later.

She never complained once. Not about the unforgiving pace he set, not about the lack of food or lack of breaks. About an hour later, they heard the rapids, but couldn't see much. The area around them was too overgrown with bamboo to walk, so they had to turn deeper into the jungle. Long minutes ticked by before they could begin angling back toward the river.

They reached the water just as Sanchez and the others were getting ready to give the final push to their canoe on the other side. Zak was already sitting in the front, looking haggard.

"Hey," Sanchez called over the water, straightening when he spotted them, his right hand lingering by his gun. "Where is Paolo?"

Had they heard the shot, was the question.

Mitch stayed quiet, letting Megan take the lead and make explanations. They trusted her more than him. She had quite a way with words when she was trying to annoy him. Let her use all that verbal creativity on Sanchez and talk her way out of trouble.

But instead of telling her little tale, she opened fire without warning.

She never did what he expected her to do. Absolutely never. The woman was bewildering.

Sanchez went down first, then the man behind him. Mitch, recovered at last, took care of the third.

"They would have never believed us. Zak wasn't in the way. I knew I could do it without him getting hurt—" Megan began to explain, but fell silent when the kid began screaming, drawing their attention.

"Help!" He scrambled to keep his balance as the water got hold of the canoe and pulled it from shore. The boat wobbled, got stuck for a moment then jerked farther away as the current took hold.

He stared back at them with horror on his face as the swift waters carried him downriver.

Without a paddle.

This must be some gigantic, cosmic joke, Mitch thought as he stared after his charge.

Except it wasn't at all funny.

Chapter Five

"Jump," Megan shouted to Zak, as she took off running. She kept one eye on him and one on where she stepped. "Jump and swim."

But the kid looked too scared to do anything.

Mitch passed her. He wasn't as much running as leaping from safe spot to safe spot. The riverbank was littered with rocks and logs and all sorts of rubble the water had deposited. Nature's hazard course.

She pushed as hard as she could, but not as hard as he did. One of them had to be safe. If he got injured, she was the backup.

He ripped off his backpack and tossed it so he could go faster. When she reached it, she picked it up. She would catch up with them eventually.

She kept him in sight for another five minutes before the rocky bank gave way to flatter, muddy terrain and he disappeared into denser foliage. She could hear him for a little longer as he dashed through the brush. After that, she heard nothing.

A bend in the river took the kid from her sight, too. Then she was alone in a massive green labyrinth of danger. She kept her gun handy, mindful of wild animals as she ran on, alert and determined. Albeit not 100 percent sure what in the hell she was doing.

The kid was gone, down the river, and she'd let Mitch go after him. Had trusted him. Treated him like a teammate. The thought occurred to her suddenly. She wasn't a fan of teammates, frankly.

She didn't mind helping others. She just didn't like them helping her, didn't like relying on them. She preferred to do things for herself. Maybe because she was a woman in a male-dominated field and didn't want to appear weak.

It wouldn't be good if she began relying on Mitch now.

She pushed harder. The man had a way of getting under her skin. He better not think that if he got to Zak first, he'd have some kind of a claim on him. She was taking the kid back to Juarez. End of story.

If Mitch didn't like that, tough for him.

She should have shot him at the guesthouse. Not killed him or anything, but hurt him enough to make sure he wouldn't be coming after her. Or, at the very least, she should have tied him to a tree after he'd shot Paolo. Coming back to Sanchez alone, she could have claimed that the two men took each other out. Sanchez would have accepted that. He would have come across the river for her, and she could have gone back to Juarez with the men.

Mitch was a major complication for her mission, but every time she had a chance to get rid of him, she hadn't. Better not be because he was ridiculously attractive. That would be crazy. She would never let a consideration that shallow affect her mission. It didn't matter that he was hot. Or that he was good at what he did. Though she respected that. But the appreciation she had for him was strictly professional. Okay, mostly professional.

All right, fine, she wasn't a saint.

She did like him. But she also wanted to strangle him. Frequently.

He'd come to help her with Paolo. Which had been a mistake. But the salient fact was that he'd been with Zak, the object of his rescue mission, and he'd left the kid to come after her because he'd thought she was in trouble.

A sweet gesture, as much as she hated to admit it. Not that she wanted sweet.

She didn't need a protector. She managed just fine on her own. She didn't want a partner.

Yet here he was, a thorn in her side.

She was carrying his backpack for heaven's sake, like some moonstruck teenage boy carrying books to a high school girl's locker. And her thoughts kept buzzing around him.

A noise ahead drew her attention. She slowed and pulled her weapon. She heard swearing, followed by, "It's me."

"Mitch?" She inched forward, ready for anything.

"I'm alone. It's okay."

She pushed through some sticky-leaved palms she hoped weren't poisonous and saw him at last.

He was sitting on a fallen tree, pressing leaves against a gash in his leg. "Broken stick of bamboo got me."

She dropped their bags at his feet and assessed the situation. Decent cut, but not life threatening. "Zak?"

"Lost him."

That couldn't happen. Simply couldn't. Everything depended on her gaining Juarez's goodwill, and Zak was the only ace up her sleeve. "Did he ever jump out of the canoe?"

"Not that I saw."

She went for her emergency pack. For a split second she considered just tossing it to him and moving on.

Oh, fine. This didn't have to take long. She pulled out some gauze and antibiotic ointment and went to work, trying to ignore the way her fingertips tingled every time they touched his skin, which was tanned and smooth with plenty of hard muscles underneath. He was so quintessentially male, everything that was female in her responded to him.

For a second she imagined his hands on her, and the image took her breath away. But that could never happen. He was a big enough distraction already.

Pulling her mind in another direction took effort, but she did it. "In ten miles or so, there are more rapids." She tried to picture the spot. She'd only been there once. A dangerous place from what she could remember.

Mitch eyed the gun at her feet. "When did your backpack get filled up, anyway? I checked it when you first showed up. You didn't have any weapons."

"Remember when I went back to the bushes to give back my breakfast?"

He winced. Then his eyes narrowed. "You hid everything important before you stepped out into the clearing. Then, after I checked, you went back and repacked. You weren't even sick?"

She smiled at him. Patted the bandage. "Done. That's

the second time I've saved your life, by the way." She stood, needing a little space after all that nearness.

"The snake wasn't that poisonous."

Still, he would have been *very* uncomfortable. She doubted that he could have walked out of the jungle unaided. "Fine. Once, then." She could be reasonable.

"I have antibiotics in my backpack, too."

"You only have your backpack because I brought it after you." Would it have killed him to acknowledge that she'd been helpful?

He tested his leg, then put his full weight on it. "All right. You saved my life. Want a reward?"

She hated that her body tingled at the prospect, even though the question had been meant as a put-down, not as a come-on.

"Sure." She swung her backpack on her back. "There's one thing I'd really like."

He gave her a careful look. Then a surprised glint came into his eyes that said he was starting to understand her unspoken thoughts. His lips stretched into a slow grin.

There was nothing for them there but trouble. Her heart rate picked up. Thank God, he couldn't see that.

"As a reward, you could stay out of my way." She turned on her heels and left him.

SHE WAS SASSY. He hadn't thought he'd liked that in a woman, but he couldn't remember the last time he'd enjoyed anyone's company this much. He was beginning to rethink the whole lone-wolf thing.

Maybe I could work with her, Mitch thought, as he tried not to think of the dozens of other things he would like to do with Megan Cassidy, none of them appropriate for two government operatives on duty.

Especially not with Zak missing.

He grabbed his own bag and took off after her. "So how bad are those rapids?"

"He'll be out of the canoe. Can he swim?"

He'd never thought to ask. "No idea." If the kid couldn't swim…

"I can't believe you lost him." She stomped forward.

"I lost him?" Just like a woman to blame a man for everything.

"I left him with you."

"You know, everything was going just fine until we met up with you." He'd found the compound without trouble, gotten the kid out and he'd even caught up with those troublesome witnesses. It hadn't been the smoothest op he'd ever handled, but he'd been managing.

Then came Megan Cassidy.

She said something under her breath that he couldn't hear and was pretty sure he didn't want to.

"You do realize that you're the biggest obstacle to my mission?" he asked her. "Not the jungle, not the bad guys. Trouble follows you. I've heard of people like that. They don't make it long in this business."

"Trouble doesn't follow me. I follow trouble. I go where trouble is, because that's my job. I conquer trouble."

"Is that how you got that scar?" He'd been curious about that from the first time he'd seen it.

"At the beginning, when I showed up at Juarez's camp, the other men didn't exactly like the idea of me joining their team."

But she hadn't let that stop her. He was beginning to think that she was the type who didn't let anything stop her when she wanted something. Not a comforting thought since, in this case, they both wanted the same thing. And only one of them could have the kid.

He was definitely taking Zak. As far as all the other things he wanted where she was concerned went, he was going to forget about those. She was too much trouble. Why did he have to meet her?

Or, a better question was, why did he have to want her?

The admission didn't please him, but there it was. He wanted Megan Cassidy, undercover CIA spook, bane of his existence, destroyer of his mission. When she'd said she wanted a reward from him…his mind had jumped to all the wrong conclusions. The images that had flooded his brain… He couldn't go there. Their uneasy alliance was complicated already.

There was only one way to handle the situation. He was going to completely ignore the attraction and deny his misguided needs.

"Want a mango?" she called back.

Fruit, in fact, was not on the top of his list of desires. "Still got one." He patted his pocket, mindful of the whole apple-and-Eve motif.

His new wound pulled with every step he took. Normally, he would have ignored it, but now he focused on the pain to keep his thoughts from Megan. A light rain began to fall, and the bugs around them quieted, looking for shelters under leaves. Birds pulled their necks in. For a while, the only sound they could hear was the patter of raindrops on all that green. He didn't like the idea of getting soaked to the skin again. He'd barely been dry since he'd gotten here.

She marched on without complaint. He did the same.

He didn't ask her what she would do if they didn't find Zak. And she didn't ask him. For people like them, failure wasn't an option. Which meant more trouble down the line—sure confrontation.

She stopped suddenly.

He went for his weapon and scanned their surroundings.

"What is it?" He kept his voice at a whisper.

"Banana spider." She pointed.

"Poisonous." He'd seen them before and avoided them like the plague. Their poison was rarely strong enough to bring down a healthy adult, but it could cause considerable damage. And excruciating pain. The most painful spider bite on the planet, according to the experts. "Go around it slowly."

She did. "There must be banana trees around here somewhere." Her tone was wistful. She scanned the jungle once she was past the spider. A little potassium would have been nice. Fighting their way through the jungle took a lot out of them.

The six-inch hairy arachnid stood its ground and stared at them. Mitch followed Megan, keeping an eye on the ground around them on the principle that where there was one spider, there might be more. "Nasty thing."

She glanced back with an amused look. "I thought as a man you'd show more appreciation for it."

He raised an eyebrow.

"Priapism is one of the side effects of its bite."

He took a double take at the spider. Priapism, huh? How come that hadn't been in his training field book?

Priapism. He shook his head. Some guys might think something like that would be fun, but it sounded painful to him. He was happy with the way his body ordinarily worked.

He didn't need any stimulators, not with Megan walking in front of him, her pants wet from the rain and sticking to her body. She had to know it, but she didn't seem self-conscious. She was focused on the job at hand.

He was focused on her shapely behind. He should never have let her walk in front of him.

Since they were near the river now, more light reached the ground and the undergrowth grew thicker. The green obstacle course didn't faze her any. She sure knew how to use that machete.

They tried to keep the river in sight, but saw no sign of Zak for the next few miles. They ate the last mangoes from their pockets, save one. He offered to take the lead. She handed him the machete and let him. She was self-sufficient and stubborn, but smart enough to know what was best for progress.

They walked another mile before they heard the cry. "Help! Help me!"

Zak. They pushed forward. At least ten minutes passed before they found him on the shore, stuck between two large rocks, half in, half out of the water, floundering like a giant, battered fish.

They rushed to him together, careful of the slippery rocks.

"I thought I was going to die," Zak shouted in between two moans. "What took you so long? My father is paying you to take better care of me than this."

Mitch held his rising ire, not the least because the kid was at least partially right. He extracted Zak and supported his weight as they walked to a more even spot where he could sit. He watched for a while as Megan carefully checked the kid over, then he took their water bottles and filled them up, grateful for the filter top that stood between them and the thousands of bacteria and microscopic parasites that lived in these waters.

"So you jumped?" Megan felt the kid's skull. "Minor gashes," she informed them when she was done.

"The water overturned the canoe. I could have drowned. You should have been with me," he accused Mitch. "When my father hears—"

"Shut up and be grateful you're alive," Megan snapped at him.

The kid pulled his neck in and blinked at her. "I'm hungry. Do we have any meat?"

She pulled a half a mango from her pocket.

"I don't think that's sanitary."

She shook her head and rolled her eyes at Mitch. "Maybe we'll run into some lemon ants."

"Are they yellow?" The kid wanted to know.

"They taste like lemons. You collect enough, it's a nice little shot of protein," she explained.

"Come on." Mitch stood. "Anyone coming down the river can see us here."

"I can't go anywhere." The kid dug his heels in. "I'm bruised and exhausted."

Mitch looked at him for a long second. To think that they were fighting over this little pile of— Seriously? He bent and tossed the kid over his shoulder, then walked into the jungle with him.

Megan was saying something in the back, but the river drowned out her words. He could swear he heard *tubes* and *tied* both mentioned in the sentence.

Once they were back under thick cover, he set the kid down. He wasn't going to carry Zak's lazy behind, not unless the kid was truly incapacitated.

"We'll take a break." He rolled a log to check under it for anything dangerous before they sat down.

"Spider!" Zak scrambled away, showing a lot more energy suddenly.

Mitch used a leaf the scoop the little thing up and shoo it out of harm's way. When he sat, the others followed his example. "You should have seen the banana spider we ran into on the way here."

"Tastes like bananas?" Zak asked, his face scrunched in a grimace.

"Not like lemon ants. The spiders live in banana trees. You wouldn't want one of those to bite you."

"Deadly?"

"Could be. It'll hurt like hell, for sure. And according to Miss Know-It-All here, they cause priapism."

"Pria-what?"

"An erection that lasts hours," Megan put in, an amused look on her face. She was no doubt entertained by the fact that particular information had got stuck in Mitch's head.

The kid perked right up. "Can we go back to look at it?"

Megan struggled to hide a grin.

They took the rest of their five-minute break in silence. Zak looked thoughtful. He was probably calculating how much money he could make if he took a couple of banana spiders back to his frat brothers.

"Time to go." Mitch stood at last, realizing suddenly that they were at a decision point. He needed to take the kid north; Megan wanted to take him south. They were going to have to come to an agreement before they could proceed any farther.

"I need sleep. I haven't slept in ages," Zak pleaded.

He did look used up and wrung out. Either they could take an hour to rest here, or he'd slow them down so much they'd lose that hour, or more, anyway.

Mitch looked at Megan. She nodded.

He tossed his backpack to the kid. "Put this under your head."

"I thought we were supposed to sleep off the ground. What if something bites me?"

"Make a nest from a couple of large leaves. You'll be fine for a quick nap. I'll make sure nothing gets near you."

The kid looked doubtful, but settled down. He was asleep in two minutes.

Megan stood and took a few steps back. She checked her gun. But when she was done, she didn't put it away. "You should leave now."

A second passed before he caught on to what she was saying. Looked like the negotiation was about to begin. His hand crept toward his own weapon. "I'm taking the kid north."

"We're going south. We'll be at Juarez's camp by nightfall."

He stood slowly. "There'll be other opportunities to gain the man's trust."

"Not before the big meeting."

"There'll be other big meetings. Zak only has one life." He moved closer little by little as he talked.

She stood her ground, but lifted her weapon. "Leave. Get your backpack. Walk away."

"You would shoot the man who saved your life? Twice?" He tried to add some humor into the situation.

Her upper lip twitched. She said nothing.

"Seriously? You'd kill me." He stole another step closer and saw hesitation in her eyes.

A second later, her tough-chick face was back. "I wouldn't have to kill you. I'd just make sure you weren't in any shape to argue with me."

"You'd leave me wounded in the jungle?" He gained another foot.

"Something tells me you've survived worse."

Then he was close enough and he lunged. He'd meant to take her to the ground and wrestle the gun away from her, but she twisted at the last second and her back ended up slamming against the nearest tree. He was holding her gun hand up, pressing his body hard against hers to hold her still.

They were nose to nose, gazes clashing.

Her breath came in quick, hot spurts, her breasts pressing against his chest. He was so focused on that sensation that a second passed before he became aware of the sharp object in his back.

Her free hand was holding a small knife. Where had she been hiding that? He'd thought he'd already seen all her weapons.

"Let me go." She squirmed.

His body responded predictably.

Her eyes went wide. Then she gave a pained smile. "Look who doesn't need a banana spider."

Damn straight.

He kissed her, more to annoy her than to seduce her. The time and place wasn't exactly right for that, although if they met again under different circumstances, he was going to revisit that option.

The knife pressed harder between his ribs. Her knee came up…and stopped. Then went down. The pressure of the knife lessened, then disappeared.

Next thing he knew, she was kissing him back. Her lips went from resisting to softening to demanding in a heartbeat. He let go of her gun hand so he could palm her breasts. They fit his hands perfectly.

Hard heat suffused his body. And need.

His head was spinning with it.

Something cold pressing against his forehead brought him back to his senses. And after a dazed moment he realized that she was now holding the gun to his temple while the tip of her knife was at his side now, just a few inches from his heart.

"Reach behind you, slowly, pull out your gun and toss it into the woods," she ordered him.

She was so good. He found it difficult to be mad at her for that. There was such a thing as admiring a worthy enemy.

He pulled back enough to look into her eyes. Instead of the triumph he'd expected, he found only desperation in her gaze. Odd. He would have, at the very least, expected her to rub his defeat in his face. She did seem to enjoy watching him suffer.

"What's wrong?" He tried not to look at her swollen lips.

"You," she said without hesitation. "You shouldn't be here. There's no way for this to end well. If I want Zak, I'm going to have to hurt you."

"I'm not letting Zak go. He's my mission. I don't leave a mission incomplete. If you want to take him you're going to have to do more than hurt me. You're going to have to kill me." He took a big step back and went for his gun.

They faced off, both knowing there was no chance either of them would miss from this distance. It bothered him more than it should have, that's for sure.

"Come with me," he offered suddenly, surprised to hear the words come out. But once they were, he went with them. "To hell with the CIA. This is a suicide mission. Juarez will figure out who you are sooner or later. If this is the kind of work you want to do, we'll talk to Colonel Wilson."

She looked away for a second, blinked hard. "I need to do this. For my own reasons. This goes beyond the CIA."

That had his mind scrambling. "You're a double agent?" He shouldn't have been surprised. She was nothing if not full of surprises. But hell, he hadn't seen this coming. "You work for Cristobal?"

"I have a private mission. In addition to the official one. Nothing to do with any of the crime lords in the district."

So she hadn't gone completely rogue. Good. He

wasn't sure how that would have influenced his decision. "Love, revenge or money?" He tried to narrow it down.

"I'm here for someone."

Love, then. The thought caused an uncomfortable feeling in his chest. He hated the idea of her risking her life for a man. He hated the idea of her caring about another man that much.

Stupid.

She wasn't his.

But he wanted her to be, he realized now. Wanted her for more than a quick adventure. *But it isn't going to happen.* The resolution didn't make him hate the idea of another man any less, unfortunately. "Is he worth dying for?"

"I have no intention of dying. Come with me." She turned his offer on him. "All I need is three days. I need to go to Don Pedro's lair and get my brother. Then we grab Zak and we're out of there."

Brother. A knot relaxed deep inside him.

"What's he doing with the don?" Hopefully his motives for being here were less misguided than Zak's.

"He works for the DEA. He was injured on his first international mission and disappeared. For the longest time we thought he was dead. Then there was a snippet of intel that Don Pedro was holding someone who fits his description." Her face transformed as she talked, her features softening as she spoke about her brother, then hardened again. "I'm not going home without Billy."

"And the CIA has no idea why you're really here." They wouldn't be amused when they found out. They liked to have their agents' full attention and loyalty. Undivided.

She shook her head.

He thought it over. "The man they're talking about, he might not be your brother."

Hurt flashed across her face. "I know he is. I can't explain how I know, but I do." She sounded defiant and at the same time desperate for him to believe her.

"Juarez might not take you."

"I'll find a way."

"You're asking me to risk this life—" he pointed at Zak "—for some cowboy mission that has a chance in a thousand of succeeding."

Her amber eyes held his. "Three days."

Part of him would have given her anything when she looked at him like that. But the trained soldier inside him knew better. "I can't."

"Do you have a brother?"

"My family has nothing to do with this." He didn't talk about his family. He didn't even think of them if he could help it. Except Cindy—who was lost to him.

"You come with me. I'll vouch for you with Juarez. You'll stay at the compound and make sure nothing happens to Zak. As soon as we're off to the meeting, you grab him and take him home. I'm not asking you to abandon your mission. I'm only asking for a brief delay."

He tried to think. He knew what he had to do. Trouble was, it wasn't what he wanted to do. He wanted to help her. But before he could come to a decision, noises reached them from the jungle.

He lifted a hand, silencing her. A group of men were

stomping through the woods, talking and swearing. Not entirely unexpected since they were a half day's walk from Juarez's camp. There would be some traffic.

They came closer and closer, until nothing separated them but a dense stand of bamboo. He stood motionless, barely breathing as he listened to their bragging and banter. They were on their way back, having collected debts from the villages upriver. From the way they were talking, Mitch felt sorry for the villagers.

With a little luck, they would pass right by. The vegetation was thick, visibility terrible. Both Megan and he were dressed in clothes that blended into the jungle. They both stood stock-still.

The men reached them, then passed by.

"Who the hell are they?" Zak asked from his make-shift bed, awakening at the worst possible moment.

All movement halted immediately. The men stopped talking.

A branch snapped. Then another. They were spreading out.

Mitch pulled back, gun in hand, his blood boiling with frustration. He and Megan took a protective stance, the two of them making sure they had Zak covered. Like a team. Keeping Zak safe was still his number-one objective. He had to remind himself of that. Because, at the moment, all he wanted was to shoot the twit.

Chapter Six

They were surrounded in minutes. Then ominous silence settled over the area once again. Megan's fingers twitched on the trigger.

Suddenly, she spotted movement to her right.

She swung that way.

"Que pasa, chica?" A tall Creole man stepped from cover first. Umberto. He was one of the oldest men on Juarez's team. "Everything okay here?"

Megan made herself lower her weapon and put a smile on her face that she hoped looked real. "We're on our way back."

Since Umberto hadn't been in camp when Zak broke out, she relayed how the kid had had some trouble with Juarez and ran away into the jungle, then how she'd hooked up with Mitch, her mercenary friend, for some help.

As she spoke, nine other men came forward, their rifles slung on their shoulders. They took their cue from Umberto, and Umberto took her at her word. She'd known him for a year and had a surreal kind of friendship going with him—or as much as you can make friends with an enemy you knew you might someday have to shoot.

She'd first shown up at the Juarez camp bringing a delivery from a Miami connection, and after a few days she'd mentioned that she wouldn't mind staying. Most of the men had wanted nothing to do with her. They were used to women working in the camp's cantina, not meddling in serious business. Umberto had taken her under his wing and protected her while the meanest of the bunch had challenged her and worked at making every waking minute of her life miserable.

Months passed before her antagonists realized that she'd never quit. If they wanted her gone, they'd have to kill her. Her tenacity eventually earned her some respect. But it was Umberto's protection and Juarez's favor that saved her. Apparently, Juarez had had some issues with his Miami connection in the past, and having her leave the man for him pleased the boss on some level.

"How about some *maté?*" Umberto offered. When people met up in the jungle, it was traditional to sit down with a cup of the herbal drink and talk a little.

Would he be suspicious if she said no? She had to take that chance.

"*Gracias,* amigo, but I'd rather get going. Wouldn't mind sleeping in my own bunk tonight." She glanced at Mitch. His facial expression remained neutral, but his tense muscles said the situation didn't please him.

They needed to get back to camp as soon as possible, before he attacked Umberto and the others and put everything, including their lives, in jeopardy. Or kissed her again, God forbid. Her lips were still tingling. What was that about? And did she kiss him back? No way. She'd swooned from hunger and leaned against him for support. That was her story and she was sticking to it.

Umberto gave her an indulgent smile, oblivious to her internal turmoil. "Can't say I don't feel the same. These old bones…" He shook his head, then headed back to the trail with his usual lumbering gait. "*Vamos,* then, *chica. Vamos, hombres.*"

Mitch shot her a hard look. He was here on a valid mission, saving a life. She would have helped him if she could have. She didn't want Zak, or anyone else, to come to harm. But more than that, she wanted to save her brother. Zak had to make it back to camp. She wasn't going to sacrifice her brother's life for a spoiled little wannabe drug dealer, no matter what state his father governed.

The kid had been quiet so far, but now he spoke up, stubborn rebellion written all over his face. "No."

"Keep moving." She shoved him forward. He seemed to fail to realize that keeping his head down was the best strategy for him. He didn't grasp the fact that the vast majority of the people present would just as soon shoot him as look at him. Which he proved yet again when he turned to Umberto and said, "Listen, man. I have money."

Umberto laughed as he looked back and gave the kid the once-over, taking in the dirty, torn clothes and sneakers that had seen better days.

"My father is the governor of Kansas."

The few men who spoke English openly laughed at that.

"This man—" Zak pointed at Mitch, fury creeping

onto his face "—took money from my father to save me. He was supposed to get me out of here. He betrayed me. Take me home and the money is yours. A million dollars."

Megan shot Mitch a questioning look. *A million?*

But he just rolled his eyes. Okay, so the kid was overestimating his worth. Still, she wondered how big a role money played in Mitch's motives. Was he really more mercenary than soldier? What did she know about the SDDU anyway? Her oldest brother, Jamie, sure didn't answer any of her questions. For a second she wondered how he was coping, how his injury was healing. The worst part of being here was not getting any news about her family back home.

Soon. All she had to do was get out of here alive with Billy.

And at the moment, the key to that was convincing Umberto that everything was fine here so they could hurry back to camp. The man was looking Mitch over carefully.

Mitch didn't even blink. "I think our little boy is homesick." His voice filled with disdain and sarcasm.

Some of the others sneered at Zak.

Umberto turned to Megan. "What disagreement did the boss have with this *chico?*"

She shrugged. "Something to do with business."

"He'll slow us down."

Meaning they should kill him here.

"The idiot shot Enrique on his way out." Megan stepped closer to Zak. "The boss will want him."

The man's gray eyebrows lifted, then he gave a slow nod. "Can't say I ever liked Enrique." He murmured

something that sounded like "rabid coyote" and spat
onto the ground.

"Forget it, *chico*," he told Zak. "Even if your father
was *el presidente* and he offered the White House for
you…" He made a dismissing gesture with his hand.

"You have no idea how much money my father has."
Zak moved closer, then stopped when Umberto's gun
rose. "You could retire."

Megan held her breath and made sure her hand was
close enough to her weapon to draw. From the corner of
her eye, she saw Mitch positioning himself, too.

Umberto shook his head.

Mitch relaxed and yanked the kid's hands back to
tie them at the wrist, holding the end of the rope. "You
should have read the career brochure more carefully.
There is no retirement from this business."

He kept Zak close. Good. He'd make sure the kid
didn't do anything worse than running off at the mouth.
If Zak tried to make a run for it, no way could she hold
the men back from mowing him down.

Umberto's gaze shifted between them, settling on
Mitch. "He's all right?" he asked Megan, his gun still
raised.

Her heart rate sped. Juarez would demand Zak,
which provided the kid with some protection. Mitch,
on the other hand, was expendable. If Umberto wasn't
sure Mitch could be trusted, he wouldn't risk it.

Mitch stood still, his stance relaxed, even though
he knew his fate was being decided. He gave her a flat
smile.

A stone-cold operator would have viewed him as
nothing but an obstacle and used this chance to get rid

of him. She found she couldn't do it. Not even for her brother.

"I've known him since we were kids," she lied. "I vouch for him."

Umberto lowered his gun at last, then started back down the trail. The men fell in line behind him.

Mitch angled for the last spot in the line.

It gave her a bad feeling. She made sure to walk next to him, keeping Zak in front of them.

"Three days," she whispered under her breath.

Mitch didn't say anything back. His muscles were taut once again, his lips pressed together. She tried not to think about how they'd felt against hers minutes earlier. It didn't matter, because they wouldn't be kissing again.

There was no reason at all why that thought should make her sad, but it did.

They marched on at a comfortable pace, keeping an eye on the jungle, ready for its dangers. They were all seasoned jungle trekkers, save Zak, who paid attention to little beyond his own complaining. Soon a breeze picked up, which moved the air around and cleared out the humidity a little. Her stomach growled. She ignored it.

She'd gotten used to going hungry in the past year. Supplies didn't always arrive to the remote camp on time, and Juarez's men weren't particularly skillful at hunting. They could shoot, but they had trouble finding and tracking game. They didn't know the animals well enough to use their habits to help the hunt, couldn't move through the woods nearly as silently as the villagers.

She didn't worry about her hunger. She was just

grateful she had enough water. Not that she drank a lot. She wanted to keep bathroom breaks to a minimum, concerned that Mitch might try something if she fell back.

They marched on without taking any breaks. The closer they got to camp, the wider the trail got, so at least the going was getting easier. Even so, Zak did slow them down. She and Mitch did their best to nudge the kid along, before Umberto could get impatient.

When the kid stumbled and she reached to hold him up, she bumped into Mitch. They pulled back simultaneously, the tension between them obvious. Good thing they were bringing up the rear, out of sight of the others.

"Three days," she whispered. It was becoming her mantra.

He shook his head.

The rain started up again, a more serious downpour this time.

No sense in stopping to wait. Rain here could go on for days. They were all used to it, and simply put on their hats. Mitch gave his to Zak, then twisted a banana leaf into a handy cone for his own head.

He didn't speak, so she, too, stayed silent as she trekked forward resolutely.

"It's the most logical course of action," she told him when she couldn't stand the silence any longer. Maybe he'd come to see her point and even help her.

But his response ended that fantasy quickly. "This is not over."

MITCH CHECKED OUT Juarez's camp. It had been built on the ruins of an old Jesuit mission. He leaned against the open door of the shed he'd been assigned for the night. He couldn't see much in the dark, but he was familiar with the layout. He'd spent days on recon the first time around, putting together a plan to get Zak out unseen. But before he could have made his well-calculated move, the kid had decided to shoot his way out, messing up everything.

In the middle of the freaking day. Everyone had known what had happened in seconds, and half the camp had rushed after them in pursuit.

But only one had caught up with them. Megan.

She was hot as all get-out. He wanted her so badly his teeth ached. Even if she'd messed up his mission in a big way. Even though he might have to hurt her to save Zak. But he didn't want to. She was worth a dozen of the useless kid.

Mitch stretched his legs, his muscles sore from all the miles he'd covered in the last couple of days. The wound on his leg still ached. He watched the night guards to see if their routine had changed since he'd last observed them. It hadn't, it seemed. Good. The next breakout would be done the right way, engineered by him. By the time anyone realized Zak was missing, he and the kid would be halfway to the extraction site.

He didn't want to think about where that would leave Megan, but the pesky thought popped into his mind anyway.

He hadn't seen her since they'd arrived a couple of hours earlier.

She'd vouched for him again, even though she had to know that he was just another obstacle in her way. Attaining her goal would have been easier if she'd let

Juarez's men take him out. Or if she'd let Umberto take him out in the first place. But not only did she not turn on him, she didn't speak against him when he'd said he wanted to guard the kid.

None of the other men was keen on sleeping in a drafty shack instead of the cozy bunkhouse. They sure hadn't fought him for the privilege. She had to know this played right into his hands. Yet she didn't betray his true identity.

He hoped she wasn't nursing some dream that he'd help her and sacrifice Zak. If she did, she was going to be seriously disappointed.

Mitch took a look at the kid through the gaps in the shed's wood slats and felt a moment of pity. On arrival, Juarez had punched him in the face hard enough to break his jaw. The kid could no longer talk, which wasn't a bad thing entirely. The less he said, the less trouble he would get them all in. He was curled up on his side, worn out and miserable, not even bothering to swat away the little flies that drove every man and woman in the camp crazy.

The trouble with having a permanent camp in the jungle was that every bloodsucker out there learned your address in a hurry and moved right in. Much better to always be on the go, in this regard at least. Mitch swatted the bugs from his face and thought of the *maté* he'd find in the cantina. The kid looked like he could have used a drink.

But Zak needed something stronger than *maté*. Mitch could afford to walk away for a short while. The shack was padlocked, and Zak wasn't going anywhere anytime soon. Looked like he'd finally hit the proverbial wall. Mitch was familiar with the feeling, as well as the pain of a broken jaw. The key was to compartmentalize the pain and keep going. But he'd been trained to do exactly that, and had plenty of practice. Zak was just a kid. Mitch walked up the path, adding a thin bamboo straw to his shopping list.

He moved in the direction of the most noise. Men were drinking around a bonfire in front of the barracks. He saw no sign of Megan, and wasn't pleased that it was the first thing he noticed. He spotted a bottle of tequila being passed around, grabbed an empty bowl from the ground and wiped it out with his shirt. Then when the bottle came his way, he sloshed some alcohol into the bowl before passing it on.

Only then did he see Umberto setting up a line of pebbles on top of a partially collapsed stone wall. Mitch counted a dozen before Umberto finished and stood aside. Several men lined up fifty feet or so from the wall. Then the shooting contest began.

Mitch glanced toward the shed, ready to return, but two shadows atop the ruins of the old Jesuit mission caught his eye. Juarez's makeshift home leaned against the stone wall, the top of which was used as a lookout. Juarez and Megan were watching the contest from there.

Mitch turned his back to them. Then, without meaning to, he ended up walking toward the lined-up men.

The pudgy bald one at the head of the line hit nine stones out of the twelve. Not bad, considering the darkness of the night and the dancing flames, both of which made judging distances difficult. Umberto put the stones back while the next contestant stepped into position. That one got ten rocks. He moved on after a couple of his buddies slapped him on the back.

Others took their turn. Most of the men were in the same range: nine hits, ten, eleven—clearly people who lived and died by their guns.

"Paolo will hate missing this," one of them called out. "Too bad he's late."

They had no idea just how late. As in, *arrival time: never,* Mitch thought, as he moved to the head of the line. He hesitated. Drawing attention to himself might not be the best idea right now. Still, he couldn't walk away now without drawing even more attention than if he simply took his turn.

He set the bowl at his feet with half a mind to drink that tequila himself later. Sweat rolled down his temples. The bonfire was too close, the flames licking higher and higher. On the upside, the smoke kept the bugs away. He took off his shirt and mopped his forehead with it, not wanting sweat in his eyes. Then he tossed the shirt next to the bowl. Okay.

One. Two. Three. Four. Five. Six. Seven. Eight. With each successful shot, the men cheered around him, toasting him. *Nine.* A cheer rose again. He looked at the remaining three stones, knowing he should miss.

But then, "You go, Mitch!" came from behind him. Megan was cheering for him.

He took out the last three stones with three clean shots in rapid succession, regretting it the second he'd done it. What was he, stupid? Now he was showing off for her?

He should never have kissed her, dammit.

Not that he could truly regret that. Those lips... Her body... Her taste... He swallowed a groan.

Maybe keeping him tied up in knots of lust was part of her master plan. Sneaky as the woman was, he wouldn't put it past her.

He glanced toward the wall, caught Juarez saluting him with a glass of something. He nodded in acknowledgment. Then he grabbed the bowl and his shirt and went back to Zak before he could make another stupid mistake.

He didn't need Juarez's attention. He'd be better off flying under the radar so he could get out before anyone had a chance to figure out anything. That was supposed to be his current modus operandi.

Give nobody reason to think too deeply about him. As for himself: think only of the escape. Except his mind was full of questions about whether Megan had been invited up to Juarez's quarters to share more than a good vantage point to watch the target practice. Whether she'd been invited up there to share Juarez's bed.

She was trying to save her brother. He couldn't condemn her. He didn't really care one way or the other, he told himself.

Except, he did.

Damn it all. Damn *her,* in particular. He'd been thinking... What the hell had he been thinking? Probably whatever she'd wanted him to think.

He was perfectly capable of taking the kid out of the jungle. And yet here he still was.

Megan was the reason; there was no getting around that. First she'd manipulated him, tangling him up in a net of lust. Then she'd probably sleep with Juarez so the man would take her the rest of the way to her goal. The thought ripped at his gut, even as cold fury spread through him, looking for outlet.

At last he reached the shed, and he smashed his fist against the wall, ignoring the splinters that stabbed under his skin.

A frightened moan came from inside.

Mitch pushed the door in, doing his best to banish Megan from his thoughts. "It's me. I brought you something to drink."

MEGAN SNUCK THROUGH the sleeping camp. Zak was back, and other things had gone well for Juarez during her absence, which meant he was happy, which meant the men were happy, which meant they'd drunk even more than usual.

Images of Mitch at the bonfire target practice filled her head—his naked torso glistening in the dancing flames, the way the muscles bunched in his back each time he'd pulled the trigger. She wouldn't have been a woman if she didn't feel anything, if she wasn't the least bit attracted.

But that was absolutely not the reason why she was sneaking to him in the middle of the night. She had information to share with him.

The night was cool and the bugs were gone until morning, which was a relief. She rounded the barracks and nearly slammed head-on into a dark bulk.

"Chica." Umberto steadied her. "All is well?"

She nodded, looking for an excuse for why she wasn't in her bed, but before she could come up with a semilogical explanation, Umberto said, "You're going to him."

She didn't say anything. Better to be taken for a fool in lust than a traitor.

"Be careful. I don't like the eyes on that one. That one has secrets."

More than Umberto realized. "We've all done things we don't like to talk about." She shrugged. "I can take care of myself."

"That you can. I taught you well."

He had. She'd learned twice as much about jungle survival from Umberto than from her CIA training. And she had come to like the old guy. He was a murderer like the rest of them. And yet, considering that this was the life he'd been born into, the only one he knew, part of her couldn't blame him. His father had been a bandit, his mother a camp woman, both dead before his first birthday, he'd once told her.

"You're tougher than most men I know," Umberto admitted, then patted her shoulder. "Be careful anyway." He turned and disappeared inside the barracks before she could have responded.

She moved on, not bothering with stealth after that. Their conversation had drawn the night guard, who was walking up the path.

"Que pasa?"

This time, she was ready with her explanation. "Checking on the kid. I worked too hard bringing him in to let him run off again."

"No worries there. I'm on duty." The guard puffed his chest out.

"Pero tu es aqui, mi amigo, thinking about grabbing a bottle from the barracks, while he's all the way over

there." She gestured with her head in the direction of the shack and smiled, keeping the mood light.

The guard shrugged, not looking the least bit concerned. "Your gringo is watching him."

She moved past the man. "I'll do a quick check all the same."

She strode through the night, toward the small storage building that housed Mitch and the attached shack that imprisoned Zak. She checked on the boy first. He seemed to be sleeping.

She looked up and sighed as the heavens liquefied for the third time that day. Rain drummed on the corrugated metal roof—small, slow drops at first. Then the rainfall picked up, drowning out the jungle sounds that surrounded them.

She went around to Mitch's side, but hesitated. The place had been used for storing weapons before a shipment of them had gone out a month or so ago. She'd managed to stick a tracker on one of the crates. Hopefully the home office didn't have much trouble following it.

She stepped closer to the closed door that was made of a mixture of old boards and bamboo, with plenty of gaps between. Inside, a hammock hung in the corner. It was attached to a hook in the ceiling with a mosquito net draping it. Since no lines from the generators ran all the way out here, an oil lamp on the floor did its best to fill the space with flickering light.

Mitch knelt in front of a bowl of water on the floor, stripped to the waist, washing up. His physique was more than impressive, more than enough to remind her that she hadn't been with a man in a very long time. Not for lack of opportunity. Plenty had propositioned her here, but they weren't the kind of men she was interested in. Even if she found one among them who wasn't a conscienceless murderer, the moment she'd given in she would have become so-and-so's woman and lost all respect and status in the camp. Juarez would never take her seriously then. Which would torpedo her mission. The only thing she should be focused on, night and day.

Yet, she couldn't deny that at the moment she was pretty distracted.

Drops of water ran down Mitch's back, wetting his skin and hair. He looked like some ancient, immortal warrior king.

She swallowed a sudden rush of desire and stepped back; suddenly she was dizzy with need. Better walk away. They could always talk in the morning.

"Come in," he said without turning around.

She stayed still. Okay, so he knew someone was out there. But maybe he didn't know it was her.

"I can smell your perfume."

Shampoo. One of her few small luxuries here. Juarez had summoned her earlier and she'd cleaned up first. Not for him. For herself. She'd been beyond grungy after their trek through the jungle. She wanted to wash the grime off, to feel semihuman again.

She hesitated another long second in front of the closed door, unsure of herself all of a sudden. The attraction that drew her to Mitch was a serious threat to her mission. She didn't like it. She wished they'd met anywhere but here, on any mission but this one.

She found maintaining a professional relationship with him challenging, but since when had she run away from a challenge? She could probably go in there and have a professional conversation without swooning into his arms.

Damn, that was no good.

She drew a deep breath and tried again. She was in control.

"Hey." She pulled the door open and stepped inside, meaning to leave it open behind her, but it closed by itself on its crooked hinges.

They were alone, enclosed in the intimacy of the small cabin.

Chapter Seven

The air inside was thick with humidity and something else…tension. It infected her immediately, set her on edge, tingled along her skin. The tenuous hold she'd had on remaining calm and collected slipped away.

Mitch shook the water out of his hair and stood. Dark fire burned in his eyes as he gazed at her. His eyes didn't miss a single inch.

She swallowed hard. Maybe coming to him tonight wasn't the best idea she'd ever had.

"I know this is not what you wanted." That was an understatement. He probably rued the day he'd ever met her. "I had no choice but to bring Zak back. My brother… Billy is…" She didn't know how to convince him. Or even if that was possible.

She tried anyway. "When I was nine and we were at my grandparents' farm for the summer, traipsing all over the countryside, I fell into an old well. Billy, Andy and I were playing explorer."

They used to do that a lot. They played explorer, soldier and policeman. She'd had her dolls, but being outside with her eight brothers had always seemed more exciting than combing some boring doll's hair.

"The sun was setting," she went on. "Andy ran for help. Billy climbed down after me, because he knew that even though I would never let on, I was a little scared of spiders. He fell halfway down the well and broke his ankle. I was fine." She shook his head at the memory. "He was five, but such a little hero already."

Mitch watched her, his gaze intent and focused.

"If things were the other way around... Even if I was in the darkest burrow of hell, on the most godforsaken spot on earth, he would come after me."

Seconds ticked by. She had no idea what he thought, what he felt. Awareness grew between them until the tension became unbearable.

It didn't look like she was going to convince him of anything. And if she stayed much longer, she might be the one who caved. *Just give him the news and get out,* she told herself.

"We're leaving for Don Pedro's place at first light," she said quickly. "The trip's been moved up."

"Juarez told you that?" He stalked closer, his shoulders stiff, his gaze never moving from her face for a second. His presence and masculine energy filled the small space.

She nodded. "I got the sense that he was nervous. Toward the end of our conversation, he took a call. I left, but waited outside the door." She prattled on. "From what I could make out, some of the other bosses are coming to the meeting, and he thinks one of them might make a move against Don Pedro. He thinks it's Cristobal." She had no reason to share that information with Mitch. His presence here had nothing to do with the local crime lords, but she didn't seem to be able to stop talking.

"I see you prettied yourself up for him." He stood within arm's reach, his voice cold—a contrast to all the heat in his gaze.

"I spent the last couple of days in the jungle. I was due for a bath."

He stalked closer still, inhaling the air around her.

Blood drummed in her ears, drowning out the rain.

"So he's taking you with him. Congratulations." His voice took on an edge of sarcasm. "How convenient."

She had no idea what he was talking about. She tried to step away from him, but he grabbed her shoulder to hold her in place. He wasn't rough, but firm.

"Have you?" His voice was a coarse whisper as he searched her eyes. The lamplight behind him cast long shadows that obscured his face.

The heat of his palm burned through her thin shirt and sent shivers of awareness down her spine. "Have I what?"

"Been to his bed?" The words came out slowly, as if he was speaking with effort.

Anger rose inside her, and she shoved him. But she might as well have shoved a kapok tree. "Go to hell."

His eyes glinted dangerously. Instead of letting her go, he moved closer. Then crushed her lips under his.

His kiss was punishing, but her body responded anyway, denied need bubbling to the surface. Then he pulled back, and ran his fingers through his hair in frustration. "Sorry. I—"

"Shut up." She moved forward and pushed her lips back against his.

He took things from there. A myriad of sensations spread through her. Her mind melted as images of Mitch flashed through what little of her brain was still working: the way he'd rushed from that bathroom at the guesthouse, naked, ready to defend her; his wide shoulders hovering above her as he'd torn Paolo off her; the way he'd looked by the bonfire, the quintessential alpha male, winning the shooting contest.

He mastered her mouth the way he mastered everything else. Hesitation wasn't part of the man, in this situation or in any other. His kiss wasn't anything like the unwanted advances of the other men in camp. They'd left her cold and annoyed. She'd left them with a black eye, or worse.

Now desire hit her like a sudden jungle storm and had her drenched in need. Mitch's body, pressed so tightly against her, felt like pure, primal power. It was overwhelming, but being overwhelmed by pleasure didn't seem an altogether bad thing.

"Megan." His voice, raw with desire, got under her skin, coursed through her veins and turned up the heat.

She opened her mouth to him and he deepened the kiss with a low groan that rumbled up his chest and fed straight into her. His lips and tongue possessed hers, conquering her until she was limp, then gently caressing her until she felt her body might fly apart with need.

She couldn't remember the last time, any time, when she'd let her defenses down so completely, had trusted her partner so fully, without reservations. Where had those gone? She'd had plenty of them when they'd first met.

She liked the guy, liked his intelligent chestnut eyes.

He was quick and sometimes funny. He was competent. He had principles that ruled his actions. She felt safe with him, which was ridiculous. They weren't more than temporary partners, their goals still mutually exclusive.

They needed to talk about that. Once her brain got back to work. For now, she let him kiss her to his heart's content, and hers.

But soon things went beyond that. She *needed* him to kiss her.

Then she needed to kiss him back.

Then she needed to touch him. That was his fault. He shouldn't have been half-naked.

His skin was warm and wet, and her palms glided over his impressive muscles. The nerve endings in her fingertips were singing "Ode to Joy" from the contact.

His hands moved to the underside of her knees and lifted her up in one sure motion, pushing her back against the wall and wrapping her legs around his waist. His need was unmistakable and gratifying.

She lost her breath when his hardness pressed against her core. A slow ache began somewhere inside her. Her hands caressed his wide shoulders, then moved up to dig into his wiry hair.

Nothing had felt this good in a long time. He didn't try to dominate her, but she knew neither would he yield. They shared some sort of a connection that was undeniable. Maybe because he was the only person in a hundred-mile radius who knew the truth about her, the only one she might be able to trust.

Her breath hitched when he carried her away from the wall and tumbled her into the hammock, which swung precariously in response. A surprised squeak escaped her lips.

"Is this going to work?" She looked up once she tore her lips from his. Could those hooks hold both of them? "I don't think—"

"Watch me." He slipped in adroitly next to her.

The material stretched to accommodate him. For about a second, she was conscious of their perilous position, but then his hand snuck under her tank top. And once his long fingers began massaging their way up her rib cage, she wouldn't have noticed if they crashed to the ground and the roof caved in after them.

She had no idea how he divested her of her light shirt so quickly or how he peeled her out of that tank top, but he did. Then he shifted her so she lay on top of him, her breasts pressing against his bare chest. She'd given up wearing bras a few months back and now was glad for it. The tight straps and the underwire were a nuisance in this heat and humidity. And now...

Now she'd found another advantage.

He gave a sound of primal satisfaction when her nipples rubbed against his chest.

Pleasure zigzagged through her in response. Wow. Double wow. Nobody had ever made her feel like this. Not Vincent, for sure. So unfair that she would have this with someone she shouldn't be anywhere near, someone she might never see again after this night.

But maybe it was better that way. Her circuits were melting, her fuses blowing. Mitch was simply too overwhelming. She'd never have full control of her life with a man like him in it.

He caught her lower lip between his teeth and nipped,

then trailed kisses down her neck. Then he pushed her higher, until the soft, wet heat of his mouth could envelop her nipple.

Sure, she'd missed a man's hands on her body. But right now she felt as if it had been Mitch's hands, specifically, that she'd missed all along. A crazy thought.

Her back arched. Her brain stopped functioning.

More heat built inside her with every tug of his lips, with every touch. Her hands explored his hard chest, the rippled muscles of his abdomen. He was built as perfectly as a man could be built. She hesitated at his belt buckle.

His hands slid down to cup her bottom and press her more tightly against him. He rocked under her. She held on to his hips, trying not to moan too loudly. No sense in alerting the night guard or waking Zak up. Thank God, the rain provided them with some cover.

"Don't think. Feel." His raspy whisper skittered along her nerve endings.

When his mouth switched to the other nipple, she felt the tug between her legs. He moved under her with just the right rhythm. Pressure built. She was going to heaven, but couldn't reach it. Not yet.

He shifted them carefully, pinning her underneath him, and pulled down her cargo pants so his clever fingers could reach the spot where she ached the most. He kissed her deeply and thoroughly as his fingers found a breath-stealing rhythm.

Now. She went for his belt buckle and fumbled. Her muscles weren't exactly obeying her every command. They were quivering.

Then she couldn't move at all. Those quivering mus-

cles contracted suddenly, held at the edge of the preci-
pice, then tumbled over it as pleasure pulsed through
her body in towering waves.

She clung to Mitch's hard body, breathing in hoarse
gasps, moaning his name.

Long minutes passed before the ripples quieted. She
was beyond sated. Dazed. So it made no sense that she
would want more of him, but she did. Deep inside her.

She shifted to wrap her legs around his slim hips.
"Take off your pants." Her voice was a breathless whisper she barely recognized.

"We don't have protection." His words came out in
a strangled tone.

She blinked. How could she forget that? She'd never
forgotten that before, not ever.

"Then let me." She moved to slip her hand under
his waistband.

At the same time, they heard Zak groaning on the
other side of the wall.

Mitch moved to the side, pulled her next to him and
gathered her in his arms. "You're heading out in a couple of hours for a long trek. Rest."

"But—"

"We'll add it to your tab." He smiled at her in the
semidarkness. "Someday, somewhere, I'm going to
show up in your life and collect."

Suddenly that seemed like a wonderful idea. She kept
her hand on his abdomen and rested her head on his shoulder. Idiotically happy, she closed her eyes and breathed in
his scent, her body still buzzing with pleasure.

When she fell asleep, her dreams were all about him.
Erotic, every single one of them.

Waking in his arms was incredibly nice after all those lonely mornings. And she'd been lonely here, despite all the people in camp. She hadn't made any true connections. For someone who'd grown up in a family with nine kids, the isolation was pretty difficult to bear. Not that she wouldn't endure much more to save her brother.

Thinking of Billy woke her up the rest of the way, and she felt guilty for indulging in a night of pleasure when her brother was suffering in Don Pedro's dungeons somewhere.

Outside, she heard the team getting ready for the trip. Jeeps were being loaded; four-wheelers roared.

"Time for me to go," she whispered. She needed to refocus, needed distance.

Mitch stirred and pressed against her, his body in the same hard state it'd been in when they'd fallen asleep. Maybe he'd been bitten by a banana spider after all.

That reminded her of Zak wanting to see one. Which reminded her of the rest of the news she hadn't had a chance to tell Mitch.

His warm hand moved up to cup her breast. She placed her own hand on top to still him. If he began to touch her again, they'd never get out of the hammock.

"The guy Zak shot wasn't just Juarez's brother-in-law," she gasped—she was having difficulty breathing as his fingers brushed against her nipple.

Mitch withdrew his hand silently and listened.

"Enrique was also Don Pedro's half brother." It was much easier to talk this way, even if she did miss his touch. "Juarez is under orders to deliver Zak to the don. The kid is coming with us."

He shoved himself out of the hammock, setting it swinging perilously, and looked at her through narrowed eyes, his demeanor growing colder by the second.

"This is what last night was about." His voice was rigid steel.

The connection that had built between them overnight disappeared. He seemed a thousand miles away. Unreachable.

A sinking feeling spread through her stomach.

"You made sure I didn't go out so I wouldn't hear the news myself. Made sure I was busy so I couldn't break the kid out before you all left in the morning." His chestnut eyes held disappointment and distaste, as if a snake he'd thought harmless had suddenly bitten him.

Denial surged to her lips. "No. Mitch—"

He dragged on his shirt and was out the door the next second, moving as if he couldn't get away from her fast enough.

Chapter Eight

Mitch strode through camp, doing his best to forget the way Megan had come apart in his arms during the night, denying the fact that every cell in his body still wanted her. He searched for Juarez, but when he found the man, he didn't approach him. Instead, he ambled over to a Jeep nearby where Umberto was struggling with a large crate of supplies.

"You need help?" he offered.

The older man watched him for a long second. Umberto obviously had seen a thing or two and had better instincts about people than most. He hadn't gotten drunk the night before with the others, hadn't participated in any of the fights that later ensued. He shrugged at last. "Sure. *Bueno.*"

So Mitch picked up the nearest bag and tossed it in the back of the Jeep, making sure Juarez saw him. "Has the infamous Paolo returned?" he asked after a few minutes, not bothering to keep his voice down. "Yesterday I heard talk of his legendary shooting skills. Maybe he and I could have a friendly contest someday."

Umberto shook his head. "He's a tough one. If he

ain't back, there's a reason." Again, his gaze stayed on
Mitch longer than necessary.

From the corner of his eye, Mitch saw Juarez catch
their conversation and frown. The boss barked a few
quick questions at the man standing next to him. Mitch
couldn't hear the low-voiced response, but it seemed
scared and apologetic.

He hoisted a crate into the car. Umberto put the jugs
of water in place. Between the two of them, the Jeep
was packed in ten minutes.

"Gracias," Umberto said as he patted down the bags
and jiggled things into place, making sure they were
secure.

"De nada, amigo."

Mitch walked back toward his shack, helping whoever he could on the way without making a big deal of
it. Megan was gone by the time he reached his quarters.
No surprise there.

He could still smell her shampoo. And he could see
her glorious breasts rising above him as she'd straddled
him in the hammock. His body grew hard all over again.

He swore under his breath and put the memories of
the night out of his mind. She'd fooled him again, plain
and simple. "But this will be the last time," he swore.

He grabbed his backpack, shoved his handgun into
the back of his waistband and left the shed. He checked
on Zak through the gaps in the wall. The kid was drinking water through the bamboo straw he'd made him
last night.

"You all right?"

"I'll see to it that my father makes you pay for this,"

Zak hissed through his lips, barely moving his swollen jaw.

He couldn't argue. He'd messed up the moment Megan had walked into that clearing at the river and he'd allowed her to join them. Mitch shook his head and moved on, making sure to pass by Juarez and his men again. He knew one thing only. There was no room for any more mistakes on this mission.

"*Adios,* then," he called out to Umberto. "Have a good trip."

"Where are you going?" Umberto asked obligingly.

"Thought I'd hunt a little while you guys are gone." He kept walking, but called over his shoulder. "A camp the size of this one can always use more meat." Hopefully, that would remind them of his shooting skills the night before.

He strode toward the woods. He was almost at the edges of the camp, about to melt into the jungle when a shout rang out.

"*Alto!*" Stop.

He took two more steps as if not realizing the call was for him.

"*Alto! Alto!*" One of Juarez's men was running after him.

"What is it?" He turned then, obligingly.

"The boss wants you to come with us. We're short-handed without Paolo."

"How long a trip? I just got in. Wouldn't mind taking a few days' break here in camp."

"You only come to the first drop-off. You guard the goods there and wait for the pickup. You can rest until we come by to get you on the way back."

So the crates and bags in the Jeeps didn't all go to Don Pedro. There'd be some sort of a drop-off of illegal goods in the jungle.

He wasn't trusted enough to be taken all the way to the big boss. Fine. The important thing was, he'd keep sight of Zak for a while longer. They were taking him part of the way, which was better than sneaking after them and trying to track them unseen. If he couldn't get Zak away before that drop-off, Mitch would figure something out so they'd take him farther.

He caught Juarez watching him from a distance, so he made sure he wasn't overenthusiastic as he accepted. The man who'd been sent after him clapped him on the shoulder with a grin anyway.

Mitch didn't return it. He was all business, every bit the mercenary he claimed to be. "So who do I talk to about pay?"

She didn't know if she should be impressed or consternated.

She was a CIA agent—she didn't get frustrated easily, Megan reminded herself. Trouble was, that left impressed, and she didn't want to be impressed by Mitch.

Bad enough that she'd been thoroughly seduced by him. While on an undercover op in the middle of an enemy camp. There had to be a whole manual full of rules against that somewhere. Not that she wasn't breaking all the rules already by secretly working to free her brother.

The two Jeeps followed each other closely on the narrow, bumpy road, followed by three ATVs. It was much easier than going on foot, even if the logging road was no more than a collection of potholes in the muddy soil. She was afraid that by the time they reached their destination, the journey might have shaken her teeth loose.

Mitch was avoiding her on purpose. He'd chosen to ride in the other car, and he never came anywhere near her whenever they hit a particularly bad patch of road and had to get out to help the cars over.

Each time, he worked harder and longer than anyone, earning some of the men's grudging respect, and the resentment of others who didn't like Juarez's approving eye on him. He brushed that off, just went along with the lifting and the pushing.

She knew the game he was playing. According to Umberto, Mitch was to stay at the drop-off site and rejoin the team on their way back. The drop-off was tonight. Mitch wanted to stay with the group longer so he'd have more time to rescue Zak.

And mess up her plans.

She'd vouched for him, back when she'd still hoped he would come around to help her. If he did anything stupid, it would be her butt on the line. Juarez would assume they were working together. He'd shoot first, ask questions later.

She would have liked to think that Mitch wouldn't do that to her. But as mad as he'd been at her this morning… He was convinced she was the enemy.

If Mitch took off with Zak… Even if she managed to convince Juarez that she wasn't in cahoots with him… She'd been the one who'd brought Zak back the first time. If the kid disappeared again, and by some miracle, Juarez didn't blame her, he'd send her after Zak for sure.

Except, she didn't have time to chase after the kid again. She needed to go to Don Pedro at any cost.

So her primary focus at the moment was to watch Mitch like a hawk and make sure he didn't spirit Zak away when no one was looking.

When their convoy came to a small creek lined with moss-covered stones, she jumped to the mud to lighten the load. So did most of the others.

"It's slippery," the driver said. "Water's higher than last week."

They'd had plenty of rain since then. Megan walked alongside the car as they crossed, in position to help if the current began pushing the vehicle downstream. Cold water filled her boots. At least she had dry socks in her backpack so she could change into them when they reached the other side. Walking around with wet feet in the jungle was asking for trouble.

Using her femininity as an excuse to stay in the car didn't even occur to her. Her continued survival depended on the men knowing that she was as tough as they were. Tougher.

They reached the other side fine, but climbing ashore turned out to be more difficult than the crossing. The mud was deeper here. The lighter ATVs made it up the bank fine, but the tires of the two Jeeps got stuck, which meant another round of heaving and dragging.

If she hadn't been watching Mitch so closely, she wouldn't have noticed that this time, instead of helping, he sneaked away into the jungle.

"Need a drain," he called back with a grin.

Except none of the men ever walked very far to relieve themselves. But Mitch went far enough that she could no longer see him at all.

She moved closer to Zak, trying to figure out Mitch's game.

He was back in ten minutes. And he was walking funny.

Maybe he'd pulled his back lifting the Jeep and walked off so the men wouldn't notice his pain. Maybe he just didn't want to seem weak. Since he didn't go anywhere near Zak, Megan relaxed and went back to work, focusing her full strength on what she was doing.

Then they were done at last, muddy, cold and exhausted. A short break was ordered. They'd build a fire so that everyone could dry up and grab a bite to eat.

Mitch sat next to Zak and talked to the kid under his breath while the others loudly joked around. They hoped Don Pedro had gotten new women to do the cooking. They hadn't fancied the last batch of cooks, who were old enough to be their mothers.

Megan shook her head good-naturedly at the comments. She rolled her eyes at the more raunchy jokes, but watched Mitch every chance she got, making sure she was close enough to stop him if he made a move. She didn't like this sudden cozying up to Zak. As good as Mitch was… She didn't dare turn her back on him for a second.

He was not going to mess up her plans.

She strode right up to Juarez as soon as her bowl was empty. "The kid's riding with me. Got some questions for him about how he escaped. I don't like it that a kid like this got through our security."

Juarez shrugged, busy with his meal. He liked his

food and it showed on his midriff. He no longer went on long marches through the jungle; he had plenty of men for that. If he needed to see to something personally, he took one of the Jeeps.

He was getting comfortable in other ways, too. He'd simply had the guard who'd let Zak escape beaten. A year ago, when Megan had shown up, gross negligence like that would have been punished by a shot to the head.

There'd been two previous trips to see Don Pedro since Megan had been at camp. No matter what she'd done, she couldn't get on Juarez to take her along. She'd been told she needed to earn his trust. Yet Mitch had easily managed to get himself invited. Only to the halfway drop-off point, but still. Juarez was relaxing the rules.

That didn't bode well for him, especially if he was right and one of the other captains was planning an internal war. Juarez had been doing too well for too long, and he was getting cocky.

Megan grabbed Zak by the elbow and dragged him to the second car so they could ride together. When she glanced back at Mitch, she expected him to be angry. Instead, a look of satisfaction sat on the man's face, which he quickly masked.

She had no idea what that was about. Didn't matter. Zak was hers.

"What did he tell you?" she asked the kid.

"To keep my head down so I don't get into any more trouble."

She watched Zak's face for telltale signs that he was lying, but didn't see any. "Try to remember that."

They piled into the cars and took off, but didn't get far before the first Jeep veered off the road and nearly crashed into a tree. Everyone jumped out of the car, swearing up a storm.

Everyone except Mitch. His knife flashed just before something brownish green flew from the vehicle. A snake.

A second passed before she recognized the shape of the snake's head. It was a fer-de-lance, a spearhead. A shiver ran down her back.

"Stay," she ordered Zak, as she jumped out to take a closer look.

The men had already gathered around the snake. Four feet long and still wriggling—the deadliest snake around. In this jungle, spearheads were responsible for more deaths than any other animal.

There wasn't a face that didn't go a little pale. She felt the blood draining out of her own.

Juarez shook off the scare first.

His gaze settled on Megan. "I owe you my thanks. This man you brought to us is a good one. He saved my life today."

Mitch.

Oh, man. She'd left Zak alone in the car and every man's attention was on the snake. Except for Mitch's, and he wasn't here.

She whipped around, expecting both him and the kid to be gone, but Mitch was right behind her. He stepped forward, bent and cut the dead snake's head off with a clean swipe of his knife, speared it on a stick and held it out to Juarez.

Juarez took it and grinned at the open mouth, at the

fangs. It was the exact kind of trophy he liked, although she had no idea how Mitch would know that.

The other men who'd been riding up front seemed equally happy with their latest comrade in arms, but Umberto, who'd been driving the Jeep Megan and Zak rode in, narrowed his small brown eyes as he watched the proceedings.

Looked like Mitch's sudden rise into the boss's favor was gaining him at least one enemy. Odd, since Umberto was one of the most easygoing of the men, not given to fits of temper or jealousy. Still, Mitch would be smart to watch his back, she thought as she headed back to the car and the kid.

Part of her wanted to warn Mitch about Umberto, but doing it without anyone hearing didn't seem possible at the moment. And Mitch wasn't talking to her anyway. He was just going to have to handle any trouble he got himself into. Her first priority was her brother.

Several hours passed before they reached the drop-off point. They unloaded one of the Jeeps. From the feel of the bags, she was pretty sure the load was drugs and not weapons. She couldn't find a way to tag these bags without being seen, so she tagged a nearby tree, sticking a microtransmitter onto the bark when she leaned against it for a minute of rest. That way, her CIA team would be able to find the drop-off location.

The sun dipped lower and lower. They needed to get their camp ready. She helped where she could and stayed out of the way otherwise. She needed to stick to Zak, who was unusually subdued, nursing his jaw and looking beat down and miserable.

She cooked, even though she never did that in camp,

leaving kitchen work to the cantina women. But now she was the only woman at hand and traditional gender roles lived on in the jungle. She didn't mind. At least she knew what she was eating. Some of the men were less than discerning when it came to food out here. She dropped dried fish into the filtered water and let it boil, adding cleaned roots and native herbs they'd brought, supplemented with a few that she found near the clearing.

While the others ate, she spoon-fed some soup to Zak. "You need to eat some of this, even if it hurts."

She made sure he had enough water and his straw, even brought him a cup of *maté* later and helped him drink it. He was in bad shape, but he could have been in worse. He could have been dead by now. She sure hoped he'd learned his lesson. And if Mitch managed to get him home in one piece, she prayed he would do something useful with his life.

"You take the second car for the night," Juarez called across the fire to her.

To be given the car to sleep in was a treat. Juarez was probably rewarding her for bringing Zak back and for adding another good man to the boss's team.

"With the kid," he added. "He better still be here come morning."

No problem there. She'd already planned on tying the kid to her wrist with her bootlaces that night.

The drop-off point, where they'd set up camp for the night, was at loggers' crossroads. Collapsed sleeping platforms were visible here and there where loggers of the past had rested. Umberto was repairing one. The rest of the men made new ones for themselves.

Megan helped Zak to another drink, but she became distracted when she heard an enraged shout.

Mitch and Umberto were facing off. Umberto cursed him with all the color of the Spanish language. Something about Mitch bumping into him and spilling his drink. "Watch where you're going, gringo!"

Mitch stood his ground, darkness gathering in his eyes. Umberto moved closer and put the honor of Mitch's mother in question. A muscle ticked in Mitch's face. More insults were shouted about gringos and all the cowards who lived in the United States He was provoking Mitch, taunting him until he couldn't take anymore and moved toward Umberto at last, rolling over him like a tank.

Umberto was older, but he was also taller than Mitch and had grown up fighting. He'd made his living with his fists all his life. He had moves that weren't taught at any law enforcement academy, and a familiarity with jungle terrain that no one could match.

The men gathered around and cheered, not a thought given to pulling the battling enemies apart. They thought this prime entertainment, business as usual. Fights were frequent at the camp.

Megan watched Mitch, her hands curled into fists. *The stupid idiot.* She could have punched him herself, given half a chance. Did he have a death wish? Umberto might have been the closest thing she had to a friend at camp, but he was a hardened criminal. She never allowed herself to forget that.

If Mitch got injured… A broken rib could be a death sentence out here. Two months back, after a fight like this, a broken rib had punctured a man's lung. He'd died before he could reach the witch doctor in the nearest village.

Her jaw tightened. She was not going to worry about Mitch, she told herself. He deserved whatever he got. But she couldn't look away, either.

The men rolled on the uneven ground, too near the fire. Umberto grabbed Mitch's collar from the back and pulled hard, trying to cut off his air. But the fabric gave instead, ripping down his back. Then Mitch was on top, pinning Umberto.

He waited, sweat rolling down his neck, until the older man capitulated. Then he stood, letting Umberto go with a cocky sneer. Which was too much for the proud Umberto, who went on the attack once again.

Mitch bent deftly out of the way, barely bumping his opponent, who fell face-first into the fire. Umberto pulled back, howling.

"Enough!" Juarez ordered at last, and others stepped between the fighters to separate them.

"I didn't mean for him to get hurt," Mitch submitted to the boss immediately, apologetic. Then he turned to Umberto. "Sorry, amigo." He wiped his forehead. "It's this damned heat."

"You let him go. He came back for more." Juarez let Mitch off the hook even as he scowled at both men. The boss watched as Umberto poured water over his burned face, hissing.

Megan grabbed her jar of salve and ran to help, shooting an angry glance at Mitch as she passed.

"Let me look at that," she told Umberto. "It's not that bad. You'll heal. Anyway, women like a man with battle scars," she said, trying to make Umberto feel better.

"Something about that one isn't right," the man told her under his breath. He was holding up pretty well considering the pain he must be in. "You watch him, *chica,* or he'll burn you, too. You'll see. You keep an eye on him."

"Te lo prometo." I promise.

Juarez kicked one of the bags that held supplies, displeasure written all over his face. "Umberto will stay with the goods. The gringo is coming with us in the morning," he declared before he stalked away.

Mitch shrugged, not seeming to care one way or the other, not looking pleased with his victory. He glanced at Umberto. "You all right?"

Umberto swore at him in Spanish and told him to drop dead.

As Mitch shuffled off, suspicion swirled through Megan. He'd wanted to come with them to the end, and now he was coming.

Convenient.

Had the fight been engineered? Maybe he hadn't spilled Umberto's drink by accident. He'd sure gained Juarez's favor in a hurry, something that had taken her nearly a full year to do. Granted, the fact that she was a woman had counted against her in a big way. The most difficult part of her job had been to overcome that.

Then she thought about the snake, the way Mitch had gone off to the woods and come back walking funny. Even he wouldn't have hidden a poisonous snake under his clothing, would he? No. She decided against it. Nobody would be that crazy.

Yet, if she'd learned anything since she'd met him, it was that he would do anything to achieve his goal.

He would stop at nothing to complete his mission and get Zak back home. On a professional level, she appreciated that.

She'd have appreciated it even more than if they were partners. But they were clearly working at cross-purposes, which meant she had to watch him 24/7.

If it came down to a choice between saving her brother or Zak, Mitch would save Zak. A fact she would do well to remember.

She made sure their paths crossed when he started down to the creek for water. "So you're coming with us to the meeting," she remarked, watching him closely. His face didn't betray a thing.

He filled his canteen, then took hers and filled that, too, so she didn't have to stand too close to the muddy creek and get her boots wet. She glanced around to make sure there was nobody within hearing distance.

"Billy always liked the jungle," she said as she looked up at the tall trees that seemed to reach the sky. "He was excited when he found out that his assignment would bring him here."

"And you? Was this what you wanted?"

She gave a sour laugh. "When I first signed up...I was thinking more plush European jobs. I'd have loved to go to Paris, in particular. Do a little shopping, a little intelligence gathering, that sort of thing."

He handed her canteen back.

"The first week of training pretty much killed most of my TV-inspired fantasies," she admitted. "Billy tried to talk me out of the job, actually. Before I signed up, and a couple of times after. He worried that I'd get into trouble somewhere far from home. And then he did."

Mitch stomped the mud off his shoes and began walking away.

"He has a girl back home, Amy. She's a kindergarten teacher. She's just the sweetest thing."

Mitch didn't wait for her to catch up. He didn't seem to be interested in her, or stories of her little brother. He was a man on a mission.

Well, she was a woman on a mission. And she wasn't done fighting.

Chapter Nine

Mitch ambled around Don Pedro's compound, hoping to catch a glimpse of Zak. He'd been carried off the moment they'd arrived at the meeting point and hadn't been seen since.

He should have taken the kid before they'd gotten this far. He'd thought about it several times during the night at their makeshift camp in the jungle, then again during the long trek that had brought them here. Yet he hadn't acted.

Something had stopped him, and if he wanted to be honest, he had to admit—at least to himself—that something was Megan. He wanted her to be able to save her brother. Even if she'd used him. If he was going to catch any flak for that from the Colonel, he would just have to deal with it.

The jumble of structures that made up the compound didn't seem to have been built according to any logical plan. It didn't seem possible that law enforcement hadn't discovered the place. The two-acre clearing in the jungle had to be clearly visible from the air. On top of the largest building, a two-story Spanish-style house complete with a balcony, there was even a helipad. A chopper was parked there at the moment.

Juarez's camp—with its roughly made wooden shacks—had an air of impermanence. He camped like a man who knew he might have to disappear at any moment, putting as little work as possible into the place and spending as little money on it as possible.

Here, only half of the dozen buildings were the traditional wooden abodes with palm-frond thatching that were native to the area. The rest were made from brick and cement. Every building had power—the hum of generators filled the air. The lights were on behind almost every window and more were strung between the buildings, holding back the night.

A semidecent road led to the compound's gate, the only entry through the barbed wire fence that guarded the perimeter to keep out the wild animals. Mitch didn't think the *policía* ever came here, unless it was to pick up bribes. From the sweet setup, it sure looked like Don Pedro had friends in high places who provided him with protection against such inconveniences as police raids.

"Tequila, amigo?" A man who could barely stand propped himself against a building and waved his bottle at Mitch.

"No, thanks. I'm good for now, I think." He gave a friendly laugh as he moved on.

The place buzzed with people; it was crowded with all the newcomers. Juarez wasn't the only visitor. At least four other captains had come with their posses, from what Mitch had been able to overhear. Cristobal was among them. A mean one, from the looks of him. His eyes said he'd shoot you if you so much as sneezed. A heavyset man, but not in the way Juarez was. Cristobal had the build and demeanor of a prizefighter. His face was scarred and his nose was crooked—it must have been broken in the past. Mitch had caught a glimpse of the man when the captains had gone up to the don's big house together.

He headed toward the cantina and nodded to the men already there, but didn't join any of their conversations or arguments. Didn't say anything but *"Gracias,"* when a quarter bottle of homemade tequila was offered to him. He settled on a log in the corner, his back resting against the rough-hewn wood of the wall, his eyes half-closed, the very picture of a man exhausted by the long trip.

He listened. Also, he kept an eye out for Megan, but didn't see her. She was probably looking for her brother.

The talk centered on guns and women. Nobody was talking about Zak, or where any prisoners might be kept. After half an hour, Mitch slipped away. A useful clue could have saved him considerable time, but from the way the conversation had gone, sticking around would just have been a waste of time.

He shouldn't have let the kid out of his sight. But Juarez had wanted him to help unload the Jeeps, and there had been no way to refuse the boss without arousing suspicion. And by the time Juarez had been done with him, the kid had disappeared into one of the buildings.

Except, he was no longer there. Mitch had checked that building first, the moment he'd been able to get away. He didn't find any bloodstains on the floor, at least, which gave him hope that the kid was still alive. They'd just moved him when Mitch hadn't been looking.

Don Pedro was busy this evening receiving his captains, who'd probably give him reports on their activities and his cut of the cash from all the shady businesses they ran. But the grace period wasn't likely to last beyond morning. Tonight, the men ate and drank. They would do that long into the night, at the rate they were going. But in the morning, they would remember Zak, the man who'd shot the don's half brother. Then there would be a reckoning.

Mitch had until then to get the kid away from here. That was all the time Megan had, too. When Mitch disappeared with Zak, her close association with him would get her into trouble. She couldn't afford to linger. He hoped she was making headway.

He stopped to adjust his left boot, glancing around surreptitiously to make sure no one was watching him. Then he ducked into a narrow space between two buildings.

Nobody called out after him.

He moved quickly, looking for entry into either building. Eventually he found a padlocked door on the right. It took him less than two minutes to get in.

The lights were out, but enough moonlight came in through a row of windows that he could see the half-dozen long tables that lined the walls. And scales, wrapping materials, all the paraphernalia of a serious drug operation.

He glanced up at a narrow walkway suspended from the roof beams. When the workers were getting these packages ready, a couple of armed guards probably stood up there, making sure nobody stole anything, making sure there was no trouble.

He walked around and checked every shadowed corner, knowing if Zak was tied up in here somewhere, he might not be in good enough shape to call out for help, even if the kid did see him in the semidarkness.

A ten-minute search turned up no sign of him. No sign of Megan's brother, either. Zak was his priority, but if he found Billy, if the man was still alive, he would help Megan. He might not have had a brother, but he did have Cindy, a sister he would have killed or died for.

He understood where Megan was coming from. Understood it and respected it. That was why he was still here, instead of already cutting through the jungle on his way back home with Zak.

It didn't have anything to do with the way his heart stumbled every time he looked at Megan Cassidy. Definitely not. That would be stupid.

He eased back out the way he'd come in and snapped the padlock closed behind him.

"*Que pasa,* gringo?"

The voice made him spin. Juarez. The meeting with Don Pedro must be over.

Mitch made a point of craning his neck around. "I thought I saw a woman come in here." He put a confused look on his face as he came forward from between the buildings, making himself sway on his feet. "I swear the *mujer* disappeared into nothing." He blinked hard. "What do they put into the tequila around here, anyway?"

The boss laughed at him. "A *mujer,* eh? Come with me."

He hesitated for a second, calculating how quickly

he could grab his knife and sink it into the man's heart, how quickly he could drag him into the shadows of the narrow space.

Quickly enough, if there weren't any others around. But a handful of men played a dice game in the dust in front of the building opposite them and, alerted by Juarez's voice, they kept looking his way.

He joined Juarez with a forced grin. "Lead the way."

Half an hour went to waste before he could get away again, leaving one relieved woman behind. With all the strangers in camp and all the drinking, the women had plenty of requests and were plenty tired. The woman Juarez had introduced him to hadn't taken offense when he'd changed his mind. He even got an affectionate pat on the back. Judging by the noises coming from the loft above the stables that housed the packing mules, Juarez was oblivious to anything but his own satisfaction.

Mitch checked the stables on his way out and found two more couples who were taking advantage of the soft hay, but no sign of Zak or Billy.

He ducked out the door, heading for another building he hadn't checked yet. The main house, the one with the balcony and the helipad on the roof, he was leaving for last. Don Pedro's private quarters had to be well guarded. His chances of getting caught would be the highest there.

He snuck into the barracks and found them mostly empty, save for the few men who'd drunk themselves unconscious and had somehow dragged themselves back here to crash. In the darkness, he stumbled over a boot someone had left in the middle of the room.

"Hey, *chica.* Come here," one of the drunks called from his bunk, his words followed by a hiccup.

Mitch moved on without response, shaking his head. He worked his way back to the narrow alley where Juarez had almost caught him and rounded the building he hadn't been able to get into before. It was dark inside. At last he came to a door in the back.

He wiggled the doorknob. Unlocked. He stepped into the darkness, closing the door quietly behind him. He knew at once that he wasn't alone. Tension hung thick in the air.

"What do you want?" The barked Spanish words came from the far end of the room. People moved in the darkness. "Turn on the light."

Not a chance. He wasn't about to make himself a target. He ducked low and readied his gun.

Someone groaned. Two muffled shots were fired. As if the barrel of the gun was pressed into something that dampened the sound, like a body. *Not Zak,* Mitch thought. Zak would be called to task in front of the don, made an example. Not Billy, either. If Megan was right, they'd had Billy for a year now. Why execute him suddenly and in secret?

He opened the door at his back and rolled out of the building a second before a bullet shattered the door frame. This one would be heard. He dashed into the bushes behind the building and laid low. Three men rushed out, but they only looked for him for a few seconds before taking off. They knew the gunshot would bring the don's guards.

Sure enough, shouts rose in the camp. Mitch couldn't move without being seen. But if they found him here…

He couldn't afford to be held and questioned. As the night wore on, Zak was running out of time.

He couldn't slip into the jungle, either. The fence was at his back. He was trapped.

MEGAN HAD BEEN HIDING behind the cantina for at least twenty minutes when the gunshot sounded and all the men she was watching ran off in that direction. Hopefully, Mitch wasn't in trouble. She shouldn't have cared as much as she did. Of course, she shouldn't have slept with him, either. There was something about him that made her break rules she'd never broken before, something that put that funny fluttering in the middle of her chest.

But it wasn't anything she could stop and contemplate at the moment.

When the area cleared at last, she headed for a double-padlocked door in the back, which she thought might lead to her brother. No other place she'd checked so far held any clues. She prayed to God this would be it.

She picked the lock and stepped inside the dark space. Her senses told her she was in a small room. Wood planks squeaked under her feet as she stepped forward tentatively. Her heart beat faster.

Every cell of her body was alive and alert. After a year of planning and jockeying for Juarez's attention, she had finally made it; she was here. Billy had to be somewhere nearby. This was it. She grinned into the darkness, then reminded herself not to get too carried away on the rising tide of hope. She needed to keep her focus, now more than ever.

She moved forward by feel, bumping into a soft, solid

mass that could have been a dead body, but turned out to be a sack of something. Her hands, held out in front of her, grazed jars. Glass clinked in the darkness. She felt a shelf. She was in the pantry. Well, all right. Logical for a room built right into the side of the cantina.

She didn't dare turn on the light, so she lit a match and looked around carefully to make sure she didn't miss any hidden doors or crawl spaces where a prisoner could be stashed.

She saw nothing. No way out of the pantry except the way she'd come in. Disappointment tightened her throat as the match went out. She only let the feeling touch her for a second. She shook off all negativity before she exited.

A couple of drunks were singing about love and war in the distance. Didn't hit a single note between them. She cringed as she snuck in the opposite direction. She had one more building to check before she moved on to the main house, the most well-protected place in the compound.

Everything she saw she cataloged, every crate of guns she found she tagged, every word she overheard she remembered. She was still a CIA operative and planned on filing a report when she got back to the office. She hoped that would make up for her gross breach of conduct here at least a little.

She made a note of the helicopter on the roof up ahead. She hadn't flown one in years, but in a pinch… She snuck toward another cement building that was a quarter of the size of the main one. This one had a double lock instead of a padlock. Her hopes rose. They must keep something important here.

But as her heart raced, she heard the sound of a few men approaching and pulled herself into the shadows.

"Then what the hell was the shot about?"

"Guard said he couldn't find anything."

"Probably Jose got drunk again and couldn't help showing off his new pistol to his buddies."

"The man could never hold his liquor. He's worse than a woman." The speaker spat into the dust as his friends laughed in agreement.

She didn't move back to the door until they were well away. She pulled her set of picks from her back pocket. But before she could put them into the lock, the door opened. The building wasn't dark—the windows had just been blacked out from inside, she realized, too late.

"Chica." An immediate grin spread on the man's pockmarked face as he looked her over. "I saw you earlier." He lifted a bottle toward her. "You want to go someplace for a drink?"

He was better dressed and more well-spoken than most of the others. He probably had a higher position in the organization, which didn't impress Megan.

"No thanks. I like to stop while I can still stand."

"A woman with principles." The man nodded. "Can't find many of those in the jungle." He watched her thoughtfully for a second. "You belong to Juarez?"

"Gotta have a protector in this business." She shrugged.

"True enough." The man looked her over again, this time with regret. "You better find your man before you get into trouble. The boys had too much to drink tonight. They see a pretty girl… They aren't thinking."

"I was just looking for him."

"He's not in here." The man locked the door behind

him, then took off for the barracks without a backward glance.

She moved on, circling around the building. When a large cloud covered the moon, she tried the front door again. The double lock was tricky to pick, but not impossible. Then she was in, with the door closed behind her.

Since the windows were blacked out, not a smidgen of light filtered in from the outside. She reached for the light switch, but couldn't find it. Some of the small buildings she'd been in had pull switches that hung from a light in the middle of the room. This place probably had the same. She moved forward.

Then a small noise made her freeze.

She held her breath, listening.

She didn't hear another sound, yet every instinct she had screamed that someone was moving toward her. The short hairs at her nape stood on end. She pulled her knife. The gun would make too much noise and draw an audience.

She backed away slowly, silently, until her back bumped into the wall. Pulse beating, she waited.

No attack came.

The silence continued until she thought she might have just imagined the noise earlier. But, no, she definitely felt a presence.

She turned toward the door. She would come back later.

A solid wall of flesh blocked her way. She bit her lip hard to keep from screaming. Then steel arms came around her to restrain her, knocking the knife from her hand.

"It's me," Mitch whispered into her ear just as she brought up her elbow to launch an attack.

"Was that necessary?" She smacked him on the chest, both angry with him and relieved beyond words. Something inside pushed her to lean against him. She checked that impulse and didn't give in to it.

"I didn't know who you were until you came close enough that I could smell your shampoo."

He'd made that up. She hadn't washed her hair since they'd been at Juarez's camp. No way he could still smell that.

"How did you get in?" She moved away from him in the darkness. Maybe a little distance would stop her from being so aware of his body.

"Back window, while you were chatting up your guy up front."

"He's not my guy," she snapped, annoyed with the situation, and the fact that she still hadn't found Billy. "Did you find anything?"

"Two extra rooms in the back. All locked up tight." His sexy voice skittered along her skin.

"Been inside yet?"

"I was about to see to the locks when you interrupted me. Careful." He took her hand and led the way back through the darkness. "Where have you been?"

She shouldn't have enjoyed his touch so much. They weren't holding hands in a romantic way. He'd already been across the room and knew the path, leading her only to make sure she wouldn't bump into anything and give them away.

Knowing that didn't stop heat spreading across her skin, however. She tried not to think of his hands on other places on her body, but she failed. The night she'd spent in his hammock refused to be forgotten.

Focus on Billy.

"I've checked everywhere but here and the main house. Did you have anything to do with that gunshot?"

"No, but I was there. Would have gotten caught, too, if not for a hole in the fence." He lit a match so they could see the lock.

There was a hole in the fence. Good to know. "What was it about?"

"Not sure. Could be Cristobal is making his move. Or private business between the don's men? Could be about drugs or a woman."

They reached the door and he let go of her hand.

She immediately missed his touch. "The don's men were shooting at each other?"

"I couldn't see well enough to tell."

She thought for a second. "I caught a glimpse of the don a couple of times, before they locked themselves up in the main house. He was definitely keeping a close eye on Cristobal."

"All the more reason for us to get moving and get the hell out of here."

She couldn't agree more. She shoved her picks into the lock and worked the tumblers, then pushed the door in.

They found themselves in small private quarters. There was a bed, a table and some shelves.

Mitch checked under the bed. He pulled out a dusty duffel bag. He claimed that, fingering something on the bottom, hesitating before tossing in some dry food, plus a box of matches. "Something for the trek out of the jungle."

Good thinking. Neither of them had their backpacks. She'd figured walking around camp with her gear would draw attention. She'd written it off as a loss. Once she found and grabbed her brother, they would be out of here. There'd be no time to go back for anything then. Mitch must have thought the same.

He looked at the last locked door left before them. "Zak and Billy are either here or at the main house."

Hope expanded in her heart. Her fingers were trembling, so this time she held the match and Mitch saw to the lock. Her hands never shook. Ever. At least, not until now. But this time was personal.

She understood, at last, why the agency didn't let its operatives get involved in missions where they had a personal stake. Everything *was* different. At least she had Mitch with her.

He opened the lock in no time. No surprise there. He seemed to be good at everything.

"Put the match out," he said as soon as he stepped inside.

She blew out the flame, frustrated that he knew what was in the small room but she hadn't seen anything. "What is it?" Was somebody coming? She listened for footsteps.

"Explosives storage."

Given a choice, she would have preferred not to go in there. But something scraped at the front door of the building. Then they heard voices.

Mitch yanked her into the dark room and closed the door behind them.

They flattened themselves against the wall, one on each side, and waited. She had her knife drawn, plus her gun handy, in case everything went to hell. *Please, God, don't let it end here. Let me find Billy.*

Three men came in, judging by the voices. They complained about the food in a mixture of Spanish and some local language. There hadn't been quite enough to eat; the soup was watered down.

"We'll go hunting in the morning," one of them offered. "We'll make a fire right in the forest and have a full meal. To hell with the visitors."

"The don said nobody leaves while the visitors are here," another responded.

This was followed by some long and colorful swearing.

She heard a familiar beep a few seconds later. Someone had powered on a computer out there. Anything was possible with a generator, she supposed. The main section of this building must be some sort of office. Long minutes passed by. The men talked now and then, but they weren't leaving. At least they weren't coming into the storage room, either.

Once their door rattled, setting Megan's nerves on edge. In a few minutes, the sound of snoring reached her. Someone must have hunkered down right in front of the door for a nap.

After a few tense seconds, Mitch pulled away and sat on the floor. She sat next to him, careful not to bump into any boxes in the dark. .

"Are we stuck?" She kept her voice low, although the man snored loud enough outside to drown out her words.

"I'll figure something out. Give me a second."

Someone turned a radio on outside. Salsa music filled the air, which meant they could talk a little without being heard.

"Billy will be mad that I came. I might be older, but he always thinks women should be protected. When I was fourteen, I got home from my first date with a guy and he got fresh with me in the driveway. Billy dropped out of our tree house like a ninja and attacked him. He was ten."

"You don't have to do that anymore."

"Do what?"

"Tell stories about your brother to make him into a real person in my mind so I'll go along with your plans and help."

He didn't miss much. At least, he no longer seemed to be mad at her.

"Looks like they're in the main house," she whispered after a moment. "Billy and Zak. That's the only place left. We could bust them out together." She went for the logical solution. The two of them together would make a pretty good team. Not that she would ever acknowledge that she was asking for Mitch's help.

"That's the plan."

His announcement gave her pause. "It is?" *Since when?*

Then something occurred to her, certain events of the past day making a little more sense. "Is that why you didn't take off with Zak in the woods when you set up the great snake distraction?"

"You've vouched for me with Juarez," he said with some reluctance.

"But keeping me alive isn't your mission. Taking Zak home is." She winced. That sure sounded like she was arguing against herself. Better shut up while she was ahead.

"We'll do this together."

His voice was steady, like the man himself. Her heart turned over in her chest. She'd set out to do this alone. She'd thought she preferred it that way. The fewer people involved, the fewer chances for mistakes.

But Mitch was... The truth was she was lucky to have Mitch by her side for this, and she knew it.

"The night before last, in your hammock, wasn't a ploy on my part. I had no intention... I went there to tell you about the change of plans."

Silence stretched between them.

"All right," he said after a minute.

Some of the tightness relaxed in her shoulders.

He shifted toward her. "I need you to answer a question for me. Honestly."

Considering who she worked for, she couldn't promise that. "Ask, and I'll see what I can do."

"How do you know Colonel Wilson?"

She hesitated for a second. "I met him a year and a half ago."

"Where?"

"At my mother's house. He came to visit my brother."

"Billy?"

"Jamie."

Another moment of silence. Then Mitch swore softly under his breath. "You're Jamie Cassidy's sister?"

"Didn't I just say that?"

"So this Billy is Jamie's little brother?"

She grinned in the dark. "We're all siblings. Do you want me to draw you a map?"

"Why didn't you tell me sooner?"

"Do you know Jamie?"

A full minute ticked by before he answered. "By name only. We're connected through…um…"

"You both work for Colonel Wilson." It annoyed her to death that she knew so little about her brother's work. If Jamie didn't want to talk about something, you couldn't get a word out of him with bloody torture. He'd been like that even when they'd been kids.

"I'm sorry, ma'am, but I can neither confirm nor deny that," Mitch mocked her, acting just like her infuriating brother.

"The colonel came to visit Jamie after he got out of the hospital." He'd lost both legs on a mission he wasn't allowed to talk about, and she hadn't been able to uncover anything despite all her CIA connections.

"I heard he's had a rough time of it."

She couldn't talk about that. The way Jamie had been the last time she'd seen him… It had broken her heart. And the worst part was there was nothing she could do to help. But she could help Billy. Nothing was going to happen to Billy. Not as long as she was alive and her heart was beating in her chest.

"We should get moving."

For a second, Mitch said nothing, and she was afraid

he was going to push her about Jamie, but when he did speak, he said, "Let's give the guys out there a little time. It'd be better if they cleared out on their own. I'd rather get out of here quietly than draw attention to ourselves."

"How long do you want to wait?" Impatience pushed her forward.

"Half an hour. If they don't move on by then, we'll find a way to take care of them."

"And until then?"

"We could both use some rest." He brushed against her back as he lay down. "Once we bust Billy and Zak out, we'll have to get moving fast. It'll be a while before we can stop to take a break."

She lay down next to him. "So what do you know about my brother?" She needed another picture of Jamie, different from the last time she'd seen him in that wheelchair with the light gone from his eyes.

"Jamie Cassidy is a living legend. He's saved the lives of hundreds. If the mission he'd been on could be acknowledged in any way, he'd be receiving the Congressional Medal of Honor."

She swallowed hard, thinking of Jamie, struggling to accept the loss of his legs, the loss of his spirit. If Jamie were well, he would be here. If Jamie were well, he would have already gotten Billy back. But now she was here to do that. And she'd get it done no matter what.

"Thanks," she told Mitch. "Thank you for telling me. It helps."

Colonel Wilson hadn't been able to tell her family anything when he'd visited, just that they should be proud of Jamie. The man had talked with her brother for two hours behind closed doors before he'd left their house. Man, she'd been steamed. Tears pricked her eyes now. She missed Jamie. Not knowing how he was doing had been the most difficult part of the past year. She missed all her brothers.

She didn't even think of resisting when Mitch pulled her into his arms. She felt a new connection form between them as she relaxed against him.

He ran his fingers down her hair. He must have read her subdued mood, because he said, "We're almost there now. It's almost over. We'll do this as a team."

"Good," she said with sincere relief. "You were a pain as an enemy."

He gave a low chuckle. "Right back at you, darling."

"I've been waiting for so long to be this close. It seems surreal. Until now, all I worried about was making it this far. Now that I'm here…" Suddenly she thought of a million brand-new things to worry about.

"There's nothing we can't handle together."

His voice held warmth and comfort and strength, so she asked the question she hadn't dared ask even herself until now. "You think Billy is still alive?"

"If he's anything like you or Jamie, they couldn't take him out with a bazooka."

That put a smile on her face. And then, all of a sudden, those stupid tears spilled over and ran down her cheeks. She rubbed them away with the heel of her hand, but more came. Great. Just great. So much for her tough-chick image.

She didn't cry. Ever. She'd lost that annoying habit growing up. Having to duke it out with eight brothers on a daily basis had taught her to never show weakness.

They teased her mercilessly if she so much as slowed down because of a scraped knee or busted finger.

Mitch brushed the pad of his thumb along her face, right through the streaks of moisture.

Wonderful. Now he knew that she was a complete mess.

But he didn't tease her or laugh at her. He kissed her.

Chapter Ten

Another man might have told himself he was only kissing Megan to distract her from their troubles, but Mitch had always employed brutal honesty when it came to women. They confused him enough without game playing, so he never lied to them, or to himself.

He wasn't tasting Megan's lips like he was a starving man to comfort her. He was doing it because he wanted to. Because he wanted her.

"We'll get them out. Don't worry about it. I don't leave men behind. Not ever," he whispered against her mouth.

She burrowed against him and he folded his arms around her, wanting to protect her even though he knew she hated that, that she didn't need protection. She was the most self-sufficient woman he'd ever met. She'd survived a year in a jungle camp with dozens of hardened criminals. That said something about her. She was nobody's damsel in distress.

He went back for another taste of her soft lips.

He wouldn't have minded if she needed him a little. He didn't have much to offer a woman beyond his protection. He couldn't offer a fancy house or a steady relationship or pretty words. He'd always been awkward around women, and he wasn't exactly the playboy type.

She tasted like mango. She tended to go for fruit during meals, and he couldn't blame her. Cantina fare wasn't exactly haute cuisine. Every meal that came out of those blackened pots was a raffle ticket to dysentery or food poisoning.

The sweet mango taste of her was intoxicating. He'd never thought that a taste could go straight to a man's head, but it did. For the rest of his life, mango would be his favorite food, he was pretty sure.

He drank her in, holding on to control. He didn't want to go too far. Or too fast. She wasn't like the other women he had run into over the years, not that there were many. He'd been working special ops at the beginning, in military units where women weren't allowed. Even now, in the SDDU, they were the exception to the rule. And since most missions were lone-wolf ops, it wasn't as if he got to hang out with them all that often.

He didn't have many opportunities to hone his seduction skills. For most of his adult life, he'd been busy fighting for his country. So being here now with Megan, trying to negotiate the rules of their cooperation while trying to negotiate the rules of their attraction, was new to him.

They broke apart for air. She shifted slightly away. Now she would tell him that this was a big mistake, he thought, a protest all ready on his lips. But instead she whispered a question.

"Did you once leave someone important to you behind? Is that why you make sure it won't ever happen again? Was it a woman?"

She'd been thinking about that? He was definitely clueless about women. Did their brains never stop?

He let her go and rubbed his hand over his face. The one he'd left behind…

He didn't want to go there. Not ever. But maybe because of the darkness—or more likely because of Megan—the words poured out from a cold, locked-away part of him.

"My mother is an alcoholic, the mean kind. My father is a drug addict. I had a sister, Cindy. She was much younger than me." Fifteen years, to be exact. "When Cindy was about a year old, my father sold her for drugs." A vast emptiness opened up inside his chest, a cold place where only his nightmares lived.

She moved closer and leaned her head on his shoulder.

"My father was too out of it to remember where he took her or who he gave her to. I ran away from home to look for her. But I never found her. The police never had a clue, either." He put his arms around her and held her tight. "I've never given up, but…God, it's been twenty years."

She pressed her lips to the side of his stubbled cheek and he drank in the comfort. Inside his heart, a couple of barricades crumbled.

"So this is why getting Zak home is a religion to you, no matter what a twit the kid is, no matter how I begged. I get it." She moved her head and lined up her lips with his. Didn't kiss him. Just left their mouths touching like that.

The gesture was sweet and erotic at the same time,

just like the woman. And the thing was, he really did believe that she understood him.

He pressed closer and deepened the kiss. She gave him everything.

Long minutes passed as their passion heated to a fever pitch. He ran his hands over her back and arms, not sure what to do next. This was the time when women wanted to hear something romantic. He wished he were better at this. *Go with the truth.* "I don't want to stop."

She stilled.

Great. Why couldn't he have thought up something sweet?

But the next second she pressed closer to him, making his body harder in an instant. "I don't want you to stop, either."

The thrill of that simple sentence shot right through him. He cupped her breasts as arousal, gratitude and other, more complicated, emotions swirled inside him.

This was dangerous, he thought. He knew this woman. Wouldn't easily forget her. He cared about her. When did that happen? Didn't matter, he supposed. It was the bare truth.

So don't mess it up. He didn't intend to. He planned on stopping way before the point of no return. He just wanted another feel of her amazing breasts. Just one more second to soak up the sensation as they pressed into his palms.

Her hand slipped under his shirt and rested against his abdomen. Her slim fingers drove him to distraction. She moved up to his chest, and as she ran her palm over his nipple, he sucked in a sharp breath.

When she began unbuttoning his shirt, he did nothing to stop her. He'd been shirtless with her before. They weren't going too far. Yet.

His hands moved reluctantly to give her room to maneuver and ended up at the hem of her tank top. He hesitated. She moved back a little and arched her back to help him. He pulled up the stretchy material inch by slow inch, taking her unbuttoned shirt with it, pulling it all over her head.

His eyes were used to the dark enough now to see the outline of her perfect breasts. The thin line of light coming in under the door helped, too, and he was more grateful for that little light than he'd been for anything in a long time. Her nipples were swollen and ready, and drew his lips like magnets.

He didn't even try to resist. He could have been happy like this, alternating between her breasts and mouth, for the rest of his life, he thought. Then her head dropped back, her back arched and her hand slipped down between his pants and his skin.

All of a sudden, he didn't have enough air to breathe.

His body flexed against hers. Those slim fingers wrapped around him.

This would be a good time to stop.

He was glad to know that a few of his brain cells were still working. Part of his brain remained alert to their surroundings and the danger around them, listening for the men outside, making sure the one in front of the door kept snoring. The rest of his brain had drowned in testosterone and need.

No. He couldn't let that happen. That would be irresponsible.

"We're going to stop now," he said.

"No," she told him. Her fingers tightened around him in emphasis.

Okay, not yet. She was right. They were still in control. They could wait a little and stop later.

Her scent and the feel of her filled him completely. When she undid his belt buckle for better access, he lost his breath. She was a whiz with the zipper. She was a whiz with pretty much everything, so he shouldn't have been surprised.

His most impatient body part sprang free. His pants, halfway down his thighs now, limited his movement. In the cramped storage room, they couldn't lie down and stretch out comfortably. He felt as if they were playing some erotic version of Twister.

He went for her pants and tugged them down, wanting to make her feel as good as she made him feel. With one hand on her breast and another between her legs, he turned her and backed her up until she sat on his lap, with him kneeling behind her.

His hard need nestled against the smooth skin of her backside, the exquisite sensation filling him up with steam. She leaned her head back to rest it on his shoulder, offering her neck to his lips. At the same time, she rubbed her bottom against him.

"We can't," he begged on a raspy whisper. She was pushing him beyond his limits. But they *could.* The duffel bag he'd fished from under the bed in the other room hid a little present.

He had left the package of condoms at the bottom of the bag because they could be useful on their way out of the jungle. Condoms could keep an injury protected if they had to cross a river. They could also be used to collect water. They were elastic enough to make a sling out of for hunting, if he ran out of bullets. Condoms had enough uses that they were a standard part of survivor kits.

"Right." She drew a slow, shuddering breath and lifted her head from his shoulder, leaning away from him. "This is beyond idiotic. I don't know what I was thinking."

"Don't apologize." His voice held a low rasp that hadn't been there before. He quietly cleared his throat. "You're an amazing woman. I—" What? He couldn't help himself? He hated jerks who said things like that.

A real man could always help himself, always made sure his woman was safe, that he did what was best for her.

Not that Megan Cassidy was his woman.

He wanted to put some distance between them but he didn't seem to be able to let her go. His arms wouldn't release her.

He pressed a kiss to her nape, but instead of letting her go when he was done, he ended up scraping his teeth along her skin.

She trembled, swallowing a moan before it had a chance to become fully audible.

"Mitch?" The heat in her voice proved to be his undoing.

"I want to." He didn't breathe. "Tell me to go to hell."

Instead, she slid back for more full body contact. His eyes crossed. He didn't care. She had her back to him and it was dark. He didn't have to worry about looking attractive. Or even sane. Which he obviously wasn't just now.

He reached for the condom. "I found something in the other room," he whispered.

She probably figured out what when she heard the crinkling sound of the packaging rip, because she made a noise that could only be described as grateful relief. She lifted away to give him room.

He sheathed himself, still not fully able to believe that they were going to do this. Now. Here.

"Your brother Jamie is going to shoot a hole in my head the size of a railroad tunnel when he finds out I touched his sister," he said, half hoping that saying it out loud might knock some sense into him at the last second.

It didn't.

"Might as well make it worth all the grief he's going to give us," Megan suggested practically.

The next second she was lowering herself onto his hardness.

He gripped her hips, stopped her when he was pressed against her entrance.

There was still time…

Then there wasn't.

His body moved forward on its own accord, and he slid into her wet heat, slowly, to give her time to adjust.

If the room had exploded just then, he would have died a happy man. And that was saying something, because he would have left his mission incomplete, and he didn't believe in that kind of thing.

She felt amazing. Perfect. Hot. Every move she made blew his mind, until his entire focus was narrowed to the friction between their bodies.

Pressure built. Tension escalated.

"Mitch," she breathed his name a second before her inner muscles began convulsing around him, pushing him over the edge.

All he saw was white heat. All he could hear was his own heartbeat drumming inside his ears.

How did I get so lucky? he thought, as he held her tight, waiting for their heart rates to calm.

A shuffling sound in front of the door interrupted their bliss. "Did you hear that noise?" a surly voice asked.

The men had turned off the radio. The snoring had stopped.

Mitch went for his weapon. Megan moved, too, then stilled again, took his hand and pulled it forward, pressed it to the floor near her knee. He felt some kind of a latch.

It could be a latch door to a crawl space below the building. He ran his finger around the edges, looking for a handhold.

It was nailed down.

She slid off his lap. He missed her immediately, but he had no time to pause and think about that or what they'd done and what it had meant.

His knife was in his hand already, and he pried up the two large nails with the tip. He felt for the edges of the door, opened it, tossed the duffel bag down and lowered himself without even pulling up his pants all the way.

The doorknob wiggled.

He reached up and guided Megan down. She pulled the trapdoor closed behind her as she tumbled on top of him.

THEY CROUCHED NEXT TO each other silently. Megan's whole body tingled. She could still feel Mitch's hands on her skin. Back there, what had happened... Nobody had ever... She'd never felt... Wow.

She blinked hard, trying to refocus on their current situation. Moonlight shone through a gap in the wood boards that edged the crawl space to the right. Beyond that, everything else was shrouded in darkness. Neither of them moved. Not yet.

"Probably rats again," a man said above them. "Can't get rid of the stupid vermin for nothin'. How many times did I tell you idiots not to bring any food back here?"

Then she heard the door close.

Mitch rustled next to her, probably working his pants up. She'd done that before she'd slipped down after him. Now she dragged on her shirt, trying not to think about all the poisonous snakes, spiders, bugs and plants that might be all around them.

She shifted toward the light. Mitch's hand shot out and held her back. He went first, taking on most of the danger.

Her brain still buzzed with pleasure. Her heart ticked as she took in his wide shoulders, silhouetted in front of her.

He was protecting her.

She hated when he did that. Still, she found it difficult to work up any indignation when she was still boneless from the mind-blowing sex they'd just had.

She drew a slow breath and nearly gagged when she caught a foul stench in the air. Something had crawled in here and died. That pretty much killed the last lingering remains of any romantic mood.

Thank God. Because she really needed to be fully present right now.

"Breathe through your mouth," he whispered back some advice. "Are you all right?"

"Fine." So much better than fine, really. But now was not the time to get into that.

So what if he was taking over for a little while?

She'd always been the protector. The oldest kid in the family. She'd always been her mother's helper, kept her little brothers clean and fed, bandaged their scrapes when they were younger. Kept them safe, which had been a full-time job with the amazing amount of trouble they'd always managed to find.

Then when they didn't need her quite so much, she'd found a job where she could keep other people safe.

Except, now her family needed her again. Although he wouldn't admit it, though he'd pushed her away and kept the whole family at arm's length, Jamie needed her support. And Billy needed her more than ever.

"Let's go," she whispered, just as boots crunched outside. A couple of men stopped right next to the building.

She froze and held her breath. So did Mitch. Any noise they made would be heard by the men. She wasn't going to make a mistake now. Not when she was this close to reaching Billy.

Chapter Eleven

Megan could hear water running. The air still stank, this time with the sharp smell of ammonia. Gross. Somebody was relieving himself on the other side of the wooden boards that closed in the crawl space where they were hiding. Just great.

Her nerves hummed. Mitch put a steadying hand on her knee as if sensing her inner turmoil.

His warm palm heated her skin through the material of her pants. A comforting gesture that also brought back thoughts of what had just happened between them in that storage room.

Her breathing grew erratic. She made an effort to calm it.

If there'd ever been a time when she needed her full focus, this was it. She couldn't afford distractions and complications. But then, why did it feel so good to have Mitch on her side?

Whoever was outside finished his business and walked away. After a minute, Mitch began moving. He made it to the opening and climbed out, but continued to crouch. She waited until he gave the all clear.

He was brushing spiderwebs from his clothes when she finally joined him.

She did the same. Yuck. She'd been living in the jungle long enough not to be scared of bugs, but she didn't have to like it. "Anything bite you?"

"I don't think so. You?" He moved forward, constantly scanning their surroundings.

She shook her head as she glanced back toward the narrow hole they'd climbed through. "I definitely wouldn't want to do that twice."

"You need a break?" He slowed.

"I need to find Billy." She kept on going.

They sneaked forward, keeping close to the shadows, until they reached a spot where stacks of firewood covered the ground in front of them. The main building stood straight ahead, outlined against the sky. Only three of the windows were lit on their side. It looked like the party had ended. The don was probably settling in for the night. Or maybe he was already sleeping and the lights had been left on for his in-house guards.

"Let's hope Billy and Zak are in there," she said as she followed Mitch, since once again he'd taken the lead.

"They have to be. Don't worry about anything now. We're here."

They rounded all the firewood and stopped in the cover of the last stack. The guards by the house didn't look like they'd overimbibed like the rest. They seemed alert and up to the task. And well armed. The security was definitely heavier than at Juarez's camp, and for a moment Megan wondered if this was standard procedure, or if the don felt uneasy about the presence of his captains at the compound and had tightened security for his own protection.

"Any ideas?" she whispered to Mitch.

"Let's do a walk around first." He stole forward, sticking to the shadows, of which there were plenty. Trees and shacks crowded Don Pedro's headquarters.

The guard at the front of the house stood by a small fire that burned in a rusted steel drum. More for the smoke that kept the bugs away than for the heat, Megan suspected. The guard watching the side of the house was smoking a cigar and looking bored. The man in the back leaned against the wall to watch the jungle.

Mitch moved quietly in the cover of some bushes. She followed him, noticing a small window low to the ground. Not enough to let anyone in or out, just enough for some light and air. The main house had a basement.

She tugged Mitch's sleeve and pointed. He acknowledged her with a nod. They checked out the fourth guard, who was cleaning his weapon, then crept back to the back of the building.

"Is there any way we could get in through that window?" Her instincts said if there were any prisoners in the house, they were kept in that basement.

"Not without some serious tools and a lot of noise. The wall is solid cement."

Which meant they had to find another way to get in and out. One of the guards would have to be eliminated. Except shooting him would draw the others. A knife between the ribs would be much quieter, but for that they would have to get close without being seen, which would be difficult since they'd be out in the open.

"Poison dart?" A few months ago, she'd accompanied Umberto and a small team to one of the local villages and she'd seen a couple of old men hunt with them.

A silent and effective weapon if one knew how to use it. Desperation had her considering every option, no matter how far-fetched.

"We could make the pipe and the dart, but do we have time to hunt around for the right frog to get the poison from?"

No. They would never find one in the dark jungle. "If we waited until daylight…"

"We have to make our move tonight. Zak's hours are numbered. Don Pedro has no reason to keep the kid around. We have to work with the assumption that he'll be executed first thing in the morning."

Couldn't argue with that logic. From what she'd seen of the way Juarez operated, enemies were dealt with swiftly in the jungle. Zak wasn't her favorite person, but she didn't want him dead, and she knew Mitch was set on his course. The breakout had to be tonight. Billy's, too, then, since once Mitch rescued Zak, the camp would be in an uproar. They had to do this together.

She drew a slow breath, trying to get her thoughts in order. She'd never been this frazzled on a mission before. She'd never worked with stakes this high. This was personal. Her brother's life was on the line.

Focus. She'd never had to remind herself to do that before. But now distractions surrounded her. Thoughts of her brother. Mitch's presence. Yet she appreciated that Mitch was with her more and more with every passing minute.

He really did make a good partner. He made a fabulous lover, too, but she didn't want to think about that just now. Someday, when they were all safely away from here, maybe they would talk about what was going on between them. It felt like something.

Especially when he caught her hand and held it gently. "Promise me one thing."

She raised an eyebrow. If he wanted her to stay behind and provide cover… No way. Billy was in there. She was going in.

"Promise me you won't get hurt," he said instead.

He cared. Her heart melted a little.

She cared about him, too. More than she would ever admit. That was a straight highway to heartache. They might never see each other again once their missions here were over. "I'll try my best," she whispered. "If you do the same."

She wanted to kiss him. Instead, she pulled her hand from his and refocused on the task. She stared at the back wall of the house, as if looking at it long enough would enable her to see through it.

"Look up," he whispered into her ear after a minute, his warm breath tickling her skin.

She did. A kapok tree stood near them with a bunch of lianas, jungle vines, hanging in every direction.

Her brain caught up with his in half a second. "You think we can Tarzan it?"

He grinned and they crawled backward, straightening only when they reached the taller bushes that surrounded the kapok. Then he gave her a boost up the tree.

Climbing in the dark wasn't the easiest thing she'd ever done. She did her best to watch out for tarantulas and snakes, hoping their luck held out a little longer. She bit her lip when her foot slipped. But Mitch braced her bottom and she didn't fall. She ignored the tingles his touch sent through her and got back to business, balancing on a side branch when she reached the right height.

Mitch inched out onto the tree limb behind her and began testing lianas that hung from above. He picked one that didn't reach all the way to the ground but was long enough to reach the roof. "What do you think?"

When she nodded, he tested the thing, putting his weight on it little by little. It held.

She moved forward to add her weight, but he held her back.

"We're not going together."

Of course not—he wanted to go first. She glared at him in the dark but didn't say anything. They both had a thing for protecting others. She got it.

He kissed her, hot and hard, before he swung, leaving her startled and swooning. She barely heard him land lightly on the roof.

The guard didn't even look up.

Mitch tossed the liana back.

She grabbed it and swung without hesitation. He caught her silently and lowered her onto the roof. Held her for a second as the liana swung back to the tree. They couldn't tie it to the roof for their exit. The guard could look up at the sky at any time, see it and realize that something was amiss.

They stood still for a second, pressed against each other. Awareness buzzed along her nerve endings. She wanted a kiss. From the look in his eyes, so did he.

They had a lot to do first. She slipped to her feet and inched away from him, careful not to make any noise. They kept low as they moved along the roof, looking for a way in. The balcony in the front, she thought, just as Mitch turned to head that way.

The compound had quieted by this point. Even the cantina, which they could see from up here, looked deserted. Strings of lights lit up the main walkways, the bare bulbs surrounded by clouds of bugs. Some of the generators had been turned off as people had gone to bed, so the constant hum was quieter than it had been earlier, but it was still loud enough to drown out most of the jungle noises. Outside the compound, the woods were dark and ominous. Predators hunted in the night, sneaking around with deadly intent, just as she and Mitch were doing.

They stopped once the balcony was directly below them. The windows were dark. This time, she went first. He held her hands and lowered her until her feet touched the railing. She made her way down from there on her own. He followed her, swiftly and silently.

The balcony door stood open, allowing them entry to a room with a large table and a couple of ostentatious, overstuffed couches. They moved quickly, keeping to the shadows with their backs to the wall.

The door at the other end of the room was locked, but between the two of them they solved that problem in a minute. The hallway outside led in two directions, with a steep set of curving stairs to the right. The lights were on here. They communicated with hand signals, then moved toward the stairs.

She'd expected to see guards in the house, but didn't. She snuck downstairs first, while Mitch covered her from above. Then she covered him while he caught up with her. They crossed the waiting area at the foot of the stairs. Saw the shadow of the guard outside through the glass in the front door and took care not to make a sound.

The first room they came across was Don Pedro's private kitchen. He ate better fare than his men, judging by the stocked shelves. Mitch pilfered a few cans as he passed through. They would come in handy on their way out of the jungle.

Down the hall, the sound of snoring came from behind closed doors. The house servants most likely, or Don Pedro's personal bodyguards who were housed in the main building with him. It looked like they weren't required to stand guard at night.

They left that room alone. The next door revealed a bathroom. Now *that* was luxury in a place like this.

The only door left stood at the end of the corridor. A solid wood door that looked at least three inches thick, with a good lock. They had to spend more time on that than on any of the other locks they'd come across so far. When they were done, they opened the door, which revealed a staircase in front of them that led down into darkness.

They had no way to tell whether a guard was on duty with the prisoners. Once Mitch closed the door behind them, they could see little, so they silently took each step with care, pausing at the bottom of the stairs.

Something moved in the back of the room. They froze, aiming their weapons blindly.

"Is Roberto down here?" she asked in Spanish, as she pushed Mitch behind the cover of the staircase. She could protect him, too. If a guard slept down here, she would just pretend that she was looking for someone named Roberto, in hopes of a quick roll in the hay. "He said he was coming up to the house."

Roberto was a common name. And even if there wasn't one among the house guards and servants, whoever was down here couldn't know if there wasn't a horny Roberto among the visitors.

"Megan?" Zak's voice came out of the darkness, somewhere to her left, the single word mumbled. His jaw must hurt like hell.

"Sis?" another voice asked.

Billy.

She stumbled blindly forward, her heart beating out an erratic rhythm in her throat as she fumbled to light a match. She had to try three times before she managed.

"Anyone else down here?" She peered into the darkness, saw a hole in the wall and headed that way.

A cell. They'd kept him in a dank cell all this time. Part of her rejoiced over finding Billy, while another part was furious at the bastards who'd treated her brother like this.

"Just me and another guy. He's hurt. Is that really you?" Billy's voice came from the hole.

Mitch lit a match, too. They didn't dare risk turning on the lights. The guards outside would see it through the small windows.

A hairy face appeared in the hole in the wall. She recognized the eyes first. She stuck her hand in without hesitation, and the next second her fingertips were touching Billy's. A tremor ran through her, tears burning her eyes.

Her brother was alive. He was here. Sure she'd believed in that for the past year, but blind faith and physi-

cal proof weren't one and the same. Her throat tightened.
A long second passed before she could talk again.

"I'm taking you home. Hang in there. Are you okay?"

"Meg." Regret mixed with excitement in her brother's voice. "It's too dangerous. You shouldn't have come." A deep, shuddering breath. "Oh, man. I can't believe you're here. I figured everyone would assume I was dead by now."

She wanted to lean her forehead against the wall and cry. But they didn't have time for such luxuries.

"Let me see the door." She let his fingertips go with reluctance and moved along the wall toward the door. Then she lit another match.

"Don't touch it. The alarm goes off if I so much as lean against the damn thing."

"Mine, too," Zak said from the other side of the basement, pushing the words out with effort. He needed medical care for that jaw as soon as possible.

She examined the wiring of the alarm. What the hell? Now she knew why Don Pedro didn't think a guard was necessary down here.

She could hear Mitch swearing under his breath as he checked Zak's door, but her full attention was on her brother. The alarm system was some sort of a homemade job, with no logic to it whatsoever. Wires, wires and more wires, all in a jumble. Her experience would mean little here. This would take more than a few minutes, maybe more than a few hours.

"I'm not giving up now," she promised Billy, racking her brain for a solution.

"Who else is with you?"

She didn't like how weak his voice was. "A friend."

"Just one?"

How to explain Mitch? "He's like Jamie."

"He's got no legs?"

"Funny to the last," she murmured, barely able to understand how Billy could still joke after what he must have endured during the past year here. Then again, he probably wouldn't have survived if he'd lost his sense of humor.

"It's too late, sis," he whispered through the door.

Like hell it was. "I'm here to rescue you now," she promised. "Don't you worry about anything."

Mitch came over. "Can't do a damn thing about that alarm. Everything okay here?"

"We'll figure it out. How is Zak?"

"He'll make it. I think we're going to have to blow our way out."

Having her brother within arm's reach at last, she was so overwhelmed she could barely think. "What are you talking about?"

"You can't get into their explosives stash." That came from Billy. "They guard it 24/7. I got that far before. They caught me when I tried to steal some of the good stuff to blow the compound up as a parting gift."

Knowing that he'd actually gotten out and had been captured again twisted Megan's heart. This time, the escape would be final. She thought of the trapdoor to the crawl space below Don Pedro's explosive storage.

"We've got our own VIP entrance. Don't you worry." She reached in through the hole again and squeezed Billy's hand before she turned to leave. Time was of the essence. In less than two hours it would be morning. Don Pedro's men would be waking up and going about their business, making sneaking around a lot more difficult. Not to mention that they would be coming for Zak in short order.

The four of them better be gone long before that.

"All we have to do," she thought out loud, organizing the action, "is sneak out unseen, steal an armful of explosives, then sneak back in. We'll blow out the cell doors, then blow a hole in the back wall that's closest to the jungle. We'll be gone before the dust settles."

"Piece of cake," Mitch said with a chuckle.

The basement was too dark for her to see his face, but she was sure there would be a glint in his eyes. The man wasn't scared of anything.

"No," Billy said from behind the wall, putting force into his voice. "You sneak out, get away from this place and don't come back here. Meg? Please."

"I'm not leaving without you." She'd come here for him. She'd planned this moment for over a year, went to bed and woke up in the morning thinking about how she could do it.

"I've been in this tiny cell for too long. I'm sick, sis. I'm weak. I can't make it out of the jungle."

She didn't want to hear it. "Then we'll carry you on our backs."

Mitch checked the basement walls with the help of another match, looking for a good spot to put the charges. She trusted him to get it right.

"I don't want you to get hurt because of me." Billy's voice filled with frustration. "Meg—"

"I'm taking you with me." They were not going to have a discussion over this. No way.

"What's left of me... I'll be no use to anyone ever again, sis. There's no point."

"I'll be the judge of that." She knew this mood, the dark heaviness that came through Billy's voice. Jamie had sounded the same the last time she'd seen him. Well, she wasn't going to let either of her brothers go out like that. They might have given up, but she was still fighting. "You just get ready."

"Meg—"

"Don't be stupid. I didn't come all this way to leave you here."

It was just like Billy to argue about his own rescue. He'd been always like that. Headstrong. Never willing to take anything at face value, never accepting her advice just because she was oldest and knew better.

"You know how much I hate it when people fight me when I'm doing something for their own good." She tried to lighten the mood. They could all use a little of that.

He gave a sour laugh. "God, it's good to see you again. I didn't think I'd get the chance. I'm grateful for that, sis. More grateful than I can ever say."

"You two can do the family thing once we get out of here." Mitch grabbed her by the elbow and tugged her toward the staircase. "Time is running out here."

"Don't waste any of it on me." Billy stayed stubborn. "If you want to get something out, get out Don Pedro's game book. It's worth a hell of lot more than I am."

"What game book?" Mitch slowed and turned.

"He's got a book where he keeps track of all his passwords to his online accounts, the location of his goods, that kind of thing. He's got a laptop, too, but he's paranoid about somebody hacking it. He keeps the most important information on paper. I overheard one of the guards talking about it a couple of months ago."

Billy coughed, and she didn't like the sound of it. But before she could ask if he was all right, he continued. "It's in his office. In his safe."

"I'll try," Mitch said. "We'll be back in half an hour. Be ready," he added.

"Does it have to be explosives?" Zak protested, but his jaw kept him from getting too loud. "What if you make a mistake and kill me?" He kept on going despite the pain each word must have caused him. "My father is rich. I can negotiate with people here. They won't turn down a bag of money."

Mitch ignored the kid and walked away, muttering something under his breath that sounded like, "Too bad money can't buy brains."

They needed half an hour to get the explosives and get back into the building. Possibly another half an hour to set everything up. Safe and effective demolition took a lot of careful prep work. It was right on the top of the list of things that didn't pay to do in a hurry.

They'd be cutting it pretty close, Megan thought as she followed Mitch up the stairs. She hoped Don Pedro's men weren't early risers.

Chapter Twelve

Mitch stopped at the top of the basement stairs and ran through their options. His original exit plan had been to grab Zak and Billy, then shoot their way out through the front door. The jungle was just steps away behind the house. They could sprint along the fence to the hole he'd found earlier and disappear before most of the drunken camp woke up, got dressed, grabbed their guns and came around to see what all the noise was about.

Except he didn't have Zak and Billy as he'd planned. They had to come back for those two, so they couldn't make any noise on their way out, couldn't be discovered.

"Back to the roof," he whispered to Megan. The liana was gone, so they couldn't leave the way they'd come, but another plan began forming in his brain.

They snuck down the hall, a pair of moving shadows stealing up the main stairs. But when they reached the top floor, he didn't head for the balcony or the nearest window.

The game book wasn't part of his mission, but he was here, steps from it. Wouldn't have made any sense leaving it behind. He'd lost too many good friends to people like Don Pedro. If he could take one crime lord down, he was more than willing to go a few steps out of his way to do it.

Megan followed without asking any questions. She'd probably guessed what he was doing, had probably been planning on doing the same thing. Their minds worked the same way in certain regards. It made them a good team.

He could see five doors on this level. One was to the living room with the balcony where they'd come in. One of the other four had to lead to the study. He was holding his knife instead of his gun. If he needed to take anyone out, he'd do it silently.

He tried one door and Megan tried another. They silently opened them just enough to see inside. Enough moonlight came in through the windows to see the basics.

A bathroom. He glanced back at Megan and shook his head. She shook her head back at him.

They crept forward.

He put his hand on the next doorknob, heard a snort from inside. A bed squeaked as whoever occupied it turned. Don Pedro, probably. He tried the knob. Locked.

Mitch looked at the last door, the only one they hadn't checked. It had a keypad entry. This one was a professional job, standard security. Don Pedro had been willing to spend money here, unlike on the rigged-up job on the basement prison. Ironically, that was the door's weakness. Mitch knew just about every standard security unit inside out. Outsmarting this one only took a few minutes.

Then he and Megan slipped into the office together.

He closed the door behind them and scanned the room in the moonlight. "Where's the safe?"

The desk was a plain top with four legs. No drawers. The few shelves in the room mostly held guns. There weren't any pictures on the wall to hide a wall safe. He circled the room along the wall anyway, looking for any irregularities.

Nothing.

"The floor," Megan said and flipped over the carpet.

Nothing there, either.

Maybe Billy didn't have the right information.

None of the furniture in the room looked large enough to hide a safe. Nothing on the wall or floor indicated a hiding spot.

"The bookcase." Megan strode that way.

He helped her push the carved-wood bookcase aside, along with the small rug it had sat on. And there was the safe: an old, manual one, not electric, built into the floor. Don Pedro probably wanted to make sure he could get to the contents even if the generator went out. Good thinking.

All they had to do was guess the numbers and dial them. Mitch could take an electric keypad apart and figure it out in minutes. Very rarely had he seen an old-school strongbox like this before. On the two occasions he had, he'd blown off the door to get to the contents. That wasn't an option here.

"Any chance the CIA offers a safecracking class?" He looked at Megan.

She gave him a mysterious smile, lay on the floor and flattened her ear against the lock, then began to turn the dial slowly.

She was very handy on a mission, he had to give her that. She did a great job and looked good doing it. His gaze hesitated for a second on the way the moonlight outlined her curves.

She worked the lock while he moved back to the door to stand watch. Then finally she opened the safe, took out what looked like a ledger book and slipped it under her tank top where the elastic of the material kept it in place.

"Here." He helped her put the bookcase back in its place, then they were out of there.

He grabbed a granite statue on the way out, the bust of a famous South American revolutionary.

She tossed him a curious look.

He just flashed her a smile, then headed for the room with the balcony.

They made it up to the roof without trouble. At the back of the building, Mitch aligned himself with the guard below. Held out the bust. Dropped it.

At the exact time when the heavy bust cracked the man's skull, Mitch let out a monkey screech to mask the noise. Then another to mask the sound of the guard folding to the ground.

He lowered himself down the side of the building, using window frames for support and jumping the last eight feet. He knew how to jump silently. Megan probably did, too, but he caught her anyway, just for the pleasure of being able to hold her in his arms.

Then they melted into the bushes together and headed for the building that held the explosives.

"I can't believe we have to go back in there again." She shuddered when they were at the hole that allowed entrance into the crawl space, a creepy, yawning mouth of darkness. No matter. He'd been in worse spots. "I'll go. You stay here and stand guard."

Her spine stiffened immediately. "I'm coming with you. You might need help in there."

He shook his head. "You always want to help everyone, but you don't want to take help from anyone. Is that an oldest-sibling thing?"

She brushed by him so she'd be first in. "I don't know what you're talking about. I'm not like those helpless women you're used to, and if it makes you uncomfortable, I'm sorry."

He grinned as he followed her.

Other than *hot* and *trouble, helpless* and *clueless* had been the first two words that had sprung to mind when he'd first laid eyes on Megan Cassidy. About the last two adjectives, he'd been severely mistaken. About the first two, he'd been right on the money.

A low hiss cut through the quiet, freezing his limbs and sharply refocusing his thoughts. *Snake.*

He pulled his knife out inch by inch, avoiding any sudden moves. "Megan?"

"I've been bitten."

His breath hitched. He heard the sound of snake scales brushing against his boot, sliced down and hit flesh. He dropped the knife to light a match to see the damage. He'd cut the snake in half, but it was still trying to bite his boot. He speared the head with his knife, careful not to go too far and skewer his own toes.

The match went out. He lit another. Now that the damned snake wasn't moving, he could examine the markings.

"It's not poisonous." His heart began to beat again.

"It sure stings." She rubbed the side of her left hand against her leg.

"The bite is swelling."

Some antibiotic cream and allergy medication would be good, but their supplies were in their backpacks, at the barracks assigned to Juarez's men. They couldn't go back there. Their gear had to stay where it was.

No one would notice that the two of them were missing until morning. The men probably figured they were having some private fun in an out-of-the-way place. But if someone got up in the night and saw their gear missing, he would want to know where they'd been.

Mitch had his most important possessions on his body: his gun and ammo, his knife and his canteen. He crawled another few feet, then stopped. They had to be under the trapdoor. He reached up and brushed his hand against the wood planks, brushing off a couple of slimy slugs carefully so they wouldn't land on his head. A plank moved. There. The door.

He got in position and slowly pushed up the square piece of wood. "Stay here," he whispered. "Hold the bag. I'll hand down what we need."

At least she didn't argue about that.

He pulled himself up without a sound, crouched and listened. Couldn't hear anything, not even snoring. The light was on out in the main room of the building, a slim line of it coming through under the door. It wasn't really enough, but he didn't dare light a match in here, so he searched by feel, first looking for the right kind of boxes, then opening them and reaching inside. He handed down several sticks of dynamite before the eerie silence began to bother him, prickling his instincts.

He glanced at the door. Inched closer to it, pushing it lightly. What he saw stopped him dead in his tracks.

Somebody was lying against the door. Mitch couldn't hear the man breathing—he held his own breath to make sure he would catch the slightest sound. He pushed the door a little wider. The man fell over with a soft thud into a pool of dark red liquid.

The single lightbulb that hung from the middle of the ceiling revealed another man on the floor near the table, lying at an unnatural angle. Other than that, the room was empty.

Mitch pulled back into the explosives room. "Come up here."

She handed him the bag first. "What's wrong?" She worked herself up, despite the fact that her left hand was now significantly swollen.

A good reminder that time was of the essence. "There are two men in here with their throats cut. I don't like it."

Then she was finally up and taking in the bloody scene. "Cristobal really is making his move tonight."

"Somebody is doing something." He let his brain work on that while he looked through the stash of explosives.

Now that he had enough light, he could see that about half the boxes were empty; half held dynamite and a small special case hid plastic explosives. Disappointingly little, but he grabbed what was there. He shoved what he needed into the duffel bag he'd stolen earlier then swung it over his shoulder and moved through the main room, grabbing whatever else he could find that would be useful on their way home: an extra knife and gun for Billy, food, a bottle of tequila, more matches, a flashlight.

He handed the alcohol to Megan, who sloshed some over her hand, disinfecting the puncture wound. It had to burn like hell, but she didn't even flinch. The alcohol would kill the germs and prevent infection. But she also needed something to counteract the allergic reaction she was having. Except there wasn't anything like that within easy reach. She would have to wait until they were in the jungle.

He reached the front door in a few more steps, turned off the light then opened the door an inch. He didn't see anyone out there. Might as well leave this way instead of through the crawl space again. In case the snake had family.

They made it out unseen and rounded the building, keeping close to the walls and moving to the back so they'd be out of sight of whatever murderers roamed the compound tonight. When he looked back at Megan, he caught her flexing her left hand. The whole arm looked stiff.

They'd better hurry.

They moved forward carefully, watching every bush, every shadow, every stack of firewood to make sure nobody was lying in wait. But they didn't run into any resistance. The first man they saw was the guard in front of the don's house, which was now completely dark. The guard now sat with his back to the wall, his head hanging back. He looked like he was sleeping. Only when they got close enough could they see the moon-light glinting off the blood at his cut throat.

The enemy was inside.

Megan looked at Mitch, her eyes wide. He swore under his breath.

All right. There was still a chance they could do this. As long as they were alive, they had a chance, he thought, following Megan as she moved toward the main door, which stood slightly ajar.

Cristobal's men would be upstairs. Their goal would be the don's bedroom and office, Mitch reasoned. The path to the basement might still be clear.

He didn't get his wish.

Two men stood in the entry hall, guarding the bottom of the stairs. And just like that, the stealth portion of the mission was over. Mitch and Megan exchanged a glance.

He took the one to the left; Megan took the one on the right. One shot each to the head. Then they ran for the basement, locking the door behind them.

They heard boots slamming on the floor. Shouting. Men headed for the front door. Cristobal's men must have thought the shooters had pulled back outside. Good.

Mitch ignored the ruckus, and stuck enough plastic explosives on the lock on Zak's cell to blow it. "Stand back."

Bang. The alarm didn't go off. Cristobal's men had probably cut the generator cords. He hadn't wanted to do that earlier, knowing the lights going out all of a sudden would alert the guards. But Cristobal had enough men to take out the guards before making his move on the house.

"You grab the kid," he told Megan, and went for Billy.

He used the other half of what little plastic he'd found to blow the lock. *Bang.* The explosion busted the lock, all right, but the bottom of the metal door got twisted and stuck in the opening.

They had no time for this, dammit. Mitch kicked the door in. "Come on."

But Billy didn't move.

"Let's go." Mitch turned on the flashlight he'd requisitioned.

Billy sat on a blanket on the floor. His clothes had half rotted off him; his hair was matted to his head. His eyes were sunken and red-rimmed. "Malaria," he said with a shrug. "I told her not to come back. Don't waste time on me. You got the boss's book?"

Mitch nodded, trying to process what he saw. His heart sank.

Confirmation that they had the book put a little light back into Billy's eyes, even as more boots slammed upstairs. The house had to be full of Cristobal's men by now. And because of the explosions, they would know that something was going on in the basement.

Mitch glanced at the wall at the back of Billy's cell and placed the dynamite strategically at the bottom of the wall, hooking together the fuses, which were in sorry shape. They did have a rat problem in the compound. He twisted and tied together the frayed chunks as best as he could.

"Zak is ready at the bottom of the stairs." Megan was

pushing into the cell. "Oh, God. Billy." She rushed to her brother's side.

"Take him out of here," Mitch ordered.

Megan was already pulling her brother up. She supported his weight, which couldn't have been much, and dragged him toward the door, her face set in a mask of hard resolve.

"Told you not to come back for me, sis. You never listen."

"There's a chopper on the roof. I'll get you home. They'll fix you up at the hospital."

Mitch whipped his head around to stare at Megan. She could fly a chopper? *Hot.* He grinned. It sure would make their way out of here easier.

"I'm too far gone," Billy said.

She ignored that and led him behind one of the cement pillars.

Mitch lit the fuse, then ran to join them. Zak was safe at the stairs. "Heads down!"

The fire raced about halfway up the fuse, then went out. Damn the rats.

He ran forward, lit another match and tried again.

Again, the fire went out before it reached its target.

Cristobal's men were banging on the basement door, trying to break it down. Gunfire sounded above. That would take care of the lock in short order.

An explosion many times bigger than what Mitch had been able to achieve with the plastic shook the building from above, nearly knocking them off their feet.

"I'm guessing that would be the chopper," Billy said,

his tone resigned. "Give me that." He snatched the box of matches out of Mitch's hand and limped forward.

"Billy, no." Megan moved after him.

Billy motioned her back. "You keep back. I know what I'm doing."

There was something in his eyes that made Mitch grab for Megan and yank her back. He wouldn't let her go.

"Fuse's worthless," Billy said as soon as he was close enough to see. He turned back, his gaze settling on Megan. "You get home safely. Tell Mom I love her. Amy, too. If things had gone differently...I wanted to marry her."

"Billy!" Megan lunged forward, nearly tearing Mitch's arm from its socket, but he held her tight.

Then Billy held the match to the end of one of the dynamite sticks directly. "I always hated the thought of dying slowly in a place like this."

Mitch threw himself on Megan, who fought him like crazy.

"I'd much rather die like a man," Billy told them.

And then the dynamite blew.

Megan screamed, a heartrending sound Mitch knew he wasn't going to forget as long as he lived.

The wall opened up, and Mitch could hear chunks of cement tumbling, although he could see little in the dust. He waited long enough to make sure more wouldn't fall on their heads, then grabbed Megan and Zak, pulling them both through the opening as the basement door burst open somewhere behind them. Bullets chased them all the way to the bushes.

They were all coughing, their eyes and throats filled with dust.

"To the hole in the fence." Mitch pointed the way.

Zak broke away and darted forward, saving his own skin. Megan pulled back. Mitch wouldn't let her go, but dragged her resolutely forward as bullets flew around them. He used his free hand to lay down some cover, shooting back.

The building behind them was engulfed in flames. The exploding chopper had shaved off the top floor. Mitch's dynamite had taken out a good chunk of the basement. The place looked ready to collapse any second.

Megan beat on his back, screaming, "I can't leave him!"

"He's dead."

"I can't," she sobbed.

His heart broke for her, but he couldn't stop to comfort her. He broke into a run, dragging her along without giving her a chance to escape.

"He died so we could make it out of there. If you go back and they kill you, too, his sacrifice will have meant nothing," he said when they were through the hole and far enough that they could slow to catch their breaths.

Her eyes were glazed. She looked at him, but she didn't look like she'd heard what he said.

He stopped and shook her gently. "Once in your life, accept help! He wanted to do what he did. He was too far gone. He would have never made it out of the jungle. He gave us Don Pedro's book and our lives. His death meant something."

She went still then, at last. Nodded. He no longer

had to hold her to keep her with him. When he started out again, she followed.

"I *will* bring these people down one day," she promised him as she wiped mud off her face, the mixture of dust and her tears.

He could hear Zak a dozen feet ahead, thrashing through the undergrowth.

Shots cut through the night. They were being followed.

Mitch shot a few rounds back that way as he broke into a run, with Megan close behind him.

HER HEART WAS BROKEN. She felt as if a black hole had sucked her in. She functioned on reflex, but her mind was a wasteland of grief.

Men were still chasing them. That made no sense. Zak had meant something to Don Pedro, but he meant nothing to Cristobal. Why would he waste men, sending them after Don Pedro's no-consequence prisoner?

"Why don't they quit?" she asked Mitch, who was half dragging Zak through the jungle. They'd caught up with him once his first burst of energy had run out.

"They must think we have something they want."

"Drugs?"

"I don't think so. There must be hundreds of pounds of that at the compound. They wouldn't risk life and limb in the jungle at night for another couple of bagfuls. They know we're on foot and can't carry much. I don't think it's the don's game book. How would Cristobal's men know we took it?"

"Then what?" She tried to see where she stepped, which was a hopeless business.

"What's the most important thing to Cristobal?"

"Power?"

"He wanted Don Pedro gone," Mitch agreed. "What if the don wasn't in his room when they went for him?"

"Like he knew something was up and took off?"

"And Cristobal's men think he's with us." They had been following an animal path, but now Mitch darted into the thick of the jungle. He held out a hand for them to stop and get down behind him.

"Let them get ahead of us," he whispered. "We'll take them out from behind. Better us chasing them than them chasing us."

He wanted the power position. She agreed. But her mind was still back at Don Pedro's place.

"We made a lot of noise. We broke out. They put two and two together," she whispered as she put it all together herself, at last. It all made some very discouraging sense. "Why can't they let the don go? They've probably killed most of his men by now. They have his compound."

"Someone like Don Pedro could have other strongholds, other men. He rules a small army, scattered around the jungle, protecting his various businesses. Whoever wants to supplant him can't afford to let the man reach his support base."

A group of men ran past them down the path. Mitch waited a minute before he got up to go after them. Megan and Zak followed, trudging back onto the path that promised easier going. Only then did they realize that a second part of the group had lagged behind. There were bad guys ahead of them and bad guys behind them. Mitch, Zak and Megan were sandwiched in the middle.

Part of her wanted to stop and stand her ground. Wanted to take the bastards out. She didn't care if she died here, too. Just now, she didn't care about anything.

Except then her mother would have to deal with the loss of two children. And her brothers would get it in their thick heads that they had to get revenge for her and Billy. And the last thing she wanted was to put any other member of her family in danger.

"Megan," Mitch whispered. "I know you're hurting, honey, but I need you to step out of it and commit to survival."

Honey?

"You're going to make it out of the jungle. You're going to survive this for Billy. I'm going to help you, and you're going to let me." He stepped closer to her, pressing his back to hers. "I take the back, you take the front." He even handed a gun to Zak, who was pulling off the path, looking ready to run away. "You help Megan."

She set her feet slightly apart and braced her back against Mitch's. "All right."

Flashlights panned the jungle behind them; she could see their beams from her peripheral vision, but she kept her gaze forward. She had to be ready to shoot at the first group once Mitch opened fire on the ones behind them.

The men shot first, and Mitch responded. Nearly every one of his bullets found their targets, judging by the shouts of pain that erupted in the night. The first group quickly turned around and backtracked, shooting at anything and everything. Zak panicked and returned fire long before they came into sight.

"Don't waste bullets!" Megan called to him, but he couldn't hear her in the din.

Megan held her fire until the men were within reach, until she knew she could do the most damage. Here they came. She squeezed the trigger over and over again.

The enemy fell.

She was numb, her finger fused to the trigger. Many died, but the ones left kept coming. They were close now. Really close.

Close enough to throw a hand grenade, she realized as a flash and a bang blinded and deafened her, and the force of the explosion knocked her to the ground.

Chapter Thirteen

The grenade almost shook Mitch off his feet. He saw Megan go down and grabbed for her. Zak dove for the bushes, spraying everything behind him with bullets.

Their enemies had expected a lull in return fire after the grenade exploded, so they'd all come up from cover. Zak's wild spray of bullets had everyone scrambling back, which gave Mitch enough time to grab Megan and duck behind some trees.

Zak was still shooting. Panic had probably locked his muscles. Mitch joined in, firing at Cristobal's men until Megan had recovered enough to continue. And then they were off, on the move again through the thick of the jungle, where every step could be fatal.

Megan led, with Zak in the middle and Mitch bringing up the rear. They were all exhausted and injured to varying degrees. The wound on Mitch's leg that Megan had bandaged up ages ago didn't hurt too badly, but it did slow him down a little. And that was more than he could afford.

Zak was running out of steam fast. He wasn't used to this pace, and his broken jaw was clearly making him miserable. But of their combined injuries, Megan's snake-bitten hand bothered Mitch the most. The whole arm was swollen now, up to her shoulder. He'd seen it when the grenade had flashed.

He needed to find a native plant the forest people called corsh to make a poultice for her. The sap of the low-growing leafy weed helped allergic reactions and even neutralized mild poisons. If only they could stop. If only he could use the flashlight in his backpack to make the search easier. But he didn't dare use it. Light would give away their position.

THE FINAL BATTLE CAME at dawn. Everyone could see at last and that lifted their confidence. Both sides wanted to end the chase. Rapid fire was interspersed with short breaks while weapons were reloaded and men searched for better cover.

Some larger rocks, or any kind of cover, would have been nice to protect them as they made their last stand, Mitch thought as he shot back and moved forward to look for a sustainable position. He burst out of the woods one step behind Megan, but slowed as he took in the cliff in front of them. The drop to the bottom measured at least a hundred yards, and the other side of the gorge was about thirty yards away.

Not a distance they could tackle in one leap.

A kapok tree had fallen across the canyon, or perhaps it had been cut that way on purpose to serve as a bridge. But that must have been a long time ago. Weather had rotted the wood. When Mitch kicked it, the spongy consistency didn't fill him with optimism.

The underside of the trunk that rested against the cliff had been hollowed by jungle critters or the elements, further weakening the structure, he realized as he looked more carefully.

He turned to the others. "We can't cross here."

"Now what?" Zak mumbled through his broken jaw, his eyes wide with fear. "We're gonna die in this stupid jungle, aren't we?"

"We'll have to make our last stand here." Cover or no cover. Their luck had run out.

Megan scanned the area, a grim expression on her face. She'd barely spoken since they'd left the compound. Her heart was broken, a dangerous condition for a soldier in battle. Her pain ripped through Mitch's gut. He wanted to talk to her, wanted to console her. But that would have to wait a little longer. Right now, they couldn't afford to take a single second to think about anything else but the fight. Cristobal's men had fallen back, but they weren't far behind.

Mitch examined the terrain. If they couldn't find cover, some high ground would do, but there wasn't any of that, either. Except...

"Can you climb?" he asked the kid.

Zak shook his head, looking ready to drop from exhaustion. He was out of bullets, too. The kid wouldn't be much help. Mitch had to get him out of harm's way.

"Get into the hollow of this tree." Mitch bent and checked it for dangerous critters. They didn't need another snakebite.

Zak glanced at the space—large enough for him to hide in if he curled into the fetal position, which he did. "Can you see me?"

"You'll be fine as long as you keep quiet."

"Where do you want me?" Megan asked, leading the charge.

He hated to see her this dispirited. "We'll be up in the trees."

She immediately scanned the tallest ones and picked one for herself. He wished they could go up together so he could help her climb, but they'd be better off dividing the enemy. So he headed toward a tree several yards away. If all went well, the enemy would enter the clearing right between them.

Lianas helped his climb; a couple of nasty snakes slowed it. He dropped them onto the trail below. With luck, they'd bite one of Cristobal's lackeys. He picked his position carefully, in the fork of a branch that provided protection from two sides. He hoped Megan had done the same. He could no longer see her. She'd done a good job of hiding in the foliage.

Megan was falling apart on the inside, but on the outside she was still a top-notch operator, taking care of business. Even seasoned soldiers couldn't always pull that off. His respect wasn't easily earned, but Megan had earned that, and more. She had his loyalty. He would see her out of here in one piece or die trying.

He'd do the same for Zak. He'd done it for all the other men he'd rescued out of hot spots before, men whose lives had been put into his hands. Yet his devotion to Megan went deeper, to a level he wasn't altogether comfortable with.

If they survived the day, they were going to have to talk about where they stood. He wasn't sure if he should be pleased or scared. All he knew was that his insides were tied up in knots every time he thought about any harm coming to her.

Endless minutes ticked by. Then the noises of the jungle changed suddenly. Birdcalls turned shrill and warned of new danger. People were coming.

For a second, Megan pulled from cover, making her face visible to him, but not to anyone below. They didn't say anything. Her beautiful face looked tough yet vulnerable.

He was falling in love with her.

And then one of Cristobal's men came into view. Mitch aimed, fired and took him out. Judging from the way the bushes moved and the force of the returning fire, there were at least twenty others behind him.

How in the hell? Cristobal must have sent fresh men in the night who'd followed the sound of gunfire and had caught up.

Twenty against two.

Those weren't the best odds, but Mitch was who he was, and Megan was who she was, and they made a hell of a team.

He neutralized two more men before a bullet nicked his heel. Good thing he wasn't Achilles. Aside from the burning pain, the injury didn't much interfere with the business of taking these goons out.

Megan got her men, one by one, with enviable precision. Each shot was a kill. Her brother was not forgotten, nor would he ever be. She was fueled in equal parts by stone-cold professionalism and red-hot revenge, a deadly combination.

The enemy saw the danger, too, and blanketed her position with fire.

If she was hit, she didn't cry out.

He tried to see how many men were left down below. They'd gotten a bunch of them, but there were still a dozen men shooting from behind cover. They had limitless ammunition and plenty of practice at shooting monkeys out of trees. The branches around Mitch were riddled with bullets. He figured Megan's hiding spot had to look the same.

One of the men below them was going to get lucky sooner or later. The only way to survive a battle against these odds was to finish it quickly.

A bullet grazed his knee. It got just close enough to rip his pants and take off some skin. Mitch took out the shooter, and the man next to him. That one had a radio clipped to his belt. Good, now the bastard wasn't going anywhere with it. They were going to need that later.

He kept on shooting at every leaf that moved. Megan didn't take a break, either. Then more bullets flew at them, and the next thing he knew, she was falling out of the tree.

His heart stopped. The ground was too far away, the fall unsurvivable.

"Megan!"

Somehow she caught herself on a branch, her boot wedged between two tree limbs. She hung upside down, gun still in hand, blood covering the side of her neck and face.

He went a little crazy then, sliding down on a liana, not caring that he was falling too fast or that the bark of the plant took the skin off his palm. He squeezed off one bullet after another all the way down, a war cry tearing from his lips.

When his boots touched the ground, he barely felt his busted heel. He plowed forward like a robot, men falling before him. Blood ran on the jungle floor. He, too, was covered in it. This small patch of jungle looked like a slaughterhouse when he was finished.

And all that time, all he could think of was Megan.

The gun had fallen from her hand. She hung listlessly from the branches, held only by her boot. If her small foot slipped from it...

He climbed the tree faster than he'd ever thought possible. "Megan! Megan, honey?"

She shook her head. Focused her eyes. They narrowed immediately as she squeezed off a shot, and when he twisted, he saw a man he'd missed earlier. The last of Cristobal's foot soldiers fell with weapon in hand and a disappointed look on his face.

Then Mitch was there, pulling Megan up and cradling her in his arms. The bullet that had knocked her out of the tree had cracked her collarbone. Mitch found two more bullet holes in her chest. He yanked up her tank top and gave thanks to God. Don Pedro's game book had acted as a bulletproof vest, saving her.

A last gift from Billy, who'd told them about the book in the first place.

"Hang in there." He made a pressure bandage, took both of their belts off and tied her to his back with them, then carried her down the tree.

"Is it over?" Zak stumbled their way to investigate the silence. "I'm hungry." He finally spotted Megan, who'd passed out from blood loss on the way down. "She doesn't look good."

"Shut up and go find the man who had a radio. We

need it," Mitch snarled at him. "And get me a boot. Right foot. About this size." He showed the busted boot on his foot. Blood seeped through the hole.

He ignored that and checked Megan's wound first. The bullet was still lodged inside her, in a way that actually prevented more serious bleeding, so he decided to leave it in. When he got her to a hospital, the doctors could deal with it. And he *would* get her to help.

He grabbed his canteen and washed the blood from her face.

Her eyes fluttered open after a moment. "What happened?"

"You got shot. Stay still." He offered her water, and she drank.

"Is it bad?" Her eyes were glazed with pain.

"Nope. You'll live to boss me around another day. Try to move as little as you can."

He limped off into the undergrowth and didn't come back until he found what he was looking for. Corsh weed for her swollen arm, and some small brown berries that had disinfectant qualities for her brand-new bullet wound.

He treated her injuries, then ripped two strips off the bottom of his T-shirt and bandaged her. Man, he hated to see her in this shape. "I wish we could rest."

She looked offended. "Have you ever seen me take a nap in the middle of the day?"

He smiled at her. He loved her; there was no way around it.

Fat lot of good it did for either of them. The situation was impossible. With the kind of jobs they had, they'd never see each other. But nobody ever said love was convenient. From all accounts, it was a major pain. He felt it.

He looked over at Zak, who was checking the dead. Beyond the jaw that couldn't be helped until they got to a doctor, the kid had no other visible injuries. So Mitch took a few minutes to deal with his own cuts and abrasions, and his heel.

"Need any help?" she offered.

She could be half dead, and she'd still be the one who wanted to take care of everybody.

He shook his head. "Don't worry. I'll live to annoy you another day."

She reached out and took his hand, her amber gaze locking with his. "I'm getting used to it. You're not always that annoying."

He squeezed her fingers. Never wanted to let her go. "I have my good days, huh?"

"Good minutes." A ghost of a smile crossed her face. "Let's not get carried away."

"Why not? I think you should get carried away." He bent over and picked her up. Took a few steps to see if he could walk without putting too much weight on his heel. He set her back down again when Zak returned with an armload of loot.

"You're not carrying me." Her eyes narrowed as she laid down the law.

"You've lost too much blood."

"Are you calling me a wimp?"

Zak dumped his bounty at Mitch's feet: a couple of pieces of beef jerky that the kid looked at mournfully since he couldn't chew, ammunition, a boot that looked like it would fit, a shortwave radio. "The rest of the stuff is covered in blood. I'm not touching it."

"This is more than enough. You did good. Let's get ready to move."

"We have a radio. Call in the cavalry," the kid argued with him, forming the words painfully.

"We have to get to a spot where a chopper can land," Megan educated him.

Mitch turned on the radio, dialed a channel he knew U.S. military in the region monitored then sent a coded message that gave their rough location. He added a special code so the Colonel would be alerted. Then he turned the thing off. No sense in running down the battery.

"I'll be carrying her." He shot Megan a look. "She's got a broken collarbone, and she's lost too much blood."

"I'm hurt, too," the kid protested.

"I'm not carrying you, so you'll just have to live with it. Grab that bag and let's get going."

"My jaw is broken."

"I never said you had to carry the bag with your teeth." Zak was a poster child for tough love. He needed some, and Mitch wasn't about to coddle him. He started out heading northeast along the gorge, looking for a way across.

In the end, they didn't need to cross. They found a flat rock ten miles down the way big enough for a chopper to land. He made another call on the radio and kept transmitting so the rescue team could track the signal to their exact location. Then they had nothing to do but wait.

Dusk was gathering by the time the extraction team

arrived. The sound of the helicopter's rotors reached them from the distance. Mitch tossed some wet leaves on the fire he'd started and sent the thick smoke upward, fanning it with a palm leaf. Soon the chopper came into view above the trees, and he kicked the fire apart so the smoke wouldn't be an impediment to landing.

He didn't know the men who jumped out to help them aboard. They weren't from his team. The colonel must have requested assistance from whatever military unit was close and available.

"Thanks. I appreciate your help." It felt odd to be on the other end of a rescue. He wasn't used to it.

The rescue team knew better than to ask any questions that didn't have to do with their physical well-being.

A medic had ridden along with the chopper. Zak demanded drugs until he was knocked out completely. Megan refused them.

"You need to go to a hospital, ma'am," the medic told her as he left her side to talk to the pilot.

They'd strapped her to a stretcher to keep her broken collarbone from moving. Mitch sat next to her and took her hand.

She closed her eyes. Her face was drawn. He had no trouble guessing the path of her thoughts. She was thinking about Billy. She had sworn not to leave the jungle without him, had planned on him being with her when she headed out of here.

He squeezed her fingers. "Your brother would be proud of you."

"I failed." Even her voice sounded broken.

"Don Pedro's game book has enough intel to clean

up half the jungle. Because of Billy, and because you came for him, you'll set back the drug and gun business at least a decade. This will save thousands of lives. Tens of thousands. This is why Billy took on the job."

She nodded. Then she opened her amber eyes and looked at him. "I love you."

He stared at her as she closed her eyes again. He loved her, too, but he was not the man she needed. He could be lost on any mission, just like her brother. No way would he risk putting her through that pain. He couldn't stand the thought of her suffering like this because of him.

Minutes passed while he looked at her, bewildered. His feelings switched back and forth between elation and despair. By the time he gathered himself, she'd fallen asleep from the combination of blood loss and exhaustion.

She slept the whole three-hour chopper ride to a small rural hospital. Medical personnel were waiting to examine her and Zak. Mitch, too, but since the Colonel was also there waiting for him, he decided he could do the debriefing before they started poking at his heel.

"I'll come back as soon as I can," he told Megan before marching off with the Colonel.

But an hour later, he couldn't find her. The CIA took care of their own, it seemed. They'd sent someone for her, and she'd already been taken away, back to the States.

Chapter Fourteen

Mitch sat in the small apartment he'd rented as a home base in between missions and looked at the printouts of a spacious condo the Realtor had done her best to talk him into buying. He'd gotten the reward money for getting Zak out of the jungle in one piece. The little twerp was fine. And now he was thinking about starting up a business that taught jungle survival.

A nerve jumped in Mitch's eyes every time he thought of the kid.

At first, he'd refused the reward money. Then the Colonel had stepped in and told him he was going to accept it because he had worked for every penny of it, and that was an order.

He didn't want the money. He didn't much want the condo, either. He wanted Megan.

Not searching her out was a daily battle. But in the end, he loved her enough to do what was best for her. He wasn't it.

Hell of a thing. He was pretty sure she was the best thing that could ever happen to him.

Funny how fate could mess up so badly.

Since he'd last seen her, he'd been on another mission and back. His heel was as good as new. His heart was in tatters.

He'd almost messed up this last job. He was losing his focus.

He needed to talk to her, he decided. So he couldn't talk himself out of it again, he grabbed his cell phone and called the Colonel.

"I need a leave of absence, sir. For personal reasons."

"Everything all right?"

"Fine, sir. It's time to visit some old friends. You wouldn't know where Jamie Cassidy hangs out these days?"

"I wasn't aware you two were close friends. You never did an op together."

"No, sir." He wasn't about to elaborate.

A moment of silence passed. "Why don't you come into my office to sign the paperwork for that leave? I'll dig out his file."

"Thank you, sir."

Now he would have to do it. Now he was committed. When he got back from his leave, the Colonel would expect a full report on Jamie and how he was recovering.

Mitch ran his fingers through his hair. If he happened to see Megan while he visited Jamie…

He stood up and headed for the door, caught himself at the last second and glanced down, wincing at the state of his clothing. Brooding home alone all week didn't do much for a person's image. The colonel would chew him out if he saw him like this.

He padded up the stairs. He could afford enough

time for a shower. He added a shave, too. If the Colonel thought something was wrong with him, the man would get on his case and insist on answers. Mitch didn't have any of those.

All he knew was that he was in love with Megan Cassidy and a relationship between them was impossible. A solution was brewing in the back of his head. But it was probably too drastic. He needed to speak to her before he made any big life changes. Leaving the SDDU wasn't a move he entertained lightly. But he would do it for her, if she thought she could accept him.

He reached the base an hour and a half later. The colonel's secretary announced his arrival.

"Colonel." He stopped in his tracks when he realized the Colonel already had a visitor. A man about Mitch's age sat in a wheelchair. He had amber eyes and blondish hair in a familiar shade.

"Jamie Cassidy. Mitch Mendoza." The colonel made the introductions. "Jamie stopped in to discuss something with me this morning. He wanted to see you, too."

They sized each other up. Jamie's handshake had plenty of steel in it.

"You were there when my brother died," he said in a tone void of emotion. But his eyes held tempered steel.

Oh, hell. If Jamie Cassidy blamed him for Billy's death, then Megan probably did, too. "Billy was too far gone to make it out. He died a hero's death."

"That's what my sister says," Jamie allowed, but his countenance didn't soften any.

Mitch's heart drummed faster. "Is she here?"

The colonel answered that. "She's in the next room, going over your report of the op to see if she can add anything. I asked for her help. The materials you two brought back are of some significance. Further ops are being planned."

The words *I want in* were on the tip of Mitch's tongue, but he couldn't say them, not until he talked to Megan, not until his future was decided.

"Sir?" He glanced toward the door.

The colonel nodded. "Go ahead, soldier."

Jamie scowled at him. He wasn't as sure about what had gone down at Don Pedro's as Megan was, apparently. Either that, or he resented Mitch asking about his sister. The man knew the life, what the unit meant, the kind of work they did. He probably would have been happier if none of his teammates met Megan at all.

Mitch understood that, even agreed. But he couldn't help himself when it came to Megan Cassidy.

He walked down the hall and knocked on the door the secretary pointed to.

"Come in."

Just hearing her voice made his heart beat faster.

She looked exactly the same as the first time they'd met. The no-nonsense ponytail was gone, and long, blond waves tumbled down to cover the scar on her neck. She had on a smattering of makeup she didn't need. Her flirty dress ended an inch above her knees. He swallowed as he stared. He'd never seen her in a dress.

Wow. All right. Okay.

She looked elegant and poised, too beautiful to behold. Way out of his league. What had he been thinking? If she blamed him… Hell, he blamed himself half the time. He'd spent a couple of sleepless nights thinking about what he could have done differently.

Almost as many nights as he'd spent thinking of her with him and nothing else but tangled sheets.

She glanced up from the stack of papers she'd been reading.

"Mitch!" She flew to him and wrapped her arms around him.

She smelled like some exotic jungle flower.

He'd thought she'd give him a cool reception, so he was stunned by the entirely different welcome. For a second, he couldn't respond.

She pulled away, a shadow coming into her eyes. She took a step back, a more businesslike look settling onto her face. "They're putting together an op to go back in the jungle. Are you going?"

"No."

She looked disappointed. "I am."

"A joint mission with the CIA?"

"I begged the Colonel to put me on the team. With Jamie's help."

His head was spinning. "I'm quitting the team."

"Why would you do that?"

"Because I want to marry you and I never want to see you in the kind of pain I saw when you lost your brother."

Her amber eyes went wide. "You're trying to guarantee that you won't die on me?"

Now that she put it that way, it sure sounded stupid.

"I'm buying a house. A condo, actually." Maybe that would help. "I'm trying to—"

"You want to marry me?" Her eyes narrowed. "When

we were in the chopper and I said I loved you, you didn't say anything back."

"I needed a little time to recover. I needed to figure out a way I could make our relationship work."

"And your way is to quit?"

That did sound bad. He wasn't a quitter. A woman like Megan wouldn't want a quitter for a husband.

"Do you want to quit?" she asked.

"No. But I can live with it," he tried to explain. "I can't live without you."

"You won't have to. I'm going with you."

"Where?"

She looked at him as if he was slow in the head. "Back to the jungle. I'm coming over to Colonel Wilson's team in six months."

"You can't." He wasn't sure he could handle seeing her getting shot again.

"Watch me." She was all cold steel on the inside. And all hot curves on the outside. A combination that would keep him fascinated for the rest of his life. Then a thought popped into his head and stole his breath. "Why wait six months?"

His gaze fell to her midriff. How much could a man trust an old condom he found on the bottom of a drug dealer's duffel bag?

Her belly was flat, but you could never tell. His heart jumped up into his throat. Spots swum in front of his eyes.

She pulled a folder from her bag on the floor and handed it to him.

His hands shook as he opened it, expecting ultrasound pictures. He blinked hard when he saw the photo of a familiar one-year-old instead. *Cindy*. The world spun with him.

"What are you doing with my sister's file?"

"Finding her."

He couldn't allow his hopes to rise. That part of his heart was dead, even if Megan had awakened the rest. "I spent years chasing down every lead. I searched hard. There was nothing to find."

"But have you ever searched with all the tools of the CIA at your full disposal?" she asked.

"And you're giving them to me for the next six months?" Hell, with something like that, he could do miracles.

"For the next six months. That's when the Colonel is shipping a team back to the jungle. He'll need that long to process all the information we brought in and devise a strategy."

Of course she would. But she wasn't going without him. No way.

"We'll do this together." Because when the chips were down, the truth was he'd rather have her at his back than anyone else he knew. "And when we come back, we get married?"

"Jeez, don't be so pushy." But she grinned. "Maybe."

His heart leaped.

"And while we're waiting for that deployment, we'll find your sister. I'm going to do everything in my power to help." She smiled at him.

He stepped closer. "I love you, you know that?"

When she stepped into his arms, he wrapped himself around her. Kissed her with all the need of the three long months they'd been apart. He was never going to let her go again. There wasn't another like her on the planet.

She pressed against him, smiled against his lips as she brushed against his hardness. His body was more than ready for her.

"And what might that be?" she teased him, between kisses.

"I'm very happy to see you."

"It's either that or you had a run in with a banana spider." She laughed at him, then jumped and wrapped her legs around his waist.

He caught her, got lost in her. *She was his*. He didn't deserve her, but as long as God saw it fit in His generosity to bring the two of them together, he would do whatever it took to make her happy and keep her safe.

He didn't know how long they'd been kissing when someone cleared his throat behind them. They jumped apart, suddenly mindful of where they were.

"There are rules about fraternization in the SDDU rule book, soldiers," the Colonel said with a hard voice. But his eyes were dancing with mirth.

"The SDDU has no rule book, sir," Mitch retorted as the tips of his ears turned red.

"Impertinent, the lot of them." The colonel turned to Jamie, who was right behind him. "Are you sure you want to rejoin a team like this?"

"Yes, sir."

"Jamie, you can't be serious." Megan ran to him, crouching next to the wheelchair and searching her brother's face.

"This man has more experience than any ten others put together," the Colonel told them in a no-nonsense tone. "He'll be an operations coordinator at our Texas office."

Mitch wrinkled his forehead. "We don't have a Texas office."

"It's on a need-to-know basis. We started up operations in South Texas six months ago. Too many of our international ops uncover terror plots with links to sleeper cells and the like in the U.S. We needed to add another office here. Texas Headquarters will investigate drug and gun smuggling as well as human trafficking from Central and South America as it relates to suspected terror activity."

"If it's top secret..." The puzzle pieces were falling into place in Mitch's mind.

"You're being transferred there effective immediately. Megan will begin working there when she starts with us in six months," the Colonel responded. "You are both experts on South American ops."

"Jamie?" Megan still sounded unsure, but a change was slowly coming over her. It seemed she was beginning to understand that this was exactly what her brother needed to get his life back on track.

The colonel knew, Mitch thought. The colonel knew and he saw to it. No wonder his men would walk through fire for him.

"There are still things I can contribute." The harsh lines softened on Jamie's face. "I can coordinate missions and play wedding coordinator at the same time. I'm good at multitasking. From the looks of you two when we walked in, the sooner we hold that wedding, the better."

"She hasn't said yes, yet," Mitch put in, just to make

sure Jamie knew he'd asked. Jamie Cassidy wasn't a man he wanted to tangle with, wheelchair or no wheelchair.

All eyes moved to her.

The colonel raised an eyebrow. "My soldiers are not known for being wishy-washy."

"Megan?" Jamie watched her closely.

"Oh, please. I'm too old for peer pressure."

Nobody blinked.

"Seriously." She patted an errant lock of hair into place at her temple, looking flustered suddenly. "He doesn't need me for *anything*. He made that plenty clear, every day we were together."

Was she serious? Mitch stared at her.

Did he want to say this with two other guys in the room? He didn't have a choice.

He went down on one knee. "Megan Cassidy. I need you more than air. Please help end my misery by staying in my life. Because without you it's not worth living."

She cocked her head, and looked like she was struggling to suppress a grin. "So you're asking for my help? Just to be clear."

"I'm asking."

"And you will let me save your life if the occasion should arise, and will admit you need such assistance freely?"

"Yes."

"Hmm."

"Is that a yes?"

A smile of pure joy broke loose all over her face as she plowed into him and nearly knocked him over, locking her arms around his neck and kissing him. "Yes." Then she kept on with the kissing.

He kissed her back hard, then remembered the others. But when he looked behind him, the Colonel and Jamie were gone, the door closed.

His body came alive with need for her. His heart opened fully, for the first time in years. "I love you and I need you."

"I love you and I need you, too." She slid her hand under his shirt.

He choked back a laugh. "Here?"

"It's a lifesaving op." She backed toward the desk. "Think of it as an emergency."

Certainly felt like it. Heat flooded him as he slipped his hands to her hips.

"So who's saving who this time?" he asked as he eased her dress up her lean thighs.

"We're saving each other," she said as she kissed him.

* * * * *

"Lily, I have a bad feeling that the reason Mia's condo was
ransacked and my father's, too, was that they were looking
for this thumb drive."

"Then you should take it to the marshal," she said, handing it to him. "I have a copy of the letters on my computer,
so I can keep working on the code."

He nodded, although he had no intention of taking it
to the marshal. Not until he knew which side of the fence
Hud Savage was on.

"Until we know what's really on this," he said, "I
wouldn't mention it to anyone, all right?"

She nodded.

"I need to get to the hospital and see my father, but I
don't like leaving you here snowed in alone."

She waved him off. "The plows should be along in the
next hour or so if you want to take my SUV."

He wasn't about to leave her here without a vehicle even
if he thought he could bust through the drifts. "Are those
your brother's cross-country skis and boots by the door?

If you don't mind me borrowing them, I'll ski down to the road and hitch a ride. My brothers and I used to do that all the time when we were kids."

"If you're sure…" She turned back to the papers on the table. "I'll keep working on the code and let you know when I get it finished."

She sounded as if she would be glad when he left her at it. He was reminded that she also had plans to talk to her former fiancé today. He felt a hard knot form in his stomach. Jealousy? Heck yes.

Except he had nothing to be jealous about, right? Last night hadn't happened. At least that was the way Lily wanted it. He fought the urge to touch her hair, remembering the feel of it between his fingers.

"I want you to have this." He held out the pistol he'd taken from his father's place. "I need to know that you are safe."

She shook her head and pulled back. "I don't like guns."

"All you have to do is point it and shoot."

Lily held up both hands. "I don't want it. I could never…" She shook her head again.

"Just in case," Tag said as he laid it on the table, telling himself that if someone broke into her house and tried to hurt her, she would get over her fear of guns quickly. At least he hoped that was true.

Start your holidays with a bang!
Be sure to check out
CHRISTMAS AT CARDWELL RANCH
by USA TODAY *bestselling author B.J. Daniels*

Available October 22, only from Harlequin® Intrigue®.
Available wherever books and ebooks are sold.

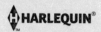

HARLEQUIN®

A *Romance* FOR EVERY MOOD™

Stay up-to-date on all your
romance-reading news with the
Harlequin Shopping Guide,
featuring bestselling authors, exciting new
miniseries, books to watch and more!

The newest issue will be delivered right to you
with our compliments! There are 4 each year.

Signing up is easy.

EMAIL

ShoppingGuide@Harlequin.ca

WRITE TO US

HARLEQUIN BOOKS
Attention: Customer Service Department
P.O. Box 9057, Buffalo, NY 14269-9057

OR PHONE

1-800-873-8635 in the United States
1-888-343-9777 in Canada

Please allow 4-6 weeks for delivery of the first issue by mail.

HSGSIGNUP